AHRIMAN
ETERNAL

More Chaos Space Marines from Black Library

• **AHRIMAN** •
by John French
BOOK 1 – Exile
BOOK 2 – Sorcerer
BOOK 3 – Unchanged
BOOK 4 – Eternal

• **BLACK LEGION** •
by Aaron Dembski-Bowden
BOOK 1 – The Talon of Horus
BOOK 2 – Black Legion

RENEGADES: HARROWMASTER
Mike Brooks

HURON BLACKHEART: MASTER OF THE MAELSTROM
Mike Brooks

NIGHT LORDS: THE OMNIBUS
by Aaron Dembski-Bowden
(Contains the novels *Soul Hunter, Blood Reaver*
and *Void Stalker*)

KHÂRN: EATER OF WORLDS
Anthony Reynolds

WORD BEARERS: THE OMNIBUS
Anthony Reynolds
(Contains the novels *Dark Apostle, Dark Disciple*
and *Dark Creed*)

STORM OF IRON
Graham McNeill

THE SIEGE OF CASTELLAX
C L Werner

AHRIMAN
ETERNAL

JOHN FRENCH

BLACK LIBRARY

A BLACK LIBRARY PUBLICATION

First published in 2021.
This edition published in Great Britain in 2023 by
Black Library, Games Workshop Ltd., Willow Road,
Nottingham, NG7 2WS, UK.

Represented by: Games Workshop Limited – Irish branch,
Unit 3, Lower Liffey Street, Dublin 1,
D01 K199, Ireland.

10 9 8 7 6 5 4 3 2

Produced by Games Workshop in Nottingham.
Cover illustration by Dan Watson.

See Black Library on the internet at

blacklibrary.com

Find out more about Games Workshop
and the worlds of Warhammer at

games-workshop.com

Printed and bound by CPI Group (UK) Ltd, Croydon, CR0 4YY

For Greg Smith.

For more than a hundred centuries the Emperor has sat immobile on the Golden Throne of Earth. He is the Master of Mankind. By the might of His inexhaustible armies a million worlds stand against the dark.

Yet, He is a rotting carcass, the Carrion Lord of the Imperium held in life by marvels from the Dark Age of Technology and the thousand souls sacrificed each day so that His may continue to burn.

To be a man in such times is to be one amongst untold billions. It is to live in the cruellest and most bloody regime imaginable. It is to suffer an eternity of carnage and slaughter. It is to have cries of anguish and sorrow drowned by the thirsting laughter of dark gods.

This is a dark and terrible era where you will find little comfort or hope. Forget the power of technology and science. Forget the promise of progress and advancement. Forget any notion of common humanity or compassion.

There is no peace amongst the stars, for in the grim darkness of the far future, there is only war.

To destroy a soul, the gods must do no more than give them a taste of the honey of victory. There, in the golden nectar of hope fulfilled and desire granted, is fleeting sweetness and eternal agony thereafter.

– from the Andolic Scrolls, c.M2,
recovered by the Imperial Conservatory in 994.M30,
suppressed by Inquisitorial decree in 781.M31

PROLOGUE

ᴛHE ᖴALLING ᗰOON

Draillita, Mistress of Mimes, now the Crone's Child, staggered up the slope as explosions strobed in the twilight. Her movements were stuttering – a stride, a stumble, a twist, her head turning to the night sky in agony. A human warrior saw her. He was one of the barbarian giants, all armoured in the red of dying suns and old blood. He was death come to end her suffering. He cursed and brought up his gun – a blunt-muzzled thing, its wide mouth filled with the dark promise of release in the silence its voice would soon shatter. Draillita stumbled anew, a fall, clawing at the grey ash, unable to go on, broken by suffering, undone by betrayal...

The blast of the gun passed above her as she fell.

An explosion in the dirt of the slope.

Even now, no release. The Crone's Child had to suffer. She rose. Star-bright tears tumbled from her cheeks. Her mouth was a shriek without end. Why must she live when all her siblings were dead?

The red barbarian fired again. Her spasms of grief twisted her aside of the shells. Explosions snatched at the grey-and-white tatters of her shroud. And now she turned, for the Crone's Child knew that she would never see the peace of oblivion. She would go on and on, walking the worlds and stars, suffering without end, a lost child, a herald of woe to all.

The red barbarian, sent by the kindness of death, fired without cease. No bullet touched Draillita. She was already next to the warrior. His eyes were crude emeralds in a face of hard edges. She howled her sorrow as her caress reached through the red armour, through the flesh and bone. She held his beating heart, just for an instant. She withdrew her hand, blood falling from the organ in her grasp. The barbarian who could not give her death lived a little longer, the second of his hearts still beating as he fell to his knees, pleading with his failing strength to allow him to fight on – and somehow, he did, red armour shivering, gun rising, and the Crone's Child did not move, for could this be the end of the long jest of her existence? His heart was dark in her hand. The drops of blood falling onto the grey ground were red tears all. His emerald eyes were just for her. She held out his heart to him, pleading for release…

A cascade of light and laughter, a whirl of motion, sharp and silver as the Thrice Fool landed between the red barbarian and the Crone's Child. He was twitching, shivering with amusement or pain or peace. His swords had opened the barbarian from collar to groin. The blood was now a wide cloth spread on the grey ground.

Another barbarian entered across the brow of the slope. Fast and rage-quick. The Crone's Child thought that this might be death's jest, that she might end here after all. Then the second barbarian fell, just like the first. His head split along a razor line that ran from one side to the other.

The Thrice Fool landed on the dead barbarian and spun. He

was golden glee and red slaughter. He twisted to Draillita, trailing the silver of his sword as he beckoned for the Crone's Child to come with him.

She lurched back, then balanced on a toe, clad in the tatters of sorrow and barbarian blood. She could go with the Thrice Fool, could dance, and laugh like the child she was. She could take the Thrice Fool's hand and become golden and red, the Daughter of the Dawn spinning in brightness without end... She reached for his proffered hand.

Fire drove them apart, tearing the air, sending ash into the sky. The brothers of the dead barbarians entered, charging over the crest of the slope, bellowing, guns roaring. The Crone's Child tumbled back; her head came up to see that the Thrice Fool was fleeing, explosions and mirth trailing him. She rose, hands appealing to the sky at the injustice of coming so close to joy and seeing it snatched away. She called on the spirits of those she had lost as she danced through the gunfire. And the lost came to her call. They were all the ghost faces of the Crone Child's life of grief: the Queen of Starlight, the Crimson Muses, the Broken Seer, a chorus of the spiteful dead. They came, shrieking in silence, arrayed in white and black, like a storm breathed from the mouth of the underworld.

The barbarians were fast, and they were strong, but neither speed nor strength could save them now. Draillita watched for a moment, anguish echoing from every gesture as she staggered and fell, and rose and took more hearts in her hands. The Crone's Child wished that it did not have to be so, that she could have laughed with joy at the bright dawn rather than shriek with vengeance at the slaughter. But she could not. She had to go on, walking the ash, dancing with death that would not come. Her role was to suffer for wrongs she had not committed and to take life from the living in revenge.

She looked at her bloody hand. Gore dripped from it. Holo-smoke and diamonds swirled through the falling droplets. The spirits of vengeance were all around her, their masks grimaces of pain. They raised their blades, and their shapes faded to black. The Crone's Child held her red hand to the sky, then folded to the ground as twilight stole the sun...

Draillita stood. The garb of the Crone's Child dissolved from her as her *dathedi* holo-suit shed the costume of the role. The shroud and tatters vanished into motes of holo-light and then nothing. The Crone's Child faded from her being. The scream sloughed from her mask. The features that were still there were blank white, a canvas waiting for paint.

The troupe's mimes were already turning away, their appearances similarly shifted out of their roles. There was an emptiness to their movements that echoed her own. She could see the Death Jesters, all in white, flitting amongst the dead like albino crows. Everything was a dance, a cycle of story and roles, but the part of the waiting player had a hollowness to it. That was what they were now – waiting in the gap between one tale's ending and another's beginning. She looked at the blood on her hands. It was already starting to clot. It reeked of the gene-violations of the so-called Space Marines. She flicked sticky trails of the stuff into the ash. There was more of it on her. She jumped into a tumble that shook the remaining gore loose.

Iyshak was there when she landed. He had shed the mantle of the Thrice Fool. The gold and red had gone from his costume. A rictus grin had replaced the expression of glee. The diamond pattern of his coat shifted between muted blues and subtle shades of near black as he moved. He had slid into the archetype of the waning moon for this interlude of cycles. It suited his artistry.

~We exit,~ she signed. As Mistress of Mimes, she did not speak or make a sound, but communicated by a system of gestures called the *lambruith*. Every detail of posture, muscle and movement held meaning so that, in her silence, she could layer nuance and import more finely than the most carefully crafted tongue. There were no fixed rules or lexicon for this mimicry: it was a language of spontaneities, an art whose expression was never the same. She held out her hand to Iyshak. He took it, and they began to walk. Around them, the fires of the tragedy they had enacted swayed amongst the ash dunes and the scattered human corpses.

They were cresting a rise when Draillita felt Iyshak's grip tense. He halted, assuming the stillness of an actor in a tableau. An instant later Draillita saw why. A figure stood in their path. It was crimson. Scarlet and carmine diamonds trailed behind it, and its shadow spread up and out into the smoke like wings. Its face was blank silver.

Draillita arched in surprise and froze. Together, she and Iyshak had become the image of the hero Ulthanesh and the song-slayer Shelwe-toc surprised by Khaine on the Sun Path. Behind them, the players of the masque came over the rise, saw the figure and the poses assumed by Iyshak and Draillita, and flowed into a crescent around them. They twisted into images of the Forest of Sorrow, their fingers twigs stirring on the smoke-filled wind, their masks images of sorrow and grief.

Within, Draillita felt unease. This was part of no cycle she had learnt. They had just completed the final act of *The Red Tears of the Child and the Fool*. Now it was complete they should have withdrawn, moving into the minor cycles of comic-tragedy, taking on the roles of Isha's scattered children fleeing the wars of the gods. Yet here stood Yrlla, the Shadowseer barring their exit. They should not have been there. There was no role for fate in this last act, and so Yrlla had not taken to the stage of battle. They should not have been here...

Yet here they stood.

The Shadowseer approached, their steps slow, the black-and-red stain of their shadow spreading wider and wider. They stopped in front of the masque at last and stood still, waiting. In this moment, when fate came as the Red Guest, they had to wait for another to challenge them.

~Why have you come?~ asked Draillita at last.

'I come with warning,' said Yrlla.

'What ill have you seen?' asked Iyshak.

'New dreams rise, and wake those that have slept long.' The Shadowseer held out a hand. It appeared as the hand of a corpse, skin and flesh withered to a claw. Clotted blood clung to its nails. Fire rose from it, licking the smoke, forming shadows in the air around them. Draillita saw warriors with horned and crested armour. They reached out towards the sky, clutching for stars that briefly showed as the smoke parted. Then beside it, other figures lay as though asleep, tinged by holo-light so that they seemed black and gold and silver. The sleepers rose and the stars vanished. The lone figure of a monstrous humanoid with a horned staff and helm remained. The stolen light of stars burned in the figure's eyes. Draillita shivered and the chorus of players echoed the movement and gave a murmur of pain. 'Such shifts of players and scene demand a response. These acts and actions cannot unfold on their own.'

~What *saedath* cycle does this begin?~ asked Draillita.

'There are several that it could become,' the Shadowseer answered, and turned, sweeping the smoke and holo-light like a ragged, red cloak. '*The Broken God's Mirth*, which sees weeping stars and swift ends. *The Pyre and the Phoenix*, where all becomes ash and uncertainty, and all who dance across its acts must leave not knowing if the dawn will replace the night...' Above and around Yrlla, shadow and light bent into images of silhouettes spinning through fire and darkness, swords of power in their hands, surging together, climbing over one another to touch a crescent moon that looked like the smile of a scythe. Then all of them falling lifeless, smearing into grey shadow, then into darkness.

'But there is another,' stated Iyshak, releasing Draillita's hand and beginning to circle, his garb and face altering with each step. 'Speak of the saedath you think we should begin.'

'*The Falling Moon*,' said the Shadowseer, and around them the chorus gave a trembling wail of sorrow. Draillita bowed her head.

~It has been many ages of mortal life since it was played. Must it be now?~

'It is not that it must,' said Yrlla. 'By choosing it, we make it the tale of what will be.'

~Fate upended...~

'A worse end for all averted.'

~But at what cost?~

'The cost of many. The cost of joy and victory.'

'We will play,' said Iyshak, circling faster, tumbling, his garb now purple and black, the crest of his hair a rainbow, a red grin splitting the cruel white of his mask. 'And so we are called to take our places. I must be the Murderer's Jest, for I am the avatar of all that shall die by the fool's mistake.' His voice was loud, ringing with mockery and spite.

'And so into this cauldron do I step as the Voice of Many Ends,' said Yrlla, and the Shadowseer leapt high. The blood mist and shadow that had filled the air dissolved into splinters of emerald and red, yellow and violet, turquoise and flame. When Yrlla landed, their mask was a tarnished mirror beneath their cowl. Around them the troupes were spinning and whirling, assuming their first roles for the cycle. From behind them, came the Death Jesters, all clad in black, all identical, for in what was to come, death held no signal aspect.

Draillita brought her hands to her face, slumped as though overcome and then straightened. Her face was a split mask, one half twisting with pain, cracked and weeping rubies and embers. The other half danced with glee, red teeth sharp, eyes glinting with malice.

~I am the Dreamer's Truth, for all must dream, and all must end.~

Ash grey and blood red unfolded beside white and black. She spread her arms and began to walk away from the others. She must go ahead, warning, a herald come too late to those who would have to suffer.

'Who are the players who know not their part yet?' she heard Iyshak call in the high voice of the Murderer's Jest.

'There are many,' answered the Shadowseer. 'But the one who first takes their place is a sorcerer, once of humankind, now a master of outcasts, son of a false king, a betrayer to all, a believer in hope. He is called Ahriman.'

PART ONE

THE EXILED

CHAPTER I

VEIL OF GHOSTS

Hargoron, First of those Born of Iron, Breaker of Anvils, listened to his ship creak under the touch of ghosts. Ice crystals crept across the viewport frames. Gossamer shapes drifted and coiled through the dark beyond. Things that might have been faces formed and dissolved. Hands reached, grew into claws, faded and sank back into the blue-green fog. The stars were haloed pinpricks beyond the murk. As he looked, the shape of a head congealed into view. Its eyes were the stolen glow of the stars, pale cataracts in a face of tattered skin around a circle of needle teeth. Hargoron bared his own teeth back.

'Sensor report,' he said, his voice a dry rasp in the quiet of the bridge.

'This eye sees, oh great lord...' called the principal augur-slave in reply, a wasted thing with a long, metal braced neck beneath a bulbous head. Its frogspawn cluster of eyes rolled across the cracked screens of its console. 'No returns within sensor range.'

It drooled a cord of spittle as it spoke, the phlegm gathering on the crust layer already thick on the console's dials.

Hargoron curled a lip in disgust and turned away, scratching a clawed finger across his chin. Flakes of rust-like scabs came away from his skin. Everything had begun to fall apart since they had crossed into the Gorgon's Shroud. Nothing in the Eye of Terror existed without adapting to living on the border between reality and the warp, but this voyage had cost Hargoron and his warriors dear. Here, the light of the stars outside the Eye was stronger than the hell-light that bled from its heart, but the tides of the warp were thick and laced with the withering touch of entropy. Wrecks rolled in the Shroud's embrace, breaking into bits as the forces of unreality sheared against reality. Ship systems failed. Corrosion seeped into metal, static into signals, and weakness into muscle and bone. He had needed to leave one ship behind in the Shroud's heart. Its engines had failed, and its hull had begun to crumble from its skin inwards, as though it were a fruit rotting dry in a desert wind. That had left him with just two craft to make the crossing back.

It had been worth it, though. Plunder from the worlds and wreck drifts within the Shroud filled his holds: great hauls of armour; weapon systems pulled from the bones of dead ships; ammunition and fuel, still good despite its time in the ghost tides. And then there were the true treasures, unique things that would let him barter for high prices with the Warlord and Ascending powers in the Eye. Enough wealth and riches to pay the gene-thieves and flesh-mechanists to give him newborn warriors. Not vagabond legionaries, loyal only to power or opportunity, but warriors loyal to him and him alone. And then... Then who knew? All that remained was to journey back across the Shroud's boundary. It was a dangerous voyage, and came with its own, unique cost.

He glanced at where the Warp Ghost stood on the steersman's

platform. Its armour was pale grey, the edges dull bronze and steel. The lenses of its helm were cataract pale. It had not moved for hours now. Occasionally it had made a gesture or spoken a handful of words commanding a change of course, but otherwise it had just rotated its head as if looking out beyond the hull and viewports, watching things move in the murk that Hargoron could not see and did not want to. Its own ship held formation off the port bow, gliding in the coiling lightning and veils of gas.

The Warp Ghost's head turned, and the pale eye-lenses touched Hargoron's gaze. Despite himself, Hargoron had to suppress an instinct to flinch. The Warp Ghost's attention moved on. Hargoron spat. The spittle fizzed as the acid ate into the deck plating. No one knew what Chapter or Legion had spawned the Ghosts' brotherhood, nor what bargain or secret gifted them their skill to navigate the warp-saturated depths of the Eye. He had never seen more than a handful of them at any time, but still they disturbed him. The Warp Ghosts would take a large chunk of his haul, but he did not doubt that without their pilots, his ships would have joined the other wrecks drifting in the slow currents of the Gorgon's Shroud. They were worth their ferryman's coin, but that did not mean he had to like their presence. There was an air to them, as though they looked not just into you but also through you. He did not like that. If he had followed his instinct, he would have put his claws through this one's throat and ordered his ships to fire on the craft escorting them. He had suppressed that instinct; you did not cross the Warp Ghosts if you wished to continue to cross the Eye and live.

'All stop,' said the Warp Ghost, suddenly.

Hargoron looked around. The bridge crew were already moving to obey. Out beyond the viewport he could see that his second ship and the Warp Ghosts craft were firing thrusters and sliding to a halt.

'What–' he began to growl, but the Warp Ghost held up a hand. Hargoron felt his hands flex as he bit down on his anger. The Warp Ghost turned its head slowly, then more quickly, looking up and to the side, then down. The ship creaked around them.

'A presence on the tides around us,' said the Warp Ghost, its voice a dull croak. 'Shadows… waiting in the fold of the Great Ocean, hiding in deeper tides…'

'What is it?' growled Hargoron.

The pale murk beyond the armaglass was thickening. A fork of yellow lightning arced through it, bleaching the view for an instant, then again and again. Hargoron turned to the steersman's platform, a demand for information on his lips.

The Warp Ghost was not there.

'Lord,' the principal augur-slave called. 'Our etheric resonators are picking up intense local fluctuations.'

Hargoron opened his mouth to snarl an order for alert. The pair of warriors from his personal guard started forwards.

Lightning sheeted the murk beyond the viewports, and in the flash, he saw the shadow of a ship. A warship. Right on top of them, sudden and real, hull flanks like cliffs, towers turning the outlines of their backs into serrated blades. The lightning flared around them, haloing them. Strobing.

'Shields!' shouted Hargoron. The ship had lowered most of her voids for the passage through the Gorgon's Shroud. Some of the crew moved to respond, but the rest just stared, dumbfounded.

It made no difference. Fire lanced from one of the warships. The thin veil of shields overloaded a second before the viewports blew in. Shards of crystal sliced through the bridge. Screams were dragged from throats as the air rushed into the void. Bodies tumbled with it, spilling blood. Hargoron clamped his hands over his head. Power fields sheathed his claws, and he was already shouting into the static-filled vox as a pillar of light blazed into being at the centre of the bridge.

He could taste bitter sorcery in the air. He moved towards the blast doors off the bridge. His two warriors flanked him, firing. He was already calling into the vox, calling his followers to face the attackers. There were gunships and bulk lifters in the launch hangars. He and his chosen warriors could run. The attackers could have the ship. He would take his greatest prizes with him and live to find vengeance.

Hargoron was at the blast doors. His two warriors were at his side, firing bolts into the pillar of light as it grew wider. A horned shadow formed in the blaze of energy, growing clearer, coming closer as though walking from an unseen distance. The pillar of light vanished.

The bolt shells halted in mid-air. Frost flashed across the deck, climbing up the limbs of thrashing crew.

A figure stood where the light had been. Crimson robes hung from sapphire armour. Horns curved up from its helm. The staff in its hand was a line cut into reality, a black wound leaking starlight.

Hargoron snarled. The power fields snapped over his claws. His warriors fired again. Hargoron began to move.

The sorcerer looked at him. Its eyes were blue stars.

Hargoron's limbs froze. The flames around the barrels of his warriors' guns were blossoms of orange and red. The sorcerer stepped towards them. It raised a hand. The bolt shells hanging in the air spun and slid until they were resting on the eye-lenses of his two warriors. Hargoron tried to force himself to move, to make his tongue call out one of the phrases of protection he had learnt from a priest of the Horned Darkness.

+I have no time for your spite,+ said a voice inside his skull. The sorcerer's fingers twitched. The bolt shells slammed through the eye-lenses of Hargoron's warriors and blew the backs of their skulls and helms out. The sorcerer was right in front of him now.

+You have something you do not understand and that I need.+

Hargoron felt the force holding him motionless give for a second. He snapped forwards, claws reaching. The armour of his limbs crumpled and sheared. The claws peeled back as his limbs froze again. He watched as they bent until they were digging into his forearms. Blood glittered as it fell, turning to shards of red ice.

He found he could still move his mouth and tongue.

'I will give you nothing!' he spat.

The sorcerer tilted its head.

+You do not need to,+ came the voice in Hargoron's skull. Then there was just a roar as he felt his thoughts come apart like a pillar of dust caught in a gale.

Ahzek Ahriman looked down at the crumpled heap of Hargoron, First of those Born of Iron, Breaker of Anvils. Here he was again, with another example of broken nobility and misguided dreams lying at his feet. He could read the past in the aftertaste of the thoughts he had ripped from the warrior's mind. Warrior... Yes, Hargoron had been a warrior once, a brother of the IV Legion, raised up during the long years of the war against the Emperor. He had never known anything but conflict with the Imperium that had created him, had never known a time when war seemed an act of optimism rather than bitterness and vengeance. Yet, he had served, and survived, and tried to hold on to the tatters of nobility that he could remember. The warp had undone that in the end, turned the will to endure into a canker that ate Hargoron the warrior and left just this broken shell of base drives and cruelty.

Ahriman shook the reflection free of his mind and let the

warlord's thoughts fall through the sift of his inner senses. Bloody memories, bitter emotions, scraps of images and cruelty tumbled past his inner eye until he had what he needed.

+Lower deck thirty-four, forward section seventy-six, ordnance magazine chamber located next to the primary hangars. Be swift,+ sent Ahriman to his brothers as he ran from the ruin of the bridge. +I will join you.+

Ctesias swayed for a second as the teleport flare faded around him. Even after lifetimes on stolen lifetimes of moving by sorcery and warpcraft, it left him with false sound ringing in his ears and acid in his throat. Part of him still thought he was back on the *Hekaton*, the acolytes shrieking as the rituals to move their strike force completed. Lycomedes recovered faster and was already moving past him, dragging five Rubricae in his wake. Ctesias moved more slowly after them. Ghost-light haloed the top of his staff. The strips of parchment pinned to his armour were charring as the warding spells inked onto them burned. He could smell the birth reek of the sentinel daemons close by.

+They have sensed us,+ he called to his apprentice. +Be ready to do as I command.+

He brought his thoughts to stillness, suppressing the sensations of nausea rolling through him. When handling the tools of summoning and dismissal, you had to be clean of emotion. To be anything else just invited the daemons of the warp to hook into your soul. Ideally, he would have liked time to prepare for what he needed to do, but as ever time was a luxury he did not have. He could feel tendrils of sensation and thought bleeding into him: the despair of a soul slowly suffocating in the void, the clammy sweat of fevered skin, the sharp pain of a failing heart spreading through the last moments of a miserable life.

The ship was lousy with ghost residue. Rust clogged the rivets on the metal walls. The canker had already been deep in its rotting bones when it had gone into the Gorgon's Shroud in search of carrion treasure, and the corrosive warp tides had only spread the rot deeper. Things had latched on to its skin and travelled with it. The Breakers of Iron, or whatever the ship's masters styled themselves, did not have the skill to purge the parasites from their vessel, but some of them had enough knowledge to bind them in place. They had made the daemons their guard dogs. Ctesias had known this when they had begun to scry their prey by mirror and smoke, but now he had to feel it on his skin and thoughts, he wished even more that Ahriman had simply burned the ship and searched the ashes. Some might have found that reaction strange – a summoner and binder of daemons whose lip curled at the warp's rancid touch. For him, there was no contradiction: a master of hounds did not have to like the reek of their beasts' excrement. He was old and soul withered, and had seen more than enough that he did not have to lie to himself. Given the choice he would have been a long way from this ship and the prize they had come for. Ahriman, though, did not give those kinds of choices. At least they would not have to remain here long.

Lycomedes slammed a ram of telekinetic force through a blast hatch. It blew off its hinges, sending rust-flecked shards clanging off the walls and deck. Ctesias went through. The passage beyond was wide. Spores drifted in the light of cracked glow-lamps. Cords of thick fungus ran through the walls and deck plating. Ctesias felt the metal sag as he hurried. He felt the warp shift. It was sludge thick. Bubbles popped at the edges of his sight. Corpse reek filled his nose.

+They are here!+ he sent.

And the Neverborn came for them. They prised themselves from the walls, dragging rolls of soft fat through layers of rust.

They flopped onto the deck, growing limbs and feelers, mouths opening.

Ctesias felt a pulse of will from Lycomedes, and the Rubricae brought their bolters up and fired. The bolts hit the daemons and exploded into blue flame. Fat cooked. Greasy smoke poured out as the things thrashed and burned. They did not vanish though, but grew, bloating, skin ripping. They wobbled forwards, dragging burnt slime across the deck. Ropes of intestine spilled from wounds and whipped through the air to coil around the nearest Rubricae. Lycomedes' will yanked the Rubricae back, but the coils were winding tighter, oozing acid over armour plates. Ctesias could smell spoiled milk and gut fluid, could hear the buzz of flies inside his head.

+Cut them free,+ snapped Ctesias. +The others are coming – the way must be open.+ He was still going forwards towards the roiling mass of daemon flesh filling the passage. In his mind the true names and words of summoning he had prepared became a chain reaching into the warp.

He spoke the first name aloud.

'Su'ka'sel'su…'

His tongue blistered. The smell of burning sugar filled his mouth and nose. Beyond the walls of reality, the daemons he had bound to his command thrashed against his will.

'Ah'kel'mur'hil'su'sel…'

He pulled the Neverborn into being, dragging them with the syllables of their names. Red slits opened in the air. Blood poured out, streaking the deck, foaming, congealing into muscle and skin and chitin. Light exploded into rainbows as it touched opalescent skin. Hooves struck steel. Long heads extended on scaled necks. Ctesias did not look at them; there were some things it was better not to see. The mass of canker-daemons recoiled then lashed forwards. The Rubricae and Lycomedes were clear.

'Feed,' commanded Ctesias, and the conjured daemons blurred forwards in a haze of mauve smoke. Booming hoots split the air and sent black specks fizzing on the edge of his sight. Razor claws met bloated flesh. Bile and scented blood splashed the walls. Ctesias let the daemonicide continue for six heartbeats then spoke the dismissal he had been holding on his tongue. The daemons howled as he yanked them back beyond the veil. He paused for a second, running his tongue over his teeth and waiting for the taste of ashes to fade from his mouth. Lumps of fat and gristle were dissolving to ectoplasm on the ceiling, walls and floor.

+The way is clear,+ he sent and began to advance, Lycomedes and the Rubricae forming around him. +We are converging on the hold. Ignis, are you on time?+

Ignis heard Ctesias' sending as a hiss in his skull. The mockery in the words and the sneer in the tone were not lost on him. He did not respond. He did not have the time or patience to. The rattle of the gunship around him rose in pitch as its engines hit full thrust. The Storm Eagle was now hurtling across the gap to their target at the speed of a macro shell fired from a cannon.

He began to count, slicing the seconds into fractions in his head, watching them form patterns in his mind's eye. Beside him in the compartment, Credence clattered, as though trying to relieve an ache. The automaton had folded its limbs to fit into the cramped space, but it barely fitted. Beside them, eight of the Rubricae sat immobile in mag-harnesses. Ghost-light burned dully in their eyes and the shallow hiss of falling dust shivered through the warp around them.

Ignis' count reached one of its sacred values.

+Wake them,+ he sent.

Ptollen nodded and began to speak names with his mind.

+Mabius Ro, Istigelis, T'latton...+ The heads of the Rubricae came up, one after another. The hiss from inside their armour grew louder. Ignis could hear the tones and sound patterns of voices calling from far away through a dust-filled wind.

+Ready,+ sent Ptollen. His will meshed with the Rubricae so that they would obey as though part of Ptollen's own body.

Ignis did not acknowledge the lesser sorcerer. He was still counting the seconds to impact. He could have watched through sensor systems and let the gunship's machine-spirits deal with the distance and time to target. He could have, but he chose not to. Everything he needed to know was in the ratios and patterns that formed and re-formed in his mind. Times, fuel weights, weapon explosive yields, all of it and more sliced into fractions and sent spinning through his thoughts. In an age long past he had been called a Master of Ruin, one who could mesh destruction with the secret geometry of the universe. The title had long since become meaningless, but the knowledge it stood for was his truth.

A second passed. Fractal patterns opened in front of his mind's eye. For a flash it was as though he were looking at the face of something truly divine.

+Loose,+ he sent. The gunship shook as the first wave of rockets kicked free of their weapon pods.

+Rise,+ commanded Ptollen, his dark blue robes rippling like water. The mag-harnesses thumped open. The Rubricae stood.

Ignis felt the patterns in his mind change, felt the values of projected distance and time bend, become a perfectly folded flower of cause and effect. He pushed his mind out beyond the hull of the gunship and into the vacuum. He had created these moments and now he would allow himself to see them become real.

The rockets hit the doors of the hangar bay. Melta warheads

detonated. The metal of the doors flashed yellow with heat. Nine nanoseconds later the second wave of rockets hit, and high explosives blew the semi-molten metal to spray. The gunship's assault ramps opened. Atmosphere howled out. Ignis could see dust and vapour beyond, curdling the light of the stars to bile green and ochre. Ptollen was at the edge of the forward ramp. There were figures tumbling into the void from the breach in the ship. The glowing hole yawned wide in front of them...

And then they were through.

The gunship fired its thrusters, skidding in the air. Ptollen jumped, his axes bright with blue fire. The Rubricae followed. They hit the decking and rose, firing at the same instant. Most of the enemy in the hangar were mortal – humans with rusted augmetics. There were three Born of Iron, though. Thick clogs of corrosion covered the dull metal of their power armour. Oil wept from their vox-grilles and joints in thick runnels. The volley of fire from the Rubricae hit them and wreathed them in blue flame. They kept coming forward, scabs of mould cooking on their armour. Ptollen met them at a run. Of the exiled Thousand Sons he was the one who most favoured the martial over the cerebral. His power and learning had always been great – great enough to earn him a place in the outer circles of Ahriman's original cabal – but that power had always focused on war. On killing. Ignis might have said that he liked him.

One of the Born of Iron swung at Ptollen. The warrior had a lightning-sheathed maul, its head a starburst of jagged spikes. Ptollen met the blow with the blade of his axe. Ignis felt the warp howl as the axe sliced through the maul. Light screamed out. The warrior tried to recover but the axe head was already in his throat, slicing down through the meat of his torso, burning flesh to smoke.

The gunship dropped to the deck. Ignis came down the ramp,

hearing the beat of seconds in his soul. Credence unfolded and followed, gun rotating up to fire. A beam of un-light shrieked across the space and hit the remaining Born of Iron warriors as they closed on Ptollen. They became brief shadows, then exploded, their matter annihilated in a shrieking blink. The Rubricae were already moving across the deck, firing on the mortal crew that still lived.

+Open the inner doors,+ sent Ignis. Credence pivoted and the beam of its cannon lanced at the blast doors that led to the rest of the ship. The metal began to distort and shake. Ptollen moved towards them, raising his axes above his head. Lightning arced from him, striking the doors and spidering across them.

Ignis felt the deck shiver as another gunship touched down next to his. This one was smaller, its lines curved smooth where the edges of the Storm Eagle were sharp. Its hull was black, edged with gold. The scars of repeated repair marked its plating. The ramp in its belly opened as its clawed feet gripped the deck. The pariah walked into sight. She was human, female, tall, thin limbed. A cloak of golden-and-black scales hung from her shoulders over a bodyglove of deep crimson. A golden helm sat on her head, its blank visor covering all but her mouth and chin. The hilt of a longsword rose above her shoulders. Ignis felt his mind recoil as he looked at her. His thoughts and senses slid off her, and he felt something hollow and hungry pulling at his soul.

Abomination… He could not help the thought even though he had been in her presence many times since she had come into Ahriman's orbit. She was called Maehekta, and she was a soul blank: without presence in the warp. Those with mundane minds struggled to be close to such creatures. To those with psychic gifts, their presence could be agony. Ignis swallowed a mouthful of bile.

'Keep your distance,' he snarled.

'Of course,' she said.

The blast doors at the other end of the hangar collapsed with a crash of lightning.

Ignis shivered inside his armour, turned away from Maehekta and stalked towards the opening.

The doors ached in Ahriman's mind as he looked at them. They were cold iron. Lines had been cut into their surface, scratched deep in the dull grey, words and symbols flowing together in a web that glowed in his mind's eye. Old words, old symbols. Rust and decay crawled over the space before the doors. Blooms of metallic fungus hung from the ceiling, and milk-white moisture beaded the walls. In places, the deck and wall plating had become as soft as skin. Amongst this, the door and its frame remained stubbornly clean and solid.

+Where is the key bearer?+ snapped Ahriman as Ctesias came from one of the tunnel openings.

There were still sounds of gunfire and screams from passages leading to other sections of the hull. Ctesias had unleashed part of his menagerie of Neverborn into the lower decks under the eye of his apprentice, and the daemons were doing what was in their nature. Ahriman had cut away the psychic backwash of the killing, but he could still feel the ghosts of razor claws sliding against the shell of his mind and hear the shivers of terror and pain.

+With Ignis,+ replied Ctesias. Ahriman could feel his brother's wariness. +They are coming.+

Inside, Ahriman forced the anger down beneath a layer of calm. His thoughts had blurred for a moment.

Of course Maehekta was with Ignis... He had to focus. Had to move through the actions that would solve the problem. He closed his eyes inside his helm.

Blink.

Blackness.

A burning line in the distance, running from edge to edge of his inner sight. Had it got closer? He could taste the dust and ash…

No, he willed.

Blink.

+The warding is exceptionally strong,+ sent Ctesias, moving next to the vault doors. Ahriman forced himself to focus on what Ctesias was saying. +We could unpick them if we had time. No guarantee that it would not trigger some nasty counter-effects. We could overload them but whatever is inside might not survive intact. Might as well let Ignis try and bore through with melta charges, though that is not going to be much better.+ Ahriman felt Ctesias' gaze sharpen on him. Their telepathic link narrowed, so that it was between them alone. +What is inside, Ahriman? Hasn't the time come for you to share that secret?+

'We…' began Ahriman aloud.

Blink.

The burning line was still there. A migraine on the horizon of his mind.

Control. He had to keep moving forwards. Had to. For them all.

'We do not need to break the doors,' he said.

'Why?' asked Ctesias, frowning at him.

'Because why break a door if you have a key?' said a cold female voice.

Maehekta advanced from the mouth of the passage. Ignis and Ptollen followed her, keeping their distance, their movements betraying their revulsion at her presence. Ctesias visibly flinched back as she walked past him to the vault doors. Ahriman kept his mind steady and did not move, even as Maehekta cast shadows onto the edge of his thoughts. The key in her hand was black iron and hung from a loop of dull chain. She ran her finger along the surface of the door, found what looked like a deep crack and slotted it home. A click, a turn and then the doors were retracting into the walls. Coolant vapour fumed out.

The space beyond was utterly dark. Ahriman's helm display fuzzed as it tried to build an image from the available light. His senses could feel the wards worked into the chamber's geometry pushing back his mind.

'A null chamber…' said Ctesias aloud. 'Well built…' He stepped to the threshold and extended a hand into the space beyond. Ahriman knew that Ctesias would be pushing his mind against the psychically dulling effect beyond the door. 'Powerful, and very well constructed. The wretches that used this ship did not make this.'

'Light,' said Ahriman. Credence buzzed. A stab-beam shone from the automaton's gun-mount. The space was large. Piles of what looked like wreckage lay in heaps across the floor. Ahriman picked his way past jumbles of broken power armour, a heap of horned skulls and bones, and stone troughs holding pieces of crystal that gleamed black in the lumen's glare. He could feel the echoes of anger and pain and spite coming off every object he passed.

'This was a spoil heap, not a treasury,' said Ctesias. He, Ignis, Ptollen and Maehekta had followed. The Rubricae stayed guard at the door. The sounds of violence from the rest of the ship had receded. 'This is just dross. They went into the veil and collected every piece of warp-saturated refuse they could find. That they thought this' – he gestured at what looked like a power fist fused with a bony growth of quills – 'was worth sealing in this vault tells you everything. Bitter gods, but the legions of the Eye deserve extinction.'

'We are only here for one thing,' said Ahriman, moving forwards as he swept his gaze around. An angular shape sat alone beside a pile of tarnished silver chains. He moved closer. The shape resolved into a regular block of crystal, eight feet at its longest point and half that wide and deep. Cracks, abrasions and dust clouded its surface, but a small window had been polished on its top. Ahriman looked in. He stayed still for a long moment, then stepped aside so that Maehekta could see. She straightened and looked up at Ahriman.

'It is the one,' she said.

Ahriman felt himself sway as he nodded. He blinked. The burning line was there, closer.

No, he thought. *No. A little more time.* His mouth was dry. He could feel heat. Could they not feel it? They must have seen. He had to… say… something. But he could not. He could not speak, could not open his eyes, could not see anything but the oncoming horizon of fire.

No, not here. Not now… If it took him now, then there would be no way out for the others. No time…

'What is it?' asked Ctesias, coming forward to investigate the crystal.

Ctesias stepped forwards and looked at what was inside the block of crystal. The polished substance was flawlessly transparent, so that he could have believed he was looking through a window into air. A humanoid figure lay within. It might have been seen as resembling a skeleton crafted from brushed steel and carbon. A black sphere sat in the centre of its forehead. Gold threaded its surface in places, forming patterns of circles and lines.

'An alien?' he said aloud, turning. 'This is supposed to save us?'

Ahriman did not answer. Ctesias began to reach out with a telepathic connection. Ahriman raised a hand. The fingers were shaking.

'It… is coming…' he said.

Ctesias felt it then, the heat pouring into his mind and body, like inhaling the air from a furnace.

Ignis had gone still. The Rubricae by the door quivered where they stood. Ptollen fell to his knees.

Ctesias had an instant to draw breath.

Then it was there.

A bomb blast inside his skull.

White light.

Roaring sound.

Charring heat.

He could see nothing but the fire.

It was known as the Pyrodomon. That was what the daemons that Ctesias had summoned had called it. It had begun when Ahriman and the rest of his Exiles had fled the Planet of the Sorcerers after trying to cast the Rubric for a second time. First the soothsayers and augurs had lost their sight of the future. Blackness had crept across their inner eyes until they could see only a few moments beyond the present. Then they had seen the burning horizon. Gilgamos, the most powerful augur besides Ahriman, had described it as a golden line drawn across a black sheet. Others had begun to see it whether they were looking into the future or not. Ctesias had closed his eyes from exhaustion one day and there it had been, bright and painful. Soon it was always there, a burn line in the dark behind his eyelids. Ahriman had called the Circle of his lieutenants. They had debated and argued, but none of them knew what it was. Ahriman had remained silent for most of that. Ctesias had found that more disturbing than anything else – not because Ahriman did not know what was happening, but because Ctesias suspected he did. Then it had come for them.

The heat had arrived first. Ctesias had felt it grow inside him, radiating from his core to his skin. Then pain flooding his flesh. Then light, roaring from the black distance. It was so fast. The gap between one heartbeat and the next. It had overwhelmed him. Pain and burning and the roar of a firestorm. It had seemed to last for eternity. When it had passed, Ctesias found himself crouching on the floor, his mouth filled with the taste of dust and ashes.

It had happened to all of them. Every one of the Thousand Sons had, for an instant, experienced the same thing. It had affected the Rubricae too. Whatever task they had been performing, they had frozen. The ghost-fire had burned in their eyes. Some, it seemed, had spoken, calling out in cracked ghost voices for old comrades, for help, for the fire to stop. That should not have been possible. The Rubricae were sealed suits of armour that held the soul shadows of the Thousand Sons who had worn them. The Rubric Ahriman had cast had reduced them to empty shells of dust. All that remained of them were echoes of their names and lives caught in an eternal cage. They could not act, only obey. But in the fire, something had changed.

Panic had set in. Theories and courses of action buzzed between the minds of the Exiles. It was an attack. It was a curse sent by Magnus the Red as punishment for the Exiles returning to his realm. It was the effect of changes in the Eye of Terror.

Then it had happened again. And again. Each time more intense, each time with less warning. And now it did not simply pass. Now it took things with it.

The fire had descended from the warp and when it had gone, one of the Rubricae had been dust. No echo of his soul remained. Others had followed. Ahriman had told Ctesias to find out what the daemons of the warp knew. He had come back with a name: Pyrodomon, an apotheosis, a metamorphosis in flame. The first of the living had been taken soon after.

It had been a sorcerer called Iskiades. He had been a diviner of dreams and a warrior of subtle arts. They had found him after the Pyrodomon manifested. The seams on his armour were sealed. The lenses of his helm glowed with a dull ghost-light. Inside there was only dust and the soft echo of his name. Iskiades, who had survived the casting of the Rubric, now just a ghost in a cage of armour, now a Rubricae.

That was when Ahriman had given voice to it at last: it was an after-effect of them casting the Second Rubric. It was an etheric blast wave from what they had done, now catching up with them. The great ritual they had enacted to try and save the Legion had not ended. It was out of control, like a fire that had taken hold of a great forest and would not be extinguished until it had burned every tree to ash. And they did not know how to stop it.

The inferno rushed through Ctesias. He was screaming behind his clamped-shut mouth. Gold and red and orange spilled and blotted across his sight. He could feel dust and sand on his skin inside his armour.

Not me! he heard his inner voice shout. It was not a plea, it was a silent roar of fury. He had spent his own soul many times and taken countless lives to hold on to life. He would not end like this. *Not now. Not me.*

The fire vanished. He was gasping, shivering. Bubbles of colour popped in his sight.

'Ctesias.' It was Ahriman. 'Ignis.'

He forced himself up, blinking. Acid tears stung his cheek.

Ahriman was there. Ctesias could see he was fighting to stay standing. Ignis lumbered into sight. His orange-and-black Terminator armour was pale with witch-frost. Maehekta was still beside the block of crystal. She looked utterly unmoved.

'That was worse,' gasped Ctesias. 'More intense than the last time.'

+Get the artefact back to the ship, we must be gone,+ came Ahriman's thought-voice, ragged, his control fraying. +Now.+

'Credence,' said Ignis. The automaton clanked forwards and lifted the block. Pistons hissed in its frame as it took the weight. They turned to the door.

Ptollen stood where Ctesias had last seen him. He did not move. He did not look at them.

They all stopped.

+Brother,+ sent Ctesias at last. 'Ptollen?'

Ptollen's head rose and turned. Pale light filled his eyes. In his mind, Ctesias heard the slow scream of dust falling without end.

CHAPTER II

ℬROTHERS

'What can you remember?'

'That I am Helio Isidorus.'

'Do you remember anything else?'

'Light. I remember light.'

'Before the light?'

'There was nothing before the light.'

'You remember language.'

'Language?'

'The words we are conversing in now, their meaning. It is the basis of speech and knowledge.'

'I do not remember how to speak. I just speak, just as I breathe.'

'Did you notice that I was speaking in High Gothic, but switched to the Hermetica Linguis of Prospero?'

'No. I heard what you said. Are the sounds you make important?'

'Everything is important. Do you realise that you have been speaking in the Hermetica since I spoke to you in it?'

'No. I speak, that's all.'

'Do you remember the last conversation we had?'

'We have talked before?'

'Yes. Do you know who I am, brother?'

'No.'

'I am Ahzek Ahriman.'

'I apologise but I do not remember having a brother.'

'You have many brothers – I am just one.'

'I do not remember the others. I am sorry.'

Ahriman watched Helio Isidorus. His Legion brother sat cross-legged at the centre of the Serene Cages. He wore a tabard of off-white. His skin was clean and unmarked by scars. His eyes were amber flecked with gold. He looked at Ahriman, unblinking. Hoops of bronze spun around him, orbiting the circular platform he sat on. Sigils flowed across each hoop. Inside his mind, Ahriman heard the song they wove in the ether, notes of power rolling over each other, caging, separating, protecting. He would need to go soon. He needed to turn to what would come next. To the future. He should go now. He would go.

Ahriman remained where he was. He wore no armour or helm when he came here, just the blue-and-red robes of a magister. The air in the chamber was cool and still, ion scented. Here the churn of the Great Ocean of the warp was reduced to a distant murmur, its power and fury excluded unless he wished it otherwise.

'Who are you?' asked Helio Isidorus. 'I would like to know.'

Who are you? The question fell into the quiet. He felt the answer come to his mind, the same answer he had given each time that Helio Isidorus had asked. Part of him thought about shaking his head, knowing that when he returned neither answer nor silence would be remembered. Helio Isidorus looked at him, expressionless, waiting.

Ahriman took a breath and gave the answer he had already given a thousand times.

His name was Ahzek Ahriman. He had been born on Terra and become a warrior in the Thousand Sons Legions. He had helped build an Imperium in the stars. He had been loyal and true to his Legion brothers, to his ideals and to the Imperium. He had been betrayed: first by his Emperor, and then by his gene-father, the primarch Magnus. The Emperor had used the powers of the warp to make His Imperium and to push His own knowledge and power to a height that touched the myths of gods. Then the Emperor had denied that same power to Magnus and the Thousand Sons. Worse, He had punished them for pursuing the arts He used. Destruction and fire, barbarity and blood: those had been the rewards for following the Emperor's own path.

Then the second betrayal of a father of his sons. Within the Eye of Terror, the minds and flesh of the Thousand Sons had begun to unravel. Mutation overran them. Warrior sages became mindless creatures of claws, feathers and living fire. Masters of the arcane arts lost control of their physical form, their shape flowing like wax under the flame. They screamed – some in silence, some with hundreds of mouths. Yet Magnus forbade Ahriman from trying to find a salvation for the Legion, and one by one more and more had fallen, until it was too much to bear.

Ahriman had done what he had to. He and his cabal of followers had prepared and cast the Rubric. The hope had been to halt the mutation of his brothers, to free them, to make them what they had been. It had succeeded in part but failed in a greater way. His Legion, his brothers, had become shells of armour in which their souls fell and fell without end. The rest, the pitiful few, had their arcane powers altered and enhanced. For this, Ahriman and his followers had earned banishment. The

Thousand Sons Legion, once dying, was now broken, divided between those loyal to Magnus, those who held their own counsel, and those who followed Ahriman. Some followed in hope of salvation, some because of the power and the possibility of power that burned from him. Others perhaps because following was all they knew. Exiles, sorcerers, warlords and seekers of hope or vengeance, he saw them all and knew that he, and he alone, could save them.

'And I am one of these Thousand Sons,' said Helio Isidorus. He said the words without expression or emotion.

Ahriman nodded. 'You are.'

'And which choice did I make? Did I choose to follow you?'

Ahriman did not answer for a moment. 'No,' he said finally. 'You did not choose to follow me.'

'Then I am one of the others – an enemy, a prisoner.'

'You are no prisoner.'

Helio Isidorus raised a hand to point at the sphere of great, bronze hoops orbiting him and the platform he sat on.

'I do not need to remember to recognise a cage.'

'You are no prisoner. You are my brother.'

'What happened to me that I do not remember you?'

'I tried to set it right,' said Ahriman. 'The Rubric, our curse of mutation, all of it. I went back to the Planet of the Sorcerers, where Magnus rules, where I was banished from. I had discovered and corrected flaws in the first Rubric. I cast it again. I knew that this time it was perfect. I believed it would remake us, that our Legion would be restored to what it had been.'

'Did it work?'

'In part.' Ahriman gave a sad smile. 'One soul, one Rubricae, returned to flesh and life.'

'Me.'

'Just so.'

'But I do not remember...' Helio Isidorus frowned. 'I want to remember.' He looked at Ahriman. 'What do you want?'

Ahriman felt himself blink.

'I want to save our brothers. I want to undo the damage I have done.'

Ctesias was waiting for Ahriman as he came from the Serene Cages. He had been waiting for the best part of an hour. His bones were aching, and he found himself leaning on his staff. He should have worn his armour, let it carry his weight, but he had decided against it – as though admitting he was tired would be giving that fact a victory. He laughed when he thought about it, often out loud. The bitterness in the sound set some of the Neverborn bound in his laboratory clicking and chuckling with delight. It was ridiculous, a contradiction – he was old without doubt, ancient even, his life long enough to swallow many of the mayfly existences of mortals. The same, though, was true of Ahriman, of Kiu, of Ignis and the rest of their kind, but they looked no older as the centuries piled into millennia. Their arts kept away time's hunger for strength. It was not that he was not strong either; that was another paradox of the joke. He could snap the arm of a human with a blow. He could pull a blade from his guts, and the wound would be closed and healed before he stabbed that blade into his enemy's eye. But the shell of his flesh withered and tortured him with pain, with the dull ache that coiled his spine. Flesh and skin sucked taut over his bones, so that with every year placed atop those he had already lived, he resembled a corpse more closely. It was one of the prices he paid, an accumulation of prices in fact, for what he was: a binder of daemons and a thief of power that had not been his. Power always had a price, both large and small, and those you paid often had a sense of humour as kind as a saw blade. You had to pay, though, no matter the cost.

He watched as Ahriman pushed the chamber doors shut. Mechanisms rotated within them. Sigils glowed with blue fire, then red.

+Is it any different today?+ asked Ctesias, the question a flick of telepathy.

Ahriman held still for a moment, not answering. Like Ctesias he wore a robe in place of armour and seemed unarmed. That was a lie, of course. Ahriman was never less than the possibility of apocalypse. Even without a weapon in his hand, the mind within and the power he commanded were greater than any blade or bolter. Even so, he was not without his tools. A blurred, black shadow hovered close to Ahriman, like a blind spot burnt into a retina, visible only to Ctesias' inner sight. Ahriman held out a hand as he turned from the door. The shadow coalesced into substance in his grasp. He held a staff now, topped by curved horns, tipped by a spear blade, and hung with fragments of crystal and bone. Light stuttered and folded behind it as it moved. Ctesias blinked, looking away from it.

+Well?+ he sent.

+He is the same as before,+ Ahriman replied, and began to walk away from the chamber. Ctesias followed him.

+There must come a point when you–+

+What?+ The telepathic reply cut through his sending.

When you must see things for how they are, Ahriman, he thought. *When you realise that whatever is sitting in that cage saying Helio Isidorus' name is at best an empty vessel, a hollow echo of a life and soul. When you let go of the hope that he will one day say something other than his name and that he can remember nothing…* He said none of it and hoped that his thoughts were as secure in his own skull as he believed.

A shiver of sound met Ctesias as they entered the main arterial passage of the *Hekaton*. Figures crowded the wide thoroughfare.

Most were human, or at least had been human. There were beast-bred there too. Most fell to their knees as Ctesias passed. Wrappings of silk pooled on the floor: ochre yellow, sky blue, orange, emerald green. Words in dozens of languages whispered into the air. Excitement, fear, loathing, adulation and awe broke over Ctesias' mind in a fever-hot wave. He felt his lip curl as they parted around him.

We are no gods worth bowing to, he thought.

+I am continuing my interrogation of the Neverborn, but they give up nothing more on the Pyrodomon. Apart from…+ His thought trailed off.

+Apart from what?+

+Apart from that they are afraid of what it is.+

+The Neverborn have no true emotions.+

+They do not. It's more an expression of their instinct for survival.+

Ahriman kept walking.

+I will keep trying to find out more,+ sent Ctesias.

+If you wish.+

Ctesias stopped. Anger fumed off his mind and he did not try to hide it.

Ahriman stopped a pace further on and turned to look at him. +Is there something you wish to say to me, brother?+ he asked.

+What are we going to do now?+ sent Ctesias. +More ships are leaving. That xenos thing still sits in the hold and you have yet to tell anyone besides the soulless one what it is for.+ Ahriman resumed walking. +Time is running out, Ahriman. There are cracks developing in your followers and forces. In fact, there were always cracks but the old ones are widening, and new ones spread.+

+You think I do not see these things? Do you think me blind, Ctesias?+

47

+I think you are letting one relic of a failure cloud your judgement of what needs to happen. I think at best you do not trust us, and at worst you think we will not agree to what you are going to do. I never was like Kiu or Gilgamos, happy to follow in the dark and think that you could do no wrong. I know you can make mistakes, and at this moment that is what you are doing. We are dying, Ahriman – the fire is coming for us all. You cannot solve this alone, and soon you will be alone if you do not act.+

+Everything I have done has been for the Legion, so that we might survive.+

+Yes, and everything you have done has pushed us closer to oblivion.+

Ahriman paused in his stride, turned. His eyes were star-fire blue. Ctesias felt the force in that gaze. He felt his mind struggle to keep balance. The power radiating from Ahriman was like the blaze of a noonday sun. He swallowed in a dry throat. This was another thing that had become worse since the assault on the Planet of the Sorcerers and the failure of the Second Rubric: Ahriman, always powerful, always first in skill of art, had begun to become something else, something more focused, like a beam of light tightened until it could burn – something that Ctesias was not entirely certain was defined by arcane skill and knowledge any more; something that stripped the moisture from his tongue as he decided to speak. His power had become terrifying. Worse was that his control seemed to be fraying.

Ahriman turned back and started to walk away, towards double doors of cold iron that led to the rest of the ship.

+The ancients passed mankind the truth that you should concern yourself only with what you can control,+ sent Ahriman without looking around. +They said that we have power over our minds, but not events. But we are not the mortals of a lost age. We are the Thousand Sons, and what we think, what we believe, what we will – that is what shall happen. Events, reality, fate – all bend to us.+

In front of them, the sigils on the iron doors flared brightly, then dimmed. The doors opened.

'If you say so,' Ctesias said to himself, and did not follow.

The quiet of the chamber settled over Ahriman as the doors sealed. He felt the configuration of his thoughts unlink from the wards woven into the floor and walls. The churn of the Great Ocean of the warp receded from his awareness. He stood utterly still, allowing himself to be aware of the beat of his hearts and the slow breaths drawing into his lungs.

Still alive, he thought. *Still flesh and blood.* The darkness did not answer. He let the moment last for a beat longer. Then willed light.

Fire rose from bowls of oil clamped to the walls. Golden light filled the space, multiplying in brightness as it bounced from the mirror-smooth granite walls. The chamber was the inside of a pyramid set upon the spine of the *Hekaton* amongst the towers and domes. Others might have thought his personal sanctuary would have been at the top of the highest tower, set above the city that grew above the vast ship. Instead, it was a modest space nestled between greater structures like a fragment of polished jet amidst a cluster of larger and brighter jewels. An enneagramic star inside a circle marked the floor, inlaid in silver.

Four stone plinths sat in line with each of the room's corners. His armour lay on one, each piece set out like the dissected shell of a dead crustacean. His helm sat on another, its horns rising above crystal eye-lenses. The third was empty, waiting for the staff from his hand. A box sat on the fourth. Lapis and bronze covered its surface with wings and scarabs, but underneath, he knew, the battered metal remained. He opened his hand and the staff rose from his fingers and glided to settle on its plinth. He closed his eyes. Here, in this stolen pool of quiet, he could feel his thoughts, and the chains of arcane formulae running through the layers of his subconscious, meshing with each other, the ether of the warp and reality, controlling and synchronising each without cease. In the silence, they whispered to him with the voices of the past.

Astraeos, lost and blind.

Carmenta, soul and mind dissolved by the ships she had tried to tame.

Ohrmuzd, his birth and Legion brother, long gone.

'Fate is for us to choose, to make our own...'

All gone, all failed by him and swept away by the current of time until they seemed like a dream slowly sinking under the surface of the present, reaching, drowning...

'Everything you have done has pushed us closer to oblivion.' That was what Ctesias had said. The truth was always a knife that cut deep.

He needed to rest, to rebalance. It was coming. He could feel it, and he would need to be ready. There was no prophecy or oracular sight to guide him now. Just his will.

I must go on, he thought. No matter what, I must go on. I must set it right. There was so little time, though, and what remained was running out. No time to plan, no time to be certain. No time to doubt. If I do not do this, no one will.

He let out a breath and opened his eyes. He was standing in front of the chest on the fourth plinth. He blinked. He had been on the other side of the chamber. His thoughts must have brought him here. He looked at the box. He had not opened it in a long time. He raised his hand. He should rest...

A gesture, and the chest's gold-and-lapis casing unpeeled with a murmur of cogs. Wards and etheric locks released with snaps of dissipating power. Battered pressed metal sat beneath the glittering shell. Ahriman reached out and lifted the lid. Off-white fabric covered the single object inside. He could smell dust and soot. Slowly he pulled back the fabric. A helm looked back at him. It was blackened and battered, beak nosed and unadorned – a crow helm for a dead warrior. He hesitated, then lifted it out. His fingers touched the scratches in the ceramite. Hairline cracks ran through its eye-lenses. It felt familiar, as though the last time he had worn it and the name that went with it had been hours before.

Horkos... A name from a different time, for a different man, a broken man who had hoped that fate would let him sink into nothing. A fool, a failure to all that he held true and cared for...

He held the helm's gaze for a long moment, then set it back under its shroud. With a flick of thought, the gold and lapis sealed over the chest again. He turned and settled into a folded-leg position at the centre of the enneagram on the floor. He did not have time, but he needed to renew himself, even if just a little. He closed his eyes and began to pull his thoughts into patterns that pulled him up through tiers of focus and control. He felt the questions and memories fall away. The quiet of the chamber settled in his mind...

And he opened his eyes in the quiet of the cave.

The only illumination was the moon-shimmer of the pool of water sitting in a curve of the rock in front of him. The silver light touched the idea of the walls, sketching water-eroded stone. A drop formed on one of the stalactites above and shone as it caught the glow from the pool. It hung, growing, then dropped. The sound of it striking water became a brief echo before it faded. Ripples rebounded from the edge of the pool, interfered with each other, and slowly dissolved back to stillness.

Ahriman let the quiet fold around him and watched the next drop begin to form. None of it was real, at least not real as most would think of the concept. The cave was in his mind, an idea constructed by will. Every part of it was taken from memory: the sheen of the stone, the flint-edged smell of the air, the texture of the silence, and countless other details. All had been real, but here they were spun together to make something new. It sat at the deepest point of his mind, with the echoes and ghosts of gene memories and half-forgotten lives. He had created it as an inner sanctuary in the days and months after their flight from the Planet of the Sorcerers and the casting of the Second Rubric. It was a place of renewal, his own place – separate and untouched by the past, present or future. The path he walked for his Legion, and the power he had to wield, left him little that existed for him alone, but the cave – silent and secret, hidden within – was his. He had allowed himself to fall into his own personal underworld. He had brought his mind to stillness, cutting away all but the vital patterns that threaded his thoughts. His humours aligned, blood and breath and nerves balanced.

'All is as it must be,' he said aloud, and his words echoed as the falling drop of water had. Here in the dark he could believe the words were true. He let out the idea of a breath. He would need to go soon, to pull his awareness up into the world of spinning thoughts and turning events, of consequences and action and the long blankness of a future reaching towards a hidden horizon. It was a long journey, just as it had been to descend to the cave. He would pass through empty palaces of memory and the dead husks of old beliefs. It would pass in one beat of one of his hearts, but he would live it as an age. Ghosts and lost things and secrets, all the things that in a mundane mind existed out of sight, buried in the subconscious, would be there walking with him as he rose to the outer world.

'All will be as it must,' he said, and stood. He needed to begin his journey back. He stepped to the edge of the pool, bent, and dipped his fingers into the water.

'Ahriman...'

He whirled at the sound of the voice, but he was already falling into the water and the word was fading into doubt. Down and on through darkness and the past...

Air gasped into his lungs. His eyes opened. His sanctuary was just as it had been. The flames still burned in the bowls fixed to the walls. The air was still, the space quiet. He blinked. Waited...

Nothing.

He blinked again, then rose from where he had sat at the centre of the enneagram. Will reached out from him. His armour rose from its plinth and split into components, which orbited him for an instant. His robes dissolved into nothing, a heartbeat before the armour assembled on him. The helm settled onto his head. The world before his eyes became spinning marks and the glow of arcane sigils and revolving geometries. Body and armour and mind unified with a murmur of neural linking and a thought. The words and characters etched into the plates caught the flow of etheric force from his mind and lit with power. Crystals set into his helm, cuirass and pauldrons inhaled it. He felt the armour bond with his mind, hardening portions of thought and will into shapes and patterns, storing strength, shielding. The Black Staff came last. He held out his hand and it was there – not moving through the air, but simply becoming present in his grasp. He stood for a moment, feeling the balance and focus of his awareness. He was about to move, then stopped and glanced behind him. Down at the edge of his thoughts he heard a voice say his name in the darkness.

CHAPTER III

KEY OF INFINITY

Ignis watched as the model of the Exiles' fleet turned through the fume-filled air. He was clad in his molten-orange and coal-black Terminator armour, and anyone looking at him for the first time would have thought he well deserved his reputation amongst Ahriman's High Circle as the last great Master of the Order of Ruin – a leveller and destroyer. They would have been right too, but not at this moment. For now, he was more concerned with the problems of creation.

The model hanging in the air above him was no holo-display but a physical simulacrum: the vessels were represented by flecks of molten silver moving on precisely balanced telekinetic arcs, which adjusted the position of each burning dot to the movement of the real ships in the void. The chamber that held the model was spherical, its walls grey iron and lead threaded with lines of gold that described the etheric geometries which perpetuated and fed the representation. It also adjusted reality, sending impulses to the crew of each ship if a vessel moved out of its place. Such adjustments were an unfortunate necessity. Ignis had long since come to terms with the fact that reality was imperfect when compared to the power and purity of numerology, geometries and ratios. That was what made the truth of number and pattern the higher truth of existence – the fact that the physical fell so far short of perfection. Watching momentum decay slowly spoil the arrangement of the ships, though, he felt himself twitch. The geometry of the tattoos covering his face changed. He sensed the shiver as the chamber sent a command for a correction in the errant ship's speed. He waited, watching to see if the speck of glowing metal adjusted position.

The arrangement was more than a matter of perfection in his own sight. The ships and their movements were part of a macro arrangement which reached out from them to the stars and the bleeding wound in space that was the Eye of Terror. That arrangement meshed with the minds and thoughts, conscious and subconscious, of all the millions of souls on board. They resonated with each other. Numerical and symbolic transformations occurred, and then altered each other. It was a vast, self-perpetuating mechanism that spooled power and meaning and purpose from the Great Ocean and stored it until he needed it. Until he unleashed that power. It was one of the most difficult pieces of ritual engineering he had undertaken, and it might have been one of the greatest works of his existence if it had not been for the imperfection of reality and mortal nature. He frowned as the errant craft's mote of fire shifted a micron back into its correct orbit.

Beside him, Credence shifted position with a hiss of gears. He glanced at the automaton. Its black shell, threaded with gold, looked like a looming shadow torn free of an armoured giant. Its gun twitched towards the circular door into the chamber. Ignis followed the gun's aim, realigning his senses to the reality outside the configuration of the model. His tattoos shifted pattern again.

A figure was moving towards them, flanked by four human guards in silver armour and blue robes. Helms hid their faces, featureless and eyeless. The spears they carried over their shoulders hummed with low-level power. Each of them was a psyker, selected from the gifted amongst the mortal thralls and trained by the lower circles of the Thousand Sons as bodyguards for the Navigator breed that steered their ships through the Great Ocean. They were the Unsighted Keepers. All of them were blind and tongueless, their power and senses channelled through their minds, their eyes lost to keep the secrets of those they protected. The foremost of those charges shuffled towards Ignis and Credence, crumpled folds of velvet dragging on the floor.

Silvanus Yeshar wheezed as he approached. Twin ebony and silver canes clacked in time with his movements, though the hands holding them remained hidden within heavy sleeves.

'I can't wait longer, we will have to go soon,' said Silvanus, looking up at Ignis. A silver veil hid the man's face, but Ignis could see the hints of features under the gauze: folds of flesh, soft shadows that might have been eye sockets. He felt his skin crawl and his lip curl as he shook his head.

'We go nowhere until Ahriman wills it. Until then, crawl back to your pit and wait.'

'The pain…' Silvanus said, and shivered. Fabric rippled as whatever flesh it hid wobbled. 'You do not understand, if we do not go then… then…'

'You will die,' said Ignis flatly.

Silvanus shook, but whether in denial or for another reason Ignis could not tell.

'The Ocean… The Great Ocean calls and I must go… We must go. The deeps are our home, its tides the life in our blood. Let us swim, let it flow through us. Please, let us live.'

Ignis took a step forward. The Unsighted Keepers flinched as they sensed his threat. Credence took a step closer, gun rotating, pistons opening the fingers of its fists. Yeshar's guards froze. Ignis looked at them and then down at the man. There was a smell in the air this close to him, a cloying reek like incense and spoiled milk.

Yeshar was, or had been, a Navigator – a class of mutant that guided ships through the warp and allowed them to bypass the limits of physics and cross light years in hours or days. The Imperium had always mistrusted them as much as it needed them. In that respect they had something in common with the Thousand Sons, but Ignis found that did not reduce his own dislike of their presence. Ahriman had taken Silvanus from an Imperial ship, and since then the warp had worked on the Navigator's flesh. Year by year, he had devolved further. His mind was now as unstable as his body. He had only two qualities of note: his skill at threading the currents of the empyrean, and his survivability. That and a note of loyalty from Ahriman towards the Navigator, which Ignis struggled to even begin to understand, had kept him alive. It did not stop Ignis loathing the creature.

'You and your brood are a component, nothing more,' Ignis said. 'You function when the mechanism requires you to. You do not bargain or plead. You wait and obey.'

Silvanus whimpered and shuffled back. He looked like he was about to say something.

+Ignis.+ The sending rang clear in Ignis' skull. He raised a hand to silence the Navigator.

+Ahriman,+ he replied.

+We must begin.+

Ignis was already moving, barging past Silvanus and his guards. Credence followed, shaking the deck with its strides.

'You understand,' Silvanus called after him. 'You do understand, don't you.'

* * *

Ignis watched as the block of crystal dissolved on the slab. The air in the chamber tasted blank on his tongue, drained of stray ions and particles in preparation for the… His thoughts stuttered for a moment. The word *examination* had come to mind, but then another had pushed into his awareness. *Interrogation…* This was an interrogation. Credence stood on one side of him, Ahriman on the other, each equally still. They had been this way for three hours, two minutes and five seconds. Ignis kept the focus of his mind on the crystal as his mind unpicked its substance.

The skeleton-like figure still lay within. Wrongness spiralled from every line of its geometry.

'A xenos,' Ignis had said when he had first seen it.

Maehekta had nodded. 'One of a race long dead.'

'But this one still lives.'

'That which was never living cannot die,' she replied.

'Its form… It is skeletal, and like a number of depictions of death from mankind's past, and from many other alien races.'

'They existed before humanity evolved,' she explained. 'Their shadows became the ideas that our minds turned into gods and dreams. It is no wonder they seem familiar. Before the galaxy made its own nightmares, these were the horrors that stalked the living.'

Ignis had not commented further.

He had asked Maehekta who had sealed it in the crystal. She had given the smallest of shrugs.

'I do not know. Perhaps it is not known by any, but I do not think that it was done by the race the specimen came from.'

Ignis concurred. Psychic manipulation of matter had created the crystal. Molecular lattices ran through its structure that kept all other energy from the objects within. Those objects themselves held no spark or mark of psychic potential or even connection – they were inert and frictionless to the ether. That implied that the two were not of the same origin.

He peeled away the last lattices of crystal. The metal figure lay still in the sterilised air. Ignis felt his mind instinctively begin to process the micro patterns and ratios in its form. Coldness coiled through his nerves in the instant before his will stopped the thoughts progressing. He had no desire to know what he would find if he let them reach their end. He sent a command to the servo-arms hanging above the slab. Chrome limbs swung down and lifted the objects that had been in the crystal with the figure: a staff, its flared cap made from a substance that looked like black-green glass; a cloak of iridescent scales; and last, a sphere. Ignis could not tell whether the sphere was metal or glass or neither. The servo-arms placed each object on its own plinth.

He waited. None of the objects or the figure moved. He checked the auspex data read-outs on his helm display. Nothing. They read as inert. Even so…

'Credence, vigilance protocol,' he said. The automaton locked its legs in place. Weapon pods armed with a buzz. The cannon on its back began a slow, watchful traverse across the room. He keyed a control, and shackles extended from the slab and secured the figure's limbs and torso. Given what Maehekta had told them of this xenos' potential capabilities, those restraints would be cosmetic.

Ignis looked at Ahriman.

+Everything is prepared,+ sent Ignis.

He could feel the power building around Ahriman as he touched his mind. While Ignis had readied the chamber for the investigation, Ahriman's attention had been on preparing his mind and the warp. Ignis noticed a tiny change in Ahriman's irises and pupils, as though he was shifting focus from the inner to the outer world.

+Come into alignment,+ sent Ahriman.

Ignis drew a breath and pulled his thoughts and sensations into a pattern that orbited his will. Sacred numbers spun in small, fast circles while his awareness turned with slow precision. Every fragment of his mind balanced with every other part. He let himself watch it for a heartbeat, then opened his inner eye.

Around him, Ahriman's mind construction extended out and out, to beyond where Ignis' inner sight could see. Ideas and meaning arced past each other like the orbs of a great orrery. Spheres of incantation swung, clashed, merged and separated, dancing with endless change.

Ignis was not a soul often moved to awe; he had seen and known too much. But as he saw what Ahriman had done, he felt something that might have been wonder. He had seen Ahriman do great and terrible things – evocations that made reality flow and whip like a ribbon caught in a storm wind. But this... it came close to perfection.

In the time taken to prepare for the evaluation of the artefact, Ahriman had conceived and created what could only be described as an etheric mechanism. Arrangements of thought and symbolism threaded spurs of will and imagination, all working and combining seamlessly. It was a work of genius made by a craftsman of the impossible. And it had a single purpose: to allow thought and memory outside of the flow of time.

+Ascend,+ sent Ahriman. Ignis closed his eyes. His consciousness rose and meshed with the construction. He heard his mind begin to echo with thoughts that were not his own. He felt the instinct to resist as parts of his soul slid from his control. Sensation flooded him: the touch of snow on his face, the sound of currents echoing in the deep belly of an ocean, cold stone and silver and the cry of a raven in a leafless forest...

Ignis opened his eyes.

Ahriman looked back at him and gave a small nod.

'We begin,' he said aloud, and looked at the metal figure on the slab. Ignis keyed a control. A single servo-limb descended from the array on the ceiling. A long carbon spike sat at its tip. Charge coils connected to the limb began to glow. Ignis felt a static hum buzz in his teeth. Despite himself, he hoped that Maehekta's information on the means to wake this... creature held true. The tip of the spike touched the figure's chest. False lightning bleached the air white.

The prisoner leapt off the slab. His body slid through the molecules of the restraints and hit the energy dome. Sparks showered through the air as the field collapsed into a flat blast wave. The prisoner landed in a crouch. His gaolers loomed above him, towering in their armour. One in orange and black, the other in blue. Behind them, their crude automaton began to turn, light glinting off the silver and black of its carapace.

The warrior in orange-and-black armour shouted. The automaton stamped forwards, piston-driven limbs shaking the deck. The cannon on its shoulder swivelled. The prisoner could feel the dark energy dancing in the weapon; he knew its shape and taste, old and familiar from wars that had scarred the stars when they were young.

The gun weapon drew breath to fire. The prisoner's senses traced the distances between every point in the room, and sliced time down until only the decay of atoms marked its passing. The short distance from him to the automaton's gun, from the automaton to its masters, from those masters to the door. Every measured value became like crystal, every facet and plane extending through countless dimensions.

The automaton fired. A beam of darkness sliced out. The air

screamed. The beam struck the prisoner's torso. The substance of his form began to unravel, crumbling into nothingness as the beam bored through it. It was so quick. For other creatures it would have been an instant, but for the prisoner it was a slow unfolding of obliteration. He had time to observe, to analyse – to know that the beam would pulse, and the black energies would swallow his body in a flash of collapsing matter. He would not survive. But he did not need to survive. He just needed to reach the sphere which lay on a plinth behind its gaolers.

His hand closed over the sphere…

And the universe was made again in a flash of collapsing time.

The prisoner became aware. His senses reconnected to his consciousness one at a time. He could hear movement around him. 'Nauth shal'cre'ta?' The warrior in orange spoke.

'Su'van'isk,' the one in blue replied.

He heard the words, and his mind began to break down the data they carried. Potential meanings rose and clustered. He could see the root of meaning in the language, but he needed more to form understanding.

'Se'sha'on ver.'

'Ka'uth van'isk, cree ur'petion. No?'

'Nev'mon usk da'she, sha'on'ver ka'na'ink? Ka-ith ne'ba…'

It was a simple language, but with some unusual symbolic systems grafted into its structure. The voices of long-dead civilisations echoed at the edge of the words.

'Function ek'ith,' said the warrior in black and orange. 'Kel of technology ral-uth bel'sharn.'

The warrior in blue glanced at the other as he replied.

'Se'sha'on se'ur'tain, and an'isk'hoy de ra'us'ason turdu'sisk.'

'Y just ver-ash daeo-nu.'

'Eh fear ta'ha'at we k-usest to.'

'That n-het comfort.'

With a little more analysis, the prisoner could have traced the roots of the language back to its genesis. That could be useful in time, but for now it was irrelevant. The prisoner needed to escape, and for that he needed one thing. He needed time.

'Is it aware of us?' asked the warrior in blue.

'Power is running through its structure,' replied the one in black and orange.

'Is that a way of saying yes, or of saying no?'

'It is the only data I have available that relates to your question. I have no knowledge of this form of... life.'

'Life? Yes... I suppose we must call it that.'

Visual input returned. Three figures stood before the prisoner. Two were of the bipedal typical norm and wore machine armour. The third was a pure machine entity, albeit a crude one – an automaton crafted of circuits and pistons. An energy lance with a fluted barrel projected above its shoulders. The prisoner watched the trio as his sight stretched into the edges of the electromagnetic spectrum. He could not perceive the submolecular yet, but that would come. He needed time, and the best way to gain that was to speak.

'I... can... hear you,' he said. 'I can see you.'

'You speak our language?' asked the one in blue.

'Its root and structure are simple,' he replied. 'Deriving its method and order of expression is likewise simple.'

'What is your name?'

'Name? Yes, a concept that your pseudo-knowledge system would value. The closest approximation that I can offer is Setekh, servant of eternity to the dynasts of the Hyksos.'

The two figures glanced at each other.

'It speaks like a human,' said the figure in black and orange.

'There are emotional markers in the tonal structure. Arrogance, defiance, disdain.'

'No, it is not talking like a human. It is talking like us. It is imitating us, are you not, Setekh?'

'You are a perceptive but limited being,' he replied.

'Everything is a matter of the perspective. From where I look at this moment, we have much to gain from one another.'

Setekh did not reply for a second. A section of his consciousness was preparing to realign the molecules of his body. When that was complete he would be able to phase through his bonds. From there... well that depended very much on where he was. On board a large ship in the vacuum, yes he was certain of that, but where was that ship? He shut down the line of thought. He would need to have answers, but they would only be relevant once he was free. For that he needed to reach the chronometron which lay on a stone plinth to the side of the slab. He would not have time to perform a significant time alteration, but he could reset events and make incremental changes for the next time he lived these moments. He calculated what he would need to do, and the precise operation he would need to perform in the instant he touched the device. As the formulae crystallised in his mind, he reflected that he might already have done these exact actions before.

'What are your names? That is the convention within your communication template, is it not?'

'My name is Ahzek Ahriman, and my companion's name is Ignis.'

'I have never encountered your species before, but you are not typical specimens. When I was last conscious there were species that existed that might have developed into your genus, but I would have expected both greater deviation from that physiology, and less amplification of gross physical qualities.

Therefore, you are not evolved creatures. You are creations, fusions of crude knowledge and biological stock. Is this line of reasoning correct?'

Ignis turned to Ahriman, the black lines of his bioelectric tattoos reformed into a different pattern.

'Do you intend to question this… thing, or does our method of analysis consist of letting it ask the questions? I do not intend this as humorous.'

Ahriman did not respond but held the gaze of Setekh. There was something about that stare. Setekh had not felt anything close to an emotion for aeons, but the cold intensity in those blue eyes…

'You infer a great deal from very little, Setekh,' Ahriman said.

'You are impressed by such trivial things. When you have aided in the building and destruction of civilisations greater than anything you can imagine, the wonder of the beasts which roam the ruins means nothing.'

'I infer that it means us,' said Ignis.

'My people shackled the stars, and broke mortality when the species you sprang from had barely left the slime pools it spawned in. Our wars burned reality, and the dominion of our kings is without limit. The ground you tread is not yours. It is ours.'

'And what is the name of your kind?' asked Ahriman.

'Why give a name to totality?'

'Because whatever you were, you failed,' said Ignis. 'Those that outlive ruin can call the wreckage of the past whatever they please.'

Setekh chuckled.

'We were, and are, and shall be. And I must thank you both, Ahriman and Ignis. This primitive exchange of meaningless emotional postures has proved most instructive. I know you now, Ahzek Ahriman, and will remember you. But you will not remember this!'

Setekh dissolved the shackles into dust and leapt for the chronometron. Ignis and Ahriman began to move. They were fast, very fast, but they were unprepared, and Setekh's hand was around the chronometron, and the calculations flowed across the contact, and Ignis shouted, and the world began to end again.

'Credence, kill protocol!'

The beam of darkness stabbed out from the automaton's gun and struck Setekh in the torso. The chronometron activated, and the present became the past.

Time peeled back around Setekh. He could not remember the earlier instances of this moment, but information existed in his awareness that could only be there if he had passed through this time already. He knew the names of the three figures who stood above him. He knew the positioning of each object in the cell and, most importantly, he knew that this was the final loop through this instance. His chronometron had moved position by increments through each of the earlier iterations of this encounter. Each time he had reached the device before he was destroyed, and each of those times he had been able to steal a sliver more time for the next instance. With each of those changes he had increased his awareness and changed the setting of the chronometron. He only needed to perform this one final operation, and he would be able to collapse this loop of time. He would be free.

'It is aware.'

'Yes. It is aware.'

Setekh's thought flow faltered. Something was out of place in the pattern of events. Something that he had not engineered. He did not have time to deduce what was wrong. Every slice of his consciousness was needed to prepare his body to phase through his shackles.

'You are Setekh, cryptek of the dynasts of the Hyksos. Can you understand me?'

'I can understand you. Your linguistic forms are as primitive as your methods of imprisonment.'

'Do you know why you are here?'

Setekh paused. The question did not fit. Lines of deduction and inference began to spawn in Setekh's mind. He shut them down. The information was irrelevant and he needed his full consciousness preparing to interface with the chronometron as he was almost ready. He just needed another sliver of time.

'You wish information,' he said. 'You wish secrets.'

'Yes, but your insight is limited.'

'And this exchange is irrelevant.'

The shackles dissolved as Setekh came off the slab. The skin of his frame flickered from dull chrome to mirror black. The automaton began to move. Its cannon swivelled, the dark energies within built.

Setekh's hand extended to the chronometron.

The beam of darkness snapped out, but it would never find its target. The chronometron was beneath Setekh's hand. His fingers closed on it.

And froze.

Frost climbed his digits. The air was shimmering. Setekh's awareness was bubbling with paradox: light blurring to dark, mass and energy interchanging and vanishing out of existence. The beam of the automaton's gun was a frozen splinter of blackness hanging in mid-air. Ahriman and Ignis were still, but light blazed around them, feathering into shadow, shifting between colours. Invisible bands of force coiled tighter around Setekh as he forced out words.

'You are slaves of the anathema realm,' he said.

'And now you see the totality of your position,' said Ahriman. 'To watch your actions has been most illuminating.'

Ahriman extended his hand, and the chronometron rose from the plinth and settled into his palm. He turned it between his fingers, head tilting as the light played over the sphere's surface. Ignis stepped closer beside him, tattoo patterns shifting across his blank face. Ahriman opened his hand and the chronometron floated up into the air, then dropped into Ignis' grasp.

'Incredible,' said Ignis. 'The effect on the flow of time is seamless. Not even a ripple in the warp. The events are simply reset and flow again.'

'And this from a bauble carried by one of their techno-viziers. Does this answer your doubts about the reality of such technology?'

'It is persuasive, but by what means does it function?'

Setekh's eyes buzzed with static as Ahriman leaned in towards him. The green lenses of the sorcerer's helm blazed bright.

'That, my brother,' said Ahriman, 'is the heart of the question.'

'You wish the secrets of time,' said Setekh. Ahriman stepped back. In truth, he had not expected the alien's response. Its mental ability was staggering. It had inferred facts from scraps of data with a speed and accuracy that Ahriman had never heard of. That made it one of the most dangerous things he had ever met.

It is manipulating you, said a voice in his thoughts. *Even as you manipulate it, it is adapting in turn. As I think and calculate, so it does too, our thoughts locked together like cog wheels.*

+The factors of risk involved are open-ended,+ sent Ignis. +The probability of disaster is acute if we allow the creature to continue to exist.+

+I understand, brother,+ replied Ahriman.

Setekh's eyes flickered.

'Death stalks you,' it said. 'You are a breed on the edge of extinction.'

Ahriman gave no reaction. What fragment of information had led the xenos to that insight? No matter the catalyst, the statement was a provocation. That meant it wanted something.

+It is going to offer an exchange,+ sent Ahriman to Ignis.

+Yes,+ agreed Ignis. +You are going to allow it to?+

'What do you want?' said Ahriman aloud.

'The direct approach,' said Setekh. 'Removing as much supposition and deception as possible. That means you have inferred that I will offer you some of what you want for something of what I need. Your intellect is impressive for one of the slime-bred species.'

Ahriman waited. After a long moment, the xenos gave a static-edged chuckle.

'You are dying. Your flesh betrays you and those you care about. You have power but you have failed to prevent the inevitable. So, you are reaching outside of your circle of power. You wish the key to unlock time…'

+We should not allow it to speak further,+ sent Ignis. +It is lacing its language with emotive and resonant patterns. It knows us. It is going to tell us what we want. The progression of events if we allow this to continue is not favourable.+

+And if what it tells us is true?+ sent Ahriman.

+Then the progression becomes catastrophic.+

'I can give that key to you,' said Setekh.

'How?' asked Ahriman.

'The device you have in your hand can manipulate the flow of time in a limited fashion. It is a wonder to you, but it is just a spark of what my kind did. Before our destruction, the master of my dynasty created a device whose potency is greater by orders of magnitude. Not simply the ability to wind back small pieces of time, or to halt it, but to recreate it – to allow the mastery of paradox and causation... We had the means to unmake what was and control what is.'

'If your kind had such power, why are they no more?' asked Ahriman.

'Power creates enemies. The greater the power, the greater the enemies. Our enemies were almost the equal of our power, and they had the means to destroy us.'

'But you survived?'

'I fled, and as my age fell to ruin I slept, and waited, and hoped.'

'Hoped for what?'

'That one day I would wake and find our enemies gone. That I could return to the ruins of my home and find if any others of my dynasty survived too. You asked what I wanted, and that is my answer. I wish to go back to the grave of my people. Take me there and I will give you the key to infinity.'

+It is not lying,+ Ahriman sent to Ignis.

+No, it is not,+ agreed Ignis. +That is what makes it dangerous.+

To most sentient species, perhaps to all, the first moment of waking would have been incomprehensible. To even the most advanced of their kind, thought – grounded in base matter and the thoughts that that matter produced – was the framework by which they understood everything: language, meaning, cause and effect. Even within the warp, especially within the warp – where the congealed refuse of consciousness gathered and festered – the initiating moment went unnoticed. It was too abstract, too purely and solely physical, but in a way that made it closer to magic than anything the warp could bring into being.

In two different points in space but at the same moment, two exotic subatomic particles held in a quantum void spun in the identical direction. They had been entangled long before and sealed in microstructures at each of their two locations. Vast distances of space separated them, distances that it would have taken light millennia to cross. That one could cause the other to change defied the base rules of the physical universe, but neither exotic particle had caused the change in the other; they simply behaved identically, bound and entangled, so that they were, to all intents and purposes, one and the same. When one changed, the other changed too.

At one location the event sparked nothing more. In the second location, systems that had been sipping energy from background radiation noticed the entangled particle change its spin. Chains of communication and consequence began to flicker through the long-cold substance of systems buried under the crust of dead worlds. The systems were simple, little more than levels of semi-intelligent monitors and governors that formed the first layers of the whole they guarded. The communications and commands blinked like the eyes of a guard dog woken from long slumber by a breath of air across the nose.

Entanglement – O

I – This hierarchy wakes – Awareness – Supplicate to II

II – Supplication accepted – authority and decision does not lie within the vaults of ordained authority of this hierarchy – Ordination to I – confirm source of entanglement location-identity

I – Obedience – Location-identity Bearer of the Black Disc, Most High Setekh – Supplicate to II

II – Supplication accepted – mandate and command not granted to this hierarchy's function – Ordained – begin waking of III

I – Obedience – It shall be as ordained

CHAPTER IV

A CIRCLE DIVIDED

Ctesias let out a hiss of pain and opened his eyes. Blood was running over the bottom of his lip and down his chin. He could feel the wound in his mouth beginning to heal already, but the damage was done. The words he had been intoning were already gone, leaving only the taste of bitter fruit and incense to mingle with the blood in his mouth. The flayed face holding the bound essence of a snared daemon floated in a bowl of quicksilver in front of him, obstinate, its presence almost insolent. For an instant, he very much wanted to pick it up and crush it. He breathed instead.

'Failure?' asked Lycomedes. Ctesias looked up at his apprentice and wiped the blood from his chin.

'If you wish to learn how I can punish insolence, then you are very close to succeeding.'

'I wished only to know if we have made any progress.'

Ctesias spat and stood, his armour shedding ash from where some of his protective parchments had burned away during his latest attempt to learn more about the nature of the Pyrodo-mon. It was like trying to unravel a knot buried in the meat of a rotten corpse and then trace a thread back to the hand that had tied it. So far, he had failed to even loosen part of the tangle.

'This is a fool's errand.'

'I thought that none could rival your knowledge and skill in the arts,' said Lycomedes, his voice neutral as he began to repaint the sigils on the chamber floor. The blood fizzed and bubbled in the silver bowl as he dipped his fingers into it again.

'Don't prove yourself a simpleton in order to insult me,' sneered Ctesias. 'You know what true knowledge and power means? It means not being foolish enough to think that because you are at the pinnacle, there is nothing you cannot do.' He shook his head, looking at the flayed face and the pattern of the waves forming in the quicksilver around it.

He swore under his breath, turned away from the bowl of fuming metal and made for the chamber door.

'Are we not going to make another attempt?' asked Lycomedes.

'It appears not,' Ctesias snapped, and did not look back as he passed the door's wards and went out through his labyrinth of rooms into the core of the ship. He was not sure where he was going or why, just that he wanted to be alone and for the itching inside his suspicions to be quiet. Doors opened in response to his will. The human and mutant thralls abased themselves as he passed but he barely registered their presence.

He had spent all his life using the warp to outrun death, to gain what he wanted and crush those who would harm him. He had prided himself on seeing clearly what others did not. The universe held no mysteries to him, or so he had thought. It had one truth: cruelty. Understand that and nothing could do you harm, or fool you, or break you. Except that it had found a way. Here he was caught between following a path of action he did not believe in and doing nothing. There was no way out. No trick to play, no hidden secret to find. They were going to be annihilated. The only hope was that Ahriman's hubris was in fact truth, that their greatest sorcerer would find a way, at last, to save them.

He laughed aloud.

'Would you care to share the jest?'

Ctesias stopped at the sound of the voice, only now realising he had let his thoughts pull his attention a long way from his surroundings. He was in a pillared hall, subconsciously picked perhaps because none of the mortal crew came here and few of the Thousand Sons. It was the remains of a temple, pulled from some dead world and grafted into the body of the ship like an unwanted organ. Pitted granite pillars rose from thick bases, saurian heads snarling down from their tops. Crude statues of humanoid figures with many arms and blank, pyramidal heads sat on plinths. Slab tablets covered in tiny circles rose from the floor like doors waiting for walls to fit into. Maehekta stood up from where she had been crouching next to one of them.

Ctesias recoiled. His instinct to leave was strong, but he held himself still.

'Jest?' he asked.

'You laughed,' stated Maehekta.

'I find my thoughts offer me the best amusement available.'

'Then I am sorry to have disturbed them.'

'What are you doing here?' asked Ctesias.

'I heard that this place was here. I wanted to see it.' She gestured at the tablet. 'Fascinating.'

'If you say so.'

'Have you read what is written here?'

'Some,' said Ctesias. 'Enough to know that reading the rest will not be any more worthwhile. Not unless you want to hear how a clutch of humans cut off from technology and knowledge – and who believed that the stars were literal eggs – thought the universe was created.' He gave a sour smile. 'Of course, your sense of value may vary.'

'Then why did your brothers preserve it?'

'They are overly sentimental.'

'Of course... Not a flaw that can be found in you.'

Ctesias nodded at the brief smile on Maehekta's smooth face and turned away. He would have to find another place for his bid for solitude. He paused, turned back. Maehekta was still smiling at him.

'What are you?' he asked. 'You appeared amongst us as the Pyrodomon took hold. Ahriman trusts you, or at least values you highly, and Ignis knows something that makes him value you, but the rest of us...' He sucked his teeth. 'We know nothing.'

Maehekta shrugged again. 'I trade in truths.'

'And that is why you are here? You traded with Ahriman for the location of that xenos artefact those Born of Iron degenerates had?'

'I traded him the location of the xenos artefact that the Born of Iron stole from us.'

Ctesias gave a single snort and a nod. 'Of course. Hence the key you had to the warded vault, and how you know about the xenos inside that psy-neutral lump of crystal.'

She inclined her head. 'Of course.'

'What is Ahriman giving you in return?'

'That is for him to tell.'

Ctesias bared his teeth briefly. 'You said they took the artefact from "us",' he said. 'Who is us?'

'I trade in truth, Ctesias, what will you give me in return?'

'Your continued life.'

'An idle threat. You fear Ahriman too much, and you are all desperate enough to do whatever it takes to help him save you.'

'I will give you nothing.'

'Then you will get no truth, Ctesias. One truthful answer, for a truthful answer. You have traded more with the Neverborn for lies.' She smiled again. The gesture made his skin crawl.

'All right,' he said.

She nodded then raised her chin, still smiling, and wiped the fingers of her gauntlet across her cheek. An image sat on skin that had been clear before: two dragons coiled around a broken skull. Ctesias flinched back. Then stared at Maehekta anew.

'You are a Curator,' he hissed.

'You cannot be part of something that no longer exists.' Maehekta brushed her hand across her cheek and the dragons were gone. The skin was smooth and unmarked again.

Ctesias nodded, eyes steady on the truth trader.

The Curators... Most of the warbands, sects and cults in the Eye of Terror survived a handful of years at most. The Curators had been one of the exceptions. The warriors in their ranks had come from many Legions, but there had been others amongst their number too, humans and half-humans. All had had a single obsession: secrets. They had gathered and hoarded them. From forgotten history to ancient artefacts, they had uncovered every hidden truth they could, by war, torture, espionage, sorcery and, chiefly, trade – other powers in the Eye had bought the aid of the Curators in exchange for their secrets.

All the Curators had learnt had been held not on parchment or data-looms, but in the minds of their initiates, crammed into memories guarded with fragments of daemon names and ritual mnemonic methods. It was said that when they gathered, they would speak their knowledge to each other, their members' positions in the order's hierarchy decided by how much each had to tell. It had been a sacred duty to them, a devotion to some demented code that they had made their idol.

In the end it had proved their undoing. Enough war leaders came to fear what the Curators knew of them, and their fear drove them to action. Some might like to have called it a war, but it was so swift and left so little behind that it took the only name that fitted the deed: a purge. The Curators had been slaughtered, their holdings razed and their members hunted down. All that remained was their name, and the stories told of the secrets they had amassed. Now, it seemed, Ahriman had somehow found a survivor from the order and made a bargain. Ctesias wondered what he had promised in exchange.

Maehekta nodded, as though seeing Ctesias' thoughts reach their end. She stepped back, turned to look around, her face set in a mild and amused expression.

'I am glad we met, Ctesias. I hoped that we could have a conversation. I know a great deal of you, even though we have never met before.'

Ctesias felt his skin prickle. 'Are you going to ask me your question?'

'No,' she said. 'Not yet.' She turned and walked away, her footsteps clacking on the stones until she was out of sight.

The ships of the Exiles gathered in the open void. All of them wore the scars of war and the changes that came from swimming the depths of the Eye of Terror. They were few compared to the grand fleet they had been, a ragged flotilla of sisters. There were craft that had fought in the skies above Terra long ago. There were warships made from the carcasses of vessels lost on the tides of the warp. There were ships stolen from enemies and clad in silver and bronze. All gathered in a sphere, revolving slowly around one another. At the centre of that sphere sat four craft, three arranged in a triangle around the fourth. There was the *Pyromonarch*, orange flames coiling over the three prongs of its hull; the *Soul Jackal*, silver skinned and haloed by ghost-light; and the *Word of Hermes*, black hulled, a spearhead of towers, armour and gun batteries. Between them lay the *Hekaton*. It had been reborn from the wreck of an Imperial warship lost to the immaterium. Only the eagle figurehead remained to mark that past. Its bones had been fused with iron and steel taken from cold stars. Towers, domes and pyramids rose in a jagged city from its back and jutted down from its belly. Silver and crystal glinted in the glow of its engines.

It was beneath the largest dome, high on its aftcastle, that Ahriman and his Exiles had gathered. Ahriman could feel the tension in the chamber, bleeding over the telepathic link with his brothers. This was always going to be the hardest part, the part where the fear of the doom that stalked them met the uncertain future. And the future was uncertain. Gone was the foresight that had once guided them through actions. Now they had to choose to step into the dark and hope they would find a path beneath their feet.

He waited after he finished telling them what they must do. Silence ached through the space. Flickers of half-thought whispered in the telepathic link between them. Ahriman let the silence stretch.

Each of his brothers stood on a silver disc in the centre of the chamber, floating at the five points of a pentagram with Ahriman at its heart. Gaumata stood in armour of deep blue, the gold of his psychic hood rising above his bare head like that of a cobra. Rubies and shards of agate glittered in the thick gold which edged his armour. A morning star with a head of blackened iron rested between his feet, and his aura was the yellow-orange of fire rising from a volcano. Then Kiu, his armour altered after their return to the Planet of the Sorcerers. Silver and emerald had taken the place of blue, and a cloak of white silk hung from his back. A sword hung from his waist, an axe from his back, life hunger aching from the entities bound into the blades. Ctesias leant on his staff, hunched despite his armour, tattoos of arcane script marching across the wrinkled skin of his head. Ignis was silent and still in his Terminator plate, his presence like the shadow of a mountain. Gilgamos wore a cloak of black feathers over his armour, which was the blue of an ocean's depths. His eye sockets were empty, their edges marked by the old burn scars of the fire that had taken his mundane sight.

+You should have told us before the attack on the Born of Iron,+ said Kiu. His thought-voice was dry, controlled, but there was unease in it too. Ahriman turned to looked at him. His brother met his gaze, his aura a kaleidoscope of fragmented colour, all bright and sharp, needles and blades of pride and insight and power.

+For that, I ask your understanding,+ sent Ahriman. +I had to be sure.+

+And you are sure now?+ asked Kiu.

+I am,+ replied Ahriman.

+A lot rests on the insight of a renegade from a vanished cult that had a reputation for treachery,+ sent Kiu. +Why did this Maehekta not use what she knew to pillage these dead aliens herself? If the Hyksos dynasts were truly as powerful as they seem, why not pick the corpse of their civilisation clean? Alternatively, why did she not sell this knowledge to the Black Legion, or the slaves of the Lord of Iron?+

Amusement shimmered from Ctesias across the telepathic bond.

+Is that not obvious?+ he sent. +Because she needs our ships, our warriors and our desperation to do something foolish.+

+We must expect treachery,+ added Gilgamos. +The bones of betrayal litter this path.+

+To be fair-handed, if we were to only deal with the honest, how far do you think we would get?+ added Ctesias. +Come to think of it, how many of us would stand in this chamber?+

Kiu looked at Ctesias, his expression rippling with annoyance that he was not trying to hide. +But I agree.+

+There is potential in this path,+ began Gilgamos, +but there is no certainty.+

+There is the certainty of extinction if we do nothing,+ growled Gaumata, cutting through his brother's sending. He looked at Ahriman, orange impatience fuming off his aura.

Ahriman had expected this. The Circle were his brothers, and they had followed him since before they cast the first Rubric. They were as different as the many facets of a gem, each reflecting a separate colour of light, each part of a whole. Back in the ages before the burning of Prospero and the war against the Emperor, many of the Space Marine Legions had prized convergence in their warriors' thoughts, insights and attitudes. It had never been so with the Thousand Sons. Their primarch, Magnus the Red, had said that to value agreement over dissent was to place walls on the path of knowledge and truth. Everything had changed since those times, but the divergent natures and insight of the Thousand Sons remained.

+Doing the wrong thing is often worse than doing nothing,+ sent Ctesias, not holding his disdain from his thought-voice. +The bones of dead xenos litter the galaxy. The aeldari, the kinebrach, the Old Ones – all of them built great empires. All of them did great and wondrous things but could not save themselves. Yet we are to believe that this one holds the means to save us?+

+Its kind once made a mockery of matter and the laws of reality,+ replied Ahriman. +They fought wars that became legends in the minds of those that came after. They broke the shackles of life and held the mastery of matter and, yes, of time, too.+

+Perhaps they did, but a corpse of a failed dream does not make you the master of that dream, or its stories truth.+

+Do you doubt my word, brother?+ asked Ahriman.

Ctesias gave a slow shake of his head. +Not *your* word, Ahriman. None of us would be standing here if we doubted that. I just doubt the source of what you have learned. You cannot trust Maehekta. She is a *Curator* – they should not be trusted in the smallest degree. Neither can the xenos who we must rely on as a guide.+

A shiver of disquiet passed around the circle.

+Trust is not required,+ sent Ahriman, edging the sending with calm command. +Nor would I ever again ask that you follow me without understanding. To see is to understand, and so I will show you why I have chosen this path.+ He flicked a thought at Ignis. The Master of Ruin's tattoos briefly became a series of parallel lines, then spiralled into a whirl of tessellating pentagrams.

'Credence,' he said aloud. Doors opened at the edge of the chamber. The circle of sorcerers turned to look. Credence loomed through the opening. Beside him floated a platform of machinery. Anti-grav hazed the air beneath it and the blue-white dome of a stasis field enclosed its top. A heap of white-grey sand lay beneath it. Beside it sat the alien chronometron device. Ahriman felt recognition hiss from his brothers' minds. They all knew what the dust was.

The platform stopped beside Ignis. Ahriman gave a nod of command and Ignis disabled the energy field.

+Watch,+ said Ahriman. He willed the command to Ignis. He felt the hesitation, almost imperceptible, then Ignis reached down. Ahriman could feel his brother controlling his distaste as he touched the alien metal. His fingers moved. There was a blink, a flick of time.

The dust had flowed together.

Another blink, another jump, and now the dust was a shape.

Then it had lines and edges, a hand, a pauldron, the outline of a helmet plate.

Blink, flick, and the fingers were moving, the half-formed head twitching with a rattling gasp as dust poured from its cracked visor. It reached out. They could all hear the gasping hiss in their heads as the remains of the Rubricae tried to rise...

The half-formed armour collapsed back into dust. Silence filled the air. Ignis released his grip on the chronometron.

+That was...+ began Gilgamos.

+Inotellon,+ sent Ahriman. +The Pyrodomon took him when it last manifested.+

Gilgamos nodded. +And this xenos device cannot reverse his state completely?+

+It cannot,+ sent Ignis bluntly.

+It is possible, though,+ said Gaumata. +The proof and potential are clear. It works. It is a beginning. Greater understanding gives greater power. So we must have that understanding.+

+The function of this xenos time technology is real,+ sent Ignis. +The inference that there is the potential to use that technology on a wider scale is grounded. I see no falsity in that statement.+

+But you do not believe the promise that it could be our salvation?+ sent Gaumata.

+I do not believe anything,+ sent Ignis. His face was blank, his tattoos set in a uniform grid. +I follow the progression of action and fact, and the pattern of the universe.+

+And that tells you what?+ growled Gaumata.

+That this is a power we cannot be certain will function for our good or ill.+

+It does not matter.+ Ahriman's sending was soft, almost cold. The others looked at him. +The possibilities of betrayal, the likelihood of deception, none of it matters. All that matters is what we intend and what we shall do. We have reached the edge of our knowledge. The fires of annihilation grow on the horizon. We must act. If any of you can see another way that we have not already taken and has not already failed, speak now.+ He looked at Ctesias then. The daemon-binder's gaze wavered. +We must act, or we must accept that we are broken. We must accept that our fate cannot be changed. And I will not accept that. We owe it to our brothers, to our Legion. We hold the possibility in our hands of unmaking the wrongs done, of making time our servant, and with it making our brothers and our Legion whole. The whims of false gods will touch us no more. Masters of ether, materium and of time, the mistakes of the past undone, our redemption earned.+

The connection between his brothers rippled with echoes of emotion: affirmation, hope and question.

+And after that?+ asked Gaumata, and Ahriman could taste the fire of hunger in his brother's sending.

+That will be enough,+ he replied, then looked around the circle, with mind and eyes. +We are in concordance?+

The affirmations came one after another: Gaumata first and Gilgamos, then Ignis, Kiu and, at last, Ctesias.

Ahriman bowed his head. +My thanks, my brothers. We will go, and we will break the shackles of time.+

The Circle raised their hands, and light and the chorus of agreement filled the forum.

'By the Light of Terra and the grand purity of all that changes, we go to the tide.' Silvanus almost sang the words as he set himself on his throne. It had once been a cradle but that, like everything, had changed. Now it was a throne, a throne for a high servant, a seat for the scion of a dynasty and someone who not only knew the truth but had also seen it.

'We go,' he said, tapping controls on the arms of the throne and the pedestals set beside it. All of them were made of a material that might have been silver, but sometimes felt like warm bone to the touch. The keys had a soft quality to them and were never the same shape or colour when he looked at them. That, like everything else within and around Silvanus, was as it should be. He settled himself onto the throne, and felt its shape alter to the changes in his anatomy since he had last sat there. He looked up at his progeny. They curled in the fluid of their tanks, coming to the glass to face him. Each of their third eyes was open, looking at him. Some champed their jaws with anticipation. Others whipped tails through the liquid, sending bubbles to the surface. Gas sacs inflated, ruffs and crests of quills pulsed. 'Patience...' he chirruped at them. 'Patience is the virtue of saints and the gold of sages...'

These progeny were the youngest of his reborn dynasty. He liked to keep them close while they grew, in part because there was no better way for them to learn, but also – he had to confess – for company. He had been alone for so long. He could not count Ahriman, nor any of the Thousand Sons, to care about him, not really. There had been Carmenta and poor Astraeos, but even then, there had been no one of his own kind. It was a strange thing about Navigators, he had come to realise: they were bred within the narrow lines of their houses, cosseted and tutored and kept closed off from everyone else. Then they were sent out, usually alone, just them and the Great Ocean and the ships they steered through its tides. They were always shunned, often hated, and their only closeness was with a clan they would rarely see.

Silvanus had been out on the Great Ocean's tides for longer than he could recall with anything approaching accuracy. He had gone beyond the bounds of what was known, he had survived, and he had changed inside and out. Once he had feared those changes – the way his flesh morphed, the way that he was not sure what was left of his mind or if his memories were really his or just colourful blooms grown on dead dreams. For a while he had thought he was cursed. He had been wrong, though, he had come to see that. He was not cursed. He was not lost. He was blessed.

Amongst the Navigators of House Yeshar there had always been a strain of piety. A few of the bloodline had followed versions of the Imperial Creed devotedly, and that devotion had always been tolerated by the house elders. Silvanus had learnt the creed of the Emperor Illuminated from his High Sister and Cousin Tutor. It had been a comfort to him many times before he had voyaged into the Eye. Before he had met Ahriman. Then, for a while, all the comfort of that faith had seemed false. What room was there for faith in the God-Emperor in the face of the full powers of the Neverborn? What good was a distant divinity's protection when Silvanus served a being who could remake reality? He had fallen into despair, for he had feared he had lost his soul, and that his mind and body would follow.

Then he had realised that the truth was before his eyes. The Great Powers of the warp, the might of Ahriman and his Legion, the Master of Mankind: all were the same. The God-Emperor's light was the light of the warp, His protection the blessing of change. His work and His angels were not the edifices of a failing empire; they were the miracles of the warp. The armour of contempt was not against the touch of the warp, but against mundane reality. The warp *was* illumination. *It* was the prime reality, the physical realm its imperfect shadow. Once Silvanus understood that, all had fallen into place. He knew he had found both salvation and revelation. He understood what no others did. There was no war between Chaos and the Emperor.

They were the same, beams of light shining through different windows of the same, great lantern.

He had considered keeping his revelation secret at first but had realised that secrecy was foolish. All was revealed in the light. All conflict was an illusion. Besides, Ahriman and his brothers were blessed with powers that made secrecy laughable. All was revealed to them, as it was to the sight of the eye of the Emperor. He did not need to speak the truth he saw. They would see it in him and know. Besides, perhaps they already knew? Perhaps this great truth was what drove Ahriman to seek the restoration of his Legion? Perhaps Ahriman was the exalted agent by which the Imperium would become the Imperium of the warp, and all disputes would transmute into enlightenment? Yes, it was more than possible, and was Silvanus not Ahriman's loyal servant? Had he not been plucked from his past life, not by chance but by fate? Had he not survived so that he could now understand the universe he saw? It could not be doubted.

He reached for the neural link attached to the throne. A film of fluid sheened the silver spike and the umbilical that trailed from it. He raised it to his head and pushed it into the opening in his temple. His nerves lit. Fire and cool water seemed to flow through his skull. The sight in his mundane eyes dimmed.

First came the connection to the ship's warp helm. Data displays lit with kaleidoscopes of symbols on screens around the throne. He felt the growl of warp engines as though they were next to his heart. Then, more slowly, like bubbles rising to the surface of a pool, came vision through the eyes of his progeny. Across the principal vessels of the Exiles fleet, they lay in cradles or hung in fluid tanks, each linked to their own ship, and to him, the sire of their line. This connection with his family had been a gift of the Thousand Sons and allowed him to guide not one ship but to steer them all. It was a miracle, but a lesser miracle than his progeny themselves. They were his, created from his body by the skills that Ctesias had bartered for with the flesh-weavers. Once, he would have thought that act by the Thousand Sons motivated by a selfish need to have a reliable means of navigation, but Silvanus did not think of it like that. It was a blessing and an act of kindness. Some of the progeny did not survive the creation process, but that was no loss. All was a cycle, and the flesh of the failed supplied the material for more to be created. He had his family. And was that not another sign that he was not cursed but blessed? He had survived. He had been raised up and given holy truth, and now he had the family that had been lost to him restored, so that he could share their sight and they his.

As the link clarified, his sight became multifaceted. His awareness spread across them all. It was, he thought, an echo of what it must be to see as the God-Emperor did.

The growl of the warp engines became a purr as the *Hekaton* came to readiness. The ships of the fleet were assembled and ready. The data for their destination was set in Silvanus' mind. All was in harmony. Now they would go back to where they belonged, to the depths of the Great Ocean, flowing with the tides that were the breath and blood of god. The ship began to move. The warp engines began to sing the song of knives as they cut into reality. He keyed the release of the shutters covering his sanctuary's ocular viewport. Metal leaves folded back.

The light of the warp flooded in. Silvanus felt it on his skin, felt the suckers on his throat open like flowers to the rising sun. He pulled in a breath, the gills on his back and chest opening, sacs in his throat sighing. He let himself see the warp with his mundane eyes for a second, feeling capillaries pop and acid tears form at their corners.

'Most holy, most high, thy servant thanks you for the beauty of this vision,' he breathed. The multiple lids covering his warp eye blinked open. He saw. 'Glorious,' he said, as the ship slipped into the tide's embrace.

In the quiet of the Serene Cages, Helio Isidorus watched the bronze hoops turn around him. Marks glowed on them as they passed each other. He blinked. The patterns that the hoops made with each other were beautiful, as were the marks and symbols on them. He did not know what they said.

'Helio Isidorus,' he said aloud. He felt the words on his tongue as his mouth made their sounds. He knew what those sounds meant: they were his name. He understood them. He understood himself. He was his name. His name was him. If he had not been Helio Isidorus he would have been something else entirely. 'Helio Isidorus.' He smiled.

He watched the hoops turn and the marks on them glow. He did not know what they said, but he knew what they meant. He knew what the turning hoops meant, and the patterns they made, and their shapes and the way they moved. He understood them.

He raised his hand and without speaking said what he knew.

The hoops stopped turning. The glowing marks cut into the bronze faded. He sat for a moment. Nothing moved. He understood that whoever had made the marks and set the hoops turning was supposed to know if they stopped doing what they were supposed to do. He understood how that was supposed to happen. He understood how the future would be different if they knew what he had done.

He decided that it would not happen. No one would know. He had decided, and so that was what would be.

He sat in the stillness and listened to the quiet in the chamber and the noise beyond. Thoughts, voices, lives. It sounded like the crackling of fire.

After a while, he decided to set things back as they were.

He raised a hand. The marks glowed again, and the hoops began to turn once more.

The noise of the outside world, which sounded like fire, faded. He was left with the feeling of time passing through him, and the sound of his lone thought rolling over and over in his skull.

'I am Helio Isidorus,' he said aloud, then smiled.

PART TWO

PATHS OF THE LOST

CHAPTER V

DOLMEN GATE

The empty world lay beneath the ships of the Exiles. Ice capped its poles. Grey clouds spiralled across its surface in great storms. Silvanus could see patches of what might be dismal, black oceans, and ripples in the cloud that might be mountain peaks rising from land masses.

'There are no ships, no debris, nothing,' he said.

'There is nothing because no one comes here.'

'I do not like...' Silvanus felt his tongue struggle to form the words. He had a feeling that its shape had been changing in his mouth. 'I want to leave,' he forced out.

'Of course you do,' said Maehekta. 'This place belongs to the dead twice over. First to the race that some call the aeldari, then to their ancient enemies. No one else could claim it now. Not even the greatest of warlords or the most potent of daemons. It is salted ground, and remains only because of what is here – a doorway into the web that runs between worlds and beneath the stars.'

'Cocytus,' said Silvanus, a tremble in his voice. 'The headwater of the river into hell...'

Maehekta laughed. Silvanus shivered at the sound.

'You are in hell, Navigator. You are one of the damned. This is not the way into a realm of torment. This is a way out.' She turned to look at Silvanus, her smile wide under the blank brass of the helm covering her eyes. 'I understand your mistake. To the souls of the underworld, the gates of paradise would seem to open only onto terror and suffering.' She laughed again. 'And they would be right.'

Silvanus turned away, still shivering. The abomination had come to his sanctuary at Ahriman's order, and there was nothing he could do to prevent it. He had considered pleading, but even as the possibility had risen in his mind, he knew that Ahriman had both predicted his response and seen it in his thoughts. Nothing was hidden from Ahriman, not any more; his sight went on and on without limit. Nothing could be concealed from him. Silvanus knew it. So, he had stifled his protests and pleas before he could voice them. He was not happy, though. No, he was as far from happy as he had been since... He was not sure. That was part of the problem of what was happening. The balance and solace he had found was falling apart, the clarity and reassurance it gave fraying to tatters. He could feel his flesh and blood shifting under his skin in sympathy to his emotions. First there had been the inaction, the droning stillness, and the tug of the Ocean on his mind as they had waited. Then, when release had come at last, their course had brought them to this hollow skull of a world and the unnatural calm that echoed around it louder than any noise. And now there was the abomination, who he had to let into his sanctuary, and would remain there for the last and worst part of what was being demanded of him.

'This... webway that lies beyond,' he began, shuffling back to his throne so that he was as far from her as he could get without fleeing the room. 'If it is neither reality nor the warp then how am I supposed to guide us?'

She stepped back next to the narrow casket she had brought with her and lifted it so that he could see what lay inside. It was an ovoid of a green-black substance the size of a fist. It might have been metal or stone, or something that was neither. Lines and incisions ran over and through it, and the more Silvanus looked at it, the more he had the impression of a fossilised insect, its legs gathered under the shell of its abdomen. It was not pleasant to look at. No resonance bloomed from it in his eyes. He very much wanted not to touch it, but he had the feeling that was what he was going to be asked to do.

'This is something that came with the xenos creature?' he asked, knotting his fingers together inside the sleeves of his robe.

'It is.'

'And it will guide us?'

'No. You will. The webway is not like a network of tunnels running under a city – it responds to those who pass through it. It is river and road and forest. It is, in a sense, alive. The paths are never the same. They move and shift depending on those who walk them and where they wish to go. I believe that to reach the right end is as much about the intent as it is about knowledge.'

'It sounds like more than belief.'

'I have made it part of my life to know things, and to know the difference between belief and certainty. I have learnt what I tell you from the lips of the aeldari themselves, some even who were still alive. I have some experience to make me believe some of what I have learnt, but knowledge without validation can only be belief.'

'You sound like some of the Thousand Sons.'

'They learnt to think, they did not invent it. A teacher may have many pupils.'

'You were from the Imperium, then?' Silvanus asked, eager as he glimpsed a shadow of something behind the words.

Maehekta did not answer but ran a finger across the belly of the object in the box.

'When we enter the webway, I believe that this object will respond. It will be drawn by its nature to reach its home, the centre from which it came.'

'My mother once told me that ships lost on the seas in ancient times would release birds from cages and follow them back to land.'

Maehekta blinked slowly.

'Something like that,' she said, and tapped the object. It gave a hollow chime that set Silvanus' teeth aching. 'It though is like me, inert to the warp, and so the webway will not respond to it. To follow it we must have a soul who will respond to it and be our living guide.'

'Me,' said Silvanus.

'You,' said Maehekta. 'The webway is as much a metaphor and puzzle as it is a network. You have been bred to deal in such vagaries, to see and sense direction. Your soul is bright. Your instincts have been refined. All these things mean that you will be our guide.'

He gave a hollow laugh. His progeny, which had been curled in their tanks, turned their eyes away from Maehekta, and looked around.

'I do not know whether I was right before.' He flicked a finger at the object in the box. 'I am not sure if this… thing is the caged bird desperately trying to reach safety or I am.'

Maehekta said nothing. His progeny turned their eyes away again, curling up against the far sides of their tanks.

'And the aeldari?' he asked after the silence had pulled across several instants. 'They see the webway as their own, and I know that they do not let others pass through their realms.'

'They may oppose us. They may not. They may not even realise we are there. The web of paths is vast beyond the ability of a dying race to watch.'

'Do you believe that or know it?' he asked. Again, she gave no reply. 'I would like…' he began, then paused. 'I think I need to look at the object, device, whatever it is. I mean with my… sight.' He brought a hand up as if he were going to touch his third eye.

'Then do so,' she said.

'It is just… It is not wise for you to be here when I… look.' He licked his lips. He was briefly aware of the suckers dotting his tongue's underside, and quickly drew it back behind his teeth. 'The eye of my kind, it can… if you look into it… you can be harmed. Killed even.'

'Why do you think that would happen to me?'

'The warp. I believe you will see what my eye sees, and that is too much for most to survive.'

She inclined her head, grey eyes steady on him. 'I will not be harmed,' she said. 'The warp is as blind to me as I am to it. Trust me.'

Silvanus hesitated, then raised the silver veil from his face. His third eye had developed several layers of lids in recent times. He opened them and looked at the object. It was nothing. A shape of dull grey amongst the spiralling colours of the warp flowing around it. The patterns of the flow were interesting, though, regular in a way he had not seen before, as though the waves of energy glancing off it always rebounded with the same pattern. It was not pleasant to see, like hearing a knife pulled across slate.

He shook himself, and was about to close his eye, when he stopped. He looked up at Maehekta. Where there should have been something, there was just a ragged absence, its edges pulling at the neon tide flowing through the room. He heard himself gasp before he could stop himself. With his mundane eyes he could see her looking back at him, directly into his third eye.

'I am sorry,' he said quickly, fumbling, looking away.

'I said that I would not be harmed.'

He nodded, about to turn and ask her to leave so that he could have what little peace he could before he had to perform his next task, but then paused. He looked at Maehekta again, fixing her grey gaze with his warp eye.

'What do you see?' he asked, his voice almost childlike.

'An eye,' she replied. 'Black, outsized, without iris or pupil. Nothing else.'

'And out there?' He nodded towards the viewport beyond which the Eye of Terror roiled and bulged across the sweep of space. To Silvanus it was an ever-shifting storm of colour and light. Stars blinked amongst folds of pink vapour that coiled into brief images of feathered and scaled beasts. Motes of light burst into golden cobwebs and dissolved into cold black. He could hear it, too. Not with his ears – or at least he could not hear it when he looked away. Sounds like voices carried on desert winds, the rattling crash of a sea breaking on stone, the shrill call of something crying in the night and the answer following. He knew if he looked away and back then the vision would be different; it always was.

He felt himself shiver. The fabric of his robes rustled. A single tear sat upon his cheek. There were words in his mouth, forming around his tongue. 'I see the wonder of infinity and possibility. Endless... Everything is there. Everything I have wanted, and everything I have lost. Nothing is really gone. It is all there. You can see it...' He looked at Maehekta, who had been watching him during his moment of reverie. 'Do you see it?'

She glanced at the viewport.

'I see a few stars, fewer than there should be, and the void.'

'That is it? Nothing more?'

She shook her head. 'I do not see ghosts or fancies of the mind. I see only what is there. The hard truth, not the dreaming.'

He blinked, the multiple layers of his eyelids closing and opening in sequence.

'I am sorry,' he said.

'I need no pity. Once maybe I would have welcomed it, but now, after all I have seen, I am glad that I do not suffer as others do.'

Then, without warning, she reached out a hand and touched his cheek. He was too shocked to move. Her fingers radiated ice into him. He felt instinct want to fight to get away from it, from her, from the grey eyes that could see none of the wonder and truth and promise of the universe. Nothing, just coldness, the indifference of life and death, an ending without continuation. He needed to get away from that before all the beauty he had found, all the truth and wonder, vanished into the vortex. He felt a scream building, rising like the shriek of an engine racing through a tunnel towards the promise of light.

Maehekta took her hand away. He shuddered with relief.

'They will have unlocked the gate soon,' she said. 'When they do, you must be ready.'

He nodded, closing all his eyes briefly again. He felt the vents down his back breathe out for him. This would be as it always was and as it always had been: the price for the chance to continue living. He had realised that, for him, survival mattered more than anything. That was why he was here, why he still lived, because no matter what was asked of him, it was better to live with the hope of living than the fear of falling into nothing. He opened his eyes and looked again at the ovoid artefact in the box. He forced his hand to move towards it. His fingers did not want to uncurl. He stopped, a thought forming in his mind.

'This... thing. It is inactive, but it will need to be functioning, responding as you say, when we have gone through the gate. If it is... bound in a sense, to the xenos creature, for this device to work, won't the xenos creature it belonged to have to be awake, too?'

Maehekta nodded.

'Yes,' she said. 'It will.'

Ignis watched the xenos' eyes glow from behind its sheath of witch-ice. They had moved it to one of the Serene Cages, deep in the decks of the *Hekaton* that were closed to all but the Thousand Sons and their most trusted servants. Before they had taken it from its crystal prison, it had been in a state of dormancy. There had been no power or energy in its substance, not even the slow decay of volatile atoms. Now it sang with power. Even when it was utterly still, Ignis could feel it, like the buzzing of a harmonic just out of hearing.

To keep it prisoner, they had placed it in one of the arcane engines of the chamber. Hoops of bronze and copper orbited the xenos, holding it in mid-air while leeching away the stray light and heat from it. For his part, Ignis would gladly have crushed it to the size of a seed. Slowly. That was not yet an option; for better or worse, they needed the creature's cooperation. While that was the case, it would remain as confined as Ignis could make it. It had given them information and had made no overt effort to break free again. That state was an illusion.

Setekh's eyes watched Ignis from behind his wrapping of ice. He had been probing into the anathema effects holding him. They were remarkably strong. He had subtly remade the reality around it. Molecules altered. Dimensions folded. Ice became metallic dust. Then both dust and ice vanished from existence. He could not yet find the limits of the bonds that held him, but he would. There was no need for him to try and break free now. His abilities were still limited. That time would come, though. Until then he had time to observe and probe the new world he had woken to. He wondered how much of what he was doing the creature called Ignis was aware of.

Ignis held his thoughts in balance. Beside him, Credence waited motionless, its gun aimed and locked. He felt part of the xenos' left arm dissolve out of existence as he tried to hold it with his mind. He caught it again as it blinked back into being. With each micro shift, Ignis had to predict where the xenos would be next and how it would arrive, and alter his telekinetic hold on it. He was equal to the task, but he knew that he could not do this forever. The projections he had followed were clear: with enough time it would get free, but for this limited period he could hold it and learn its capabilities.

Ignis felt another shift and was realigning his will and thought to counter it when it stopped. Credence gave a clatter of code from beside him. The xenos' eyes had brightened.

'You have come to the door,' said Setekh. Its voice was almost quiet. 'You have found the lock and turned the key.' Ignis did not answer but remained watching Setekh through the rotating hoops of the cage. 'I can sense it. Perhaps in the same way that you sense using your extra-dimensional abilities. Our journey progresses. You have manifested a degree of ability beyond what I had expected.'

Ignis looked into the cold light of the xenos' eyes and did not reply. Beneath his feet, he felt a rumble as the ship's engines began to build power.

* * *

Ahriman felt the gunship shake as it dropped through the clouds. Altitude data pulsed in gold at the edge of his helm display. He could feel his mind contracting in. The ethereal sense that skimmed insight from the world around him was pushing against a leaden presence slowly surrounding him, pushing his senses and the reach of his mind inwards. It was coming from the world they were descending to. There was a hollowness beneath them, cold, lifeless. It felt like sinking into the deepest parts of the sea, the light fading to nothing beneath the aphotic zone, pressure building to crushing force.

'Just like old times, Ahzek.' His head snapped around, ready to see a figure in armour in the mag-harness beside him, bolter in hand, eyes laughing as they looked back at him. The rack was empty. Ctesias looked up from across the compartment, his helmed head tilting in question. Ahriman shook his head in answer and began to rebalance his thoughts.

Their altitude was dropping fast. He felt the gunship bank, turning into a landing spiral. Ready lights blinked to amber. He released his mag-harness and stood. Aside from Ctesias and Lycomedes, the compartment was empty. They had brought no Rubricae, uncertain if they would respond in the planet's deadening aura. The only other object in the compartment was the sceptre they had taken from Setekh. It lay on a tracked casket, fastened in place by bands of plasteel.

'Approaching target site,' came the pilot's voice over his helm vox. *'Auspex reads negative for heat, movement and energy.'*

Ahriman looked down at the sceptre. It was glowing. Deep in the grooves etched into its haft, faint green lights had sparked to life.

'Take us in,' said Ahriman into the vox.

'By your will,' replied the pilot. The gunship began to drop faster. Ahriman felt the blackness wrap closer around his mind,

pushing him down into the depths, down where there was no light, just the peace of oblivion. And from somewhere at the back of his head came the memory of the voice he thought he had heard.

'Just like old times, Ahzek...' A voice he remembered from the cave of his solitude on the *Hekaton*, a voice that should not have been there or here, a voice he knew but could not recognise or remember.

The light in the compartment flashed to green. The gunship slammed to a halt, sitting on its thrusters as its chin hatch opened on grey light and rain, then settled slowly to the ground.

'Is there something wrong?' asked Ctesias after a moment.

Ahriman shook his head.

The world outside was painted in rain-washed monochrome: iron, slate, granite, mist and storm cloud. A beach of wet shingle stretched away from them, curving between black mountains and the grey churn of a sea that blurred into the sky. Rain slid across the view in pale curtains, pattering from Ahriman's armour. A second gunship dropped from the cloud layer and skimmed along the shoreline before coming to station. Maehekta jumped from a side door and moved down the beach towards them. Ctesias and Lycomedes came to stand next to Ahriman. The casket holding the sceptre trundled between them.

'It is in there?' asked Ctesias, motioning at the mountain rising into the rain and cloud above them.

'The key site should be close, yes,' said Ahriman.

Ahriman looked up at the mountain. The flank facing them was the dark grey of graphite, its cliff overhangs and crags formed by slow erosion that had scattered lumps of stone onto the beach. There was a geometric consistency in the shapes of the rocks, he noticed, from the largest to the smallest, as though their structure were fractal, the micro echoing into the macro.

He looked down at a lump of fallen rock lying near his feet and willed it into the air. It rocked in place, his mind and will slipping on its substance. The ether was distant, its power muted. He brought his mind to a sharp point of focus and the stone rose to eye level, rotating. It was almost a perfect polyhedron. Almost.

'Impressive,' said Ctesias. 'The Curator said this world is supposed to be inert to the ether.'

'It is,' replied Ahriman, turning back to the mountain. The polyhedron dropped to the ground. 'It is like a stone in the flow of the river. Enough force, and the river can shift the stone slightly, but it cannot break or swallow it. Understandable – the webway is built in harmony from the warp. If you are going to construct a door into the etheric, it needs to be tethered to a lodestone. This entire world is that lodestone.'

They climbed up inside the mountain, following a narrow gorge that led from the shore. Rain ran down the walls to either side. The grey light of the sky became a line above. Ahriman took the lead, picking between fallen boulders, following the shadows of steps cut into the gorge floor. There was no vegetation, he noticed, not even moss or lichen. No animal cries broke up the droning patter of water on rock. Ahriman could feel the circle of his will growing smaller the further they progressed, until there was just the sound of his own thoughts in his head. Links between deep thoughts and the warp thinned, becoming mere cobweb strands. The sound of the sea on the shore they had left had long faded. He felt a part of him want to scream.

They went on, step by step, until they passed a spur of rock and saw what they had come for. The gorge walls arced around, enclosing a space that Ahriman could have crossed in ten strides. Polygonal columns rose from the middle of the space, the tallest of them seeming to form the shape of a door just wide enough that two humans could have walked through it abreast.

'Is this it?' asked Ctesias.

'Does it still work?' asked Lycomedes. Ctesias' apprentice sounded uncomfortable, as though he was trying to keep his voice level.

'The only way to find out if the lock still opens is to turn the key,' replied Ahriman, lifting the sceptre from the casket. It was light, almost weightless; he had the feeling that he could have bent it with his fingers, but if he had swung it against one of the stone blocks it would have been the stone that shattered. The threads of light running along the grooves in the haft were shining. Flecks of crystal gleamed in the surface of the stone as he moved the sceptre close to it.

'The information we have on the operation of the gate is not exact but...'

Ahriman turned in a circle. The sceptre was a cold presence in his hand, focusing the deadening atmosphere of the world. With the power of the ether distant, his mind felt small, reduced to mundane thoughts and processes. Those thoughts and the mind that held them were not mundane. They had been selected, tutored, enhanced and trained to be a weapon to cut the universe. His eyes took in the shapes and angles of the stone blocks, ideas, facts and possibilities sliding through his awareness, combining with each other, growing and breaking apart again as they passed through sieves of finer and finer logic. It took a second for him to know what the mechanism would be.

'There is much to be valued in secrets,' he said, stepping past Lycomedes and Ctesias towards the columns that made the shape of a door. 'In what is hidden, in what we cannot see.' He looked up at the stone and raised the sceptre in his hand. 'There is protection, and there is power. We know this, and the creatures who built this place knew it too. They put that understanding into what they made, but their insight was flawed. They believed they were higher than others, that none could touch their brilliance. They were right, up to a point, but it is not in the large things that such hubris comes undone. It is in what you do not see...'

He paused for a second, his eyes finding the precise point relative to the pillars and walls. He reached the sceptre into the air between the columns. Nothing, just the gleam of the lines in the rod's metal reflecting from the flecks of crystal in the rock. He stepped back. He could...

'They fought and feared those who wielded the ether. The anathema realm, the creature Setekh called it. They feared it and loathed it, and like all things that one fears, it consumed their thoughts and sight until it was *all* they could see. They made this place both to perform its task and to steal the weapons of their enemy. They thought that if anyone not of their kind tried to unlock their gate, they would do it with the power of the warp. To do anything else seemed to them impossible, and what you think is impossible is the flaw that undoes you...'

He held his eyes steady on the space between the columns, forcing his senses and his mind not to slide into what it knew to be and not be there, forcing it to see what was... and he reached out with the sceptre. The metal hit stone. Another column stood where there had been nothing before. It rose to meet a block that rested on it and the two other pillars. Together they made an irregular arch with three openings. In the middle of the stones a hole opened in the floor, no wider than a bolt shell. Carved lines radiated from it, linking circles and semicircles.

Lycomedes stepped back with surprise.

'Where was it before?' he asked.

'It was always here,' said Ahriman. 'It only required to be seen by more than one observer for it to become tangible.'

'Dimensional phasing,' said Ctesias. 'Two physical realities coexisting at the same location in space and time, separated by the perception of the observer. I have encountered the concept, seen fragments of related theory, but to achieve it without using etheric methods...' Ahriman thought he could almost detect admiration in Ctesias' voice as he gave a slow shake of his head.

'Now,' said Ahriman, 'let us see if we can turn the key.'

He slotted the tip of the sceptre into the hole in the stone floor. Green light shone from the lines and grooves. Ahriman felt a jolt in his mind, like the echoing of a vast bell. He pushed the sceptre down. The light spread out across the stones, racing across patterns that had hidden in the mountain rocks. The ground shook. The sceptre rose from the hole into the air as the green light grew stronger. Ahriman took it and looked around.

'We must go,' he said. 'The gate is opening, and we must be in orbit by the time it is ready.'

When they reached the gunships, the sea had drained from the shore. A ribbon of grey water lay along the horizon of a black plateau. Columns of stone rose from the seabed. Green light glowed from them. The rain had ceased, and the clouds were thinning. Stars shone in the dark, cold and bright in a way that was hardly ever seen in the Eye of Terror. Ahriman could feel the leaden pressure of the world changing, shifting like the turning of a great wheel. The gunship took off as, below it, the Dolmen Gate opened.

The sphere of the world broke. Splits opened its surface. Rock and remaining water tumbled down into the chasms. No fire or molten stone poured from them. On they ran, broadening and linking in straight lines until they stretched across the planet entire. Green lights glowed on the surface and arced into the air. The warp was weeping as Silvanus looked at it. Multicoloured light peeled back from the growing presence of the gate. He could hear the machine-wrights and tech-devotees howling in their code dirge as systems on the ships overloaded. Half-etheric systems and the warp-infused engines that powered their workings were failing. Silvanus felt sick. Sweat sheened the folds and frills of his skin. There was blood and fluid oozing from the breathing pores on his back. He wanted very much to look away from what he was seeing, to be anywhere else but here watching reality and the warp disassembling. Disassembling... Yes, that was it... Matter manipulated beyond its normal laws and limits, the warp, the great and forever ocean of the warp, pushed away and negated. He was seeing something that should not be, not in reality or in dreams, and he could not help but observe.

The planet came apart. Blocks of matter the size of mountains shunted out, realigned, spun like the moving parts of a vast engine. Blackness filled the spaces within and between. It hung against the curdled light of the Eye, a puzzle toy discarded by a god before it was solved. Then it turned inside out. Space and geometry folded in to where the planet's core had been. Where there had been a sphere, now there was a funnel opening into a darkness beyond that of the void.

Silvanus stared at it. He realised that he was weeping. Around him, his progeny churned their fluid tanks – some to get away, some to press their eyes against the glass and look. This was like nothing Silvanus had seen before. Navigators existed to behold the impossibility of the warp and chart a course through it. That alone made many of them numb to the new or novel. What was the new or the mundanely shocking when you could see the bubbling cauldron of living thought and nightmare under the skin that most souls believed was the dominant reality? The longer you looked into the warp, the more it showed you all the truths it hid. Echoes of the tortured dead, palaces of lost dreams, futures and pasts, gilded wonder and bloody terror. Silvanus had gone further even than the oldest of his kind. Much further. He had charted courses through the riptides of gods and seen worlds where the immaterial and the physical were fused, and the living changed what was real by whim, will and accidental dream. He had seen the daemon heralds of the gods and spoken to them. All these things had changed him and taught him, so that now he knew that the physical was not the prime reality, but the lesser sibling of the warp – a grey shadow to the Great Ocean's majesty. That realisation had given him so much, had stolen some of the terror from what had become of his life, had lent it meaning.

It did not help him as he looked at the gate. It stole the softness and comfort of his beliefs and left his throat dry and his mind screaming with the hollow instinct to run. It was like nothing he had seen. No, it was a negation of all that he had seen. This hole bored in warp and reality meant that everything he had come to accept might be wrong, just another layer of lies and incomplete lies piled on top of the others.

'I…' he began, his tongue struggling to form words. 'We cannot…'

Maehekta looked at him. As before, she had removed her helm so that he could see her face. Her grey eyes met his.

'You must,' she said. 'What you feel now will pass once you go through.'

'What if it's… I cannot see into it. It just goes on and down and on and down…' He was breathing hard, feeling the bird of his heart beat its wings against the inside of his chest. 'I… If I go in, I may never reach the end… may never come out. It has no shape, not in any of my eyes.'

'It is only a door. Pass through and we will reach another place.'

'What if that is not true?' he blurted. Tears were still streaming down the folds of his cheeks.

'It is true,' said Maehekta. 'I know.'

'How can you?'

'Because I have been there,' she said.

She reached towards him. He flinched back. His progeny thrashed in their tanks, beating the liquid to foam. The cold deadness of her presence was like ice on his skin. He shivered, then was still. There was something soothing in the touch. His mind stilled, his breathing and heartbeat slowed. He nodded.

'All right, just one small step through the door...' He glanced at her again. 'It is just a door, isn't it? I mean, like you said, we go through and are in another place. I do not know... Every time I look at it, I just can't help but feel that once I go through, I will be... There is a way back, isn't there?'

'There is,' she said.

He clamped his teeth shut and forced himself to reach out a hand towards the ovoid lump in the box. He wasn't looking at it directly, but he could see it at the edge of his sight... Holy Throne of Terra and the twin-headed prophet of change but it was moving; he could see it moving in his periphery, legs unfolding, skittering and twitching as his fingers got closer. He clutched the eagle-winged eye talisman on his chest with his other hand. The points of the feather tips bit into the skin of his hand and drew a little blood. He could feel the coolness of the sapphire eyes in the eagle's twin heads. He would do this. He would survive. He was watched over and protected.

'Throne of light, by all the currents of the warp and the wings of the righteous that soar above and the eyes that watch us and the golden light that waits and guides... protect and see for me as I seek to see with your eyes.' He touched the object in the box, felt its needle legs wrap around his fingers, felt pain whip up his arm as they bit into flesh and nerves. He lifted it, bowed his head, and brought it up towards his face. The thing leapt from his hand as though trying to get away. He felt Maehekta's hand grip it and him, adding her strength as they forced it closer. His progeny writhed in their suspension fluid. He opened his third eye. He was screaming now.

This was the price for survival, the bargain he had made and remade many times over since Ahriman had taken him. Do what was demanded no matter what and live. He would live. He would survive.

The artefact was ripping his fingers to shreds. Blood was scattering over him. He wanted not to do this, not to be here, not to have been taken from his ship all those ages ago, not to have agreed to serve to survive, not to have lived. The artefact met the socket of his third eye. He almost blacked out. Its legs spasmed, then clamped on to his forehead as though trying to close back on themselves. Blood poured down his face, into his mouth. He tasted tin and copper. For a moment, he thought it would rip the front of his head out. Then, suddenly, it went still.

He panted, blood puffing from his lips. The blank darkness of the device covered the sight of his third eye, but he could sense or feel something. Slowly, with bloody hands, he picked up the neural-interface spike from the side of his throne. He found the opening in his temple and slotted it home. The navigation systems of the *Hekaton* flowed into his being, familiar and comforting in their shape and sensation. The eyes of his progeny scattered across the fleet became his own. He felt the murmurs of their thoughts and instincts. He raised his head and gaze. He saw the Dolmen Gate through the many facets of his multiplied warp vision. He felt the legs of the artefact dig into his forehead and the bone of his skull. He could feel it, like lightning and ice and falling. He shuddered one last time, then spoke, knowing that Ahriman would hear.

'We are ready and await your command, lord.'

He felt Ahriman reply in his thoughts.

+Take us through.+

Silvanus took a hiccupping, hissing breath, and obeyed.

111 – This hierarchy wakes – Ordination to 11 – locate Bearer of the Black Disc, Most High Setekh. Determine precise current time

11 – Obedience – location of Bearer of the Black Disc at trans-reality gate coded as pagoth-nul-setep

111 – Supplication accepted

11 – further insight – the gate was opened – inference – Bearer of the Black Disc, Most High Setekh, passed through the gate into the anathema-sub-realm of paths

11 – further insight – elements of an alien species accompanied Bearer of the Black Disc, Most High Setekh

111 – Supplication accepted – Ordination to 11 – identify alien type and origin

11 – Obedience – alien species unlisted in this hierarchy's information-tomb

111 – Supplication accepted – Imperative Ordination – a direct communication must be opened with Bearer of the Black Disc, Most High Setekh

II – Failure of comprehension – This hierarchy does not have the means to obey

III – Ordination to II – wake two additional instances of Hierarchy III – designate current instance as IIIc

II – Obedience

IIIa – This hierarchy wakes

IIIb – This hierarchy wakes

IIIc – Ordination to IIIa – Ordination to IIIb – inference and reasoning required – assimilate current information

IIIb – assimilation complete

IIIa – assimilation complete

IIIb – the means for waking the dynasty does not exist

IIIa – the Sautekh injunction – their existence be ever blighted – still remains

IIIc – these hierarchies cannot wake the dynasts

IIIb – only the Bearer of the Black Disc, Most High Setekh, exists outside of the injunction – only they may pull back the shroud – only by their means may the Hyksos wake and rise – eternal be the dynasts – obedient shall we ever be to them

IIIa – we must form direct communication with Bearer of the Black Disc, Most High Setekh

IIIb – the means are limited – the motive canoptek units are held within the Sautekh injunction

IIIa – there are scarab canoptek units within the anathema-sub-realm of paths – they may be ordained to action and reach the Bearer of the Black Disc, Most High Setekh – they can be activated by this hierarchy – their location in the anathema-sub-realm of paths can be transmitted to the Bearer of the Black Disc, Most High Setekh, via our limited entanglement

IIIc – the Bearer of the Black Disc, Most High Setekh, will have to engineer the alien craft's intersection with the scarab canoptek units

IIIb – such matters are not for this hierarchy – we must decide, we must ordain

IIIa – so reasoned – so ordained by this hierarchy

IIIc – so reasoned – so ordained by this hierarchy

IIIa – so it is ordained

CHAPTER VI

WEBWAY

Air gasped in Silvanus' lungs. He came to his feet. The nightmare drained from him. Sweat soaked his clothes. The sound of his heart was almost deafening. He was panting as though he had just sprinted to the edge of exhaustion. It was all right, though. He was awake, and the dream was fading back to where they lived. He looked at his hand and let out a breath of relief. It was just as it should be, the digits a little longer than a planet-bound human would consider normal, but nothing else. Not what it had been in the– He blinked. Not what it had been in the dream. He brought his hand up to his face, paused, the fingers hovering just over his cheek.

'It was a dream, you idiot,' he said aloud.

Then he laughed at himself and touched his hand to his cheek. There, just as it should be – no gill folds, no fronds of feelers. Just his cheek. Everything else had been left in the dream. He got up. His quarters were dark, the lights dimmed to the night watch of the ship. He could see the rumpled sheets covering his bed, the shadow of cabinets against the walls, the frames of paintings brought from the family enclave on Terra – a parting gift from his mother to match the importance of this post. A battlefleet no less, a grand cruiser no less, the battle group flagship no less. He smiled to himself. He had done what was needed from him and more.

He winched the shutters back from the viewports. Starlight poured in. He stared at the points of light for a long while. He was still smiling. From here, everything would progress as it should. He would guide this great ship, the principal of the battle group's Navigators. He would rise, and his status within his house would rise with him. The old Heirs Apparent could not live forever, and one day... Well, who knew what he would become?

He turned away from the viewport, hesitated. There was something lying on the floor, something pale that caught the starlight. It looked like the broken shell of an egg, but an egg the size of a head. He bent down and picked it up. It was light. He turned it over. It was a mask. An ovoid mask, its delicate features set in a serene expression. Black lines crossed the eyeholes like neat, painted-on blade scars. Silvanus stared at it. Why was it here? He could not remember it being his or bringing it into his chamber. Had it been a gift – a surprise from his mother or one of his kin, left for him to find? But it seemed a strange gift, and why leave it on the floor as though cast aside?

He frowned, then stiffened. He was sure that the mask's expression had been serene, but now its brow was pinched in a frown... He raised an eyebrow, watched the mask to see if it raised an eyebrow too. He laughed, giggling at himself. He turned the mask over, looked at the inside. It was a perfect impression of the outside, a face made from the negative space, except that it looked like it was laughing. He brought it up to his face so that it was almost touching his skin. He looked through the eyeholes.

There was a figure standing in front of him.

He pitched backwards. The mask tumbled from his hands. The figure was still there, utterly still. It was very tall, humanoid but not human. White and black diamonds covered its skin. Grey and red ribbons hung from it, tangling and pooling on the floor. Its face was not there. Just a smooth, black absence at the front of its head.

'What…?' he gasped. 'Who…?'

The figure stepped forward, unfolding from stillness, slowly, every movement perfectly smooth. He felt the air stop in his throat. It picked up the mask from where it lay on the floor, rocking with fading momentum, its inner face still laughing. The figure picked it up, looked at it just as Silvanus had, shivered with silent laughter, then brought it to its face. It looked at Silvanus through the holes in the mask's eyes. He began to scream. The figure was over and above him faster than he could follow. It crouched, still again. It reached out a hand, index finger raised, and something in the movement was like a shouted command that silenced the scream coming from his throat. The figure placed its finger over his lips. The mask of its face had changed – one side black, the other white; one side grinning with red fangs, the other cracked and weeping. He was shaking as the figure stood.

A dream, a dream, a dream… was all he could think. He began to weep.

'Silvanus!' The sound of a voice shouting in the distance from the other side of sleep…

The masked figure tilted its head, and he could tell that it was watching him. He felt like a bird with a broken wing that would never fly again, something small and to be pitied before its neck was broken.

'Silvanus!' The shout was louder now, closer. The figure looked around, shrugged, and the world folded back into a dream that was not a dream at all.

Light poured in, unfolding in burning diamonds. Sound came with it and he *was* screaming now, the sound ripping from his lungs. The figure in the mask was crouching over him. Motes of light winked around it, billowing like an ephemeral cloak caught in a wind. The figure's hand was blurring, as though it were that of a phantom. A grey mist filled the chamber, spiralling and rolling. It tasted of sugar and smoke. Lurid ghost images popped in his sight. Silvanus could hear blows on the sealed inner doors. His guards, shut out of the chamber when he had taken to his throne to steer the ship through the gate into the webway. But he had not been alone.

'Silvanus!' he heard Maehekta shout.

'Here!' he gasped. The figure on him twisted.

A blur of lightning and sharpened steel cut through the fog. The figure leapt into the air as Maehekta's blade sliced through the space where it had been. The door shrieked as it gave way with a shower of sparks. Maehekta was above him, her great sword drawn and shining with lightning. The figure hit the ceiling of the chamber, kicked off and spun down. Maehekta sliced at it, but it slid under the blade, spun back, and its foot slammed into her chest just below the heart. Maehekta shot backwards; landed in a crouch, gasping. One of Silvanus' guards came through the fog, spear raised. The figure flicked itself backwards, drawing and firing a pistol before it touched the floor. Razor discs hit the Unsighted Keeper under the bottom edge of its helm. The guard dropped, gurgling, blood gushing out. The figure pirouetted, its pistol whining as more discs shrieked through the fog in a wide circle.

Silvanus scrambled backwards, limbs tangling with the neural-link cable that had fallen from his head. Maehekta charged forwards, an energy field snapping into being in front of her. Razor discs struck the shield and became flares of blue light. She spun her sword, flowing from cut to cut without pause. The figure tumbled backwards, dodging under and around the blade, its shape exploding in a blur of red-and-white fragments of light. Silvanus saw Maehekta's mouth curl beneath her helm as she whirled the sword, reversed the grip of her hands and brought it around in a scything cut to the legs. The figure leaped away, landing on the frame of the viewport, crouching like a gargoyle on a cathedral spire. A spill of iridescent fabric fluttered to the ground. The figure looked down to the severed edge of one of its sashes, then tilted its head in mocking appreciation. It raised a hand and pinched a small ovoid between its fingers. Maehekta lunged at it.

The crystal of the viewport blew out behind the figure. It flung itself through as Maehekta's sword sliced the space it had occupied. Its foot slammed into Maehekta's throat as it arched and tumbled back, spinning in a cascade of shattered crystal. The mist filling the room was sucked out. Maehekta pitched back from the viewport, stumbling then falling into a loose heap that did not get up. Silvanus, gasping, began to heave himself up next to her. The sight that filled the viewport made him flinch.

The hull of the *Hekaton* reached ahead of them, plunging into a glowing fog. Another vessel filled the space above them, pressing down like a crenellated sky, close and coming closer. He could see aerials, cooling pipes and gun turrets. The whole surface was rippling, cracks opening in armour plates, clouds of gas venting. For a moment he thought dust was falling from it. Then he realised it was not dust but pieces of armour and stone, each the size of a tank. They were hitting the *Hekaton*, slamming into the upper hull of the ship like stones thrown into a city of sand. Clouds of debris exploded from toppled towers. A great booming shriek sounded, rolling and growling like the gasp of a dying god of iron. The ship above them was coming apart, screaming as its hull twisted and sheared. And the *Hekaton* was plunging on towards it.

'Holy Throne!' he shouted, scrabbling back to his throne, trying to find the neural-link cable. His progeny were thrashing in their tanks, blood foaming the fluid pink. The alien device fastened over his third eye was twitching, twisting as though trying to pull itself free. There were corpses on the floor: his dead guards, still leaking life fluid; others had formed a ring around him, spears facing outwards, their protection come too late. He found the cable, slid it into the opening in his temple. The connection to his progeny opened. He saw and wanted to weep all over again.

Helio Isidorus was facing towards the opposite wall when Ctesias entered the chamber. The hoops of metal spun on. Ctesias could taste the cage's power pulsing over him like the heat from a plasma lamp. He did not like it. As much as his craft was the chaining of daemons, he had never been easy with that same art applied to the living. Oh, he could cause suffering without end and feel almost nothing, but there was something about caging a being that could make its own choices that sat poorly. He was not sure why. Perhaps it was a need to hold on to a scrap of nobility despite all his deeds. That or a price exacted by one of the more imaginative Neverborn he had bargained with. No matter the cause, he did not like the cages or what they implied. Worse, he did not like that he had helped make them. Still, that did not stop him coming back here, always alone, though never for long. He was not sure why he did, other than he felt he had to come and see the prisoner in the gaol he had helped make.

Helio Isidorus sat on the platform which floated between

the turning hoops. His legs were folded beneath him, his back straight. Ctesias watched him for a long moment, opened his mouth, then stopped and shook his head. What was there to say to someone who could only remember their name?

'Is there something you came to say?' asked Helio. He turned towards Ctesias, a look of mild concern on his face.

Ctesias looked into Helio Isidorus' eyes. There was something about his expression that made him want to blink: an innocence and openness, like looking into the eyes of a child or an obedient hound. *Is this what is left inside the Rubricae?* he thought. *Just a memory of a name and obedience?*

'No,' said Ctesias. 'I did not come to say anything.' He began to turn away, stopped again, blinking at the instinct that made him glance back. 'I am sorry,' he said.

'For what are you sorry?'

Ctesias shook his head. This was a conversation without point or end, just like all the others, just like all those that Ahriman had tried.

'Nothing,' he said.

'What is your name?' asked Helio Isidorus.

'I am Ctesias.'

Helio Isidorus frowned again, blinked. 'Is it?'

Ctesias nodded, but Helio Isidorus was shaking his head.

'It is something else...'

'No.' Ctesias felt the word come sharp from his lips. He was not sure why, just that something in Helio Isidorus' voice meant he did not want him to go on. Why? This was just the same as all the other conversations with the former Rubricae. 'I am called Ctesias,' he said, aware that he had carefully picked the phrase to be true and wondering why.

Helio Isidorus nodded. 'Yes, you are called Ctesias,' he said. Then nodded again. 'And you are not Ahriman.'

Ctesias felt his skin prickle. His heartbeats were rising.

'You remember Ahriman?' he asked carefully.

'Who?' Helio Isidorus said, face and eyes open in question.

Ctesias felt himself release a breath he did not realise he had been holding. A strange sense of relief flooded him. He had thought for a moment that... But no. This was just the same as always. All memory beyond the immediate past gone, leaving just a flash of light and a name.

'Ahriman is someone who comes and talks to you,' he said.

Helio looked down and away, as though puzzled. 'I am sorry, but I do not remember him.'

Ctesias began to turn away again. 'You do not and will not. I am sorry,' he said again.

'I remember you.'

'I am here, but once I am gone you will forget me, too.'

'No.' Helio Isidorus shook his head again. 'I remember you.' Helio looked up. His face was expressionless. 'You are the one who dies.'

Ctesias froze. His blood was cold. The beat of his hearts suspended between beats.

Alarms sounded through the chamber. The walls and deck shook. The comms system in his armour activated with a shriek of static. He flinched and the frame of the ship shook again and did not stop shaking. He glanced back at Helio Isidorus, but he had looked away, utterly unconcerned. Ctesias cursed and ran for the door and whatever disaster had come for them now.

The ships of the Exiles had gone through the gate together. Beyond was a tunnel drilled into the starlit night. Nebulae and stellar dust swam through blackness stained by the colours of birthing and dying galaxies. The ships slid down the throat of the tunnel one after another. From his viewport, Silvanus had looked out in wonder. He had seen great and terrible things in his life, had investigated the warp again and again. In a very real sense, he had been born to perceive madness and paradox. There was wonder and majesty in the immaterium for him; to look on it was to see the stuff of heaven, but the webway… Its peace struck him first. Wild tides ran through the Great Ocean, and the threat of death existed in its calmest seas. Uncontrolled, primal: that was the warp. In contrast, looking into the webway was like looking at a perfectly designed garden. It was architecture, rather than nature. The warp was still all around them, but while it normally broke and frothed, here it flowed like filtered and purified water. It was… incredible.

The ships slid on. The tunnel must have widened to fit them, but Silvanus could detect no change in its size. Mist rose and enclosed them. Silvanus' wonder faded. The mist grew thicker and the view of the cosmos outside the tunnel walls dimmed. The walls of the webway clouded and blurred so that they blended with the mist. He could not tell if the walls were there at all any more. He felt alone, even linked to the sight of his progeny. The *Hekaton* almost felt as though it were not moving, as if it were becalmed in a cloud. The alien device covering his third eye squirmed but offered no other sign of direction. Even the normal noises of the ship seemed muffled. The world had become grey, diffused, a ghost realm slowly dissolving the sensations of living.

Then a light. A blink like a rainbow star.

His eyes had snapped to it, but it had gone. A second later he had felt the ship moving towards where the light had been, and realised that he had steered it that way. He wondered why he had not hit the wall. The light came again, dancing in the distance. His progeny on the other ships were watching it too. He made himself focus, made his progeny focus.

Focus…

He kept having the feeling that there was someone right next to him, watching him. Maehekta had withdrawn to a side room so that her soul-dulling presence did not interfere with his sight. But the feeling remained...

Foolish... Silly... There was no one there, no one smiling just off his shoulder. He did not need to worry... He did not need to focus... Navigation... Ha! He did not even know what he was supposed to do now. The alien device on his head did not seem to be doing anything. He tapped it with a finger. Giggled. Tapped it again.

The light was back, winking in the mist. He had no idea what he was doing or supposed to do... Absurd, hilarious. He laughed. His throat gills ruffled as the sound rose and kept coming. He shook, tears rolling from his eyes. He was not sure why he was crying, just that it seemed the only thing he could do... The light was ahead now, glimmering like a sunbeam pouring through a diamond. Red, green, blue, yellow and purple shards sparking and spinning... Just looking at them made him not want to stop laughing and crying...

He had heard the sound of a door releasing and resealing behind him. It must have been Maehekta. He should have turned around to see why she was disturbing him, but he could not speak over the sound of his own laughter. And he did not want to look away from the lights. The sparkling light was coming closer, bursting into smaller shards, each pinwheeling. There were stars dropping from above too, tiny glimmer-flecks of rainbow light, spinning over and over. It was dazzling and he just wanted to watch and to keep laughing.

Some of the stars landed on the hull of the ship and began to spin across its towers. The mist was inside his chamber, somehow spreading up around him, and he could smell something that might have been the chemical mockery of a flowery scent.

Something had touched his cheek then. There was someone there, someone right there next to him, and he had tried to turn his head. Out of the corner of his eye he had seen the hull of a warship looming out of the mist above, close enough to touch, and then he had been falling and laughing and laughing until the dream took him and he woke.

By that time, the *Hekaton* was seconds from crashing into one of the other ships.

Silvanus saw it all through the eyes of his progeny. Some vessels were travelling upwards. Some had turned so that they were driving back into the ships following behind. All of them jumbled like a handful of children's toys thrown into a sack. How had it happened? The question screamed at Silvanus for a second, and then the first of the ships struck each other.

The *Fire of Nine Suns* was a destroyer. She was small for a warship, only a kilometre long. The *Three Crescents* was four times its size. The *Fire of Nine Suns* struck the prow of the larger ship like a driven spear. Chunks of armour peeled from the *Three Crescents* as the smaller ship cored into its forward decks. The larger ship, trying to manoeuvre at the last instant to avoid the collision, twisted as it ploughed on, ramming its own mass into the *Fire of Nine Suns*. The two rolled over, locked together, shedding debris. Then something critical in one of the ships exploded. The prow sections of both blew apart. The wrecked hulls spun away from the detonation. The remains of the *Three Crescents* hit the tunnel wall. The etheric substance of the webway shook. Golden fire radiated from the impact point as the ship tore into the tunnel wall. It became a golden gauze of fire, shredding the hull. The *Three Crescents* pushed on, extruding across the reality membrane in a spill of fire. Silvanus felt the voiceless scream of his progeny that had been on board the ship in the instant before its body was forced through the golden curtain.

Then the tunnel began to contract. The walls had turned black. Some ships hit, broke, metal breaking into sparks. Others tried to pull away, but there was already no room to move. Hulls met. Metres-thick armour plates buckled, broke, became scraps as the walls pressed in and in, twisting, grinding like the gizzard of a great worm. Debris slammed together, rolling and churning into a mass of crumpled metal. Explosions lit off as macro-munitions and plasma generators detonated. The mass of wreckage bubbled with fire, melted, shattered, fused.

Silvanus could hear his progeny calling for him, for the protection that he had told them the twin-headed Emperor would give them. The sound rang in his head. He almost blacked out. Breaking hulls, splitting reactors, the pain of his family as it burned…

The scarab device on his forehead dug its legs into his skull. His focus snapped back to the sight in front of his own eyes. He was just in time. The ship in front of the *Hekaton* was a cliff of metal. Close enough to touch.

'Throne save me!' shrieked Silvanus, willing the *Hekaton* downwards.

Thrusters flared along the ship's hull. Flame and gas and plasma poured into the mist. The fire of the *Hekaton*'s main engines shrank, but its momentum pushed her on even as the thrusters fought to bend that course.

'Nine-fold Emperor save me!'

The wall of the other ship's hull filled Silvanus' world. An aerial spire projecting from its surface struck a gun turret just behind the *Hekaton*'s prow. Tower and turret ripped free. Pieces of rubble spun back, bouncing along the ship's back, ripping into other structures like wrecking balls. The bronze face of a grotesque roared across Silvanus' view, grinning at him as it whirled past. The hull of the other ship was above him now, blurring as Silvanus forced the *Hekaton* downwards. He could see the tunnel ahead of him. It was narrowing. He felt the *Hekaton* shudder.

'Come on! Please!' he pleaded. They were almost clear of the other ship, almost clear into the tunnel beyond. They would be through before the passage closed… 'Please!'

For a second, he thought he could see figures on the other ship's hull above him, tiny brightly coloured figures, dancing and leaping from tower to precipice. He thought, even though it was impossible, that he could hear laughter. High, cruel laughter. He saw some of the figures drop towards the *Hekaton* as it passed beneath, whirling as they fell, crackling with pixelated colour. Silvanus' eye caught one of the figures landing a half a kilometre towards the prow. For a moment, he was ready for it to shatter into shining fragments. Then it tucked into a tumble, landed on one leg and exploded up into a jump that sent it bounding away.

Pain stabbed through Silvanus. He let out a cry. The device on his skull was biting deeper and deeper. Blood was pouring down his face. It was yanking his head and eyes up towards the tunnel ahead. Except there was not one tunnel ahead; there were three.

CHAPTER VII

$\mathcal{H}$ARLEQUINADE

The laughing murderers entered the *Hekaton* and began their slaughter. They slid through wounds in its hull. The thrall crew and beast-bred that met them first saw only broken blurs of light before they died. And how they died. Split from crown to groin. Limbs severed in bladed whirls. Sacks of skin falling to the deck filled with the bloody pulp of organs. Spines yanked through flesh and armour. Clouds of gossamer wire, as soft as a child's hair, enfolding bodies before shrinking to pinpoints and leaving red jelly to wash the walls and deck. Clouds of gas billowed through breached doors. Sweet scent filled lungs, and horror the eyes of those that inhaled it. Through this the dancers sped, never pausing, always laughing.

Ahriman saw it all as his thought form blurred through the ship. It took the shape of a murder of crows, each feather a fold of darkness and starlight, silver-clawed with eyes of blue flame. In the physical world he had not moved. His eyes were still open, still seeing the dust falling from the ceiling of the bridge-temple. The shouts of the machine-fanatics filled his ears, but inside his mind he was racing through the *Hekaton*. Frost sheeted the stone walls as he passed. The invaders were quick, but they were still physical, and no matter how fast they moved they could not outrun thought. His focus narrowed.

He found the first of the enemy in an aviary of one of the beast-bred clans. The aviary was a spiral that wound upwards through the dead spaces of the ship, curving like the inside of a seashell. Bones and chewed trinkets gleamed in the golden resin of its walls. Beams criss-crossed the space. There were beast-bred perched on some of the beams. At a glance they might have looked human, until you saw the clawed feet and beaked faces. They were already drawing weapons and cawing their war cries as the laughing murderers sprinted up the spiral to meet them.

A beast-bred chieftain hooted in anger and launched herself down at the invaders. Her herd followed. One of them fired at the nearest dancer. The dancer leapt over the stream of bullets. It landed on a beam, balancing on one foot long enough for its blurred image to resolve into a figure in iridescent turquoise and white. Its face was a red scowl under a green mane of hair. Razor discs sang from its pistol. Two of the beast-bred fell, gurgling, blood gushing. The chieftain gave a cry of rage and pointed her hand. Will and belief fused in the chieftain's mind and pulled substance from the warp. Lightning flashed from her fingers towards the dancer. To Ahriman's inner sight, the lightning unfolded slowly. He saw the chieftain's mind forming the crude patterns of emotion and meaning that let her pull energy from the warp. It would not work. By the time the lightning reached across the gap, the dancer would be gone and more of the herd would be bloody carcasses. Ahriman would not let that happen.

His thought form roared down the spiral. Frost flashed into

being on the walls. Ghost-light spun across the beams spanning the drop. He reached his sight forwards, into the next seconds before they happened. He saw the possibilities unfold and chose one to allow to exist. The chieftain's head jerked up, and Ahriman knew that for an instant her mind saw him: a cloud of black feathers and starlight and blue flame. Ahriman reached out with his will and pulled the lightning out of being as it formed beyond the chieftain's fingers. He spun it through his mind and loosed it. The lightning struck the dancer. For an instant, it fell still alive, a broken and bloody doll. Then Ahriman's mind struck it. He did not try trickery or any of the subtler arts of mental invasion; there was no time, and there was no need. His will tore open the dancer's, ripping through thoughts, tearing its alien tongue from its skull, and slicing into its psyche.

Laughter… laughter that was sorrow and longing and a purpose given to a soul who had lost their way… The weave of past and present… Masks worn one after another, the thoughts and memories and truths of each still clinging to them like tatters of skin to a skull…

The sense of sorrow that came with the thoughts was almost overwhelming. He pulled free and let the broken wreckage of the dancer's mind collapse. In the physical world, its body fell. It struck a beam spanning the aviary spiral with bone-breaking force, and tumbled on, not dancing now, not laughing, just falling. Ahriman heard the ripple of glee in the minds of the beast-bred, gloating and exulted.

He had a name… *Agaithari*, the name the aeldari gave the followers of their Laughing God: Harlequins, dancers of doom, and players of mythic war.

There were more of them coming, leaping up past the falling corpse of their kin. Ahriman watched them for an instant. He understood them now. He could see the legends and stories unfolding in the flick of their kicks, in the shifting colour of a sash, and the angle of a sword. It was a tragedy in motion, a dying story given last breath in war. What he had to do would be like breaking the neck of a songbird. There was always tragedy in necessity. But it had to be.

He fell on them, a storm of ghost wings and claws. Some of the psychic potential that lurked in all aeldari must have let them see their doom as it came for them. They jerked aside, trying to blend their reaction with the movements of their dance. His will flowed into the substance of their bones and flesh, and became fire. The bodies exploded as the last of the dancers came level with them. Bone splinters and red steam blasted out in clouds of bloody shrapnel. The dancers fell, their holo-projectors creating broken kaleidoscopes of light to trail behind them.

Ahriman pulled his mind and sight back from the aviary. For an instant he allowed himself to float above what was happening across the ship. In the space of minutes, the enemy were already deep inside. Some had reached the decks that were the domains of the machine and cyborg sects that tended to the ship's engines and core systems, but were making no attempt to reach the main plasma conduits or other vital machinery. Instead, they were killing the machine initiates they came across and cutting power trunks so that other sections of the ship became dark or filled with random strobing light.

One group had reached a hangar space and bored a hole in the blast doors. Jetbikes and arrow-shaped skimmers screamed in through the breach and shrieked down corridors. He could feel stronger minds amongst them, too, pushing their thoughts out into the ether, flooding it with contradiction and hallucinations. Even as he reached his mind to call on his brothers, he felt the ether shift and chuckle. Here, in the sub-reality of the webway, the current of the warp was bending to their will. It made sense. He and his brothers were trespassers here. This was the Harlequins' ground. He could not see or sense the rest of the fleet, but here, on the *Hekaton*, they were on the edge of disaster.

Moving in scattered groups the dancers were following wild, random paths that had no clear purpose. They did have purpose, though, a single overarching purpose to shelter the lesser goals of each group: mayhem.

Helio, thought Ahriman. Because in his mind's eye he could see what the dazzle of the dance hid. They were making for the Serene Cages.

Ctesias cursed as he ran. He reached the end of the passage leading from Helio's cell. The ship shook again. He could hear blurts of noise over his armour vox, chopped with static and distortion. There was fighting in the ship, he could tell. Somehow, the supposedly simple entry into the webway had gone wrong. Instinctively, he reached into the store of his memory for a Neverborn's name, but the power guttered even as he tried to call on it. He cursed again and drew his bolt pistol. He was not surprised, just angry that he had not been ready. Now, he was caught here, in the Serene Cages. Here his abilities were limited – not absent all together, but if this was as bad a fight as it sounded, they might as well have been. Ignis was here too, but the cages were close to a kilometre of subdivided corridors and doors. Ctesias might as well have been on another planet. He saw two Rubricae standing sentinel either side of the door ahead. He reached out to them with a tendril of will and spoke their names aloud.

'Rehat, Askestemes, heed my word!' Compared to how the Rubricae were normally commanded, with telepathy and direct will, this felt like the act of a child. The two Rubricae rotated their heads to him.

'Follo–' he began.

The door behind the Rubricae blew in. Molten metal sprayed out in a burning orange flower. The Rubricae nearest the door lurched. The other began to turn. A blur of light burst from the hole in the door. Ctesias fired, pumping bolts into the breach. The blur of light unfolded into a figure, its face a mask of malicious glee. He fired a bolt at its head. It cartwheeled aside, grinning.

'Kill it!'

The Rubricae fired. Bolts exploded with blue fire. The gleaming figure leapt towards the ceiling, fast enough to evade the rounds chasing it, dazzling with speed. Then a bolt exploded just beneath it. A coil of cyan fire reached from the explosion and snared its foot. Flesh burned to ash and the dazzling figure was falling. Bolt-rounds sawed into it before it touched the ground. It fell the last half-metre as a drift of grey ash. The Rubricae stopped firing.

'The door!' called Ctesias. The Rubricae began to turn. A wailing shriek split the air, then another and another, blending into a pulsing scream. The Rubricae nearest the door seemed to shiver, then jerked, then began to collapse. Ghost-light leaked from the slices in its armour joins. Dust was running from the rents like grey blood. Ctesias could hear a shrill sound in his mind, like a scream swallowed by a sandstorm. Another figure tumbled through the breached door, dragging a cloud of black-and-white flecks behind it. It landed on the fallen Rubricae, coalescing. Diamonds of white and black covered its form. A skull mask grimaced beneath a purple coxcomb. Bells of bone tinkled with dry laughter as it stood. The weapon it held was as tall as it was, a slender barrel tapering to a flared snout. It fired into the second Rubricae. A howl like the dead in torment sliced the air. Razor-edged stars hit ceramite. The Rubricae juddered, bleeding dust and ghost-light.

Ctesias fired at the skull-faced dancer but it had already leapt into the air, like a released spring. It kicked the staggering Rubricae with enough force to crack its faceplate. The Rubricae cannoned back. Another figure somersaulted through the breach behind the first. It touched the ground for a single stride, long enough for Ctesias to fire again, but it was already kicking into a tumbling sprint that took it up the wall and over the ceiling. The empty sockets of its mask did not move from Ctesias as it arced through the air.

Death... thought Ctesias, the moment slowing. He had thought that when his end came it would be at the hands of someone or something he knew: an old enemy, a false ally, one of the Never-born taking its vengeance. But here, in the end, death would be at the hands of strangers, delivered with the indifference of a scythe swept through a stalk of corn. Enough to make you laugh... So he did and drew the power of the warp that he could reach. The runes on his staff lit with cold fire.

The twin dancers rose, weapons aimed. He spoke a word inside his skull. A fork of black lightning reached across the space between them. The pair leapt into the air at the same moment. They fired as they moved. Discs and stars and razor-edged spirals shrieked. Ctesias felt them hit his armour, splintering, gouging. His bolt pistol rose to fire. He could see a grinning face beyond the barrel. He would take one with him, at least.

He felt something strike just below his arm. No pain, just a thump, like a finger flicking his flesh. His pistol did not fire. The dancer in his sights had not moved. Its skull-socket eyes looked back at him. He tried to squeeze the trigger. His fingers would not move. The dancer tilted its head. Ctesias' arm was locked in place. Cold was flowing through him from the point just below his arm. He could not move his head. He could not close his eyes. The second dancer stepped close to him, its movements delicate and slow. It reached out and picked something out of the join under Ctesias' right arm. It held it up to him. It was a spiral disc, off-white, like polished bone. Blood and plum-coloured fluid seeped from the holes. The dancer rolled the disc across its fingers like a coin, then reached out and slowly cut Ctesias' cheek. The cold began to spread through his head, becoming a fever ache. His veins were burning as the venom spread.

The dancer stepped away from him, its sibling beside it. They both bowed as though they were receiving applause. Ctesias began to shiver in his armour. Lights were popping in his sight. The world was blurring, shapes pinwheeling to sharp-edged fragments. There was no pain, but it was coming like a wave gathering out at sea.

The pair looked at one another and gestured to each other in perfect synchronisation. Then the venom finally reached Ctesias' brain and the world and sense tore to pieces.

Ignis looked up as a tremor ran through the deck.

Engine strain, he thought. Shearing force from sudden directional change.

The *Hekaton* was manoeuvring hard.

'You are lost,' said the xenos from within the orbiting hoops of its cage. 'The anathema web is a kind realm. It fights what is not of its own. You will end here and all your kind that you brought with you.' It paused, the glow of its eyes pulsing briefly. 'This is certain unless you let me make good my bargain and guide you.'

'No,' replied Ignis.

'I am aware of the device of mine that you have activated,' said Setekh. 'The object that you might call a scarab. You do not understand its purpose, and you do not have the true knowledge to make it work. It will not save you from the place you have taken us.'

'No.'

'This… vessel of yours is under attack. The air vibrates with the echoes of explosions transmitted through the metal structure. The ways were never peaceful. The spawn of our enemies infested them once, and some may even now. Naive creatures of flesh that thought themselves destined to rise to the heights… fawning over the scraps of power and approval from their creators, always willing to carry the blades of war. They were easy to despise, but to underestimate them was always a grave error. If they survive in this age, then you should not repeat that error – it will undo you. I can get you safe through the ways between stars and through the enemies that try to stop you.'

'No.'

'You must, or you and I and all that you have brought with you shall end. You are lost in a web of infinite malice. You do not have the intellect or knowledge to survive it. I do. I wish to reach the same goal as you. We have made an accord. Release me.'

Credence clattered from beside him, weapons armed and fixed on Setekh.

Ignis felt the calculations and projections flow through his mind, as the choices became symbol and number and data. He let the projections spool out to their end. Then shook his head once.

'No,' he said.

'Then you will die here,' said Setekh.

'As will you.'

It laughed for a second.

'I am already beyond death.'

* * *

The venom touched the edge of Ctesias' mind and for the first time in a long, long time he felt fear. Despite the craft of that corpse of an Emperor to remove such emotions from His warriors, it was still there, buried down in the meat.

He could not move. He wanted to move but could only see the shapes of the death-masked dancers moving catlike away from him.

The walls of the corridor were bulging at the edge of his sight. He could feel thoughts form and connect and mutilate in his head, screaming then dissolving into froth.

'One and two and three and do you remember me?' The voice filled his head, rolling with echoes.

The shapes of the Rubricae on the floor began to rise, shadow and light reversing.

'Nam... Name... Naaame...'

There were no walls... There was no substance... Not even stars, just abyss... on and on, and around and down to the bottom.

'One, two, three, give the keys to me...'

No.

He wanted to say no, but his mouth would not move, and the thought in his head sounded weak, and the sing-song voice almost sounded like his own.

And then he knew what was coming, and the fear became terror.

His power and survival had been built on control. He was a summoner and binder of daemons. His craft and art was to take entities made of raw emotion and occult power and make them do as he commanded. Some of that was a matter of knowledge: rites and spells of evocation, command and dismissal, but knowledge alone could get you killed or worse. Many had learnt that lesson over the ages. The screams of some still could be heard in the warp if you had the ear to hear them. The bones of others spoke their own silent warning. Ctesias kept a small collection of such remains as a reminder that pride in dealing with daemons led to only one end. No, knowledge was nothing without control of yourself. That was the great learning: your control was the limit of your command and power. So Ctesias had made his mind a thing of total control. He had stripped his thoughts of delusion, his actions of any of the comfort of false virtue. Many thought him cynical and power hungry, and he was, but he had long ago decided that it was a small price to pay. If he did not have mastery over himself, he would be vulnerable. Vulnerable to what he shared his thought space with.

Down in the depths below his mundane memories, Ctesias kept the true names of his daemons. Such names held power all of their own; they corrupted, and squirmed, and tried to turn the soul inside out. So, he had broken his memory of them into pieces. A separate cell of memory held each fragment. All he needed to use one of the names was the location of its components. Other sorcerers held true names in grimoires or in objects; Ctesias had made his mind his grimoire, and his own thoughts the key to the cypher that held them. No one could take his knowledge from him, or use it against him, because only he was the master of his thoughts. He was in control.

In the ringing dome of his mind, he could feel the links of control slip from the fingers of his will.

'Yes, yes, that's it… Let your thoughts be free… Wouldn't you like that…? Wouldn't you like to see what it's like to be free?'

No, he said. *No. No!* But no words came, just the sudden grind and hiss of armour as he collapsed to the floor.

He could feel the daemon names coming loose of his control now, rattling in their divided cells like finger bones shaken in a dice box.

There was fire in his veins. The venom had reached his spine, was flushing into the sheaths and connections of his nerves. The rational part of his mind knew what was happening, was aware that his organs were altering. His cells were becoming furnaces pouring even more molten fire into his flesh. Acid spittle drooled from his tongue onto the deck. His eyes were still open. Colour whirled in his sight. He thought he saw the two dancers step away, as though wanting to watch from further away.

He was going to end here, burned from within or eaten by vengeful creatures from beyond.

The dancers tilted their heads. Behind them was the cell that held Helio. He wondered if they would open it next.

White light… Sudden and bright, as if a door had opened onto the surface of a star. The dancers became black silhouettes. Then the light vanished, and the death-masked dancers were gone, as though they had never been. Their shadows were still there, frozen on the passage wall opposite the open door to Helio's cell.

Great bubbles of colour swelled and burst in Ctesias' sight.

He did not know what he was seeing now.

Bones rattling… names…

Do not… do not say the names…

'But they want to be said. They want to be free…'

Ctesias tried to blink… just to blink…

There was a figure in the doorway.

It looked down and towards him. Its eyes were blue stars…

It looked… it looked like… it looked like…

'I am Helio Isidorus,' said a voice.

Then Ctesias blinked and found that he could not open his eyes again.

* * *

'What are the three steps to power?'

It was a question that Ahriman had learnt the answer to even before he had gone to the Legion. He and his brother Ohrmuzd had been sitting at the feet of their tutor, Euboaea, on the terrace of the family manse under Terra's sun, as she had asked the question. They had been nine years old. He remembered glancing at Ohrmuzd, and his brother flicking one of the counting pebbles at him. Euboaea – young, clever and patient Euboaea – had caught the pebble before it reached Ahriman. They had looked at her sheepishly, ready for a telling off. She had just held the pebble up. Sunlight had glinted off the oval of blue lapis.

'Everything you do is an expression of power. Even just catching a stone. What was the first thing I needed to do, to do that?'

'See it,' said Ahriman quickly. 'You needed to see it.'

Euboaea had raised an eyebrow. 'To see it?' she asked and closed her eyes. 'What about if it slipped from my fingers now?' The stone dropped and her hand flashed down, catching it again. 'I couldn't see it, so how did I catch it?'

'You felt it,' said Ahriman. 'You felt it drop from your hand.'

'Good,' she nodded. 'So what do I need to do first if I am going to catch the stone?'

'Perceive it,' said Ohrmuzd. 'You need to perceive the stone before you can do anything to it. It doesn't matter if you see or feel it.'

Ahriman had glanced at his brother, but Ohrmuzd had a calm, focused look on his face.

'Very good,' Euboaea had said, and smiled at Ohrmuzd. 'The first step to power is perception.'

Ahriman's mind split and exploded out across the *Hekaton*. Everything was a blur. In the core decks, the mortal warriors and beast-bred felt ice shiver through them as he touched their minds. He looked through their eyes, smelled the floral reek of hallucinogen-laced smoke, heard the laughter and the shrieks of pain. He was Lycomedes with a squad of Rubricae, rushing to the main arteria; he was a brute mutant on the ammunition decks; and he was the machine-cultists with their eyes filled with static. The minds of all other beings of this ship bowed under him. He was all of them, and they would follow his will. The ship was drowning in mayhem and cacophony but seen through a thousand eyes and senses, the confusion drained away.

'And once we have perceived clearly, what next?' Euboaea had asked, tossing and catching the stone.

'Will,' Ahriman had said, and the pebble had frozen in mid-air.

In a thought he spoke the names of the Rubricae on the ship. There were hundreds. Some walked the ships as guardians to their living brothers, but most stood in lightless chambers and halls, immobile, the lights in their eyes dimmed to a dull glow. Now their heads rose. Ghost-light blazed from their helms.

Euboaea had watched the pebble rotate in the air in front of her. Ice crystals had begun to fog the blue stone. Ahriman had felt his eyes prickle and his forehead pinch as he fought to keep it still. In the corner of his eye, Ohrmuzd was grinning.

'Perception, and then the will,' said Euboaea, unhurried, even as Ahriman gritted his teeth with the effort. 'Without clear perception we cannot know what we have to do, but once we sense things clearly then we must set our will.' She had looked between them. 'Why do I say "set our will"? What does that mean?'

'It means you put all of yourself into what you are going to do, no matter what,' Ohrmuzd had answered. Euboaea had smiled. Ahriman had felt his fingers bunch as he had tried to keep his focus on the pebble. He was holding his breath. Clenching his teeth.

'And why must you set your will?' she had asked.

'Because if you don't then you won't be able to take the third step of power,' Ohrmuzd had said.

'And what is that?' She shifted her gaze. 'Ahriman?'

He gasped, lungs exploding, eyes running, body shivering. The
pebble began to fall. Ohrmuzd's eyes had snapped shut. The pebble
had exploded into dust.

'Action,' Ahriman had said, panting. 'The ultimate step of power
is action.'

'Just so,' Euboaea had said as the dust of the blue stone pattered
gently to the ground.

The Rubricae moved. First one step, the joints of hundreds of
suits of armour creaking as they shook off immobility. Then a
second step, made in dozens of different chambers. The decks
shook like a struck bell. Then they took another step and another,
and they were running, every stride synchronised. The sound
rolled through the ship, beating like a drum.

The aeldari Harlequins heard and must have sensed the
counter-attack. In places they simply vanished in clouds of light
and smoke; in others they did not have that choice. In the main
arteria, where they had been coating the stone floor with the
blood and limbs of mortal crew, the Rubricae started firing.
Shrapnel and coiling fire filled the thoroughfare. Tendrils of
blue flame whipped out, reaching for the dancers as they spun
through the air. Some bounded to the ceiling, landed for an
instant and then rebounded. Jewels of light scattered in their
wake. Ahriman perceived the fire and dance through the Rubricae's eyes. They did not see, not truly. Substance was as mist,
colour drained to a smoke grey. Walls and floor, weapons and
masks, and all the rest of the physical world held shape only in
the echoes of all the hands that had touched it. The living shone
in their sight, bodies and souls casting pale shadows through a
grey-ghost world. Some amongst the Thousand Sons called it
the Grave Vision. That was not the truth. Not to Ahriman. The
Rubricae were not dead. In their eyes the Harlequin dancers were
not blurs of light or the whirl of limbs in motion. They were

tangles of gossamer light, moving with the speed of birds, their glowing threads fraying to nothing in their wake. They were the slain, grimacing as they tried to outrun death's embrace, their laughter hollow. He pitied them.

His will flicked through the Rubricae. Their guns silenced. The Harlequins whirled. Razor discs cut into armour. Dust and ghost-light bled into the air. A beam of bright white fire lanced into one of the Rubricae. Armour shattered and melted. The Rubricae slumped to the floor, and Ahriman felt its silent cry in his mind as he watched the dance unfold. He had its pattern now.

He reshaped his will. The Rubricae shifted. In corridors, passages and junctions they stepped forwards. Razor discs tore at them. Some fell, the damage done to them enough to send them down to the deck, screaming in silence. The rest moved on, implacable, weathering the squall. Ahriman could see them and the Harlequins in his mind, could see the unfolding seconds counting down to the point where the lines of fire and escape would intersect with perfection. The moment came. The Rubricae fired again. Flame and thunder rolled through the *Hekaton*. The blue fire burst from each bolt shell and flowed into the explosion of the one that followed. The inferno caught lithe bodies as they tried to tumble away and burned them to ash before they could touch the floor. Ahriman felt the shiver of the coordinated volley in the air of the bridge-temple, and the fire inhale fury from the ether. He had won. Now all that remained was to turn it into annihilation.

The servitors and machine-serfs he was holding ready were poised to key the controls of bulkheads and doors. In a second the internal shape of the ship would change. Air would vent from some passages. The pressure in others would become enough to collapse lungs and hearts. Open ways would shut, as others opened. By his will, the ship would become a killing maze. Within a beat of a mortal heart the enemy would be no more. He reached with his will...

Laughter filled his mind, echoing in his skull. Light and colour and sensation flooded his inner sight. He could feel a presence spiralling through the ether around him. Barbs of memory struck him: the pyramids and towers of Tizca falling into fire... Magnus looking down on him as they stood for the last time on the plains of the Planet of the Sorcerers... his brother Ohrmuzd smiling. All sliced through him, shrill and bright. The chains of his will did not break, but the impulse that had been about to annihilate the Harlequins slipped a link.

He cut the memories away and raised his mind's eye in time to sense a presence like a shower of silver and rose petals passing him, and see the image of a mirror mask. Then nothing but laughter draining to a chuckle that blended with the echoes of fading gunshots. And just like that, the Harlequins were gone, sliding away in the gaps between the forces closing on them, speeding from the ship as though they were made of light and air.

Setekh felt the ship shake. It was under attack. He could sense the tones of the weapons being deployed by the attackers. They were familiar. Old weapons in the hands of old enemies. Lethal, but not of grave concern. The power of the Thousand Sons was great too. Of more concern was how he would reach the canoptek swarm. They were a limited resource, but he needed them to communicate with any of the rest of Hyksos that were awake. He had received the swarm's location in the webway. Now he just needed to bring the Thousand Sons to that place. In that respect the current attack was useful. It would allow him to alter their course.

Data from the scarab unit attached to the human creature

called Silvanus buzzed through him. Through the unit he could see the tunnels branching through space and time ahead. He could hear the flesh things' whimpers and gasps of fear. He could sense the buzz of terror down nerves. So weak, so limited. So easily used. Setekh commanded, and the amulet attached to Silvanus' head obeyed.

In front of him, Ignis and the automaton watched and saw nothing. If he had had a mouth, Setekh might have smiled.

The three tunnel openings yawned in front of Silvanus. The scarab on his forehead felt like it was trying to chew through his skull. The walls were narrowing. The edge of the hull hit one of the walls. Pieces of molten armour tore free. The scream of the ship was alive in his mind, and it was plunging on... He stared at the openings, certain that if he kept looking the three ways would split into six. There was no way to make a choice, no light to follow, only the tumbling hulls of ships and the promise of death.

'Not like this... please...' he pleaded.

Then he closed his eyes and chose.

CHAPTER VIII

$\mathcal{N}$OWHERE

Silence in the ship. Ahriman held his mind still. In his thoughts, he touched the triggers of hundreds of guns, could feel the pounding of blood in a mortal's ears, and smell the blood and cordite. The dancers had gone. Just like that, they had spun back out of the ship as if they had never been. He had not seen that as a possibility. It was disturbing. He sensed the engines cut out. The vibrations of primary systems faded from the walls and floor of the *Hekaton*. Lumen lights dimmed then went out. Consoles in the bridge-temple blinked and shut down. In the machine enclaves the tech-shamans heard their engines mewl and spit in protest, and then become as silent. A shiver ran through Ahriman's armour. Red warning symbols glowed at the edge of his sight: critically low power, emergency energy protocols active, functional impairment. Whispers and nervous hisses ran through the bridge-temple. Ahriman quieted them with a snap of thought. He could not allow panic, or questions, not if any of them were going to survive. He held his thoughts and mind very, very still. Without releasing his connection to the Rubricae or those others he had been using, he pushed his will out and up to the Navigator's tower.

+Silvanus?+

+Silvanus, where are we?+ Ahriman's voice filled the hollow space of Silvanus' skull. For a second the Navigator did not respond, keeping his eyes shut. Everything was quiet. No spike of connection to the ship via the neural link, no feedback from the helm controls under his hands. Perhaps when he opened his eyes, everything would turn out to be another dream. Or perhaps another nightmare waited on the other side of his eyelids.

+Silvanus. You are alive. You will answer.+

'Yes, lord,' he said aloud, and his voice sounded too loud. He opened his eyes. 'Yes…' he said softly. 'Where are we…? I… I…' He looked around. It was dark. The lumen globes had failed. Even those that floated on suspensors under their own power had gone out. One of them lay on the floor near his navigation throne, its sphere cracked from the drop. The only light came from one candle that was still burning beneath a shrine to the Two-Headed Emperor of Fortune and Light. He let out a breath of laughter and made the sign of the aquila. He shook himself and spoke, knowing that Ahriman would hear him. 'I don't know where we are, lord. All the lights and systems are down.' He levered himself up and went to the shattered viewport. Blackness filled it, edge to edge. He put his hand out, fingers tense, but they touched nothing. He let his hand drop and leant on the frame, next to the broken crystal clinging to its edges. He looked out. There was nothing. A thin breath of air touched his cheek, made him flinch.

+Do you have control of the ship?+ asked Ahriman.

'No. No... I... There is no power, all the neural links and controls are dead.'

He shivered, aware suddenly that he was no longer linked to his progeny. He looked at their tanks, expecting to see them in distress. They were all looking at him, finning to keep themselves steady in their fluid. Some had their teeth bared. He almost flinched.

+Silvanus,+ cut in Ahriman's voice. +Where are we?+

'I... I do not know. There is nothing outside the hull.'

+Nothing?+

'There is air, lord. I mean I can feel it, breathe it too. It smells like...'

Dry bones, and dust, and rust, came the answering thought.

+Where did you lead us?+

'I didn't. I mean I don't know.' He was gabbling, he could tell. 'I didn't lead, the walls were narrowing, and there was one way and then there were three, and–'

+Enough,+ sent Ahriman, and Silvanus felt his tongue freeze; a second later, the needle points of Ahriman's will boring into his recent memories filled his head with shrill pain.

And it happened all over again, inside his skull, fast-wound over the top of the present, every moment and terror since they had gone through the gate. It was over in the time it took his heart to beat. He vomited. Acid bile leaked from the blowholes and gills on his back.

+Find the null Maehekta. The aeldari struck her, but she would have survived. Find her.+

'Find her, lord?' he said, suddenly aware that another breath of air from the empty viewport was stirring the cloth of his robe. 'I am... What is happening, lord?'

+Your guards are dead. The hoists to your tower are disabled. Find the null, Silvanus. She will protect you.+

'Protect me from what, lord?' he managed.

The dry air settled the cloth of his robe in the silence that followed.

Ctesias felt the touch of sea spray on his cheek. He opened his eyes and looked up. Above him, the sky was blue. Sunlight danced on the surface of the water lapping against the rock he lay on. He pushed himself up. The sea extended away to meet the sky. He looked down at himself. Black robes, clean limbs without scars or tattoos. He turned. A fortress rose towards the heavens. Pyramids grew into towers, stretched into bridges that spanned the air. Ctesias frowned but began to climb the steps up to the small door that opened in the nearest wall.

'That door won't open,' said a voice behind him. He turned. A face looked up at him from a small boat bobbing in the swell. The face was young, balanced on the edge between child and manhood. The sun and salt of the sea had deepened the bronze of the youth's skin, and there was a dry crust of salt on the sun-bleached tabard he wore. 'There is another way in. I can take you if you like.'

'I don't think so,' said Ctesias carefully. He was trying to pin his memories in order, but something was missing. There had been the dancers dressed as death, but then...

'As you please,' said the youth, and he began to push away from the rocks with an oar. Ctesias looked down at himself and up at the stacked spires of the fortress.

'Wait!' he called. The youth stopped, head cocked in question. 'I mean... Ahriman? Is that...?' The question failed under the boy's steady gaze. 'No...' he said. The flicker-blur of memories was still not settled or clear in his head. 'I mean this is a mind-scape. The fortress, it's Ahriman's, in his mind... I was injured. He must have brought me here.' He looked at himself. 'I just thought that you might be him, that... he might have pulled part of my thoughts into here after...' He shook his head and rubbed his hand across his forehead. 'I can't remember.'

'I have to go,' said the boy after a moment. 'My family and brothers will be waiting for me. I have set the pots, but I'm supposed to be back to shore by sunset. Another couple of years and I'll be old enough to come out and pull them up at night.'

Ctesias looked at the boy in the boat. The light of the sun on the sea was very bright, the air hot.

'You are a memory golem,' he said. 'Meant to deal with any mind who ends up here but not hostile.'

The boy shrugged. 'There is another way in,' he said. 'I can take you. I have time before sunset to get home.'

'Why am I here?' Ctesias asked, but shook his head again before the idea of the youth in the fishing boat could try and respond. 'Ahriman must have brought my mind into this place for a reason, but then why is he not here?' The wind tugged at his robe, and a wave broke slightly higher on the warm stone. 'There is something about this that is familiar.' He blinked. 'No matter, that's the thing about the mind, about Ahriman too – everything has a reason.'

'Are you from Tizca?' the youth asked.

Ctesias looked around at him, then back at the sea, and then at the line of the coast that the impossible fortress rose from. He laughed.

'Of course... He built part of this place from the memory of Tizca. The sky and sea and shape of the shore at least. Though the coast was not like this since before the Imperium came. Not even the land could escape that change.'

He turned and climbed down the rocks. The boat rocked as he stepped into it. He dropped onto the narrow board bench at the stern. The youth watched him for a second then began to row out from the rocks. He trailed one oar and circled the other, aiming the small boat down the shore to where the rocks rose to a cliff. Arches of stone reached out into the sea, and as they came around, Ctesias could see the mouth of a cave.

Above the cliff, the fortress stretched up against a sky that was showing no threat of fading to sunset as the boy had said it would.

'I wasn't from Tizca,' he said as they started to move into the cave. 'I was born on Terra.'

'I have never heard of a city by that name,' said the boy. The cave did not end, nor in fact was it truly a cave, but a passage cut into the rock, its bottom half open to the tide. Round holes cut into the roof let the sun down in brilliant columns. In the distance was darkness.

'Terra's not a city. It's another world, a planet far away, no matter where you are. Though to be honest I do not know where I was born on it, or what I was like before the Legion. They took a lot in making us, and the rest I sold.'

'I did not know there are other worlds.'

'There are thousands of them. Millions of cities, billions of people.'

'I would like to see them.'

'No... no you wouldn't. If you were alive, I would say that you would get precisely nothing by seeing those places. Crammed with suffering and all the problems of human life just made bigger. No, I think that if I had known only the sea and a familiar circle of sky, I would not care to see what was on the other side of it.'

'Why did you leave your home then?'

Ctesias shrugged. He was looking up into the light coming from the openings in the cave roof as the boy rowed on.

'I don't know why I left, or at least I don't-'

'Remember,' said the youth, and the tone of his voice snapped Ctesias' head around. The boy was looking at him, the light falling from the openings in the roof lighting his face for a second, then vanishing as the boat moved into the shade.

Sunshine and darkness... one after another, and the rhythm of the oars dipping into the water.

'Don't you want to remember, Ctesias?'

His mouth was open. His throat was dry.

The face that had peeled back from the shadow into the sun had not been the youth. It had been Helio Isidorus.

'Get up, please get up.' Silvanus tugged at Maehekta's arm. There was blood all over her. He just hoped it was from the tangle of his guards that she had fallen in. It had taken him a while to find her. The kick from the masked dancer had sent her halfway across the room. The armour on the front of her neck was crumpled. Without it he was sure she would be dead. As it was, he was not sure if she was alive. 'Please...' He reached out to try and take the helm off her head. She came up with a snap of muscle, a knife that he had not even known was there in her hand. A blue power field buzzed over the blade. Her other hand gripped the folds of flesh under his chin. The touch sent a spear of ice-cold pain stabbing through his eyes. She held still then let him go and got to her feet.

'Power?' she said, looking around.

'All down,' he gasped, 'ship wide.'

'The attack?'

'They went... They just went, after I took the turn in the passages, they just went.'

'The rest of the fleet?' Maehekta moved to the viewport.

'I don't know. The tunnels... there was one way and then there were lots... I had to pick... I had to.'

'It is trying to stop us, the webway and its guardians, the ones in the laughing masks. That's why they left us, because we were already confused and weakened enough that the tunnels themselves could deal with us.'

'You make it sound as though the tunnels are alive.'

'They might be.'

'So they are trying to kill us.' He heard the pitch of his voice rising.

Maehekta gave a single shake of her head. She was intent on the darkness outside of the viewport. Silvanus glanced out, but the view was just as blank as it had been before. You could not even see the towers set towards the ship's prow.

'Maybe, but there are other ways of dealing with unwanted parasites.'

Silvanus felt a breath of wind. He looked out and down. He could see more clearly than he could before, he realised, as though his eyes were altering in response to the new conditions. His hand went to his face then quickly dropped. His eyes had grown, they and their sockets spreading across his face, so that they could gather all the light they could from the dark. He realised he had not blinked in a long time.

He was about to turn away when he stopped.

He took a step back. The wind blew again, and that pulled his eyes up to the darkness above. Maehekta was looking down, checking her bolter.

We are still moving… said a voice in the back of his thoughts, cold and rational. *The engines cut out, but we must still be drifting forwards at the same speed we were before. It's just not being able to see anything that makes it seem that the ship is still…*

Silvanus saw something in the dark ahead of them, something that for the second he glimpsed it seemed like a grey ghost clinging to his sight. He realised what it was in the second he had to draw breath.

The hull of another ship broke from the dark. Sudden and silent, pushing through the black like a shark rising from deep water. Holes pocked it and blooms of grey-green rust clung to its skin.

Silvanus' cry was stolen by the sound of shearing metal as the *Hekaton* struck it prow-on.

CHAPTER IX

*I*MPACT

The *Hekaton* ploughed on into the wreck she had struck. The dead ship had been made by alien hands in the fringes of a star that was barely part of the galaxy. It was a hollow ovoid twenty kilometres long, and grey skinned. When it had been whole, that space inside had held bubbles of fluid and gas as habitats for its crew. The outer hull was a lamination of metal and carbon, like the shell of an egg holding a yoke. Whatever luck or hope had brought it into the webway, it had not found its way out. Weapons and debris had put holes in its hull. The gas and fluid had drained from the pockets inside. Any of the crew that survived the loss of their vessel had drowned in the air of the webway. Later, other lost and hungry creatures had stripped and eaten what remained inside the ship, leaving it as a husk resting in the dark.

The prow of the *Hekaton* punctured the ship's hull like a spear striking a hollow skull. She punched in, driven by momentum. Towers and turrets sawed through its skin as the *Hekaton* rammed into the space within. Silvanus ducked as he saw the wall of the alien ship speed closer. Aerials and masts towards the prow were snapping as they struck the oncoming wall. He curled up in a ball.

'Oh God-Emperor! Oh God-Emperor!'

The impact never came.

A buttress on the *Hekaton* caught on the shell of the alien ship like a saw tooth snagging in bone. The dead vessel rolled over, pulling the *Hekaton* with it. Locked together they began to fall. Kilometre-high stacks of scrap and wreckage loomed out of the dark as they spun past. The two ships caught a pinnacle of debris and ripped it free.

The sound of the impact rang inside the *Hekaton*, like the echoes of a raging god striking a gong. On the outer decks, crew became pulp as the shock waves ripped through them. Towers were torn free from the hull. The mutants in the deep decks called out to the gods and spirits to spare them. In the forward castle, Exalted Brother Sultaris and twenty-seven of the Rubricae under his command fell into the dark as the tower-bastion they had stood in shattered.

On the bridge-temple, Ahriman felt the ship begin to tumble. His boots locked to the deck an instant before the world turned over. His mind ascended, spooling power to it. He reached out to the minds of his brothers, and their minds became a mirror of his. Their thoughts meshed and the ether shuddered as their joint will yanked it into shape. Mortal acolytes and beast-bred shamans across the ship fell, spasming, their minds overloaded. Some died then, blood running from tear ducts and mouths. Others shrank, fat and muscle dissolving from bone. The Thousand Sons drained them of life and power in the space of a heartbeat. Thrall cultists screamed as a blur of colours and symbols filled their eyes. Shadows shook with voices calling out in chorus, every word forming a sigil in the ether that met another, merged and spun on to meet the next.

At the eye of the storm was Ahriman. He could feel the *Hekaton*, the air beyond it, the wreckage of the alien craft and the masses of debris and ruins looming around them as they fell: spurs of broken matter the size of mountains, jagged, waiting to rip the *Hekaton* in half. The ether was thin here, its full tide held back by the webway. Ahriman felt the power of his brothers flow into his orbit. Too little for what needed to be done, but all that there was. He held himself still in the moment, allowing the storm to turn. Part of him wondered if Magnus, or even the Emperor, had ever felt the same, had just wished to let the storm turn around them and remain in the stillness, untouched, eternal and at peace. He held the moment and reached out.

Frost sheeted the hull of the *Hekaton*. Leaves of metal and carbon falling from the alien hulk broke into motes of dust. The *Hekaton* groaned as etheric force gripped it. In his mind, Ahriman held the idea of the ship and felt reality force itself against him. Metre-thick armour plates buckled. The shell of the alien ship cracked. A great spur of bone-like matter loomed ahead, ten kilometres across, crooked like the beckoning finger of a corpse.

Ahriman could see the spur in his mind's eye, could feel the tug of momentum and the mass of the ship tumbling towards it. He reached for stillness and control, a storm of power wrapping the ships in immaterial energy. He felt the Black Staff in his hand, its power reflecting his, adding to it for as long as he could focus...

At their simplest, the powers of the psychic, the sorcerer and the witch were the same: they used the ether to change reality. No matter the root, that was its result. Formulae, spells, artefacts, subtle arts and training all were just ways to make an idea real by will. Simple. But reality was stubborn. The greater the violation of nature, the more power it took, and that power writhed like a snake when grasped. So it was not enough to have power; to wield it you needed the will to focus the idea of what you wanted, and the will to make it so. The greater the idea, the greater the power, the greater the will... To stop a pebble from falling you needed to make the idea of the stone not falling more real than that of gravity. Once, when they were still children, Ahriman had dared Ohrmuzd to hold three stones in the air for longer than him. After five hours they had both collapsed, red haemorrhages staining the blue of their eyes. They had been punished when they woke, and the lectures on foolishness and danger had lasted months. Now, in the ether-starved reality of the webway, Ahriman held the idea of the *Hekaton* still and set his will against the reality of millions of tonnes of metal spinning through darkness.

He felt parts of his mind scream. He felt thoughts buckle. He was drowning, going down and down into the depths beyond the light, where there was only crushing darkness and silence.

He felt an echo of pain, perhaps his, or perhaps the last agony of one of the mortal psykers caught in the storm rip, heart bursting as life essence poured into Ahriman, sustaining him for just a little longer...

The hull groaned. Ghost winds howled through darkened passages. The cries of the mortals shivered in the dark.

The ship slowed in her fall. She vibrated. Etheric ice fell from her in sheets. The shell of the alien craft spun on its own momentum, wrenching it free of the *Hekaton*. Pieces of hull shell flaked away as the craft collided with the spur of bone matter. It folded in two, crumpling and cracking for an instant before it tore in half.

In his mind, Ahriman could feel the flow of the warp dwindling, as though the webway had felt him drawing power and was strangling the flow. His hold on the ship weakened. It rolled over as it dropped. Wreckage of the alien craft plunged past it. He held his will firm, but what passed for gravity in this realm had hold of them. A ragged sea of detritus rose to meet them. He sliced speed and force away from the descent. He could feel his hearts beating in his chest. Blood pounded through his skull. He tasted iron in his mouth. The pressure was everything now – black, blinding pressure. He had to let go... He would not let go...

The *Hekaton* struck the debris plain. Its keel fins gouged through the layers of dust and wreckage, shearing off a moment before its prow stabbed into the ground. The stern kicked up. The prow bit, and the hull hung, its weight balanced by momentum for a second. Then the great ship thumped down. The force lashed through its structure. Bodies slammed into ceilings. Bulkheads cracked. Ruptured pipework vented gas and fuel into her guts. Hundreds died in a second, more drowned or suffocated in the minutes after. The *Hekaton* shuddered as Ahriman released his hold on it and lay still, pieces of wreckage falling around it like snow.

The *Hekaton* settled where she had fallen. Metal bones and skin that had not felt the pull of gravity for centuries groaned as its bulk slumped into the layer of grey dust and wreckage. It lay creaking, filled with darkness. Ahriman felt the buzzing presence of the tens of thousands of mortals on board quiet for a second. Down on the deep decks, eyes looked into the black and ears listened for the sound of another impact. For a second, they were all balanced between anticipation and panic. One more sliver of time and the latter was all there would be. Thousands of souls trapped in the dark, sealed in places where there was no light and air that would be becoming lethal with every extra breath taken. They would tear themselves apart, the ship too, more than likely. He had to prevent that. His own mind was reeling from the power he had exerted to stop the ship steering. He could feel imbalances in thought, emotion and reason. The humours of his body were spiralling out of control. He could feel the ether pulling thin as he reached for it to renew him. The part of him that was, and always would be, mortal and human screamed at him to stop. That he had nothing left. That he was drowning.

Stop. The command echoed in his mind. And everything did.

The thoughts spinning at the edge of his fatigue.

The roar of sensations from his senses.

The pull of time, and the undrawn breath on his lips.

He held himself at the centre of the whirlwind of the present.

Then carefully, in an eternity that passed in the length of a lightning flash, he pulled his mind and being higher. The fatigue fell away. The thoughts fell away. Everything within was wiped clean, footprints in sand brushed away by a gust of wind.

He held still for a moment then breathed his will outwards. Micro incantations formed in his thoughts as it billowed forth. He did not try to sense what his mind was passing through. There was no need for understanding. Only control mattered. There was no time to consult with his brothers or draw on their help. There was only him, caught in the narrow gap between the past and future. Only him and the pandemonium if he did not act – and, as ever, there was no choice.

His mind blasted through the ship, picking up the emotions and thoughts of the humans, beast-bred and mortal creatures that called it home. He ripped fear and panic from them. Some fell as though asleep; others halted what they were doing and stared into the gloom, trying to find the severed end of the moment they had just been living. Some, a few that would survive, would later talk and tell others of an age left in the dark and the sound of an angel passing through blank dreams, the beat of its wings like the wind rattling sand through the skulls of the dead.

Ahriman was on his knees on the command dais in the bridge-temple. The space around him for three metres was a rippled mass of warped metal and evaporating ice. The ship hull creaked around him. Slowly, with blood on his tongue and teeth, he drew breath.

+Brothers,+ he sent, and heard and felt the answers of twenty-five of the twenty-six that were on the ship. There was no answer from Ctesias.

+Lycomedes, find your master.+

He felt the acknowledgement and scattered commands to the rest of his living brothers. He reached out his thoughts to Ignis.

+Ignis.+ Ahriman's sending filled his consciousness. +What has happened to the ship?+

+Total system failure,+ Ignis sent. +Most machine-based mechanisms have shut down or ceased to function. Our armour is operational but impaired. It is as though the whole craft had taken a haywire pulse before impact, but that is not possible on this scale.+

+Manifestly it is,+ said Ahriman. +Get to the machine decks. Restore power.+

Ignis paused for the length of a second. +The prisoner?+ he asked.

+Is it still functioning?+

Ignis looked at the two cold points of light still gleaming from where the orbiting hoops held the xenos.

+It is.+

+Go to the machine decks. If we do not have power, then we are lost.+

+As you will,+ replied Ignis, and he felt the mental link sever. He touched his mind to the incantations running through the rotating hoops. They were still functioning, but whether they would continue to, he did not know. The behaviour of the warp within the webway was not something he understood. He did not think even Ahriman did. He would simply have to trust and hope. That made him uncomfortable. He moved to the door.

'Do you wish to know what is happening?' Setekh's voice stopped him, and he turned back. 'The sub-dimension we are passing through has ways of responding to threats and intruders. It can remake its structure, can create paradox effects. There are places within it where it can swallow irritants and unwelcome presences. This ship, for example – it has been made power-less by a macro pulse of what you would call haywire energy. The sub-dimension will allow the organic matter inside this hull to expire. Eventually your bones might be expelled into reality. The principle is not unlike a biological worm excreting the earth that has passed through its gut. Alternatively, you stay here, snagged in its coils.'

'You speak as though these tunnels are alive,' said Ignis.

'They are.'

Ignis was silent.

'Haywire,' he said, at last. 'How do you know to use that word?'

'Fractal induction. I have had nothing to do except assimilate the information available. From one fact I can know all things. The principles of your cognitive models are encoded in your languages and your technology. Given enough time, I could extrapolate everything you know. Even the secrets that you do not know yourself.' He paused. 'I know how to get us through the sub-dimensional tunnels. Free me and I will save you, your comrades and this ship.'

Ignis did not reply. His mind ran through the cadence and

details of the xenos' words. They were perfectly pitched to open Ignis' hunger for understanding and to needle his pride. The creature wanted him to ask more, wanted to lead him down a path of questions and answers that would, at the end, result in Setekh being free. It was impressive.

Ignis turned away. He needed to reach the machine decks.

'You will have to agree,' said Setekh. 'Ahriman will command you to.' Ignis paused at that and looked back at the xenos. Its eyes were bright and steady. 'He is committed. You doubt. He will do anything that is necessary to achieve the end he has set himself. It will drive him to discard your objections.' It paused. The light in its eyes flickered. 'I know it.'

'You lie for your own ends.'

'From one thing I can understand everything. Remember that.'

Ignis walked from the chamber then. Credence followed. Once they were beyond the door, he began to run, his armoured strides shaking the dark.

Silvanus pushed himself up. The floor of his sanctuary canted downwards towards the shattered viewport. He could feel bones clicking and grating as he moved. Somehow, during the entire terrifying fall and impact, he had been conscious. Rattled between walls and floor like a die in a box, he had felt every pitch and twist of the ship as a hammer blow. The bodies of his already dead guards were pulped heaps amidst the debris of his possessions. Maehekta pulled herself from where she had grabbed the throne and somehow had the strength to wrap data-feed cables around herself. Her armour had fresh dents, but she was moving.

'You are alive,' he said, half amazed. He took a step. Something in his back crunched. He winced at the pain. It faded and when he moved again, he could tell that whatever had broken had softened and found a new place to sit in his flesh. Maehekta shook her head at him. There was blood on her face, under the edge of her helm. He was about to ask her if she was injured when he looked across the room and wailed.

Some of his progeny's tanks had broken. Small, pale shapes lay in pools of fluid. He hurried over. He felt the broken joints in his fingers pop and re-form as he tried to lift the bodies back into the broken tanks. His grip kept slipping on their wet skin. He closed his eyes. Tears ran down the folds of his face. The other progeny were battering against the sides of their tanks.

+Silvanus.+

Ahriman's voice in his head, sudden and harsh. Silvanus bit his lip. His eyes were clamped shut as though he could squeeze out the pain.

+Silvanus!+

'Yes,' he breathed. 'Yes, lord.'

+Is Maehekta alive?+

'She… she is.'

+Get her and get down onto the outside of the hull.+

'What? I mean, lord–'

+Power is down ship wide. I need to know you are safe.+

Safe… of course. Ahriman, chosen of the Nine-Fold Golden Throne, wanted Silvanus to be safe. The Emperor protected, He truly did.

+Once the ship is powered, you must guide us out.+

The golden warmth faded in Silvanus' chest. His eyes went back to the lifeless body of his progeny still clutched in his hands.

'I… must…' he stammered. 'Of course… lord.'

+The hoists are not working from your tower. I am going now to force a way out of the ship via the hangar space. You will meet me on ground level outside the eleventh port hangar bay.+

'Yes… yes of course, but outside, lord?' Silvanus' eyes went to the dark space beyond the shattered viewport.

+We are going to recover Sultaris and my brothers that fell from the ship. You will help us find them.+

'Me?'

+Your sight may be useful.+

'Useful... Yes... I am useful.'

Silvanus was quiet for a long moment. He could see the dim shape of the hull below. A grey luminance had spread through the black, though he could not see its source. The hull top was three hundred metres down.

'How–' he began.

'We climb,' said Maehekta. She had pulled a coil of rope from one of the pouches on her back. Silvanus looked at the drop then back at the rope. It looked very narrow.

'I...' he said, but Maehekta was already tying the rope to a pillar. She tested it and dropped the coil out of the viewport.

'You... you go first,' he managed.

She shook her head, and dropped out into the dark without a pause.

Several racing heartbeats later, Silvanus followed.

Five kilometres from the *Hekaton* the canoptek swarm woke. They had made their nest in a saurian skull that sat amidst a jumble of bones and debris. Each unit of the swarm looked like a scarab beetle the size of an open human hand. There were several thousand inside the skull, legs clutched tight as they slept. And they had slept for a long time – long enough for star kingdoms to rise and fall. The swarm was not intelligent, not in real terms. Each scarab had a limited set of decision-making abilities. Together the swarm could pool those abilities to perform its task. During the wars against the Great Enemy, they had watched enemy movements within the webway. They had performed their task, and they had survived, parasites that clung perniciously to the etheric tunnels. Then the orders of their masters had ceased. The swarm had found a hiding place and slept. Now an order from a higher level of their kind had given them a new task.

The constructs of the swarm cast their senses out and found the alien ship, just where they had been informed it would be. They detected large numbers of biological life forms. Their instructions were to avoid all detection. The swarm remade itself, creating smaller and smaller scarab units until the whole swarm was a mass as fine as sand. It took no longer than it would have taken a biological being to breathe. Their shells were black, and when they flowed out of the skull it was as though they merged with the dark of the air. Around them the carcases of dead machines and creatures sat still, pale, as the swarm coiled through them towards the ship.

CHAPTER X

MIDDEN

+I have found Master Ctesias.+ Lycomedes' sending touched Ahriman's mind. He swallowed. Colours were bubbling at the edge of his sight, and he could still taste his own blood on his tongue. Fatigue clawed at his will, even as he pulled his mind into balance. +He is injured and not conscious.+

+Where was he?+ he sent.

+The Serene Cages, close to Helio Isidorus' chamber.+

A moment of pure cold, and the sensation of a bottomless pit opening beneath him.

+Helio Isidorus is–+

+Unharmed. He stays where and as he was. The xenos did not breach his chamber. Master Ctesias killed them before they could try.+

Ahriman heard the breath leaving his lungs in his helm. The abyss beneath him closed.

+And your master?+ he asked.

+I...+ Ahriman could feel the uncertainty in Lycomedes' sending. +He is alive, but I cannot reach his mind.+

Ahriman turned the information over in his head. At the edge of his awareness he heard the whisper of a presence and saw a Rubricae half buried under a mound of shattered rubble.

+Get him to safety and protected,+ he sent to Lycomedes. +I will attend to him later.+

The thought connection broke. Ahriman turned his attention back to the Rubricae at his feet. It tried to move. Its armour was damaged, rent apart in places. The power threading the suit was trying to remake itself but failing. The voice of the soul within was faint.

+Kasthaeph,+ he said. Ahriman placed his hand on the Rubricae's helm +Stillness, brother. All shall be well.+ He closed his eyes, and through the veil of exhaustion pulled a strand of will. The debris rose, parting above the half-buried Rubricae. It stood. The rents in its armour were glowing, the armour plate struggling to reknit.

Silvanus half knelt nearby, coughing beneath his veil. The null, Maehekta, stood three paces from him, hands on her weapons, head scanning the ruins. Bloody and battered, she still seemed more comfortable amongst the canyons of debris than the Space Marines.

The bulk of the *Hekaton* was three kilometres behind them, the cliff of its hull barely visible. Even with his helm augmenting his eyes, he could barely see more than a few hundred metres in any direction. There was something in this place that worked against senses of all kinds. He could have used his mind to sense further but the warp had receded so that he could only call on its weakest currents. With time, he could have unwound the forces at play, but he did not have time, and he was using the power he could call to sense the presence of the Rubricae that had fallen from the ship. They had almost located them all, though he feared they would not find Sultaris alive. It had been a long fall, and Ahriman did not know how large this corner of the webway was. He was increasingly sure that the answer would change if one ever found it. Coming this far out was a risk. None of them might survive, but he was not going to lose more of his Legion to this place. Not if effort and will could save them.

Something moved in the shadow of a line of broken spurs that projected from the ground like the ribs of a half-buried corpse. Ahriman held still. He reached out with his senses. Echoes and ghost sensations crowded his mind... It moved again, before his mind could touch it. A figure... A figure in power armour, its shape broken by distance and darkness.

+Sultaris?+ he sent. The figure had stopped moving, still in the deeper dark beneath the arch. He went closer, then paused. At the edge of awareness, he felt the brush and rustle of feathers and heard the far-off cry of a raven. His thoughts and senses sharpened to a point. He took a pace forwards and saw. It was not Sultaris.

Battered red armour, a patchwork of repairs and damage. Marks barely visible under the dust and dirt. And above it, looking back at him, a blackened helm with a beak-like snout. It looked at him, the servos in its armour growling protest. It held out a hand. On it was a rough disc of silver.

'Lord!' The cry came from behind him, loud enough to make his gaze twitch aside. 'Lord, we have found him!'

It was Silvanus' voice, high in the still air.

Ahriman looked back around to the figure in the black helm, the figure that should not and could not be there.

It was gone. He looked down. The piece of silver lay on the ground. He picked it up. It was tarnished and had been crudely hammered into the shape of a coin, but he could see the trace images of oak leaves still visible beneath the marks of the hammer blows. Cold flooded his mind, his thoughts turning over and over.

+Brother,+ came the sending of one of the lower circles, a warrior called Lemek. +It is Sultaris, we have found him.+

Ahriman turned. He could see two of his brothers and the Navigator clustered around a fold of debris. He turned, began to move, began to run.

+Back to the ship,+ he ordered.

'Lord, he…' began Silvanus, stepping back, and Ahriman saw what they had found. He saw the crest of a high helm projecting from amidst the powdered detritus. Cracks ran through it, and the eye-lenses were empty. Blue lacquer still clung to it in places. The fingertips of a gauntlet rose from the ground just beside it. Lemek reached down and pulled the helm free. Dust fell from the empty space within. It looked like it had been there not hours but centuries.

+It is like the others,+ sent Lemek. His head was bare, the sapphires bonded to his dark skin gleaming pale. His aura was rolling with muddied red. +Like Ptollen. Pyrodomon took him.+

But I did not feel it, thought Ahriman. *I did not feel the fire of Pyrodomon rise, and we always do…*

+Get him back to the ship,+ said Ahriman. Two Rubricae began to pull the rest of the empty armour from the ground.

'Lord.' It was Silvanus. The Navigator had moved slightly away and was gazing off into the darkness. Ahriman did not turn. Everything had become still inside his mind. He looked at the rough silver disc in his hand. A coin hammered from the silver leaves that his brother Ohrmuzd had worn on his armour before the Flesh Change had taken him.

This is not possible, he wanted to say. It was not possible because he had left that piece of silver sealed in his chamber on the ship, locked and warded. Yet here it was in his hand.

'Time, causality, the observer and the observed,' said the memory of his own words, spoken long ago to his brothers and disciples, under the approving eye of his gene-father. *'We must treat our assumptions on all these matters with suspicion.'* For a second, he imagined he heard laughter, like the chuckling of a bird. *'The past cannot be changed. If you changed the past, then the present would already be altered. But we see no signs of such alterations. Even in cases where ships caught in an etheric distortion in the warp arrive before they left, the line of causality is maintained. The truth is that if we could manipulate threads of events through time then we would see evidence of it in the past that we have already experienced.'*

'Can you see that?' Silvanus said. Ahriman and the others looked around at him.

He just pointed.

Movement… Tiny flickers of movement down at the edge of sight where the visible bled into the ragged dark.

Silvanus moved forwards, trying to see more clearly. The Thousand Sons were looking the way he was pointing. Couldn't they see it?

It was like sand blowing through the cracks in a rock… tiny specks moving through the canyons between towers of wreckage, but at this scale each speck was not sand…

'Do you…?' he began.

+Get back to the ship, now!+ Ahriman's command whipped across Silvanus' mind, and he was turning, running, stumbling. The Thousand Sons were moving too, Rubricae closing around them, guns raised, eyes blazing with ghost-light.

Maehekta was next to him, her bolter in her hands, looking back. He glanced behind him.

Figures… Hundreds of blue-grey figures bounding and climbing over the wreckage, their shoulders hunched, their skin pale like that of the belly of a fish, flowing towards them in a tide. There was a smell on the sterile air, a smell like stagnant water and salt.

The Rubricae began to fire. Lines of blue-tinged flame streaked into the dark. Flowers of yellow and pink burst amongst the tide. The flames boiled out, writhing and twisting. Hissing cries rose with the sound of flesh cooking from bones in the blink of an eye. He saw one of the Thousand Sons gesture, and the fire whip through the air, snaring bodies. A group of Rubricae were dragging the remains of Sultaris. Ahriman was with them. The light of the fire pushed against the dark. The ship was ahead. Silvanus' limbs were screaming, outbreaths gasping from his mouth and the gills under his robe. The tide of figures was level with them, spilling around the circle of Rubricae as volleys of fire punched into them. They were running ahead, towards the *Hekaton*, trying to cut them off. Silvanus could see them clearly now. Blind faces with rows of holes in place of eyes, needle teeth in wide mouths, feet and hands tipped with claws. Their muscles were famine taut beneath their skin as they bounded across the plain of wreckage. They were fast and the fire eating their brood did not turn them back.

Silvanus stumbled, heaving breaths shaking his body. Maehekta yanked him to his feet. He squealed at the dead cold that spread from her touch, but she was pulling him up and on. They were almost at the ship. There were figures coming out of it – beast-bred, bellowing and hooting as they charged. Ahriman must have called them. The tide of blind creatures met them at a run, and the two waves tore into each other. Claws and teeth raked open red wounds. Teeth bit, and jaws came up bloody. A ripple passed through the tide of creatures as the scent of blood filled the air. They swarmed over each other, ripping and tearing, and the beast-bred were being submerged, made into bloody ribbons, sinew ripped from bone by needle fangs and grinding maws. Silvanus stumbled, looked back the way they had come for a moment and almost froze. More were coming from the mountains of wreckage. Beside him, Maehekta started firing. The roar of her boltgun pummelled Silvanus. This was a curse, a lived penance from the Emperor for having sinned and failed. The way back was closed, filled with a rippling, bloody mass of the creatures. The Rubricae were still firing, holding back the tide with rolling blasts. He began to call out prayers between his gasping breaths, pleading, apologising, promising anything for this to not be his death.

Ahriman stopped, turned. The Rubricae were still moving, still ringing Silvanus, Maehekta and the other Thousand Sons. The tide of creatures surged forwards. Ahriman raised his staff. A halo of wan light surrounded it. Silvanus felt a ripple at the edge of his senses, like a gust of wind. The nearest creatures slowed, heads twitching, huffing air through the holes on their snouts. Then they turned, leaping back into the others coming behind them, their hunger turned against their kin. Blood and skin flew into the air as the tide began to eat itself.

Ahriman turned away and charged towards the ship. An open hatchway loomed ahead, the promise of safety beyond. Volleys of fire ripped into the knots of creatures swarming and tearing at each other.

+Inside,+ he sent. +They will not be occupied for long.+

Silvanus did not need to be told twice and stumbled into the welcoming dark, before collapsing onto the floor. Behind them, half the Rubricae formed a line across the opening. The others were pushing the blast doors shut. They sealed with a clang. Silvanus heard something hit the other side before he had even taken a breath. He saw Ahriman standing, the lights of his eyes shining in the dark, looking down at something silver in his hand.

Ignis could smell blood on the air when he opened the hatch to the machine decks.

'Vigilance protocol,' he said aloud. Credence clattered in reply. Ignis sent will down the crystal core of the axe in his hand. Its edge lit. He could see the outlines of machine stacks beyond the hatch, backlit by the red-coal glow of fire. He felt a muscle in his face twitch. These decks were the domains of the Xrut-cari. The machine-tribe ruled them all. They kept themselves sealed away from the rest of the ship and no one entered their domains. The only exception was the Thousand Sons, and even then, Ignis thought that was as much about fear as respect. The Xrutcari were temperamental, dangerous even, but without the power from their machines, the rest of the ship was dead. Air would curdle to toxin, life to silence and death.

He moved down a gantry between two towering electro capac-itors, both dark and silent. The ion reek of power discharge hung in the air. He could smell burning oil and meat too. That meant the Xrutcari had started killing each other. It had not taken them long.

Ahead, he could see a wide platform. A fire glow was coming from beneath the grating. He heard a clanging cry, like a bubble of air caught in a steel pipe. A circle of figures stood on the platform. Sheets of copper and silver feathers hung from their shoulders. Half masks of beaten metal with bulbous, frog-eye-lenses covered their faces above mouths filled with frayed cables and steel teeth. The tallest amongst them was half as high as Ignis again, a stilt-legged priest with lank mechadendrites hanging from its spine. The metal of its feather cloak chimed as it turned to look at Ignis and Credence. It held crude knives of lapped flint in each hand. It buzzed a stream of noise. Ignis did not respond. There were seven bodies chained to the ground. A spark had been set to an oil sump below, and tongues of greasy, yellow flame were cooking the meat from the bodies. He noticed that most of the cloaked figures were struggling to stand or move. Whatever had taken out the ship's systems had done the same to the Xrutcari's augmetics.

The stilt-legged priest buzzed at Ignis again. He ignored it. He could hear a scratching moan right at the back of his skull. The Neverborn that nested in many of the ship's mechanisms were squirming in their suddenly cold prisons, starved of the furnace heat and the tang of electrostatic or code. They were getting hungry. The Xrutcari could feel that hunger, too. The machines were their patrons – the Neverborn within, their saints – and they knew that if they did not do something then they would all die. In the sudden dark after the machines had gone silent, they had done the first thing they could think of: they had begun sacrificing their own.

Ignis had to admit they had a point. A lack of air and power and life-sustaining processes would kill all except the Thousand Sons on board, but if the Neverborn in the ship's guts broke free then there would be no one left to die of asphyxiation. The problem was that the deaths of a few lower-grade devotees was not going to do anything.

'You know me. You will hear and obey my will,' said Ignis. His voice rolled and sheared through the canyons of metal. An angry clicking came from the machine stacks above. Credence rotated its gun upwards. Figures crouched atop the cliff faces of pipes. Copper glide wings folded against their backs, and clusters of dead eye-lenses shone in the fire glow. They looked like the idea of moths sculpted from scrap metal. Ignis could sense the presence of dozens of minds, looking down at him.

The stilt-legged priest hissed at him again, trying to form the values of its tribe's code-cant. Ignis could sense panic and anger in its mind. Augmetic sections of its brain had shut down. It was running on a mutilated mind. The rest of the tribe were the same or worse. Ignis could feel the aggression and fear rising in their surface thoughts. Perhaps they did not recognise Ignis or what he was. It did not matter. His own mind was counting the seconds and minutes since the ship had gone dark. Every instant shifted the odds away from survival. He could hear the rasping calls of the daemon things in the cold machines. He needed to act.

The priest took another wobbling step, still hissing. The gathered figures on the machine stacks tensed, ready. A bubble of fat popped as the oil flame ate deeper into one of the bodies chained to the floor.

The Xrutcari's instinct had been right, he reflected. The solution to the immediate need was sacrifice, blood and death to feed the daemons in the mechanisms, and their arthritic fire to set the wheels turning again. It was a simple calculation of necessity.

'Credence...' he said.

The automaton gave a single clatter of acknowledgement.

A surge of broken code-speech hissed around the chamber.

The stilt-legged one took another stride across the deck.

'...kill protocol.'

Setekh became aware of the scarab swarm as they billowed through the dead spaces of the ship. They had entered through a break in the hull and slid through its inner structure until they reached a duct above the chamber that held him. Five layers of metal plating lay between them and the chamber. The swarm began to break down the plating. The metal was crude, produced by the action of heat and pressure. Imperfections riddled it. That made the process easier. Within moments the swarm had pulled apart the molecular bonds of a hexagonal area of metal. A hole formed. The swarm slid through, rebuilding the gap behind them. They repeated the process until they breached the ceiling of the chamber. They spread into a flat layer across its surface. Their shells shifted their chromatic pattern to match the metal. Then they sealed the hole and began to scan.

Setekh watched them. He could sense the clicking of their reasoning as they collected data. He could not order them directly, yet, but he knew the assessment that the swarm would make and the action they would take.

A single scarab unit detached from the whole. It spiralled down towards the limit of the turning bronze hoops, paused as one of them arced past, then dived. It flared with light. The air around it paradoxically thickened. It activated its matter-consumption devices, but there was nothing for it to consume. It hissed, rolling over, needle legs kicking as the anathema forces crushed it. There was a flare of green light, then just a pinch of grey metallic dust hanging in space. Above, the watching swarm made their assessment, and selected their action. They shifted on the ceiling until they were directly above Setekh. Then they descended, climbing one over another so that they formed a stalactite growing from the ceiling to the sphere enclosed by the orbiting hoops. The tip of the swarm met the sphere of anathema force inside the hoops. The tip started to glow as the units forced themselves forwards and burned and crumbled. On the ceiling, the swarm had begun eating the metal plates. They broke down the molecules and passed them to units that were replicating themselves at the tip of the stalactite. The swarm pushed deeper into the space, units replacing those consumed at a rate just fast enough for it to stretch down as a metallic thread. Setekh waited.

Vibrations trembled through the ship. He read attempts to reignite the vessel's generators in the patterns. That attempt would need to succeed soon. The ship was grounded in one of the detritus zones of the webway. If it could not be made to rise again then his plans could not progress. That was an unacceptable possibility.

The end of the swarm thread was just above his eye. He watched as a unit appeared from over the disintegrating bodies of the swarm. It crawled across the last sliver of space... and touched his forehead.

Setekh's authority expanded through the swarm. They began to remake themselves. The group outside the sphere spread, chewing into the metal and expanding, replicating and building objects that were far beyond their prior ability. Setekh drained what knowledge and context existed in the swarm.

The swarm completed their construction – a entangled communion interface. Not refined nor powerful enough to send the highest of mysteries and concepts, but enough to link him across space to the canoptek keepers. He spoke to the keepers of his dynasty for the first time in a long age.

Bearer of the Black Disc, Most High Setekh – heed the authority of my place in the ordination of all things.

   III – Obedience, and supplication

   II – Obedience, and supplication

   I – Obedience, and supplication

   III – all under the division of these abase and await command

   Bearer of the Black Disc, Most High Setekh – heighten reasoning of all divisions by two knots of degree – so it is ordained

   III – Obedience – self-initiation of ordained authority – this division is now V

   II – Obedience – self-initiation of ordained authority – this division is now IV

   I – Obedience – self-initiation of ordained authority – this division is now III

   V – replication of structures and units to fill I and II ordained

   IV – Obedience

   III – Obedience

Bearer of the Black Disc, Most High Setekh – what of the Hyksos, to whom the doors of the eternal are not closed, do we still bear the chains of imprisonment?

V – Supplication and obedience – the Hyksos, for whom we exist and to whom we are obedient beyond time, sleep still – the chains and guardians placed on us still stand – only those divisions present remain – the gaolers do not wake

Bearer of the Black Disc, Most High Setekh – do the gaolers function?

V – they function

Bearer of the Black Disc, Most High Setekh – heed this authority and my command – prepare and restructure all divisions under your ordinance for the rising of the one who is the Most High, Who Sees the Arc of Stars and May Turn Them Back Through the Wheel of Night

V – Supplication and obedience – as it is ordained by the command of the Hyksos and the Bearer of the Black Disc, so it shall be

IV – Praise and obedience at the rising of the Most High

III – Praise and obedience at the rising and the return

II – Praise

I – Obedience

Bearer of the Black Disc, Most High Setekh – I return, with the means to open the way – until the time of my arrival – when I will speak the command and ordain that the sleeping shall wake – let nothing warn the Gaolers Who Hold the Keys – this is as it is ordained

V – Obedience

CHAPTER XI

OPENER OF WAYS

Setekh broke the connection. The exchange with the distant canoptek minions had happened in an instant. Setekh gave a final command to the swarm before they withdrew. Then they were spooling up to the ceiling again. They opened the breach they had made before and flowed out again. They buzzed through the ship, a smoke blur that flowed through cracks and flaws in weld seams. Lingering heat and radiation guided them. The *Hekaton*'s reactors and engines had barely cooled since they shut down. To the swarm, they shone like suns behind thin mist.

They reached the machine caverns and spread into a cloud. There were flesh-entities in the space, but radiation and metallic dust were thick in the air. None of the entities noticed as the swarm spiralled down to the machines. They were crude. Very crude but the damage done to each machine was simple for the swarm to find. The scarab units oozed into the machines' cores and began their task. In the war with the Great Enemy their function had been to break down machines of other species. Now they made them anew. Micro cutters split fused wires. Energy jaws chewed corrosion from gears. Cracks fused. Broken connections knitted. It took minutes. It would have taken less time, but they had been commanded to stay hidden. Once the repairs were complete, the swarm built power. Motes of charge grew in tiny metal thoraxes. Millions of metal legs scratched against each other as the power grew. Worms of lightning jumped between scarabs. Then the swarm convulsed. The power jolted through the crude machines they had repaired. For a silent instant, nothing. Then the machines growled and ignited.

Ignis felt the plasma light in the reactor's heart. He heard the daemons that lived in its shell keen. The blood on its casing flashed to ash. Power vented through conduits with a roar. Ignis turned and looked up as arcs of lightning snapped between spires of machinery. The remaining Xrutcari tech-devotees were trembling, chirruping in their static-laced tongue. He felt a flat deadness fill the air. Ten paces away a cylindrical charge coil, the height of a Battle Titan, sparked then shrieked as blue fire roared through its core. Above and around them lumen globes were flickering to life. Air-cyclers coughed into action. Towards the back of the cavern, Ignis saw a red glow kindle as the main engine cores drew power into their hearts. The deck began to tremble. Pipes damaged by the crash burst. Coolant fluid began to fall, pattering down amongst the keening Xrutcari like the first rain come after a drought. Information began to fill Ignis' connections to the ship, growling and weeping as malefic-data djinns spun through the cables and systems. He began to see what was happening outside.

He blinked. Beside him, Credence gave a cog-work growl.

'Follow,' Ignis said and began to run as around him the false rain fell, and tech-devotees sang in joy.

* * *

Still gasping on the deck of the loading hangar, Silvanus looked up as lights flickered in the ceiling. They fizzed for a second, then glowed bright. He almost wept.

Ahriman and the rest of the Thousand Sons with him were already moving. A scratching clang shook the hangar's blast doors.

'They will not leave now they have scented blood,' said Maehekta. Ahriman paused in his stride and looked at her. He had pulled his helm off. Sweat beaded his skin. He looked exhausted. That sight was enough to make Silvanus whimper. 'Other things will come too. We must get out of here now.'

'Out?' Silvanus felt the word come from his mouth before he could stop it. He looked around wildly at Ahriman and Maehekta. Terror had stolen the fear of speaking. He looked between them. 'How do we get out? Did you see the ships out there? The bones? Nothing gets out of here.'

He was breathing hard.

Ahriman looked at him for a long moment. Silvanus looked back and for once did not blink. The sorcerer's eyes were very blue. He braced for the coldness to reach along that gaze. Inside he felt voices scream at him that he had blasphemed, that he was going to suffer for speaking to the warp's prophet. Then Ahriman did something that sent the spear of terror deep into Silvanus' chest. He nodded and turned away. Silvanus thought he saw Ahriman close his eyes for a second.

'The webway is psychomorphic,' said Maehekta. 'It responds to our intentions, our natures, our desires and fears. This place is the midden of those that lost their way and lost themselves. It is responding to traces of despair in your minds. That is what keeps us here.'

Ahriman looked up at her.

'That's it? We just have to not despair?' Silvanus laughed suddenly. He could feel his breath shortening to panicked gasps. His voice was rising. Anger was doing it. 'Not despair at being lost in a labyrinth with monsters swarming outside. We just need to have hope and the magic door opens! And then, once this *miracle* arrives, how do we get out of these tunnels? This thing did not guide us true before, so how is it going to now?' He slammed his palm onto the scarab clamped to his skull. 'How do we get to wherever it was that was so vital we reach in the first place?'

He slumped down, exhausted, panting, tears pouring. Part of him wanted someone to shout at him. To ask how he dared say such things. Anything other than what he knew he would see if he looked up: cold eyes regarding him with complete indifference. For what seemed like an age there was just the sound of his own sobs and the buzz of the ship's systems waking.

'You are right,' said Ahriman. Silvanus looked up. 'You are both right. We will find the door out of this dead end, and we will reach our goal.'

'How–' began Silvanus, but Ahriman was not looking at him.

'Take him back to the tower,' he said to Maehekta. 'Make him ready to steer the ship.'

Then Ahriman turned and walked away through the stuttering light. The Rubricae and the other Thousand Sons looked at Silvanus for a long moment, then went after their master.

+Ahriman,+ sent Ignis. +The ship is functioning. I project the engines will be ready to give us lift within ninety-five minutes, but without a way out we must channel power to our defences. The creatures on the outer hull will find a way in if they have not already.+

+The ship will rise.+

Ignis' stride faltered. He had been making for the upper levels and the hoists to the bridge-temple. Around him the bones of the waking ship creaked.

+If there is no path out of this part of the webway,+ began Ignis, +then we must–+

+I can open a way.+ Ahriman's sending cut through his own. Ignis felt the edge in the thought, like a blade cutting through a knot of rope. +Once we are out, we will need to travel at speed through the webway to our destination. There are enemies in here and the longer we are in their domain, the higher the likelihood of them attacking again.+

+The Navigator has proved unreliable.+

+The passages respond to the intent of those that travel them. So I will be the intent.+

+And who will steer us?+

+The xenos itself,+ replied Ahriman.

+No,+ said Ignis.

+Its kind subverted these paths before. It knows how to get through better than any of us. We do not have time to learn those secrets, yet. We must use it. It wants to return to the ruin of its civilisation. It will agree.+

+It is a creature that cannot be trusted and is of great malice and ability,+ sent Ignis.

+Its treachery is predictable, its malice a problem that can be held and prepared for.+

+Preparation requires time,+ sent Ignis. +That resource is absent.+

+We have what we need, brother. The Navigator will be an interface. He is already connected in part to Setekh. All that is needed is the will to put it to use.+

And there it was, thought Ignis. There was the truth of all that Ahriman did: the impossible overcome by will.

Ignis had not been part of the cabal that had cast the first Rubric. He had become an Exile without the need of Magnus the Red's banishment. He had joined Ahriman later. His reason had been simple: he preferred to fight at the side of his own kind. That and perhaps pride in knowing he could do what few others of Ahriman's followers could – he could act without emotion or concern beyond the logic of his beliefs.

Then they had cast the Second Rubric and had to run from the Planet of the Sorcerers. A second exile to add to the first. Others had fled Ahriman. Ignis had remained. He had a place, a role. That had fitted his need for order. He had made a poor mercenary. At some level he had needed to fit and to be part of a greater whole. Ahriman had provided that. It had not mattered what their purpose was, only that they had one. Until now.

Now he saw the limit of the pattern Ahriman's actions created. The first Rubric and the second, and now this quest for the impossible: there was a fractal aspect to all of them. Each was a repetition of the past. The details changed but the intent did not. Each goal was an attempt to heal the past, and each one demanded more and more. Factors spiralled, values changed, and the progression spun on and on. Every success held within it the seed of the next catastrophe. Ahriman had always been like this, unchanged and unchanging. Ignis reflected that the pattern of his own life had been the same.

+I will follow your will in this instance,+ he replied. He felt Ahriman's thoughts rise to reply, but his mind spoke first. +But if we survive and get free, I will...+ For the first time in his memory, Ignis hesitated. +I will go.+

A moment of silence.

+As you will it,+ came the reply at last. Ignis thought he felt a blink of emotion snap across the mental connection. Perhaps shock, perhaps something else. Ignis was not certain it had even occurred. Emotion was not a domain he had ever understood. +Take the xenos from the cages. Make any agreement with it that is needed. Bind it. Bring it to the Navigator's tower.+

+As you will it,+ replied Ignis.

* * *

Setekh could sense disorder in Ignis from a look. He had examined and analysed the warrior's face and physical mannerisms over and again. He could read Ignis without the warrior needing to say a word. Ignis exhibited great control, but his thoughts still spoke in ways he did not realise. That was one of the greatest flaws of flesh – you could not control its nature. Errors oozed from the pores of skin like sweat.

'You wish me to guide you,' said Setekh.

'That is Ahriman's command.'

'It was inevitable that you would come to me for this. It will be, but for that to be done I must be free.'

Ignis' face was still, but the orbiting hoops slowed. The anathema pressure holding Setekh shifted. He dropped to the disc at the centre of the circle and rose. Ignis was watching him. The barrel of the crude automaton's main weapon was steady. Setekh felt the itch of the dark matter held in its reservoir. The disc floated to the floor. He stepped off. There would still be anathema power surrounding him, he knew, subtle chains that he could not perceive, but that was to be expected.

'Take me to your puppet guide,' he said.

'What do you want for this?' Ignis asked.

'Only what you have already agreed,' said Setekh, raising his hands as though to show them free of manacles. 'I am the last of my kind. I wish to return to the ruins of my home.'

Ignis looked at him for a long moment. Setekh watched the geometries of the warrior's facial tattoos shift from circles to jagged lines. Then Ignis moved aside and Setekh walked past him to the door.

Silvanus stood in the ruin of his sanctuary. Pieces of debris lay scattered from the shattered viewport. Bodies were strewn across the floor, lifeblood sticky on the carpet. The ship shivered. Blood drops shook from the ceiling. The engines were lighting. Silvanus turned. Then his mouth opened. He felt himself half fall back against his throne. His surviving progeny twisted in their tanks. He tried to gasp but could take no air into his lungs.

A figure folded into sight. Its body was a mockery of a skeleton in metal. Its eyes glowed with buzzing fire. The scarab attached to Silvanus' skull burned cold against his eye and forehead. He could see the figure in the warp too, or rather could not see it. It was a black shape around which distortions rippled and shivered, wave patterns folding and merging. It was not just an absence, like Maehekta; it was a violation. It was the xenos prisoner. The creature of a race already without life before it perished. And it was here. In the space that Silvanus thought his own.

The xenos halted. Behind it followed Ignis. The Master of Ruin's face was a cold mask. His electoos had formed into vertical lines. His aura smouldered black and crimson.

'What...?' stammered Silvanus, looking at Ignis, but it was the xenos who spoke. Its voice crackled like static caught in a cable.

'Bring it closer,' it said.

Ignis looked at Silvanus. His eyes were dark and unblinking. 'Go to it,' he said.

Silvanus did not move. 'What is happening?' he asked.

'It is here to show us a way through the tunnels,' said Ignis.

Silvanus shook his head. 'Ahriman...' he began.

'This is his will,' said Ignis.

'No...'

Ignis gave a single nod, and something in that gesture stilled Silvanus. In all the time Silvanus had spent with the Exiles, Ignis had remained a figure of cold reason. Sometimes that reasoning was understood by only himself, but it was reasoning all the same. Ignis did nothing that did not serve a line of logic or pattern of thought. Other Thousand Sons acted from emotion, from bitterness and pride to sorrow. But not Ignis. He was like a cog that turned by the will of higher orders and principles. Except in those few words and that look, Silvanus thought he saw a flicker of something almost human in him, a ghost of emotion. That, almost more than the presence of the xenos, terrified him. It was as though he had just seen a mountain fold into the sea.

'The...' the xenos began. The buzz of its voice clicked for a second. If it had been human, Silvanus would have thought it was smiling. '...biological control interface will have to be connected and activated so that your ship will obey.'

Silvanus was still looking at Ignis. He wanted to shake his head.

'Do it,' said Ignis. Silvanus nodded, and forced himself back into the throne. The neural interface slid into his skull. His nerves closed on it. As ever, the kaleidoscopes, the meshing of sight with his progeny, the bridge to the ship's helm controls. The xenos moved closer, until it was just beside Silvanus. He could feel sweat pouring down his face. The xenos was right above him. It began to raise a hand. There were flakes of psycho-active ice on its joints. Silvanus kept his gaze low. This close, the presence of the thing was filling his eyes with painful colours. The ship gave a lurch beneath him. Shards of glass leapt into the air and hung for a second. A low growl shook the ship. Another lurch and the tremble of engines as the *Hekaton* tried to pull herself from the debris.

'Look at me,' said the xenos. Its head rotated on its neck to regard Ignis. 'It must comply.'

'Do as it says,' said Ignis.

Silvanus forced his head up.

The xenos was staring at him. The ship shook again. The

thrum of engines was constant now. It moved a hand. Pieces of ice formed on its fingers and fell as its joints uncurled. Silvanus could see the blur-shimmer of psy-force restraining the thing's movements. He was breathing hard, gasping. The scarab attached to his head was becoming heavier, pulling his face down. The xenos extended a single digit. Its bones were grey metal under a fine layer of carbon black and gold. It was almost beautiful. The device on Silvanus' forehead was a cold lump of ice and fire. The link to the helm poured a babble of data into the base of his skull. He felt as though he were being stretched. The xenos' finger touched the scarab on his forehead.

Reality folded.

He might have cried out.

He could not tell.

He had been born and trained his whole life to see the universe differently from other humans. Where they saw chaos in the warp, he saw tide and flow, meaning in abstract patterns, sanity in madness. His time in the Eye had pushed him further, had allowed him to see the inverted truth of the universe. None of it prepared him to see as he saw in that moment.

Blank darkness. Lines and curves and shapes that were not part of reality slid along planes, reversed, spun and extended into the distant abyss, and in that abyss... Nothing. Just emptiness undiluted by light or variation. Everything that made meaning, gone. He was seeing into a place where there was nothing except vastness, and the slow scream of stars. He was nought, a passing bundle of atoms with a delusion of life and power. Nothing could survive. Nothing could live.

He was now just a link of meat and nerves between the eyes of death and the path beyond. He wanted to call to his god and feel the comfort of pain, but he could only look and obey.

* * *

The *Hekaton* pushed up from the ground. The starved creatures swarming on her skin shrieked. Some bounded down towards the ground, leaping between towers and crenellations. Others tried to force themselves into cracks in armour. The ones behind them tore at those trying to squeeze into the gaps. Blood and intestines sprayed into the air. Engines and thrusters ploughed burning ruts into the debris layer, then heaved the hull up inch by inch. Gun turrets snapped free. The ship rotated, shedding debris. Backwash from its engines whipped dust storms through the piled wrecks.

In his sanctuary, Ahriman knelt. He could feel the ship trembling as it rose. The walls of the webway were already responding. The pressure and texture of the ether was altering. Grey mist billowed through the canyons of wreckage around them. Then the pocket of space began to contract. Gossamer walls hardened. A spire of wreckage groaned as pressure built in its roots. A shriek of shearing metal. Chunks of debris the size of tanks began to fall, striking the ground and the *Hekaton*.

The webway was going to try to kill them now. It was going to crush them and let their bones mix with the dead that had come before. That would not happen. He would not let that happen.

'*The webway is psychomorphic,*' Maehekta had said. '*It responds to our intentions, our natures, our desires and fears.*'

He opened his hand. The rough silver coin gleamed on his palm. The box sat in front of him. He reached for its lid, then hesitated. What would he see inside? Was the helm still there? Was it gone? Out there in the midden, he had thought he had seen it looking back at him as he had been passed the coin.

The ship shook again. He needed to act now. His hand remained still on the lid of the box. Time – one of the last great mysteries. He had studied for centuries, had seen how it bent away from the simple line that most people thought it was. But this… This coin in his hand and the figure in the blackened helm, it might mean something else. Paradox. Past and future merging. If he opened this box and the helm was still there, it meant no one else could have taken it. That meant it had been him. He had been the figure that had given himself this silver coin. A token of proof. It might have many meanings, but he was certain that if he opened the box and found the helm then the coin meant one thing: hope. Because if in the future he had not taken the secrets of time from the Hyksos, how would he have returned? His future had begun to guide the past. If the helm was still inside the box that was proof, and proof was more than hope: it was certainty.

Except, what if you are wrong? came the question at the back of his thoughts. *What if the helm is gone? What would that mean?*

He took a breath, held it still in his lungs and then opened the box.

From the Navigator's tower, Ignis saw a lump of debris hit the flank of the ship. It burst apart. Shards tore through structures on the upper deck. The *Hekaton* pitched. A tier of batteries tore free, turrets and gun barrels rolling down the hull in a slide of metal. In front of him the xenos had pulled back from Silvanus. The Navigator was unmoving, rigid in his throne. The vile clone-things in their tanks were battering themselves bloody against the glass. Behind him, Credence shifted as the deck plunged.

Silvanus' senses were no longer his own. Silver fibres had stabbed from the scarab into the root of his third eye. He could feel them worming into the meat of his brain, creating new pathways, hot-wiring his senses. He could see the webway now. White lines curved in space-time. Paradoxes became openings and spaces in unreal membranes. It was agony. He felt his hands move on the helm controls, and felt the ship sliding down one plane of reality towards another.

There is no way out! his voice screamed inside his head. He felt a coldness guide his hands and instructions pass from him to the helm. The ship was still moving. Out beyond the hull the pillars of debris were still falling. The *Hekaton* was sliding forwards as shards of ship carcasses fell about it. They were going to plough straight into the webway's wall. He felt the silver threads push deeper into his skull. Pain exploded through him. He wanted to vomit but could not. They were going forwards, but only the annihilating boundary of the webway waited for them.

Ahriman pulled his mind into the ether. He was cold, shivering in his armour, his mind sucking power to him like an exhausted man gasping for air on a high mountain. He had a little further to climb. His thoughts found Silvanus. The Navigator did not respond as Ahriman touched his mind. That did not matter; he was linked to the ship and Setekh. All they needed now was to open a way.

Ahriman's mind rushed out, reaching for the webway itself. His thoughts and senses were birds, wings pulling ghost-fire as they spiralled through the dark.

Outside the ship, the fall of debris was a deluge. One of the spires of wreckage shuddered, held, then collapsed. Twenty kilometres above the *Hekaton* a crooked spine of matter sheared from the spire top and fell. Its heart had been a ship carrying plants and biomes. When it had died the plants had taken over the wreckage for a while, tangling the kilometres of the hull with pale roots and branches searching for a sun that was not there to find. They had died long ago, their trunks and vines fossilising around the frame of the lost ship. It had stood for an uncountable age. Now it shattered as it collapsed. Hundreds of metres of rock rolled over, shearing into spines and slabs. A piece hit the prow of the *Hekaton* and slammed its nose down. Dust and shards exploded out. The ship's engines roared as they pushed the vast bulk back up. Ahriman's mind touched the edge of the webway enclosing them. It rippled back as though fleeing. For a second, he could feel his senses reaching. Then the webway surged forwards.

Pale light enveloped Ahriman, grabbing on to his thoughts and wrenching them out beyond the grasp of his will. He felt the root of his mind vanish into the distance. The force pulling him on was like nothing he had ever felt, deeper and stronger than the will of any mortal, beyond the power of a daemon – like the riptide of a sea.

This is how this place makes its ghosts, he found himself thinking. The minds of the unwary pulled past the point they can get back.

He was far out now, almost past where the thread of will could pull him back to his body and the stricken ship as it floundered, heaving as debris struck it in an avalanche. He could barely make out the way he had come. There was just the ghost-light surrounding him, pulling him towards a horizon he knew he would never reach. He could not even tell where the real was. The webway had plucked his soul like a feather from carrion. No way back...

In the quiet of his sanctuary, his hand closed around the silver coin. In front of him, a box lay open. From inside, a battered and soot-blackened helm looked up at him.

Hope...

The ghost substance of the webway tightened around his mind. He could feel the thread of his soul stretching. His thoughts buckled...

Then...

* * *

The path opened in front of Silvanus like a flower to the sun. It was… even in agony there was no other word for it… beautiful. He felt himself feeding power to the engines and the *Hekaton* responding. The ship was thrusting forwards into an open space while behind it the cliffs and spires of debris fell.

I am alive, he thought. Relief shouted in his head. *I am alive!*

+Listen to me, Silvanus,+ said Ahriman. He could not answer. Could do nothing. It felt like his brain was being crushed in two as the pressure of the xenos and the sorcerer grew. +If any of our ships survived, they will be here. You can reach them through your kin. You can bring them to us.+ Silvanus wanted to reply, but all he could manage was a tremble of half thought. +Open your eyes. Bring them to us.+

The webway changed. In his altered sight he saw planes of space merge. The tunnel ahead of the *Hekaton* expanded and there were other ships, ships he recognised. They were the ships of the Exiles: the *Soul Jackal, Pyromonarch, Scion of the Ragged Sun, Weigher of Souls.* Not all the ships that had gone into the webway, but more than he could have hoped.

Down deep in his mind, Silvanus felt something bright open its eyes…

Many eyes. Views scattered across different sanctuaries and ships. He could see through the gaze of his progeny again.

They were alive. Impossibly, his family were alive.

Under the deadened layer of the xenos' hold on his mind, he felt a thought push through the dark, bright and burning.

A miracle, he thought.

PART THREE

TOMB WORLD

CHAPTER XII

*D*UST

Ahriman paused in what he was saying, the words catching on his tongue. Helio Isidorus looked back at him, waiting. The hoops of the cage rotated slowly. Ahriman shook his head, closing his eyes for a second. When he opened them again, Helio was still looking at him just as he had before.

'You were telling me something about yourself,' said Helio. 'About something that happened.'

'We made it through, most of us – more than I thought while we were in the webway. Not all though.' He felt himself blink and shake his head. 'Five ships did not rejoin us.'

'What happened to them?'

'Lost, destroyed, both.' He blinked again. In his mind he saw the dead ships gathered in the pocket of the webway like bones in a gullet. The silence of that place touched him afresh. 'Perhaps they found another way out.'

'How did you find the others?'

'The webway responds to what you want, and why. It brought us back to them.'

'And before that you were trapped because you believed you were trapped?'

Ahriman looked at Helio. His brother's eyes were dark, lacking in all judgement or guile.

'It is possible.'

'And the other ships, the ones with our brothers on, did they believe they were lost and so the webway made that real?'

'I do not know. It is…'

'Possible?' Helio said the word.

Ahriman nodded. Then he paused, looking at his brother for a long moment.

'You are talking differently, Helio,' he said finally.

'Am I? I do not remember us talking before.'

'Perhaps more of you is coming back.'

'It is… possible.' Helio smiled, gave a small shrug. 'And these wants and beliefs that the webway responds to, they are not just about the journey. They are deep down. They are what they believe about everything, not just where they are going.'

Ahriman nodded.

'How long ago was this?'

'We passed through the gate three days ago according to our own measurement of time.'

'Three days ago…' Helio looked away, frowning at nothing, then shaking his head. 'Three days… three days… three…'

Ahriman had been waiting for this. The brief light of recall was fading in his brother's eyes. In a minute they would start the same conversation again. He should go. There were preparations to make.

The remaining ships of the Exiles had appeared inside a cloud, passing from the reality of the webway to a void of cold starlight and drifting plumes of gas on the edge of a star system. The star was an angry orb of fire slowly curdling into the last cycle of its decline to a cold ball of neutrons rolling through the void as a tombstone over its own grave. One planet circled the star. Long-range auspex and scrying told that it was utterly lifeless. It was not just that nothing lived on it now; it was as though nothing had *ever* lived on it. The remains of the Hyksos were on that planet. Even if Setekh had not confirmed it, the choice would have been clear. The landing forces were forming even now. His brothers were making ritual connections between cohorts of Rubricae so that they could be commanded en masse. War machines were rising from dream-comas. They were fewer, far fewer, than he would have liked. There had been other losses during the passage and there were only four of the Circle to stand with him.

Ctesias still had not woken, though he lived. The aeldari venom yet ran in his system, trying to unmake his flesh from the inside out. His cells were fighting it but only as fast as they fell. A holding action that could at best allow for an eventual victory, at worst delay defeat. Fever heat bled from him. Ahriman had entered his mind but found it still and bare of thought, a fortress of chained secrets still locked but with its master gone. What had happened to him? Had his mind flown as his body fought the alien poison trying to unmake it? Had his thoughts been caught by the webway's net and set drifting through the labyrinth realm? There was no time to find out, not now. Time had run fast and thin. But still, with so much that needed to be done, Ahriman had chosen to come here, and to talk to the one person who would not remember or judge him for what was happening.

And to remind yourself that there is hope, said a voice at the back of his thoughts. *To remind yourself that things can be changed.*

'I am trying to remember…' said Helio.

Ahriman waited.

After a long moment he forced himself to rise.

'I must go,' he said.

Helio looked at him. He nodded slowly.

'Yes, you must. I understand.'

Ctesias felt cold. The boat rocked beneath him as it touched a set of stone steps. The youth's face was in shadow again, the light coming from behind was bright, scattering off the water against the cave wall and ceiling.

'Who are you?' he asked. The youth had jumped onto the stone steps and was fastening the boat's painter to a post. A small entranceway sat in the rock wall at the top of the steps, closed by a wooden door. 'Where is this?'

The youth stopped and looked down at him.

'You know where this is. It is where you wanted to be. So that is where I brought you.' The boy pulled a heavy key on a string from where it hung under his tunic and slotted it into the lock on the door. 'Come…'

The door hinged open.

Ctesias did not move. He felt very cold. The youth tilted his head, dark eyes reflecting a shard of the sunlight falling into the cave.

He was young, thought Ctesias. Young but on the edge of not being so. The age when the world started to change from whatever simplified truth you had known before into a world more complex, more cruel. The age when a youth might be taken by the Legions and become something and someone else.

'Please,' said the youth. 'This is the way.'

After a moment, because he could see no other choice, Ctesias followed. The youth stood aside as he reached the door. He hesitated again on the threshold. He could see a flight of clean-cut stone steps on the other side. The youth waited, saying nothing, until Ctesias stepped through; then he pulled the door shut from the outside, and Ctesias heard the lock turn before he could push against it. It did not move when he tried the handle, and a blow on the wood did nothing. He stepped back, closed his eyes, and tried to extend his will into the mindscape around him. When he opened his eyes, nothing had changed. He began to climb the stairs. Up and up, one foot after another. He passed windows that opened onto sky and sea, and others that framed stars and darkness. There were doors, too – some closed by painted wood, others by metal or black stone. He heard sounds behind some: voices, the calls of birds and the sound of the sea breaking on rocks, or perhaps hands beating against walls.

At last, he reached a door that was open. He stepped through. A white marble floor extended to a balcony framed by an arch. Delicate pillars rose from the floor to a vaulted ceiling. Suns and moons and stars drifted in gold and silver gilt. The sky beyond the balcony was the same blue it had been above the sea.

'Are you lost?'

He turned at the voice. A man was standing in the room beside a stone table. He wore a white tunic swathed with a blue toga. His feet were bare, Ctesias noticed. A neat beard framed an open, curious expression. He might have been no more than three decades old.

'Who are…?' Ctesias began, then stopped. 'You are Helio Isidorus.' He let the word hang, almost not wanting to hear the reply. The implication of the confirmation, of what it meant, was not something he wanted to be fact.

The man frowned and set down a wax tablet and stylus on the table.

'That is my name,' he said. 'Do I know you? I am sorry, I don't remember.'

Ctesias licked his lips and found that his throat was dry. He felt as though he were balancing on the edge of a cliff above a long, long drop. He cut away the instinct to run or to demand. He did not know what he was dealing with, and until he did, every decision could be lethal.

'This… palace, is yours?' he asked at last.

'It is,' said the man, and he smiled.

'You created it?'

'Created it?' The man looked around the room. A breath of wind from the balcony rocked the stylus on the table. 'Can you create anything? Nothing can truly be destroyed or made. Everything is just transmutation from one form into another. All of what is here already was and is. I simply arranged what I found.'

'Found?'

'Yes. This…' He moved and put his hand upon the frame of the arch opening onto the balcony. 'This was part of a manse on the side of a burning hive. It looks better here, I think.'

'But where did you find it?'

'Somewhere out there,' he said, and gestured to the view beyond the balcony. Ctesias looked, and the blue sky and sea were not there.

Blackness and burning fire.

Ctesias snapped his eyes shut but the sight was in his mind, seared like a neon scar left from looking at the sun.

Dust falling through a void, tumbling without end, each mote a memory, each burning… and the palace, for all its size, an island floating in the infinite dark as a universe fell past it in fragments.

'This is your mind, your memories…' he said, still reeling from the sight. This was what it was to be a Rubricae, to be an endless abyss through which broken grains of memories and identity fell like dust cast into the dark, never to hit the bottom. Helio Isidorus was in some ways no different to what he had been when he had been that endless fall of dust held in a shell of armour. Flesh and bone had replaced ceramite and metal. He was still a cascade of lost memories, held together only by a name. Except that now he was changing, and that change set cold into Ctesias' bones. He rose slowly. 'You are remaking yourself. That is what this palace and mindscape represent – you are rebuilding an identity from all these pieces of memory. The boy in the boat was you from before you became part of the Legion. The sea is the sea from how you remember Tizca being then.'

'I want to remember, but I do not know if what I find is mine to remember or someone else's. They might be others', or yours. I take what seems to fit when I find it.'

'And bringing me here, doing this…'

'You need help. I remembered you. I decided to help.'

'You said you remembered that I was the one that died.'

'I do not remember that now.'

Ctesias paused. The face of the man who was Helio was open, smiling, calm.

'When you lived before, you were not gifted with more than a sliver of psychic potential. But this…' He gestured at the palace and where he stood. 'This is power that I have seen in very few.'

'I do not know what you mean. It just is. I understand what I understand and can do what I can do. Sometimes that changes.'

'Changes?' breathed Ctesias, the word wrapped in cold laughter. 'How much has been changing?'

'Since you have been here…' Helio looked into the distance, considering. 'Some. I find things. Do you know what this is?'

There was a helm on the table. It had not been there before. It was blackened and battle scarred, but besides that cosmetic damage it had none of the horns, adornments or distortions common to the equipment of the Legions of the Eye of Terror. The snout tapered to a conical point. With a favourable eye it might look like the beak and skull of a bird.

Ctesias' thoughts were racing. He needed to leave here. No matter what else, Ahriman needed to know about this. The implications of the mindscape of the palace, of what Helio had done and could do…

'It is a helm from a suit of Mark Six Astartes-pattern warplate,' said Ctesias, looking around for a way out. In a mindscape there was always a means of exit, a metaphor for escape built into the fabric of one's surroundings.

'Is it?' asked Helio.

'Sometimes called the Corvus design.'

'Corvus… relating to the genus of avian typified by crows and ravens. Birds associated with prophecy, fortune and sometimes ill omen – sometimes thought to be the messengers of the gods. Carrion eaters who feed on the dead.' Helio picked up the helm and turned it over in his hands. 'Ahriman the crow warrior, brother to ravens, why do you not wear this face when it fits you so well?'

Ctesias looked around at the mention of Ahriman's name. He felt cold.

'Why are you here? What is your name?' Helio looked up from the blackened helm. Ctesias stumbled back.

The eyes in Helio's face were golden pits of fire. For an eye-blink the fortress was not there, just the dark and stars swirling like golden dust scattered from a hand, and two eyes shining through them, burning.

Then it was gone, and the walls were there again, and the man in the blue toga who was Helio Isidorus was frowning with puzzlement. Ctesias did not wait; he ran.

'Wait!' called Helio Isidorus. Ctesias reached the balcony and jumped. Behind him he heard Helio's voice calling out. 'Who are you?'

Dust kicked into the sunlight as the gunships descended. They landed in a spiral, touching down one after another, each separated by a perfect span of distance and time. Strike fighters held station above. The raw sunlight reflected on the inlaid gold feathers on their wings. Above them, the stars glared down from the black void.

Ramps opened as soon as the gunships were down. Rubricae marched into the light and spread out in overlapping circles. The lesser sorcerers of the Exiles moved with them, directing their brothers as they moved. Shells of telekinetic force unfolded around them with a shiver of frost on the air. War machines were released from the belly cradles of landers and began to move in-between the Rubricae.

Last came a trio of larger gunships. They landed at the centre of the spiral as the outermost craft dusted off. Terminators lumbered from inside them and set themselves in a wide circle. Behind the slow-moving warriors, shapes walked into the light. They stood taller than the Terminators, their bulk filling the mouths of the open assault ramps as they stepped down into the dust. The ghost-light in their sensor slits fuzzed and pulsed like signal static. Sparks and curls of spirit flame flickered on their skin. Weapons hung from their shoulders: manes of silver tentacles, fists with chisel fingers, guns with shrieking avian faces for muzzles. A living sorcerer walked at the side of each of them, their minds pulling the spirit sealed within the machines. These were the Osirion, the twice remade. Before the Rubric they had been Dreadnoughts holding the remains of the Legion's heroes who had fallen to the edge of death in battle. Now they were walking cages holding the spirits of the near dead. Slow to wake and difficult to control, they rarely came to war. The air crackled around them. Motes of dust floated up from the ground as they halted.

A single gunship touched down at the centre of the arrayed warriors and machines. Ahriman walked into the hard light. His will and mind were already meshed with those of the sorcerers commanding the units on the ground. A familiar low, rattling sound – like sand churning along the bottom of a seabed – touched his mind: the Rubricae whispering their names into the dark. He let it surround him as he stood, then walked down onto the dust. Five followed him: Kiu and Gilgamos, Maehekta at a distance from the others. Ignis and Credence were last. Ahriman watched the Master of Ruin with his mind's eye but could read nothing but careful control in his aura.

+I have a last request of you,+ Ahriman had sent when they had come out of the webway.

He had found Ignis preparing shuttles to take him to the Word of Hermes. The Master of Ruin had not responded at first. Ahriman had waited.

+You wish me to come with you to the xenos world,+ Ignis had replied at last.

+Yes.+

+You have enough forces to waste a continent. My presence or absence will not be significant.+ Ignis had paused in checking the shuttle and looked at Ahriman. +An excess of force if it is as dead as it should be. I do not see how my presence alters the factors at play.+

+Because I trust you to do what must be done,+ sent Ahriman. +I always have, brother, and there are things that I trust you alone to do.+

Credence had filled the silence that followed with a low series of clicks.

+Tell me,+ Ignis had sent at last.

He had not seemed shocked by what Ahriman said next. If anything, *he seemed to think it logical, something that had Ahriman not told him, he would have inferred. The answer had been enough for Ignis to agree. One last service to the Exiles' cause, and then he was gone.*

Ahriman came to a stop beside Kiu as the gunship lifted off.

+Atmosphere is not breathable,+ sent Kiu.

Ahriman bent down. The gauntlet of his armour released with a murmur of clicks. The air was cool on his skin. He picked up a handful of the sand and let it slip through his fingers. It glittered as it fell, tiny, polished spheres catching the silver glare, dark and sparkling like graphite or haematite.

+I can sense no residue of life in anything,+ sent Kiu. +Nothing has been here for millennia on millennia.+

+Look,+ sent Gilgamos, and they followed the impulse in his sending.

What had seemed a rise of mountains had shifted in the distance. Wind had started to gust. The dust rattled against his armour. Ahriman could feel the slow beat of his blood and breath on the inside of his helm.

+What is that?+ asked Kiu.

+It is a storm,+ Ahriman replied, then turned to Maehekta. 'Bring the xenos down.'

She gave a single nod and keyed her vox.

High above, the last gunship began its approach. The strike fighters tracked it until it touched down. Setekh descended its ramp. Four Rubricae bracketed him. The xenos did not pause or look around but walked towards Ahriman. It tilted its head, eyes glowing, then without prompting, pointed towards where the storm was rising.

'The entrance is in that direction.'

Ahriman looked around. +Follow,+ he sent, and they began to walk into the rising wind.

* * *

The world felt Setekh's presence. As he followed the Thousand Sons, he detected the micro vibrations of warning. He could sense the minute processes of the guardian protocols activating. There were a few canoptek units of his dynasty awake on the world. The betrayers had needed to leave layers of underlying systems functioning so that the whole planet did not collapse. They had subverted the dynasty's own servants to aid their gaolers. That had been a mistake, one of many. The Triarchs had presumed that none of the upper hierarchy of the Hyksos would be free to subvert those simple units. A mistake. He was close enough now that he could communicate with them at will.

Bearer of the Black Disc, Most High Setekh – heed the authority of my place in the ordination of all things.

V – Obedience

IV – Obedience

III – Obedience

II – Obedience

I – Obedience

Bearer of the Black Disc, Most High Setekh – I approach with the means to enter our domain – the wardens must be prevented from responding to our presence

V – understanding and supplication – the wardens will wake – these ones do not have the means to prevent it

Bearer of the Black Disc, Most High Setekh – delay their waking for the maximum duration possible

V – Obedience

He kept the connection open now. He would need it soon. He was close, so close. Just a little further. Behind him, the swarm of dust scarabs swirled through the wind and followed.

Dust hissed across Ahriman's armour. The world beyond the lenses of his helm was a swirl of grey. The shapes of his brothers moving close to him were smudges in charcoal; those further away dissolved in the granular murk. Only the runes glowing in his helm display and his mind's senses showed him the force moving with him. Both of those senses were fraying, too. The runes dancing across his eyes would vanish, or dissolve into pixels and re-form into shapes that had no meaning. The cords of will connecting him to his brothers were growing thinner. The Great Ocean of the warp was sometimes ebbing, sometimes ripping, like a current shearing around a reef hidden under the waves. Close by, the xenos walked, shackled by the aligned will of the Circle. It rotated its head when Ahriman looked at it, its eyes two points of blurred green in the murk. There was a mockery to that look even though it had no expression.

+Halt!+ The command came from Kiu, sharp and clear over the dim pulse of the mind link, followed by the wordless command to readiness. The formation stopped, guns rising, eyes living and lifeless fixed on the swirl.

+Brother?+ asked Ahriman.

+There is something there, close by.+

Ahriman's head and senses turned in the direction communicated in Kiu's sending.

The dust and sand billowed past his armour. He could see and sense nothing beyond the curtain of the wind and the presence of his brothers.

A world of matter, and matter alone, he thought. *No trace of life. No colour in the warp. We are almost blind here.*

He was about to give the order to move again, when the grey cloud shifted, thinning and retreating like a shroud pulled back.

A vast shape loomed above them. A first it looked to be merely a stack of stone, black-grey like the dust that had etched its surface. It went up and up, pointing at the sky. Then Ahriman saw the curve and geometry of its bulk, not made by wind or geology but raised by design in a curve, like a crooked finger of a god's corpse. The wind shifted again and another stack appeared from the gloom, facing the other, and beyond them more – an avenue of gigantic, uncapped arches.

+Why did we not see these from orbit?+ asked Gilgamos, and Ahriman could feel the soothsayer's unease.

+Because they are made not to be seen by machine or mind,+ said Ahriman. No one replied, but he could feel the mental connection shift as his brothers rebalanced their thought patterns.

'We are close,' Setekh said, its voice modulated with the sound of the wind and dust so that it was clear.

+Follow,+ willed Ahriman.

They moved down the avenue between the pillars. Other shapes loomed around them, structures half or completely buried in dust drifts: ziggurats, the needle tips of obelisks, slab-sided platforms the height of tanks. Yellow runes swept Ahriman's vision, searching but finding no threat. There was a threat, though; it was all around them in the white-noise roar of the wind.

'There,' came Setekh's voice. Ahriman felt the xenos' arm move against the forces wrapping it and allowed the limb to move. It raised. A single digit pointed ahead of them. The edge of a wide plinth of black stone could just be seen under a rippled layer of dust. 'That is the seal to the entrance.'

Ahriman willed a halt, and the force began to unfold into a pattern of overlapping circles surrounding him. Overhead and up into orbit, the gunships and strike fighters on station began to wind a watching gyre. He looked around. Eye-lenses glowed a grainy green through the murk as Setekh looked back at him. Ahriman held the xenos' gaze for a long moment then moved to the plinth, followed by the rest of the Circle and Maehekta. He vaulted up its edge and onto its flat upper surface. Dust eddied across the dark stone. It was smooth despite what must have been millions of years of abrasion. Square grooves ran across its surface, catching the dust and sand. Ahriman could see the pattern of a sigil, its shape repeating and repeating in finer and finer lines so that any part of it seen up close would be like looking at the whole. He could feel the slab surface as a blank, leaden presence in the warp. Ahriman turned to Setekh.

'This is no door,' he said. 'It is a seal. Placed to keep others out and what it guards within.'

'That it is,' said the xenos.

+If this is the heart of its kingdom and they were lost long ago,+ sent Ignis, +then who placed a seal over their grave?+

+Not the enemies they were fighting,+ sent Kiu. +This follows the same elements of design as the rest of the objects and structures we have seen.+

+The xenos themselves placed this seal over the grave of their own kind,+ sent Gilgamos. +And that means that not all them were dead and gone.+

The wind gusted. Ahriman could hear it moaning as it slid through the surrounding megaliths.

+We have come too far to turn back,+ he sent.

None of the others replied. Ahriman turned to Setekh.

'Open it,' he said.

'I cannot. You must do that.'

Ahriman looked at the slab surface beneath his feet. The stone substance was not impervious to the ether, but there was a resistance in its matter that made touching it with the mind unpleasant: cold, like salt water in a deep, dark pool whose surface had never been disturbed by a ripple, and in which nothing could live. It made his skin crawl. For an instant he paused, aware of the doubts in the minds of his brothers, the unresolved questions in his own. He could stop, he could turn back...

I cannot leave the future to chance or turn aside for doubt, answered his thoughts.

His will billowed out, caught the thoughts of his brothers' minds, and pulled them up into alignment with his own. Their thoughts dimmed. Their wills meshed with his as he brought his thoughts into focus.

Light, he willed.

His thoughts became blinding. He raised his hands and staff. The rest of the Circle had turned their faces and hands to the sky. Crackling brilliance filled their thoughts. A column of turning air was spiralling above them, boring up through the dust cloud to the cold starlight above. Grains of sand were rattling on the stone.

Ahriman shifted his thoughts. Lightning leapt into the air from each of the Circle. The arcs met, forming a sphere that poured white light out through the grey curtains of the storm. Then the lightning struck down into stone. It rebounded, cutting into the air. Ahriman could feel the structure of the stone seal resisting. He poured his will against it, battering into its matter and essence, inhaling the strength of his brothers. The plinth glowed. The sand covering its top became fluid, became gas. And still the lightning struck. Ahriman could feel the effort of sustaining his power and focus. Nerve and flesh and instinct screamed at him to stop. It was like trying to push against a cliff, his muscles and body on fire, sense and mind shouting that it was impossible. He silenced both thought and feeling. His will floated free, serene, eternal, utterly unyielding.

A split opened in the stone. The lightning poured into it and spread into cracks so that the branches of a blinding white tree seemed to be growing across the plinth beneath the thunderbolt's fall. The stone shattered. Splinters showered up into the air. Great slabs tumbled. A chasm opened beneath. Then the lightning vanished. Thunder and the rumble of falling stone filled the sudden quiet.

Ahriman felt the power vanish from his mind. Fatigue washed over him. He felt his body draw breath, his hearts rising to a storm beat. He held himself still and waited for the feeling to pass. One of his knees had folded to the ground, his hand gripped his staff. Around him, his brothers were rising from where they had fallen. Above them the wind was pouring dust back into the space left by the vortex and lightning.

Ahriman rose. The broken stone seal lay before him, a dark hole at its centre. Dust was already beginning to fall into the opening. He looked back into the darkness, then dropped through.

Shadows closed over him, and the sound of the wind drained to quiet. He looked around. A chromed skull looked back at him from the dark.

CHAPTER XIII

UNDERWORLD

Ahriman stopped. Behind him, Kiu and a pair of his disciples descended the ramp of rubble. Maehekta and Setekh followed at a distance. Ignis and Credence followed last with a block of Terminators. Gilgamos would stay with the bulk of their forces on the surface.

Kiu halted beside Ahriman, head rotating as he took in their surroundings. The chamber they had breached was hexagonal. Niches lined the walls. Skeletal metal figures stood in them, their heads and hands resting on shields and the pommels of weapons. Layers of dust covered them, but the blast from the breach had stripped that shroud in places. Ahriman took a step closer to the metal skull that had greeted him.

+Guardians,+ sent Kiu.

+Or wardens,+ replied Ahriman. +Look at the colouration and markings. Quite different from Setekh. His kind were called the Hyksos. These specimens are similar, but they are of a different order.+

+They could simply be the marks of a different caste of these creatures.+

+That is possible,+ sent Ahriman.

+They appear inactive.+

+We should trust nothing here,+ added Ignis. +We could simply destroy them, and remove the possibility of them activating.+

+No,+ sent Ahriman. +We do not know enough of how any latent defences might function – and there will have been defences.+ He looked up at the broken dome of the ceiling. The wind was blowing in spills of grey sand. He could feel the song and touch of the ether becoming distant, as though closed behind dull blocks of stone.

We are walking into a realm of the dead, he thought, remembering words once read by a forgotten myth-weaver of Terra. *And the light of our minds grows dim.*

Ahriman turned his gaze to the single exit from the chamber. It was a black opening framed by the geometric lines. He looked back at where the xenos floated in its bindings of telekinetic force.

+Keep it close,+ he sent to his brothers.

Then he turned and made for the waiting door.

They walked down and down into the hollow heart of the world. Silence wrapped them, deep and drowning, as though it had drained from the night between stars and pooled here, becoming thicker until it was as substantial as the stone of the floors they walked over. They passed over chasms that went down past the reach of Ahriman's eyes, and through passages whose walls stretched up and up. Every structure and surface was of the same near-black stone, cut and shaped and smoothed into vast blocks and panels. Grooves ran over the surface of everything, lines linking circles and crescent arcs. There were few signs of machines: a few metallic fins or hollow cylinders worked into the stone structures, but nothing that would imply moving parts or power transfer. In fact, there was nothing at all – no remains of xenos creatures or constructs besides those in the first chamber.

The further they went, the more Ahriman was reminded of the ruins he had once seen on the Ionus Plateau on Terra. Tunnelled into the rock of what had been the edge of a seabed, they had been of a scale too large for humans, and without any sign of why someone had bored them into the stone. They too had been empty with just the sound of the air running through open doors and empty passages, moaning.

They kept on. Ahriman could feel the dull heaviness of the structure above and around him. It was like trying to breathe in thin air, each inhalation a gasp. His mind was linked back to his brothers on the surface, but that connection was becoming thin, like a fraying thread paid out behind them the deeper they went. The power contained in his staff pulsed like the building pressure of a migraine.

He took another step and stopped. His will flashed out, and the rest halted. Guns rose. The focus of Kiu's and Ignis' minds rose.

The tunnel walls were no longer there. Somehow, they had crossed through a doorway without noticing. He looked around slowly. A vast space opened beside and above him. In front, the floor narrowed to a ramp that sloped down. Kiu and a pair of Rubricae stood in the arc of a doorway. The glow of their eye-lenses was the only source of light to sketch the corners and walls around them. He looked back at the blank space in front of him. He could have sent light shining through it with his mind, or freed his senses to swim through the dark like a blind swimmer feeling their way through a flooded cave. That would cost him, though, and he needed to save his strength.

+Illumination,+ he willed. One of the Rubricae stepped forward, braced, and fired its gun. The round flew high and burst into a phosphor-bright sun. The Rubricae fired twice more. The three lights drifted down, flickering.

A great plateau extended away in front of them. There must have been a ceiling above, but it was so high that the light did not reach it. Vast shapes of stone projected from the cavern: tetrahedrons, hundreds of metres to a side, and spheres that curved through air and wall like moons trapped beneath the earth. Pyramids and square-topped ziggurats rose from the floor of the plateau. What might have been roads cut between the structures. And it went on to the edge of the light and sight: a silent, dead city under the skin of the world above.

+The structures are intact,+ sent Kiu. +No signs of violence or disaster.+ He let the implication hang in the thought connection.

Ahriman looked around at Setekh.

'Almost nothing of your kind seems to remain besides these structures.' The xenos' gaze seemed brighter here than it had on the surface.

'If any of our treasures survived, they will be in the remains of the Court of the Phaeron. There...' said Setekh, extending a hand and digit to point at where a split-sided ziggurat rose from the plateau. Ahriman looked at it, fixing it and the path to it in his thoughts. Above, the phosphor rounds were arcing downwards, their light fluttering and dimming. Ahriman nodded to himself and stepped down the ramp and into the city.

In the high tower aboard the *Hekaton*, a flash of pain drove through Silvanus' sleep. He gasped and opened his eyes. Blood wept from the wounds in his forehead where the alien device had bonded with his skull. The pain was worse now the device was gone. The wounds left by its legs had not closed and when he tried to sleep, the pain would become a storm. A cold metallic taste lurked in his mouth, too. He shook himself and shifted to the edge of the sleep-couch. His remaining progeny stirred in their tanks, watching him with cataract-white eyes. He looked down and shivered.

'Great Emperor of all, forgive me and bless me with thy power that can change all, sorrow to joy, agony to peace.'

He fumbled for the aquila hanging on the chain around his neck. It was not there. A sudden wave of panic and scrabbling ensued, until he saw it lying on a shelf on the other side of the room. It must have fallen off earlier in one of the... incidents. He had insisted that serfs clear his chambers of the debris from the alien attack and the mishaps of the trip through the webway. It had been done, and the most basic of repairs completed, but there were still brown crusts of blood on the carpet, and nothing had yet replaced the furniture and items that had been smashed or riddled with projectiles. A razor disc from the masked alien that had invaded his sanctuary remained embedded in the ceiling above the couch. Apparently, it had sliced the fingers from the first serf who tried to remove it and resisted the tug of servo-claws. The main oculus-window had been repaired though, not least because without the layers of armour crystal Silvanus would die from vacuum exposure every time the blast shutter opened. He chuckled at that, and then wondered why.

The candles he had set burning beside the aquila had gone out. He did not want to get up, but he needed the comfort of the twin-headed god's mark.

He rocked himself to his feet and shuffled over to the shelf. He was breathing hard, and he could feel the blowholes on either side of his spine sucking air. Sweat was running into his eyes, and when he wiped his hand across his face it came away pink with perspiration-diluted blood. He hissèd a curse at all that had befallen him and picked up the aquila. He felt better straight away. The gold was warm in his hands, and the sapphire in its eyes seemed to wink at him. He smiled and kissed it. He was not alone, not at all. He was not unfortunate, but blessed. The Emperor's many eyes were watching over him. There was nothing to fear, nothing at all. He closed his eyes and let himself bathe in the sense of peace. All was golden. All that was darkness would change to light. He opened his eyes and hung the aquila around his neck.

He was just starting back to the sleep-couch when he stopped. There was something lying on the floor, under the couch, where it must have fallen. It was small, pale, smooth. He could not tell what it was, and it must have been hidden from anyone not standing exactly where he was now. A broken piece of an ornament perhaps, or a chunk of crystal from when the window had blown out? He moved closer, stooping so that he could get a clearer look, but it was at just the wrong angle to see unless he was lying flat to the ground.

He knelt, leaning on the couch, his other hand reaching beneath it. He blinked, his fingers feeling the threads of the woven carpet. He touched something. He tried to hook his fingers around it, but only managed to push it away. He tried again and his finger found what felt like a hole. He tugged gently, felt it slide nearer, and then pulled more firmly until it was free. He straightened, flushed by the effort and the minor victory it represented. He smiled and looked at what was in his hand.

A white mask looked up at him with empty holes for eyes.

He gasped. The mask tumbled from his hand as he scrambled away from it. It lay on the ground, rocking back and forth. He was panting even harder now, eyes wide – not wanting to look away, not knowing if he had the breath or strength to scream.

Back and forth…

There was no one to hear him even if he did scream.

Back and forth… the mouth moulded into the face seeming to shift from happiness to sorrow.

They were gone to the surface, Ahriman, the others… Just him… just him left.

Back and forth…

Not fortunate, not blessed, not watched over but cursed.

And the mask was glowing now, the white of its shape become the white of lightning and the glare of starlight.

Guns rose. Ahriman felt kill impulses breathe from Kiu's mind into the Rubricae that walked with them.

+Hold,+ willed Ahriman.

The fingers of the Rubricae and Terminators froze on the triggers of their weapons. The rising spiral of Kiu's thoughts held steady.

They had entered an oblong plaza cut into the other structures. Machines hung from arches that ran down its centre like a spine. The machines each had six limb-blades bunched beneath them like the legs of a dead spider. Each limb was an arc of metal four times the height of a Space Marine. What looked like gun pods nested close to a central abdomen that encased the hunched form of a xenos creature similar to Setekh. The shroud of metal dust was heavy on them, but menace still radiated from their every line. Ahriman could see thirty hanging above the plaza.

+There are more,+ sent Kiu, turning his gaze. Ahriman saw the niches set in the arches from which the spider machines hung. Skeletal figures stood in the openings, their heads bowed. +They are all like the ones that were in the first chamber. Same colouration and markings. And there are differences in the construction of these arches. It is subtle, but they are distinct. As though they came after the rest.+ Kiu turned to look back and up at where the ziggurat rose in the distance. +We should set charges and be ready to destroy them.+

Ahriman considered this for a second.

+Agreed,+ he sent. Kiu and his Rubricae began clamping melta and plasma charges to the alien creatures.

Ahriman moved ahead of them. A low, dull throbbing had begun in his skull. According to the image of the plateau's roads and structures he had in his mind, this was the avenue of obelisks that ran to the foot of the great ziggurat. He had estimated it to be a kilometre and a half long, but something in the angles of the structures had thrown his sense of scale off. Distances that had seemed short now turned out to be much longer. The kilometre that should have been left until they reached the ziggurat now seemed three kilometres. It was no accident either.

+Reality here is not set true,+ sent Ignis.

Ahriman did not reply but stepped onto the avenue. A part of his mind expected a reaction, a change to the stillness and silence. None came. He took another step, looked down and stopped.

His will shifted to his staff and blue light kindled between the horns on its top. The cold light pushed the darkness to the edge of a circle. He moved forwards slowly, watching the light of his staff peel back the gloom.

'Maehekta,' he said into the vox. He heard the null mistress move up behind him. She was being careful not to come too close, but he could feel the already weak pulse of the warp ebb.

'Look,' he said. Carved figures and images lay on the ground at their feet, incised into the stone. They were composed of the same circles, lines and crescents that made up the marks they had seen throughout this underworld. Except that here they were not simply glyphs but an illustration. His eyes moved across each part, processing, seeking pattern and inference.

'A pictographic message,' said Maehekta.

'Like those used by any number of other sentient races throughout time to tell their story,' said Ignis, moving up next to them. 'Or to praise their gods and enforce the narrative of their civilisation.'

'No,' said Maehekta. She had crouched down and was running an armoured finger along one of the grooves forming the image of a humanoid figure. 'It is not meant to communicate to their own. For that, they used their own language. They made this for others, for simple minds. For us.'

'To break down and interpret an entire symbolic system is not simple,' said Ignis.

Ahriman almost smiled inside his helm. 'If this was intended to be read and understood by beings that the makers considered inferior, then analysis will not help. All we need to do is let our minds see what was there.' He shifted the focus of his thoughts and looked at the marks on the stone again.

A cluster of lines became a figure, became a spectre of death and oblivion…

'It is a warning,' he said. His eyes were moving faster now, the meaning unfolding with each image that emerged. 'That any who come here will perish. That they shall become nothing. They will be unmade and all that they value with them.' He paused, moving forwards, stepping over the images he had already read. 'It says that there was a king who dreamed of a kingdom greater than was his due. He became obsessed by the powers of entropy but did not see the limits of his own power, and in his ambition, he sought to make a spindle to gather the threads of time. Three greater kings, one of which never spoke but was wise above all, forbade the upstart to continue his quest. But the upstart would not listen to wisdom and worked until his foolish ambition was almost complete. Their hands forced by the upstart, the three greater kings took his kingdom from him, but being merciful and wise sent his kingdom and all those who served him down into eternal night. Over the empty seats of the upstart's dominion, they set their wardens. Unmakers of being and reapers of the living. And those wardens watch still, and any who come into this place would better slay themselves than take a further step.'

He looked up at Maehekta.

'There is more,' she said. She had moved to where one of the bases of the obelisk met the floor of the avenue. Its side was a hundred metres across, seemingly bare, but as Ahriman moved closer, he could see that countless lines were cut into the surface, so faint that they were like shadows caught in stone. Maehekta was tracing a series of the lines, the tip of her finger hovering a hair's width above the stone. 'These marks were once clearer but something has stripped layers of matter from the surface.'

'An attempt to excise them,' said Ahriman. His eyes were tracing the ghost images now, his thoughts parsing linguistic precedence for meaning.

'I believe that this pattern and this' – Maehekta's finger looped across a section of stone – 'are names. They are repeated twenty-one times in this section alone.'

Ahriman saw it and recognised one of the patterns from the marks on Setekh's frame and possessions.

'One is the mark of the Hyksos,' he said. 'This was their realm. Those that destroyed them must have stripped their name from this place when they placed their warning. The other pattern...'

'Is a title,' said Maehekta. She gestured, and Ahriman traced the ghosts under her fingers. Sounds and inferred meanings flicked across his mind as he parsed the symbols, looking for a root to latch on to. 'All translations are imperfect, but the closest I can make it would be Osorkon – a bearer of the Black Disc.'

Ahriman heard the word, his mind matching the sounds to the symbols he saw. He looked up, thinking that for the first time since they had entered the underworld of the Hyksos, he had heard an echo, far away and dim, like an inhaled rasp of laughter. Setekh was watching them, limbs hanging loose in the woven cradle of force. The green glow of its eyes was steady.

'Your kind were not lost to a great war with an ancient enemy,' he said to Setekh. 'It was your own kind.'

'As you know, Ahriman of the Thousand Sons, Lord of Exiles, nothing is as simple as our enemies would like others to believe. The truth is also immaterial. We are gone. This is our tomb.'

Ahriman turned from Setekh and made for where the steps rose up to the top of the ziggurat.

This is a court of the dead, thought Ahriman as he stepped into the chamber at the summit. Pillars rose from the floor. Spurs of dark stone arched beneath a ceiling like ribs supporting the inside of a chest. Clouded crystals sat at the points where the arches met. Incised marks covered everything, circles and lines running down walls and across the floor. They reminded Ahriman of blood grooves cut into a slaughter table. Dust lay heavy everywhere, a choking, granular shroud that barely stirred as Ahriman stepped. The dulling pressure in his head was increasing. The flow of the warp was now little more than a trickle into his thoughts.

Twin rows of hexagonal crystals ran down either side of the chamber, and at the far end, there was a cube of a green-black substance, twelve metres to a side. No dust clung to its surface. Its mirror-smooth front reflected the pinpricks of Ahriman's eye-lenses as he looked towards it. He felt Ignis halt at the threshold of the door. Setekh was beside him. Maehekta had remained outside the chamber; for what he needed to do, he needed his tie to the warp to be as strong as possible.

+No doors,+ sent Ignis. +No locks or defences.+

Ahriman looked around.

Setekh was already looking back at him.

'You stand where you wished to stand, Ahriman, in the heart of a kingdom made before your kind could strike fire or raise a wall of mud.'

'And you have what you sought, Setekh of the Hyksos. You look on the works of your kind, and the dust that is all that remains of your pride.'

The sliver of will passed from his mind to Ignis as the last word left his lips. Ignis turned, fist running with blue fire in the instant before it slammed down. Ahriman felt and heard the thunder crack of will in his brother's mind. Setekh's gaze flared briefly as Ignis' fingers crushed its torso. A static-filled rasp was the last sound to come from the xenos, an electric death rattle of laughter. Blue fire flared across its remains, as Ignis poured the fury of his will onto them. They glowed, flaring white and then crumbling. Ahriman felt Ignis' mind pull back into the orbit of calm, aching with effort in the thin ether.

+Without it, how will you find what we seek?+ It was Kiu, his voice distant, but his senses attuned to all the Thousand Sons in the throne room. He was seeing what Ahriman and the rest were, hearing what they heard. +This is just ruins. If there is anything of the devices they made, there is no sign of them.+

+What of the xenos remains we found near the entrance and in these caves?+ sent Ignis. +They were positioned as guardians. Whether literal warriors or grave sentinels, they were placed there to watch over something.+

+There are always corpses in tombs.+ Dismissal laced Kiu's

sending. +If this is the heart of an alien empire then its works have gone the same way as its dominion.+

+What of the structures placed in this underworld? They have not decayed. They have a function. Something must have maintained them,+ sent Ignis.

+There is nothing here,+ replied Kiu.

+Then why place the guardians over it?+

+Ritual significance. An insult to an enemy destroyed. If what the pictographs say is truth, then the Hyksos were traitors to their kind. Death is not punishment enough. The earth must be salted, and markers raised as a message to others. Like us... Like when the Wolves came to Prospero.+

+History has a pattern,+ sent Ahriman. He had stopped to look at a crystal worked into the wall. It was vibrating slightly, almost below the level of feeling. +No matter the gulfs of time or species, the ways of punishment and betrayal are the same for those that dare what others will not.+

+You sound as though you admire them,+ sent Gilgamos.

Ahriman placed his hand on the crystal, stilled his breath and muscles so that he could feel the tremble run up his fingers.

+I admire the depth of their insight. They went further than we can likely understand. At least in their domains of knowledge.+

+And now they are gone, and the secrets their own kind punished them for with them.+

Ahriman stood. +They are not gone,+ he sent. +They are here. Right here where we stand and the secrets of time with them.+

Ahriman could hear the distant whisper of Kiu's annoyance; the thinness of the warp here was grating on his nerves.

+There is nothing but cold stone. I can feel the passages and chambers leading off here. They are just as this one. I can sense no veils in the warp. If something is here, then what is hiding it?+

He does not see, thought Ahriman. He thought of his pupil

and friend, his mind as quick as the wind off the sea, but now that insight and intellect had turned inwards. See too clearly and you will grow deaf.

Knowledge is power, but only if you have the will to not let it make you weak.

+The rest of this xenos breed did not destroy the Hyksos. Perhaps they could not. Perhaps they did not want to. Perhaps they wanted to give them a chance to repent. They feared them though, so they made them a prison.+

+Where?+ asked Kiu.

+Here,+ Ahriman replied, and drew his hand through the air. +The prison is here, one sliver of time out of sync with the rest of reality.+

He closed his eyes for a moment and shifted his perception.

+Look,+ he sent, and opened his eyes for his brothers to see. For an instant they all saw two spaces. In one, the centre of the chamber was empty. In the other sat a black cube.

+You knew of this?+ asked Gilgamos, his thought-voice distant as it came from the surface.

+What is that?+ asked Kiu.

+A keyhole,+ sent Ahriman.

Ahriman looked at Ignis and gave a nod, then walked towards the cube. The light glowing at the top of his staff dimmed as he went closer. There was a shape within, dim at first, a shadow of an object drowned under green water. He stopped a hand's reach from the surface. There were shapes there, down in the crystalline depths…

Ahriman looked back.

I have come this far, he thought. +Give me your strength, brothers,+ he willed. Along the chain of sorcerers stretched through the underworld, his will passed, leaping from mind to mind, up and out onto the surface.

There, Gilgamos heard it and was ready. His mind reached up into orbit. In the ships, the chieftains of the beast-bred and the leaders of the countless cults heard the will of their master and threw their souls out to be caught by the waiting net of incantations. The light of their lives poured into the ether and twisted, following the line of will down to the surface of the dead world, an invisible lightning bolt following the cord of a kite thrown into a storm. From mind to mind it passed, until it reached Ahriman.

He felt it fill him, felt the storm surge flood his skull, felt the limits of the possible recede to a horizon. Ghost-fire wreathed him. His mind was climbing to the pinnacle, the future he had reached for coming closer by the tread of seconds. He raised his hand. The tips of the fingers glowed. Light pushed through the crystal. Ahriman's mind was a prism, pulling power and thought into a single beam. The crystal flickered. Its inner and outer dimensions reversing, its colour blinking between dark-ness and opacity. And now it was not in front of Ahriman but all around him and he–

Silvanus tried to shut his eyes. He could not. He had frozen. A circle of blue-green light spun from where the mask had fallen, growing wider and wider, blurring like a coin tossed onto a tabletop. Space unfolded behind and inside it, coiling back so that it was now not a disc, but a hole bored through reality, a tunnel into the beyond. For a second, nothing moved. No sound stirred the silence. Then the dancers burst from the opening with a shower of light and shrieks of sorrow.

Silvanus realised he could not hear his own breath. Mist billowed from the tunnel mouth. Colour blurred through the mist. He saw a lithe figure clad in tatters of red and white, black tears running down its face. Then another, spun in rainbow;

and then another, whose cloak billowed into a gale of red and gold diamonds as it landed. The three figures crouched, covering their eyes, or mouth or ears. They looked as terrified as Silvanus felt. On the edge of the chamber, eyes wide, body frozen, he watched. He had no choice. He was the audience for this moment. Something else was coming, he knew it. He wanted to run. He wanted not to be there, not to see what was going to come from the glowing portal. Silvanus thought he saw a shadow in the mist. He felt his lips tremble. Down in the pit of his mind he was remembering – no, feeling – pieces of old stories that had scarred him as a child: the hollow dog seen under the moon; the tall man who walks from the snow with red hands and bullet-hole eyes; the shape rising from deep water beneath a calm sea.

The fourth dancer stepped from the portal.

It did not run, though there was the promise of speed in every fraction of its step. It was wrapped in black, diamonds of colour bleeding from its edges; tall, a blade given life, its face a mask without emotion or pity, two horns rising from its brow under a black cowl. Hollowness… emptiness… the pity of a razor. It stepped into the ship and then went to the door, which blew into shards at its touch. The three other dancers rose from their places in a bound. Colour and noise howled through the chamber, and they were gone, tumbling in the wake of the solitary figure. More dancers came from the tunnel mouth, a leaping cascade of blurred limbs and leering masks. Silvanus clutched himself, trying to shrink into the wall, to melt out of notice.

A figure landed in front of him and cocked its head like a dog. Its eyes were black stars in a red-and-white sorrow.

'Please…' managed Silvanus. The figure laughed, flipped backwards, pistol rising, and shot him before he saw it land.

* * *

Reality folded. Ahriman's eyes, which had seen the impossible many times over, could not process it.

Light and dark spindling together. Matter foaming. Dimensions flexing like light over the surface of a bubble. Then a line drawn across everything. Beyond colour. A shiver of sensation across his arms. Blackness, spiralling, like a jug full of darkness and stars, swirling as it filled and drained. Migraine blur. Colours pushed past the chromatic scale.

Then nothing.

Then standing on the floor of a chamber. He could feel it beneath his hands and feet. He had fallen to a crouch. He made his body move, made it stand. He swayed. The Great Ocean of the warp was a distant point of light, the way that the sun could become a pinprick of light when seen from the bottom of a deep well. Enough... just enough of a connection. His skin shivered. The glow of the helm display became a cloud of orange static, then cut out. Blind – he was blind or as good as, and he was alone. He could not use his mind to sense or see his way here. The gauntlets released from his hands. The air that touched the bare skin beneath was cold. Very cold, as though it had sat still and unstirred, molecules slowing to the slowest of tumbles, all energy bled out. He reached out and began to feel his way. One step, two, muscles heavy as he moved.

His hand touched a solid surface. He ran his fingers along it. A wall... cut with channels, linking and diverging. No damage. Hard, clean edges. No warmth. Images formed in his mind from the touch, like sound picked up by a needle from grooves in a phonographic cylinder. He saw vast shapes rising to the cold stars: dark, shaped stone, draped in the tide of night – a city rising out of dream, inhuman. Figures on streets, their movements like the slice of shears and the click of cogs counting down time. He let the impressions recede to shadow and moved forwards. The sound of steps clacked and faded into the distance. He could feel silence and emptiness arching over and around him. It was very cold. The death of stars cold. He was just about to take another step when he stumbled, half falling to one knee. His flesh was shivering inside his armour. His limbs felt numb.

This is what it is to drown, he thought. Or to be a fish pulled from the water into air, gasping for the ocean that was life. He reached out a hand again, but this time it found only emptiness. There had been a wall to his right, but it was not there now. He became still, slowing everything unnecessary while he thought. He did not have long, less time even than he had thought. This was a fold space, a pocket dimension or series of dimensions. Just there, next to him, Ignis would be standing in the chamber at the top of the ziggurat. It was not done by the power of the warp, it simply was – a violation of both etheric and material truth. Depthless... lightless... like the image of the abyss where the ancients had thought fallen gods were chained. He could feel heat leaching from his flesh. The helm display was fuzzed with static, icons fading. The armour's power system was draining even as he looked at its read-out. He did not have long before it would become a dead weight, then a tomb for the freezing flesh within. Light, he needed light. His fingers felt heavy as he reached for the phosphor flare on his waist. It ignited into white light, fizzing as it burned. It began to dim at once, shrinking from brilliance to a low, sullen glow, like a candle struggling to burn without air.

There were... pillars on the edge of sight, curving up, and spaces beyond them sketched in deeper dark.

Ahriman moved forwards. The tip of his staff scratched on the stone floor with each step – marking a path back... but where was that? The light withered as it touched the edges of objects that resembled plinths and arches without doors. His armour was getting colder, the flesh within too. The thread of will leading back drew taut, thinning the further he went. He stood on what must have been a wide platform, its surface glass smooth, but holding no reflection. The shadows of what might be vast buttresses curved overhead, but there were no walls that he could see. Just the dark, draining his sight away to infinity. It felt like vertigo, every direction a drop down into an abyss without end. This was not just a cavern: it was a world under the world. He knew then that he could walk and walk and never find the edge.

His armour chimed a warning: power at critical levels. The alarm burbled to quiet. Ahriman focused his will and took another step.

A faint sound, like something sharp and heavy dragging over stone, came from somewhere in the distance. Ahriman paused, waited, looking in the direction that the sound might have come from. It did not return. He turned.

A wide hole lay at his feet, plunging down into nothing. It had not been there before.

Carefully he knelt, muscles trembling. The light of the fading flare did not reach down far enough to show anything but the smooth walls of the shaft. He held the light out above the drop, then let go. It fell, dimming the deeper it went, until...

It landed. Ahriman looked, blinking the helm display to zoom even as it fuzzed. There was... something. Not one shape but an impression of several things, like lengths of chain tangled in tar. The power warning on his armour chimed again. He reached down and took the scarab Silvanus had used from his belt. The golden lines on its back gleamed in the glow of his eye-lenses. He looked back at the fading light of the flare then threw the scarab down. He watched it fall, until the flare went out and the dark wrapped him again. The helm display shimmered then vanished. He did not move. Then a sound came up out of the pit. A rattling, like a chain clattering over a turning cog, growing and multiplying. Something was rising up, accelerating, the metallic rattle of it now deafening. There was light too, grey light that found only edges, pulsing, flexing the impressions of pillars and arches so that depth and distance flickered.

He jerked back.

Then it was there, in front of him. Scythe legs gripped the stone floor. Tentacles unfolded. A shape loomed above. A figure of dark metal, the lines of its frame blade thin. Spider legs and tentacles hung beneath its torso. It moved with a stutter, like the teeth of a cog wheel jumping as it unravelled into being.

CHAPTER XIV

$\mathcal{P}$HAERON

The figure turned a single, blue eye on Ahriman. It sat upon a throne, a great crest rising from its shoulders. Sigils covered it and the rest of its body. A few of the marks glowed dimly. A golden crown topped the staff in its hand. A sphere of dull blue energy rotated between the crown's prongs. A sound like the rasping of data through a failing vox-horn came from it. Ahriman shook his head, then spoke.

'I have met your kind before. If I speak, you will be able to reconstruct my language.' The figure's blue eye pulsed. Another rattling hiss, but this time there were the ghosts of phonic tones in the noise. 'Can you understand me yet?'

The figure on the throne shifted, its movements stiff.

'I…' The word emerged from a swell of static. 'I… understand. Who are you that comes to our realm?'

'This is a pocket dimension,' said Ahriman, ignoring the question. 'It is a space outside the continuity of other space.'

'You have intelligence.' A cackle of electrostatic laughter. 'It was inevitable that whoever found us would have the rudiments of intellect. Enough to understand the scope of what we created, even if they lacked the ability to comprehend it fully.' The xenos' head swayed, as though trying to imitate the shake of a human head. To Ahriman it looked more like the movement of a snake before it struck. 'Cattle species, things of sludge and mud, cobbled together from imperfect materials, self-replicating... like...' The alien's head dropped. The light in its eye pulsed and dimmed. 'Mould... growing... stars... the light of...'

Ahriman felt the cold dark press close. Heat was draining from him. His nerves and neurons would be firing more slowly. The xenos continued, as though to itself.

'A long age, an age beyond age since there was any other awake, and now the first creature to come before me is a lesser thing. Fragile in its flesh, fearing the things it cannot undo about its nature...' It looked at Ahriman and the blue light in its cyclopean eye was a hard point. 'You came for our secrets, thinking they could heal your flaws.'

Ahriman did not reply but waited.

'I can see it in you,' said the xenos. 'It is there in the micro-detail of your words and thought. We were not so different to you once. We feared death. Feared it more than we valued anything we could find in the living world. We sought to conquer it.' The xenos raised a long finger and tapped the matter of its chest, then gestured up at the space around them. Blue light glowed from the edges of pillars before fading. In the brief light Ahriman saw figures, curled into niches or kneeling on the floor as though they had shut down while abasing themselves. 'This was our victory,' said the xenos. 'Not life, just continuance. We did not see that our enemy was not the frailty of our bodies. It was the enemy that harvests and eats all. The true enemy of existence.'

'Time,' said Ahriman.

'Just so. What is death but a consequence of the flow of time? What is frailty but a substance's inability to endure time's touch? Death lies not in life, or matter, but in time.'

'And, like death, you sought to conquer it,' said Ahriman.

'Conquer...' said the xenos, its voice rasping with an electro buzz which Ahriman realised was laughter. 'Conquer, no. Such an enemy does not deserve to be conquered. It must be shackled and made to abase itself.' The xenos was moving away now, and in the shadow its shape seemed to shrink so that its back appeared bent, its cloak rattling as it dragged over the stone floor. It moved its head, looking up into the infinity of silent darkness around it. 'Are we not the masters of all existence in our kingdom?' Ahriman thought of stories of Old Terra, of kings and queens alone in enchanted palaces, their kingdoms falling around them and only the echoes of their memories as courtiers.

'But you are here,' said Ahriman, 'and your realm is dead and buried.'

The xenos turned, its eye bright for a second.

'Our punishment for daring to seek what others feared. The transference from flesh took many things from us, but it did not take our pride. If our endeavours had succeeded, then what of them, what of the three kings and all their power?' The xenos' head twitched from side to side, like a being at the edge of its days, its body slowly failing along with the mind within. It was not looking at or talking wholly to him. 'The Hyksos would have unwound the Triarchs' power, spun back all that the other dynasties had done and remade our past as it should have been. No kingdom of machines, sleeping and hoping for better, but dominion beyond the limits of time and space. Death not merely overcome but banished. A universe in which there were no enemies that we could not overcome. Eternity as our empire.'

Ahriman swayed. Grey-white fog was spiralling through his awareness. The leaden cold of this place was creeping into him. The strand of connection to reality was becoming thinner, the threads fraying.

'Instead...' began Ahriman.

'Instead, our vision was denied. The Hyksos punished to exist outside of reality. No light nor heat, just the cold decay of atoms in this tomb within a tomb.'

'You...' Ahriman replied, then had to pause. His lips and tongue were numb, sluggish as he formed words. 'They let you remain awake though, and aware, imprisoned with all of your court and power but unable to break free. Starved of power so that your abilities faded...' Ahriman shook his head. 'What must that be like for a creature like you? A mind built on an architecture that makes the lives of other beings just an instant of your existences... All those ages that have passed while you drained the power from all of your subjects until there was just what you are now... a shadow living in darkness, waiting for what?'

'To be free,' said the xenos.

'I can give you that,' said Ahriman.

'You are nothing.'

'You know that is not true. Even in this limited state, you broke down my language and analysed my reaction. Without me telling you, you know what I want and that I can do what I promise in exchange.'

The xenos tilted its head, the gesture almost human.

'You are brilliant, for your kind. A rare mind, with knowledge and insight beyond what many of my kind would have thought could grow from the sludge soup of matter.' The xenos shifted and came closer. It was tall but its back bent over, and its movements jerked and dragged. Ahriman noticed that not all its fingers could open as it reached out and touched his faceplate. 'Brilliant but limited. You have succeeded in entering this prison, but you cannot leave with what you look for. You cannot leave at all. This flesh shell of yours is failing. You are dying even as you stand before me. You have a connection to the anathema realm, and by manipulating that connection you think you can break open this prison, or flee once you have what you seek.' It dropped its hand. 'It cannot be done, and I cannot tell you of or give you the treasure you would steal from us.'

Ahriman could feel his mind fading. Could feel the sensation of hands and limbs become separate, distant.

'Why?' he managed to say. His legs were buckling. The cold reality of the place was unravelling him, draining him, and the thread of light was not enough.

'Because the great work of the Hyksos Dynasty is not here, and it is not in my authority to give it in exchange for my freedom even if I wished it.'

Ahriman felt his flesh begin to shake. He could see it now, could see what he had not seen before – the mistake, the great mistake that had led him here…

'You are their king, their ruler…' he said.

'No,' said the alien. 'No… I am a servant, a most loyal servant who served to the utmost of their ability. When the other dynasties of our race turned on us, they condemned us. They locked us away to wither and our master with them. This was supposed to be our phaeron's torment, watching himself and his realm wither until at the last, when the other dynasties had won the war with the Great Enemy, they would release him and bring him amongst them, broken and humbled. But for all their power they were deceived. One of our phaeron's most trusted advisers and servants took on his semblance, and so let him slip free of his prison before it shut. Our king wrapped himself in sleep until our enemies retreated or died. He knew a time would come that someone who wanted to steal our work from us would find him, someone with the strength to overcome the guardians our enemies set to stop our prison opening... And found him you did. I can see his sigil on you, threaded through the surface layer of molecules on that shell over your flesh. He brought you here and now he will claim his throne again.'

Ahriman felt his legs give way. Grey and black spiralled through his sight. Warning runes lit in his eyes, fuzzing a last red warning: power failure, vital signs critical... His body was trying to shut down, trying to pull him into the protective embrace of a sus-an coma. The last thread to the warp snapped. The light of the xenos' eye was the blue of cold stars shining in a lifeless void.

'Who... are... you?' Ahriman forced out, though in his unravelling thoughts he knew the answer and could see.

'I am Osorkon. I am cryptek and herald to the phaeron of the Hyksos, who is and shall be the Eater of Time. I have waited here long, I and these other subjects. Our King Setekh, Bearer of the Black Disc, is come again.'

The scarab swarm rebuilt their master. They did it silently, and without anything becoming aware of what they were doing. The phaeron had dissolved into micro-particles when Ignis had struck him. It had been a powerful blow, but the matter of his being had settled across the chamber, mingling with the dust. The scarab swarm, which had followed him, had begun to find and gather the dust of his body tighter as soon as their motes fell. Together they formed a grey, powdered sheet, chromatically matched to the stone of the floor. Inside that layer of dust Setekh rebuilt himself. Information pathways formed inside the dust, multiplying in complexity as his intelligence regrew. The scarabs began to reconstruct his body.

He would not take the form he had before. That had been merely a costume, a cloak to hide his nature. When he rose now, it would be in the shape of the phaeron of the Hyksos. He would have to act quickly.

Ignis was still where he stood by the door. A light patina of ice crystals had formed on his armour. His Rubricae slaves were with him. The guns of the automaton, Credence, panned slowly from side to side, but its sensors were too simple to detect what was happening.

Setekh commanded and the swarm units obeyed. Slowly, his form cohered. The sheet of dust on the floor rippled. Concentric rings formed, then re-formed. Particles began to run together, cohering into shape and substance. A figure rose from the floor.

Ahriman felt the instinct to breathe. He fought to stand but could not. The cryptek was hunched over him.

'My lord and phaeron came here with you,' rasped Osorkon. 'But you never realised that it was you that overcame those who would stop him. You breached the outer doors so that he could turn the final key and reclaim his kingdom. What dream or hope brought you here has failed. You are too weak to know that only with the patience of eternity can you have true power and victory. We have waited so long... and now your short wait for death is over.'

The darkness was crushing Ahriman down and down. He was sliding away from the world. The xenos' gaze was a cold blue light vanishing above. Down and down, always down, down to the silence and quiet.

Falling...

Down to the darkness of a cave without entrance and exit.

The dark hole within...

No sanctuary now, but the last place his mind could cling on to.

He could hear his thoughts quietening.

Water dripped from the stalactites into the pool. Ripples and echoes…
Last thoughts…

'Ahriman.' He heard the voice, sudden and clear, echoing. It was familiar, so familiar, but he did not recognise it. He tried to turn, to look, but his surroundings had become thin and grainy, sand running through his fingers. His thoughts were slow and would only form one after another.

'Who are you?' he called in his thoughts.

'A question that you know the answer to but cannot see.'

'Another mind… No thought projection could reach in here.'

'I am here. With you.'

'Then you are a ghost echo of my subconscious that has…'

'No.'

'Then, you can't be…'

'In time, you will know, but not before. You cannot know.'

'I…'

'There is only one thing you must know in this moment, Ahriman.'
He felt cold, and wanted to say something, but could not.

'It is not over,' said the voice. 'Not yet…'

A thread of light reached down through the dark, a last thread that a sliver of his mind could pull on.

His eyes opened.

The cryptek recoiled. Ahriman's hand lashed out, driven with a last scrap of will and strength that he did not know he had. His fingers punched through its eye into the substance of its skull. It tried to pull back. He closed his hand, muscles driving frozen armour. The alien's skull burst into fragments. Ahriman felt his hearts stop as he threw his mind down the strand of thought that still connected him to reality.

+Ignis!+ he shouted in warning.

* * *

Credence gave an urgent clatter as Ignis heard Ahriman's warning. His eyes snapped open. Something was rising from the floor. Something darker than the surroundings expanded into the space above, its substance granular, billowing like sand churned into water. Ignis felt as though he were falling, then flying, then clinging to the ground beneath him as it became a cliff. And the darkness grew, expanding, sliding across angles that could not exist. It rippled forwards. Cold blue light crackled in spinning murk, writhing. Sounds screamed in his ears, babbling in a cacophony. Symbols and images flashed in the lightning snap. Nerves lit with sensations, a deluge of tactile information. He could not hold on to it, could not process it, but there was meaning in the storm, like a voice slowly resolving out of static. The cyclone of particles divided, grouped, flowing together in a kaleidoscope of matter. It might have lasted a second or an aeon, but it ended as abruptly as it had begun.

The sound vanished. The whirl of granular matter slowed, draining from sight as a shape formed in the murk. A crowned figure stood in front of him, limbs unfolding into the light. It was twice the height of Ignis. A cloak of ragged silver scales hung from its shoulders. A mass of black, segmented coils dangled from its torso in place of its legs. The light sheared from the bones of its form, as though it did not want to touch them. It was an absence, visible by the lighter shadows that framed it, an impression pushed into the world. Gold lines and circles rolled across the shadow of its body, molten fire against depthless night. Its face was gold. Blue eyes burned in its sockets. On its crown rose a crest and circlet holding a black disc ringed by a hairline of gold. It raised its sceptre. Blue lightning flashed through the air, touched the walls. Worn grooves in the stone shone with blue light. The walls were shaking. The black cube at the chamber's centre flexed. Arcs of green energy reached out from the walls and struck the cube. Its dimensions inverted so that it seemed both a solid and a void.

Ignis brought his gun up and fired. Bolts struck the space around the crowned figure. Explosions bulged from the air as burning blisters.

'Kill protocol!' he called. Credence's cannon snapped into line and fired. The beam of darkness speared across the chamber. There was a sound like shearing glass. The beam halted in mid-air, buzzing like a trapped insect. The air around the figure thickened and rippled. The beam bored on, pulsing. Ignis stopped firing. His will snapped a command. Three Terminators came through the door. They fired as they moved, the bolts shrieking as they ignited with warp fire. A rippling wall of dust rose from the floor and swallowed them.

Green energy arced along the walls and floor. The black cube of space was flickering as its dimensions broke into impossible geometry; it was a sphere with straight edges, a polyhedron with only one side, a dot that was a sphere, the sphere a cylinder and the cylinder a flat circle. Ignis felt the ratios and paradox of the shapes begin to erode his reason. He sensed his mind trying to accommodate factors and values that should not be. There was one thing his instincts told him: the cube, what Ahriman had called a keyhole, was opening.

The Rubricae and Terminators were still firing, all of them in a rhythm. Explosions bubbled the air. The beam of darkness from Credence's cannon bored closer to the crowned figure. It had not moved, its attention and energy focused on opening the hidden dimension.

In the back of his mind, Ignis heard the voices of Kiu and Gilgamos.

+The ground is moving...+

+Spatial anomalies...+

+Energy manifestations...+

Then the world changed. The crowned figure flickered. The light in the chamber vanished – fire, energy, all of it gone as though it had never been there. The warp ripped away like ocean water pouring off an island pushing up from the depths of the sea floor.

Then light. Blue, cold, razor sharp.

The walls had gone. They were no longer in a chamber but at the bottom of a tier-sided pit. The floor was a kilometre across. Sharp obelisks jutted out of the walls on the lip of the pit high above. Light was running over the edge of every surface, pouring into etched sigils, and flowing up and up. Spheres and octahedrons detached from the walls and floors and floated into the air. The blue light leapt up, flooding niches where figures stood, heads bowed, hands resting on the hafts of weapons. Ignis stood reeling as the light poured on and out. There was no sign of Kiu's force, which had been on the steps of the ziggurat. Just him and Credence and a circle of Rubricae.

The crowned figure stood before them, looming taller. It looked nothing like the alien he had helped Ahriman interrogate, now. It was shining, blinding at the same time as seeming to eat light. It raised a hand. Silver-and-black spheres rotated above its fingers. It looked at Ignis.

'Kneel,' said Phaeron Setekh.

Invisible weight fell on Ignis with the force of an avalanche. His armour screamed. Servos locked and blew. His muscles tore as he fought to stay upright. The air in his lungs was lead. His hearts thundered as they tried to pump blood through his veins. He knew what was happening, could understand the properties of gravity and mass altering around him. This was no power he had seen in sorcery. It was not of the beyond; it was reality itself made to bend like a child's toy. He could not resist. The warp was flowing back. He could sense it roaring closer like a flood wave after an earthquake, but it was not here. Without it he was just matter, and this exiled and returned king was its master.

A beam of blackness sliced through the air and hit Setekh, dead centre. Credence stamped forwards. The phaeron juddered as the energies of the beam and his form warred. Ignis felt the crushing force ease. Air gasped into his lungs; he began to rise. The returning tide of the warp was there, roaring closer.

Setekh's form twisted towards Credence, hand rising, the spheres orbiting its fingers a blur of silver and black. Rust and decay flowed over Credence's joints and plating as it tumbled through decades in the space of nanoseconds. Credence gave a shattered cry of dying metal.

'No!' shouted Ignis. The tide of the warp broke over his body and mind. Formulae of annihilation flew through his thoughts. Shards of telekinetic force speared at Setekh. The Rubricae snapped into motion, firing. Bolt shells burst around Setekh in a drum-roll inferno. Ignis' mind caught the warp fire as it burst into being and pulled it into a cage of white light. He could sense reality shifting around Setekh, rules breaking and remaking themselves faster than he could perceive. But he did not need to perceive, only to predict. The patterns in his mind altered, blinking through dozens of possibilities in the second of pause between heartbeats. It was like one of the ancient games of Terra in which pieces warred across squares and grids and meshes as the players made moves based on calculations that grew from every possible change of position. The air changed density and temperature as Ignis' will and the alien's manipulation of reality broke existence into an expanding sphere of shattering light. The Rubricae fired again.

A beam of blue energy whipped down from the tiered walls of the pit. Ignis shifted his will and the energy exploded from a dome of force. His eyes jerked up. A creature of blade legs and armour plates was skittering down the steps of the tier. Clusters of blue lights dotted its head, and the barrel of a weapon jutted from under the shell of its carapace. Around it flowed a tide of glowing eyes and legs. Another beam lashed from the creature. Another shriek of lightning as it struck the dome of force around him. He willed, and the Rubricae pivoted and fired up. His focus snapped back onto Setekh, but it was too late. The cage of warp energy surrounding the xenos collapsed.

Setekh came forward in a blur, jumping between instants like a blown pict-feed. There was a blade in the phaeron's hand, its edge a ghost glow, like something both there and not. Ignis raised his fist. Lightning wreathed his fingers. Setekh cut.

And Ignis knew that he could not stop it. All projections reached zero in his mind.

A wall of pale light met the blow. There was a sound like a lightning bolt being yanked back into the sky. Setekh spun around. Ignis' skull pounded with the beating of countless wings. Ahriman stood behind Setekh. The staff in his hand was a line of night. Darkness and blinding light surrounded him in a ragged halo.

Ahriman felt the next beat of his heart begin. He held his gaze and his mind still, a point fixed in the storm, the edge that past and future balanced on. He had slowed all sensation. His mind was a pool of dark water, a mirror to the world. In its surface he saw the image of Setekh: reality cracking around the phaeron like a shroud, the cold arc of its blade, and the hiss as it glided a fraction closer over the stones. Its image pulled at old ideas and archetypes: father of time, the eater of all, the death waiting at the end of the slowing beat of a clock, Chronus, the World Serpent, the hungering dark of a sea under a sky without stars or moon.

'Their shadows became the ideas that our minds turned into gods and dreams,' Maehekta had said. *'It is no wonder they seem familiar. Before the galaxy made its own nightmares, these were the horrors that stalked the living.'*

Ahriman felt the immediate future expand in front of his mind's eye. He chose how the next moments would unfold.

And his choice exploded into being.

Figures with long-hafted weapons stepped from niches on the tiers above. He felt Ignis' will command to the Rubricae. Volleys of bolt shells sliced up the tiers. Fire burst. Metal creatures melted. A beam of green light lanced down, struck a Rubricae. Layers of armour crumbled into ash. The Rubricae reeled. The ghost-light seeped from the breach in its chest, reknitting ceramite as the green energy stripped it away. The Rubricae raised its bolter and fired back. Another arc of pink-and-blue fire blossom unfolded through the xenos creatures. There were too many, though. Beyond the rim of the pit, he could see flashes of cold light and hear a rolling rattle as more of the dormant aliens woke. A tide of insectoid creatures surged down towards them. The figures with the long-hafted weapons were moving to Setekh's side.

Ahriman split his will. The stone floor around him shattered. Shards exploded up. His mind caught them and flung them out. They met the enemy in a blizzard of black needles. They punched through. Ahriman's mind caught the fragments from the impact and threw them up into the creatures behind.

Setekh flew forwards, space and time skipping. The phaeron's blade sheared the light into jagged spectrums as it cut.

Black lightning arced from Ahriman to Setekh. It vanished into nothing. Setekh was within a blade swing. A wall of tele-kinetic force snapped into being to meet the blow. Reality around Ahriman and Setekh came apart. Space broke into blocks that split and split, as though it were a pixelating pict image.

Ahriman was pouring matter into reality from the warp as fast as Setekh's technology broke it down. Cubes of flame tumbled like snowflakes. Energy beams became smoke.

In the mirror of his mind's eye, Ahriman saw patterns rippling through the fragmenting chaos: fractal motifs, wave patterns, the imprints of two minds – one bound to mechanical reality, the other soaring in the tides of dreams. Through it, the face and blade of Setekh slid closer, nanosecond by crumbling nanosecond.

He would not be able to stop the blade; of that he was certain. Ahriman gripped his staff and threw his mind into the warp. His body dissolved into a cloud of beating feathers and silver claws. The blade passed through it as the unkindness of ravens spiralled up. Setekh raised a hand. The spheres of silver and black spun to a blur, and… time was remade.

Setekh flew forwards, space and time skipping. The phaeron's blade sheared the light into jagged spectrums as it cut. Black lightning unfolded from Ahriman's hand towards Setekh. The fork of energy vanished. Ahriman felt the strand of will yanked into another space. Setekh was within a blade swing. He rammed a wall of will into being between him and the xenos. Setekh raised a hand. The spheres of silver and black above his fingertips spun to a blur, and… time was remade.

Ahriman gripped his staff and threw his mind into the warp. His body dissolved into a cloud of beating feathers and silver claws just before the blade could cut him. Setekh raised a hand. The spheres of silver and black above his fingertips spun to a blur, and… time was remade.

Setekh flew forwards, space and time skipping. The phaeron's blade sheared the light into jagged spectrums as it cut. It was there, flickering between being and not. Just as it had been each of the times before.

Ahriman watched it all happen again. From where half of his

mind was in the warp, he had seen each of the earlier times the clash had occurred. He had seen Setekh come closer each time. He had seen the flaw in the xenos' movement. Now it was time to change the end of the sequence.

Setekh cut.

And Ahriman rammed the bladed tip of his staff into Setekh's chest. Ahriman focused for an instant, and the xenos exploded in a burst of black flame.

CHAPTER XV

ᴅEATHLESS ᴅANCE

On the *Hekaton*, the dancers of *The Falling Moon* slid from the portal they had opened in the Navigator's tower and down into the main mass of the ship. No one saw them. The Thousand Sons' attention was fixed on the planet below. They felt nothing. They noticed nothing. And in that absence, the players moved into place.

Those outside of the aeldari who had heard of the Harlequins knew them for their way of war: draped in colour and slaughter, dazzling, a raucous expression of murder and laughter. It was true, but like most ideas it was limited. Their truth was that story was war. And in story and in art, absence defined meaning. The absence of a sound coming from the mouth of a human crewman, as a monofilament wire punched through his skin and unfurled inside his body. The absence of colour as the dancers' holo-projectors folded the light to shadow. The space left by the minds of the Thousand Sons as they focused on the world they orbited. All these things were blank spaces waiting for the brushstroke to give them colour and shape. The darkened stage, still unlit after the curtain raised…

In the guts of the ship, Draillita, Mistress of Mimes, now Dreamer's Truth, peeled back the metal covering the plasma conduit. Pipes and machines cramped the space around her. She had to crouch, her red-and-white cloak coiling around her in shades of grey as she took the Vessel of the Sun's Fury to the conduit. She bowed her head in sorrow as she armed the device with a touch.

Iyshak, Master of Players, now the Murderer's Jest, reached the great domed junction of sealed passageways. He crouched beside the tunnel mouth just beneath where the dome began to climb. It was crystal, etched with symbols. His soul could feel the ache of those images. His mask shifted to a grin of mockery. So much knowledge. So much protection. So little of it meaning anything. The gold and red of his motley blended with the gilding coating the walls and pillar tops. Below, he could see the suits of armour that were the spirit prisons for the Thousand Sons. There were nine of them, each placed at the edge of the junction. A lone living soul stood at the junction's centre. The floor was polished obsidian, a black mirror. Doors sealed the passages off the junction. Each was a slab of metal and stone. More marks covered them. From here you could move to all the truly vital parts of the ship. From here you could tear her heart out.

The mask of his face grinned. The edges of its mouth were sharp points. Murderer's Jest raised his hands. Tiny flecks of red spiralled from the gesture then faded. When he lowered his hands, they held a sphere, balanced on a fingertip. White light and mist swirled within. He reached out into the air above the long drop to the floor beneath the dome.

* * *

Yrlla, Shadowseer, now the Voice of Many Ends, cut the last of the locks and pushed the door wide. Air rushed past, whipping Yrlla's sashes. The void looked back at the Shadowseer. Stars slid across the mirror mask as they turned to look down the length of the warship. Their sisters and cousins gleamed as brighter stars against the firmament. The planet sat beyond the prow, grey and cold, a smudge against the dark as though its face refused the light falling on it.

Yrlla listened to the nothingness, then sprang out into the void, caught the spear of an aerial mast, whirled around it, and finished at its tip. The Shadowseer's mind was a mirror to the currents of the warp flowing past, letting them slide under the awareness of the Thousand Sons. That mask would now have to change. There were already currents and patterns of power at play in the warp, great and terrible acts of sorcery that Yrlla could not undo or rival. That did not matter, though. The nature of a jest was not to dominate but to subvert: to make power seem foolish, strength clumsiness, majesty hubris.

Yrlla's mind slid out into the flow and whirl and surge. The minds and workings of the Thousand Sons rose like burning islands from the tide. Such arrogance. In the gaps and openings between them, Yrlla unfolded veils of meaning. Each one sent a shiver through the Shadowseer. This was the end of the first act of the cycle of *The Falling Moon*, the time when new enemies entered, when pieces of the past died, and blood and ash lay on the ground. It was not an ending. It could not be. Within the mythic cycles there were great meanings, greater than even the minds of the aeldari could hold clear; the wisdom- and sorrow-taught lessons of gods: once begun, you had to play a tragedy to the end.

+Harken,+ sent Yrlla, +the song rises.+ And the players heard, and readied for the last dance of the act to begin.

* * *

The charge Draillita had placed on the plasma conduit detonated. If anyone had been watching and able to perceive what was happening, they would have seen the first stage of detonation as a blink of white light. Bright enough to blind, it strobed for a second as it ate itself, then annihilated the casing of the conduit. Then the plasma roared out. The blast ripped down the conduit. Billowing, indigo energy ripped through the decks. Plating crumpled. Metal became slag. The already damaged *Hekaton* groaned. Sections of lighting and shielding failed. The blast wave roared on, hit hatches in the outer hull and blew them out in a spray of liquid steel.

Iyshak tipped the sphere from his finger. He drew his swords and pushed off the wall. The sphere began to fall. Iyshak tumbled after it. The Thousand Sons sorcerer standing at the centre of the space below looked up. The sphere shattered into a ball of lightning and a swirl of mist. The sorcerer raised his hand, light gathering in his palm. Iyshak's sword struck the sorcerer's elbow and sliced through in a flare of lightning. Blood fell like shattered rubies.

The sorcerer was fast. A stave lashed at Iyshak as he touched the floor. He kicked up, somersaulting over the blow as his coat and motley rippled into red and gold. He was above the sorcerer, grinning down at it as his paired swords scissored through its neck. More blood, spraying in an arc as the Murderer's Jest landed on the floor a second before the armoured body collapsed.

The cloud of light and mist that had burst from the dropped sphere froze. The head and weapons of the Rubricae juddered as they turned towards Iyshak. He cocked his head and sprang towards them. Behind him, the frozen sphere of lightning became a tunnel in the air. Iyshak's laughter was the sound of thunder as figures of broken light spun from the tunnel mouth.

* * *

Yrlla heard Iyshak's laughter and felt the ship creak as the plasma conduit detonated. The Shadowseer's veil poured across the ship. It was an illusion but also a mockery. Anyone or thing looking towards the *Hekaton* would see the ship burning, or firing, or see nothing at all. Those looking out from inside would see enemies firing weapons on them. Even the Thousand Sons' most subtle sorcerers would find their sight filled with ghosts and shredded nightmares. It was a grand working, one that the Shadowseer could not have woven without using the power of the Thousand Sons themselves. Their sorcery permeated everything around them. The Shadowseer's veil did not challenge that or break it, but simply subverted it: sliding into the gaps at the edge of the eye, pulling the tattered warp into new shapes, billowing like pieces of bright cloth caught in a gale.

Aboard the *Soul Jackal*, one of the deck acolytes looked into the crystal sphere of its scrying device and saw ships closing fast, guns lighting. A cry went up from the augur-slaves. Machines and scanners screamed warning. Who was the enemy? How had they got so close? There was no time to find answers. The *Soul Jackal* fired. Macro shells shrieked across the void. Some exploded in empty vacuum, but part of the volley struck the *Hermetica* and stripped her shields. The *Hermetica* returned fire. Plasma bombards lashed energy at what looked to its crew like an alien craft of silver. The plasma struck the *Hekaton*. Its shields, syncopating from the damage to one of its main plasma conduits, flared and then crumpled. Plasma burst across her flank. Turrets and buttresses melted and sagged into space.

Through the warp, the Thousand Sons still in orbit called out warnings and questions. Jumbled laughter answered them, while in the guts of the *Hekaton*, the players of *The Falling Moon* danced.

* * *

On the surface of the dead world, Gilgamos felt the ground tremble. Dust shook into the air as triangular structures thrust upwards from the black sand. The sand writhed around the circle of Rubricae and Thousand Sons, then erupted. Clouds of beetle-like bodies rose from the ground, chrome wings buzzing louder than the wind. Green light glowed in their abdomens. They spiralled and flew at the rising obelisks. Emerald lightning arched from the points of each structure. Swarms of chrome bodies flashed to dust, but more followed, churning through the air faster than they vanished. They landed on the sides of the obelisks. Mandibles and energy beams bit into stone. A cloud of the chrome beetles struck the edge of the telekinetic shield above them and exploded into shreds of metal and flame.

They had to remain until Ahriman returned, no matter what. Endure just a little longer, just as they had always done. That is what they had to do. Gilgamos just did not know if they would.

He had been a watcher of the future since the Legion took his memories of being human. He had watched as the horizon of that future had grown closer and closer. He had held his inner eye open as the fire of Pyrodomon burned away foresight. He had seen the present and the future become a dark tunnel to walk through. They called him a soothsayer, but in truth he was now just a sorcerer, and a warrior who did not know if he would live past the next heartbeat.

The ground heaved again, whipping sand into whirlpools in a dry sea. Gilgamos' will snapped out. The guns of the Predator tanks rotated. Weapons on the Osirion Dreadnoughts armed with a whine.

A shape burst from below. It was serpentine, its body as thick as a tank. Chrome plates covered its back. Thousands of blade legs covered its underside. A green light burned at its head as it spooled into the air from the ground. It arched then whipped down towards the Thousand Sons. The creature's mouth struck the telekinetic dome. Red and golden sparks showered out. Its legs scratched across the invisible barrier. The guns of the Predators fired. Las-blasts struck it, shearing away legs and pieces of carapace.

Gilgamos sent another pulse of will out, and the circles of Rubricae and Terminators fired. Bolts and missiles converged, enclosing the creature in rippling fire. It twisted, portions of its body dissolving in blue-and-pink fire. Then he felt something release in the warp, like a plug pulled out of a basin of water. The creature vanished. In the eyes of the Thousand Sons, it ceased to be. The dome collapsed, sucked out of existence. The creature folded back into being and crashed down, its bulk slamming into the Rubricae. One of them twisted under it, the shell of the warrior's armour cracked, glowing dust pouring out. Razor mandibles sliced down and wrenched the Rubricae up into the air. Green light pulsed in the creature's jaws. The Rubricae spun over and over as webs of virescent energy unpicked its armour. The rest of the force was firing. Lightning and rays of fire poured from the staffs and hands of the sorcerers. The energy vanished as it met the creature, draining into nowhere.

Above and around them the constructs were swarming over the pillars and obelisks as they pushed from the ground. Arches of lightning whipped through the billowing dust. Gilgamos felt the flow of the warp break around him. It was like being caught in a riptide. It was not just the centipede creature. The planet and everything on and in it were pushing the currents of the Great Ocean aside, like an island rising from the depths of the sea, its mountains sending bow waves out, its bulk breaking tides and creating whirlpools. He felt his mind spin and tumble over and over as he held on to the thread of thought and power linking him to his brothers.

The centipede creature reared up. Explosions splashed against its carapace. Behind it the sand rippled. Concentric rings formed for a moment then collapsed inwards. Three more creatures burst through the dusty surface, swaying as they pushed into the air. They coiled down onto the ground, blade legs a blur as they ran towards the lines of Thousand Sons. Gilgamos looked at them, then reached out with his mind. His thoughts touched the Osirion. He felt the dry echo of the twice-dead warriors encased in their enchanted sarcophagi. The hiss of their souls was ice cold.

+Hear my will,+ he sent.

Of all the entombed Thousand Sons, the souls caught in the Dreadnought shells burned hottest, their anger glowing embers. The Rubric had stripped away everything but the pain of their first deaths, granting them an eternity of suffering. Gilgamos' command set that pain free.

The Dreadnoughts charged. Piston-driven legs shook the ground. The centipedes twisted to meet them. Beams of green energy and spears of plasma reached across the closing gap. Two beams of light converged on the lead Dreadnought. Armour flaked to powder. The machine powered on, its skin crumbling from it as it charged the xenos. It pulled back its fist. A centipede creature reared, mandibles and blade legs tensing. The Dreadnought slammed into it. Its fist rammed up into the creature's core. Chisel fingers slammed closed. Silvered metal crumpled with a scream. Inside its sarcophagus the soul of the twice-dead legionary roared at the reality it loathed. Pistons bunched. The fist ripped back. The centipede writhed. The fist rammed into it again. The creature's body whipped around the Dreadnought, constricting. Its needle legs scored across the war machine's sarcophagus. A sphere of cold energy deep in the creature's core activated. A nulling pulse blew through the Dreadnought. The runes and warpcraft binding spirit to metal went slack.

Intent and fury dimmed. Strength drained from pistons. It was only for an instant, but it was enough. The creature squeezed its coils tight around the Dreadnought. Its legs burst through armour. Plates and servos twisted. Alone in the silence of its shattering body, the ghost of a warrior cried out. The dust and light of its memories fell and fell.

Gilgamos felt the echo of those memories: the kick of a bolter in a hand, the glare of light from a main sequence star, the spear of pain and the fall that had begun but never ended. Then blackness.

The centipede creature uncoiled from its kill, pieces of broken armour shaking from its legs as it twisted to face its next target. Twin lines of crimson energy hit the creature and bored into it. Concentric rings formed briefly in the air around the beams. Metal deformed. The second Osirion Dreadnought advanced, piston feet churning sand. It rammed a curved blade of shining gold into the creature. Power flowed from its soul core. The cutting edge glowed white hot. Green energy gushed from the creature. Then the Dreadnought ripped the blade down, through its body and out. The creature flailed and fell.

From the centre of the circle, Gilgamos saw the light of battle flare and linger in the rolling sandstorm. He could just feel the link to Gaumata in the sky above but could not reach down into the tombs where Ahriman had gone. Before him, another chrome monstrosity reared, its body dancing with impacts and explosions. The wind howled and, in his mind, he looked again to the next seconds of future and saw nothing.

CHAPTER XVI

$\mathcal{P}$YRODOMON

Ctesias opened his eyes. He had been falling... Yes... falling after he had jumped from the balcony in the mind-palace. He remembered Helio Isidorus' shouted question following him.

'Who are you?'

The vision in front of him resolved. He was lying on his back. Above him, wooden beams rose to a circular skylight in a vaulted ceiling. Motes of dust drifted in the shaft of light. The breath he drew was cool and dry, and smelt of parchment. He was not out yet. This was still the mindscape. Helio Isidorus' mindscape. How he had arrived at this new part of it was blank, a transition as sharp as the slice of a sickle. A razor flicker and here he was... No way out just by jumping from a high place. He had to find a better way.

He remembered the light in Helio's eyes... burning...

Whatever Helio was, whatever the Second Rubric had done to him, he was changing – had changed already. What did that mean?

If you don't get out, the answer does not matter, he thought.

He pushed himself up. He was in a long and high chamber. Shelves covered the walls, criss-crossed by wrought iron ladders and narrow walkways. Letters and numbers had been incised into the wood of the shelves, index codes for the sorting of books. It was a library. He almost laughed. He had known and kept many libraries. Before Prospero burned, he had been one of the Keepers of the Archives and Scrolls. It was an inconsistency that had always amused him that those who had the title Librarian in the Legion did not actually perform those duties. This library's books, though, were not on the shelves but heaped on the floor, pages splayed like the wings of slaughtered birds. Words marched across the pages between illuminations and gilded symbols.

He moved to a pile of books, squatted down, and picked up one of the volumes. He began to read, stopped, and frowned. He was not sure what he had expected. Reproductions of books that Helio had studied, perhaps: histories, treatises on philosophy or warfare, poetry even. This book was certainly none of those. At a glance, its pages looked like any other of the kind printed by one of the great presses of Uthero or Tun, typeset words stamped clearly on thick paper. The sentences and words made no sense, though. A phrase would complete and the next was nothing to do with what had come before. Some just trailed off. Others were just words, filling columns like bits of broken rubble poured into the hollow inside a wall.

An axe, its head a chest-wide span of black iron, its cutting edge curved like a skull's smile. I cannot remember what it is to breathe; only what it is to drown in an abyss, to sink without hitting the bottom. ...muscles bunched. against metal. I am rising out of the dark. is low. I am an outline held in a dream of falling. begins. Where was he? His name, what was his name? wanted to shout, but he was drowning in the blind dark. His name... a ragged drip, drip, drip. started. remained on the iron dais. 'He does not hear either.' There is no turning back. There never was any turning back. '...is just an echo, the sound of a name caught in a bottle.' A sketch in the darkness. Low. A hiss. Where now? Heaped. Hope. They... voices... calling... me... Except... just there on the edge of hearing was another sound, a murmur like a cry caught in a wind.

Voices.

On it went. He turned the page and more filled the next spread, and the next, and those that had come before. None of it fitted together or had a pattern that Ctesias could see, but... there was something to it, a texture, a feeling that built in his head as he took in more of the text. Voices... Yes. It was like hearing voices all speaking at once.

He closed the book. The cover was red leather, and unmarked. No title or author or volume code. He picked up another book. It was the same. Even the illuminations made no sense: figures without faces, creatures that faded into smudges of colour, patterns of symbols that ran off the edge of a margin as though to continue on another page that was not there. He closed that one, too, and looked up at the empty shelves and the piles of books on the floor. A puzzle, that is what this was, a puzzle that was almost unsolvable.

'And, of course, the way out of this place is to solve it...' he said aloud.

'You can solve it?' The voice came from behind Ctesias. He closed his eyes for a moment when he heard it. He had seen no one else when he had looked around, but, of course, *he* was here. He was certain what this library was now, or rather what it represented. Ctesias turned.

'You are Helio Isidorus,' he said. A figure stood beside a pile of half-fallen books. He was old, his robe grey and ragged over bent shoulders. Fine grey hair circled a bald pate. The flesh of the face had pinched over the bones, but the eyes were the same as those of the boy in the boat and the man in the palace.

'That is my name,' said Helio. He had a pile of books clutched in his arms, and his grip shifted as he looked around. 'Do I know you? I feel I should know you.'

'You do, but you do not remember me,' said Ctesias. He gestured at the books. 'This is your library?'

'Mine? I don't think so, or rather I don't know. But I am the only one who has tried to put it back together. No one before you has come here that I can remember. I have been the only one.' He shook his head. 'No one else… and I am old…' He looked around. 'You said you could solve it. If that is so, then you are a most welcome guest.'

'I didn't say that I could solve it. I am not sure even what the problem is to be solved, but I am here to help.' He told the lie and watched for a sign that this version of Helio Isidorus had detected it, but the old man simply shuffled to a table and placed the books he was carrying on top of an already tottering pile.

'Help?' he said and gestured at the drifts of open pages around them. 'I do not need help. I need a solution.'

'What is the problem?' asked Ctesias.

The image of the aged Helio gave a hollow laugh that turned into a hacking cough.

'These.' He gazed at the piles of books. 'Everything without a place. It is all here, but out of place. Sometimes I think I have found a whole volume and then I realise that it is not complete…'

Ctesias noticed the equipment on the table then, the knives, brushes, jars of adhesive and presses, all the tools of the bookbinder's trade. Two volumes lay there, their spines and covers lying beside them, bindings cut, pages laid out and weighted down, words razored from some places and pasted in others. He moved closer and looked at a page that had been sliced into neat ribbons. There were a few complete sentences.

I am Helio Isidorus. I am a brother to warriors and a son of Prospero. I am of the gene-lineage of Magnus the Red. I was of the Circle of the Golden Sun and an initiate into the Tenth Sphere of Mysteries, though the fire of my mind did not burn with the light to let me pass further. I served in the wars that made the Imperium and did the will of the Emperor...

Ctesias nodded to himself and looked at the next page. Only a few lines on this one were complete.

I am Helio Isidorus. I am a creature who has turned on his creator...

Ctesias looked up, and then around at the books – thousands and thousands of books, millions of pages, trillions of words...

'How long have you been trying to remake this library?' he asked.

'How long?' The aged image of Helio looked at him, frowning. 'I do not understand. This is what I have been doing and what I will do. There is nothing else.'

'Word by word, line by line, trying to put a life of hundreds of years back in order one line at a time...' Ctesias laughed, the sound brief and cold. 'That is not a puzzle that I think I have an eternity to spend completing.'

Helio frowned. 'I do not understand what you are saying.'

'This...' Ctesias turned, pointing at the books and walls of empty shelves. 'This is a way of your mind trying to put itself back together. Just like the palace made from stones of the past. These books are your memories, Helio. Jumbled and out of place. You pick up a book, open it and find snatches of memory, some of them so small that they are incomprehensible, others clear and vivid, but none with order, none with context. It is here, all your life is here, but without order, contents or index to make it mean anything.' He let out a breath, closed his eyes and rubbed a hand across the closed lids. 'And you are trying to put it back together from the inside, trying to find individual grains of sand in a desert... And it seems that you have trapped me here with you in that impossible task, because without being able to remember then you are not going to be able to let my mind go. Somehow the Rubric made you powerful, but gave you back your mind with none of the pieces in the right place or a guide to where they should go.' He dropped his hand and opened his eyes. 'That, at a certain level, can only be seen as a type of exceptionally cruel joke.'

The aged Helio looked at him for a long moment, still frowning.

'I do not...' he began, then shook his head. 'Fanciful – what you say does not make sense.'

'No,' said Ctesias. 'No, it does not, but it is true.'

'Then why... why don't I know that already?'

'Because that memory is somewhere in here, broken into words and mixed in with all the rest.'

The image of Helio shook itself and shuffled over to the table of dissected books.

'Then I must keep going.'

'No,' said Ctesias. His eyes had fixed on the page of one of the books that lay on the floor. An idea had just dropped into his thoughts. 'You will never reach the end of that task, and neither will I.' Helio looked around at him. Ctesias bent down and picked up the book and held it out to Helio. The old man hesitated and took it. 'Read it.'

'It is like the others...' Helio blinked at the page. 'Though most of this page is coherent.'

'Who is it about?' asked Ctesias.

Another shake of the head, another blink.

'I don't understand.'

'The problem is that you are the answer, Helio Isidorus. The code that reorders the words and pages in these books, the index that knows where they sit, that is you. The only thing that makes sense of these pieces is that they happened to you.'

'To me?'

'You cannot understand the pieces of your memory from out-side – you have to see that they are yours. Once they are yours, they will have an order, because you will give it to them.'

'How?'

Ctesias smiled. 'Read the words,' he said.

'I already have.'

'Read them aloud.'

The aged Helio blinked, then, with a slight shake of his head, looked down at the open book. He bit his lips, took a breath.

'I am Helio Isidorus…' he began. 'I remember blue. The blue was sky, slashed red by fire. I could smell smoke. There were pyramids on the horizon. Fire leapt from cracks in their sides. The dead were a slick carpet on the ground…'

The words went on. For a second, Ctesias thought he had been wrong. Then the image of the library began to fade from the edge of sight.

'The warrior stood amongst the corpses…'

The light was changing. The shaft of sun that had fallen from the skylight in the ceiling was growing wider. The shadows were rippling to tongues of smoke. They were not standing amongst shelves and books now, but on a floor of cracked tiles.

'The gun in my hands shook with a thunder rhythm…'

Sheets of shattered crystal and brass spars arced above towards the blue dome of a shining sky. There were dead warriors on the ground and blood and ashes in the air. The image of Helio in front of him was no longer aged but young, robed in red and ivory.

'I remember the pain,' said Helio, and with that word they were standing on Prospero as it burned.

In the underworld, the blast wave of Setekh's dissolution broke over Ahriman. Arcs of blue lightning whipped the air and ground, then sucked into a singularity where Setekh had been. A sound like the shattering of glass played in reverse stole all other sound. Then the singularity exploded. Its blast wave came out in stutters, each ripple a frozen moment. It struck Ahriman, pulled him into the air and held him there. A constellation of debris hung around him. Then it was past, and he was falling, and the wave was blinking up the tiered sides of the pit.

Ahriman hit the floor. Slices of thought and memory fell through him like leaves from a gale-blasted tree: Setekh spinning backwards and forwards through time, the sword, the glow in the xenos' eye before it blasted apart. Ahriman saw all the futures where he had fallen, cut open and bleeding out even now. Part of him thought he could feel blood leaking out of him in slowly fading beats. Part of him knew he was alive and whole. Which was the truth?

+Ahriman,+ said Ignis' voice. The flat tone of the sending was enough to centre his mind. Ignis' hand steadied him, pulled him up. The flesh inside his armour was numb. His vision blurred as he looked up.

The xenos on the tiers were falling. Some had plummeted to the ground. Others staggered then collapsed. A high note sawed through the air. High above them, floating spheres and octahedrons were blazing with blue light. The ground was vibrating.

+We must reach the surface,+ sent Ahriman.

+Setekh...+ began Ignis.

+It will return. This entire world is a mechanism for its survival.+

They climbed the tiered sides of the pit. The Rubricae and Credence flanked them, spitting fire into the surviving aliens. The underworld of the Hyksos lay before them, not shrouded in dust but gleaming with cold light. Things were moving in the distance. An electrostatic keening pulsed through the air. Ahriman could see across the city to the great door to the surface they had come through. He began to run, Ignis and the Rubricae with him.

+Ahriman.+ Ahriman felt Kiu as he appeared from beside a row of rib-shaped pillars. Maehekta was with him, sword drawn and lit. A group of Kiu's Rubricae stopped to turn and fire at a target out of sight. +There is a host down here and it is waking,+ sent Kiu as he formed a triangle with Ahriman and Ignis. His Rubricae formed circles around them as they moved.

Ahriman did not answer. They could all hear the drone of metal on stone. The Great Ocean of the warp was retreating from their minds, as though some process had come online again, and was pushing it back.

They were closing on the door to the surface, running down the great avenue. One of the pyramids split down its centre, blocks sliding aside from a black opening. A shape dragged itself into sight from the gap. It stalked forwards, blade legs scissoring it into a run. Figures loped after it, backs bent, arms swinging long-barrelled weapons, eyes blue stars.

Ahriman's, Ignis' and Kiu's minds reacted as one. The Rubricae turned and fired. Kiu spun his blade and an arc of cold fire sliced through the advancing figures. Ignis turned, Credence locking into place at his side as they faced back into the tomb city. Hundreds of eyes gleamed in the dark. Beams of green energy stabbed at him, bursting across the wall of force that sprang from Ahriman's hand.

* * *

Ctesias blinked his eyes to a sunlight stained by smoke from a burning city. Helio Isidorus stood three paces from him, looking down at the book in his hands. The red and ivory of his robes stirred, though the air was still.

'Helio?' said Ctesias.

A blink and then Helio looked up. The hand that had been supporting the book dropped to his side. It fell, pages fluttering and then dissolving to dust.

'Yes,' said Helio Isidorus.

'This is your memory,' said Ctesias.

'It is?'

'Yes,' said Ctesias. 'This is from when the Wolves came to Tizca.'

He knew what the memory would be, but it was only as he spoke that he let himself turn and see the full extent of it.

It was enough that he almost wished he had not looked. Nothing moved. Every mote of ash in the air, every coil of flame was motionless, but apart from the stillness, it could have been real – *more* than real even, sharper, like an edge that could slit skin. It was not like a memory or a dream, it was a living presence. Ctesias knew exactly where they were and when. They were in one of the lesser pyramids that had stood to the seaward side of Tizca. A glance at the sun and shadows told Ctesias that it must have been part of the Collegia Azurine, where the Legion and its followers had gathered to discuss the nature of the mind and the limits of knowledge. A macro explosion had blown the side of the structure in. Broken pieces of crystal hung in the air, some in mid fall, some exploding into glittering shards where they had struck the floor. There were Thousand Sons too, moving through the curtains of smoke. Their armour was red, edged in silver and ivory, their emblems bronze and gold. The Wolves of Fenris were also there. Smudges of grey armour in motion amongst the smoke, fur cloaks and axe smiles swinging.

Beast teeth and bones hung on cords from their necks. Some had removed their helmets and come to battle with faces bare, knotted tattoos framing canine snarls.

Helio was looking around, discomfort pinching his features. 'This was a battle,' he said.

'The greatest of battles for us,' said Ctesias, 'or so we thought. What was done on Terra was worse, but for us, for the Thousand Sons, this is *the* battle of our history.'

Helio turned his head. 'I was part of this?'

'You were a warrior of the Legion, and yes, you were part of this.'

'The Thousand Sons, that is you and me, and them?' He pointed at the crimson-and-ivory warriors.

'Yes, and more still in the rest of the city. By the time this battle is done, there will be a lot fewer.' He shook his head. 'You might think them fortunate. The longer I outlive them, the more I do.'

'And them?' Helio nodded at the warriors in grey breaking through the smoke.

'The Wolves of Fenris, Russ' Dogs, the Rout – so many names you would think they were trying to win a competition only they cared about. They are the judgement and vengeance of the Emperor, our master and creator.'

'Judgement for what?'

'For being sorcerers and breaking His command to turn away from the supernatural powers we had developed.'

'And for that, *this* was our punishment?'

'I am one of the few who thinks that it was not unreasonable. We *were* and *are* sorcerers, and we *did* violate the Emperor's commands in spirit as well as fact. I am afraid that when you do remember, you may find the brotherhood you return to less than the wronged ideal we so love to cling to.'

'This was a just act then?'

'I do not know about just. Predictable might be closer.'

'You do not seem to be a man driven by ideals.'

'I am not. I like to think that if you are going to tell lies, it is best not to tell them to yourself.'

'Then what do you want? Why are you helping me?'

'Because I want to get out of here, and I can't do that without you letting me out, and I think that the only way that happens is if I can help you to remember. It is a matter of self-interest above all.'

Helio held his gaze still on Ctesias, then gave a nod. Whether it was agreement or acknowledgement, Ctesias could not tell. He watched this image of Helio as it turned back to the vision around them. He could feel the cold and hollow abyss waiting to swallow him if he let himself think about the implications of Helio's abilities. For now, he just needed to keep going, moving through the labyrinth of Helio's lost identity. Once he was free, then... then he would let himself think of what a former Rubricae, with a broken mind and catastrophic levels of power, meant.

'Who is this?' Helio pointed at one of the figures frozen amongst the shattering pyramids. Fire had smudged the red of the figure's armour with soot. He held an axe in one hand, its edge a flare of blinding light. Shards of crystal surrounded him, arcing in and forming a sphere, fingers of lightning linking each one. There were corpses at his feet, a body in the remains of the crimson armour of the Thousand Sons, rents open to pour a darker crimson onto the tiled floor. Further away a warrior in grey was just ending its fall. A red chasm bisected its torso from collar to groin. Plaited grey hair whipped back from the lean face as it howled its last. Through the smoke more warriors in grey were closing, their helms and shoulders marked with red and black in jagged toothed patterns. Ctesias looked at the tableau and drew a slow breath, half expecting to taste the blood and smell the smoke, but it was blank and sterile.

'That is Ignis,' he said, nodding at the figure surrounded by crystal shards and lightning.

'Ignis...' said Helio Isidorus slowly, then shook his head. 'I do not...' He frowned and turned, looking down at the dead warrior at Ignis' feet. 'This...'

'Arcanakt, and this must be the moment after the Wolves took him. Ignis was a lone fighter even then, but he and Arcanakt understood one another, I think.' He shook his head, looking around. It was all so real, so pin sharp, almost truer than the reality had been. He half wondered what would happen if he picked up one of the bolters and put a shell through the eye of one of the Space Wolves. Would that warrior have dropped dead in the battle all that time ago, felled by a round fired from another point in time? He shook his head at the fancy, squeezing his eyes shut for a second. He needed to find a way out of this, find a bridge back to his own mind, then find Ahriman. This was not a maze or a prison. It was a puzzle box made of a broken mind. He had tried to run but only found more places to be lost. No... the way out was to solve the puzzle, to find the answer that this part of Helio needed. He opened his eyes.

Burning Prospero was still there. He squinted. Beyond the smoke he thought he could see the spire of the Occlussary. Would he reach it if he tried to walk there now? Would he find himself as he remembered, fleeing as the tower of secrets burned? No, he doubted he would. This was a mindscape, built of memories that had been real, that had been lived, and memories were limited. He turned.

'You must be here somewhere...' he said aloud, eyes scanning the smoke and frozen billows of dust. 'To remember this, you must have been here...'

He shifted and then saw the cluster of warriors thirty metres behind Ignis. Red armour and ivory, golden serpent crests above plough-fronted helms… He saw the warrior at the front, bolter in hand. He moved closer… looking into the green eye-lenses as though he would see the face beyond.

'And here you are…' he breathed. 'This was you.' He turned. Helio Isidorus stepped forward, robe brushing through the ash hanging in the air. He was frowning, eyes fixed on the warrior in red armour. He shook his head, but to Ctesias the gesture looked more like confusion than denial.

'Why can I not remember?' he said.

'But I think you can,' said Ctesias. 'You can remember this moment down to the dust. Just like you could remember the sea of Tizca before and the boat you rowed across it. You can remember everything, but the memories are grains of dust, books without order, numbers or index. It is all there. You just have to find the connection between them. You have to find yourself.'

Helio was still looking at the warrior in red, who had been him at this moment. Slowly, hesitantly, he reached out as though he was going to touch the faceplate of the warrior's helm. He seemed to hesitate.

'The Rubric changed you,' said Ctesias. 'I do not know how, but I do know that it has made you dangerous. A mind without purpose will walk in dark places, and at this moment you are powerful and lost. But you have come here, you are closer to finding purpose… At least I think you are. You just need to find and take the next step.'

Helio looked at him then, confusion creasing his face.

'I am afraid. Why am I afraid?'

'To be alive is to feel pain, and once the past belongs to you again, well…'

'I do not want pain.'

'No, but I think you want to be alive again.' He gestured at Ignis and the other Thousand Sons. 'I think you want to come back to us, Helio Isidorus.'

Helio looked at him for a long moment. Unblinking. Ctesias wondered at what he had just said. It had surprised him, and what surprised him most of all was that he believed it. Somehow, somewhere along the way he had found that he wanted and believed in something greater than power and self-serving survival. He wondered when it had happened.

Helio Isidorus blinked, then nodded and raised his hand again.

'I want to remember,' he said and touched the face of his memory.

The air shivered. Then sound roared into Ctesias' ears, and the Wolves were running, howling, their axes red smiles stained by fire. The shards of crystal around Ignis blasted forwards. And now Ctesias could smell the smoke and the blood and the reek of murder. Only Helio's past self did not move, but simply stood as he had been, utter stillness in the centre of a breaking storm, the bare hand of the person he would become resting on his faceplate.

'Helio!' shouted Ctesias. A Wolf was running towards them, teeth white and sharp in a snarling mouth, axe rising.

Helio Isidorus' head rose. Furnace light filled his eyes. His past self was gone, as though erased by the turning of a page in a book.

The world stopped again. Sound vanished.

'I was here,' said Helio. His head turned, his burning gaze moving across the scene. 'This happened.'

Ctesias did not reply.

Helio turned and looked at Ignis and the other Thousand Sons.

'What happened to them?' he asked.

'Some lived through the burning of Prospero,' said Ctesias. 'Those that did were changed by the Rubric, just as you were.'

Helio stepped close to the unmoving warriors. 'Why?'

Ctesias felt a reply forming. He was going to say that they had been devolving into monsters, that they had been dying, that it had been an attempt to save them... He stopped and spoke the only truth he knew.

'I do not know why.'

Helio nodded, not looking around. 'So many lost. So few remaining...'

'Some survived the battle and the Rubric.' Ctesias gestured at the figure at the centre of the blizzard of crystal shards and lightning. 'Ignis remains and lives still.'

Helio looked around. The light in his eyes glowed brighter.

'I do not remember that,' he said, and the voice was cold and blazing, ice and fire, blinding, burning. Ctesias felt a shiver pass through him. The stillness of the memory suddenly felt dangerous, a thread pulling taut. 'I do not remember him being as you say.' Helio was beside Ignis now, eyes glowing brighter. 'I remember that he could have had the strength and power to save his brothers. I remember that he did not have enough strength. I remember that for all his might, he was weak.' The light of the world was growing brighter, bleaching colour from the red armour and the falling blood.

'He lives,' said Ctesias, feeling a note of urgency in the words. 'He is one of Ahriman's allies. He is–'

'I remember light and darkness and falling.' Helio's hand was rising, reaching out towards the memory image of Ignis. The light was blinding now, and Helio Isidorus was a shadow in the glare, its outline blurring to black feathers. 'I remember all that was...'

'No–'

'And all is dust.'

He touched the memory of Ignis, and the tissue of the past blew into fire and embers.

A flash. White light filling Ignis' eyes.

Quiet.

Just the sound of sand rattling across the ground as the wind rose.

Credence's pistons vented gas as they braced the automaton.

A beam of energy reached through the air. Green. Fizzing.

Everything was getting further away while staying in the same place.

Ignis looked down at his hand. There was fire glowing in the gaps between the digits. He froze.

+Ignis, brother?+

Another stutter of light. A blink. Blinding. He could feel the breath in his lungs. His hearts beating louder and louder.

No pain, nothing, just light.

Light.

He was...

Fire.

+Brother?+ A word shouted into his thoughts, and he was falling but not moving. He raised his hand.

It was glowing. It was burning.

Flash.

I remember fire...

No. He needed to... He needed... Ahriman...

Flash.

It was white, the stark white of a sun's heart; it roared from a black sky...

'Credence.' He tried to say the name, but when his mouth

285

opened, the only sound he could make was the roaring of flames drawing breath as the furnace door opened. *Credence!*

I fell to my hands and knees. The ground beneath me was red dust, the colour of rust, the colour of dried blood. Pain, hotter and sharper than any wound filled me...

There were the other Thousand Sons. Credence was turning to him, gears clattering, weapons ready. Ignis raised his head to look at the automaton but...

I could not see, the fire took my eyes first, and then it took my tongue before I could scream. Inside my armour, my muscles bunched, straining against metal. The fire burned through me. My skin blistered. I felt mouths open across my body, a thousand mouths each with razor teeth, each babbling a plea for the pain to stop. The fire pulled through my body like hands through wet clay. I was suffocating, as if sinking in sand. The acid touch of panic burnt my flesh. I could not breathe. I could not move.

Ignis tried to stop it, but the memory was roaring through him, burning.

Everything burning. Everything burnt to grey ash in the light.

'Ignis,' *the crumbling embers of his brain and soul shouted.* 'I am Ignis! This memory is not mine. It did not happen. The Rubric did not remake me ... I survived... I...'

Everything stopped.

Like a razor drawn through the memory, a hard line severing the present from everything that came before.

He felt nothing.

He stood slowly, unbending from where he had fallen into a crouch. He felt nothing. He was nothing... just a dust rattle of the memory of a name in a suit of armour.

'Ignis...' *breathed the voice of the dust as it fell without end, and he fell with it.*

* * *

The image of Ignis came apart in front of Ctesias and blew into the wind. The scene of Prospero began to crumble, flecks of colour billowing away around the ragged hole where Ignis had stood.

Helio Isidorus turned towards Ctesias. His robes were whipping in the air, glowing like a naked flame. Behind him, pieces of the memory scene tumbled back into darkness, falling into the void that was all around them now. Everywhere he looked, dust fell and spiralled, motes glowing, burning. Ctesias felt it bite the idea of his skin. The roar of it filled him, shaking him, pushing him to his knees.

'I remember you, Ctesias,' said Helio.

Ctesias forced himself to keep standing. 'This is–'

'Memory, Ctesias.' Helio reached out a hand and held it in the cascade of dust. 'These are our memories, the memories of all the Thousand Sons. All the living, all the dead and those trapped in-between. It is everything. All our suffering, all our meaning, all our knowledge.' Helio closed his hand, then cast the dust it held up. Ctesias looked and saw... and saw...

Tizca under a blue sky, seen out of the tower room...

Terra, home of humanity, the sky streaked with gunfire and the scream trails of daemons...

Two boys sitting watching a storm approach from a veranda...

Magnus alone, his head hidden in his hands...

He saw Ignis and Amon and Sanakht and Khayon. All of them held in grains that caught the eye then began to fall.

'It's you...' he breathed. 'You are Pyrodomon. It is you. You are what is coming for us. What you remember becomes real. The Second Rubric...'

'I am the Rubric, Ctesias. The first Rubric and the second. I am the power that threads all the brothers of our Legion for all time. What the Rubric did was bind us together, body and spirit for eternity. The Rubric is a fixed point in the warp. As soon as it was complete it always had been...' The corner of Helio's mouth twitched in the shadow of a smile. 'A bomb that never finishes exploding, its blast wave reaching backwards and forwards through time.'

'And the second casting... It did not save you from the Rubric, did it?'

'Save me... The Second Rubric simply brought its power to one point, into one of the souls that fall through it even now. I am the voice and face of the Rubric. I am all its power. I am the flame that burns away all that was. It was meant to free us from time, for fate and change. That was what you all wanted, that was what you all were trying to create.' A true smile now, serene and terrifying. 'You succeeded. You created salvation. You created me.'

Helio spread his hands. The dust spun about him, turning into a spiralling cyclone. Light was glowing under his skin. His eyes were holes into a star's fury.

'You said that you could not remember,' called Ctesias over the sound of the wind.

Helio laughed. 'I could not. But I remember now. The dust coheres, memory and awareness come together and make a person who thinks they live. What is a life but its memories? I am out here in the dust with the rest, divided down into the smallest pieces, a library of jumbled books and words. We are all just dust in the wind, Ctesias. But I am the centre of all that we were and are. I am the voice of us all, past, present and future. I am the bringer of the end.'

'And what is at the end?'

'Salvation. All of the Thousand Sons made one, unchanging, eternal.'

* * *

Ahriman saw Ignis come apart. Grey ash swirled.

+Brother! Ignis! Brother!+ Ahriman shouted with his mind, trying to push to where Ignis had stood, but the burning winds pushed him back. He could taste the power in the flames ripping through the warp. It was familiar... so familiar... Dust and fire and ashes... The texture and taste of the Rubric, as it had been when he cast it the first and the second time. The taste of salvation that had lost its way.

I did this, said a thought in his mind, cold and cutting.

He could not see Ignis now, not with his eyes or mind. He could see only fire. Credence pivoted to fire at the closing xenos. The space around the automaton danced with golden-and-green light as beams of energy splashed against the shell of its shield. Scorpion creatures of black and gold flew forwards, the beams of Credence's cannon passing through them as though they were not there. Kiu lashed his mind at a cluster of the xenos as they solidified for an instant, but Ahriman's focus was not there.

The shroud of ashes thinned around Ignis. A figure in armour stood there, head bowed in its socket.

+Ignis!+ called Ahriman. The head of the suit of armour came up. Ghost-light shone in its eyes. The roar of falling dust filled Ahriman's mind. He felt his movements falter, felt his thoughts ring hollow in his skull. *Ignis...* This could not be...

+Ahriman!+ called Kiu, and the sending pulled Ahriman's senses back into focus. The fire from the Rubricae had stopped. He called to them by name, but they would not move. The only answer to his call was the roar of flame. In his mind, all he could hear was fire and the rattle of blown dust.

Pyrodomon...

Around them, the wakened alien dead closed in.

* * *

Ctesias looked up at Helio Isidorus. The space beyond Helio opened, and he saw... A pillar of fire turning in place. A blinding cyclone. He felt his mind struggle against what he was seeing: a psychic singularity, a self-sustaining point in the fabric of the warp. Fragments of the past and future, the souls of the dead and the lives of the living. He looked at it and his vision pulled into it, spinning him into its orbit. In the fire he saw them, all his brothers.

Kiu standing beside Ahriman...

Lycomedes halting in his step on board the *Hekaton*...

And the rest a tumbling spill of names and images...

Akhor'menet...

Amon...

Manutec...

Aphael...

Gilameht...

Khadeth...

Khayon...

Mabius Ro...

Mordeghai...

Onoris...

Hakor...

Aarthrat...

Ezorath Qu'rastis...

Hasophet...

Omarhotec...

Daedophet...

Kahotep...

Nezchad...

Sanakht...

Ignis...

Menkaura...

Ashur-Kai...

Phosis T'Kar...

Uthizzar...

Tolbek...

Khalophis...

Hathor Maat...

Thousands and thousands of souls, the fallen and living, the broken and lost, the Thousand Sons of past and present and future.

Ctesias saw them and saw that it was about to come: Pyrodomon, the fire come to take them all. The wind ripped at him, pulling him closer to the burning pillar. He felt himself begin to fall into it and knew that in an instant there would be no way of turning back. Part of him wanted to let it happen, to slide beyond the event horizon down into the maelstrom of flame and pain, to be blasted into countless memories. Dust to dust, and ashes to ashes...

Fire. Sudden and total, filling Ahriman's inner sight.

The Rubricae stopped moving. Froze. The light in their eyes was blinding, but they did not move.

+The light...+ Kiu's thoughts were ragged. +I... I cannot see.+

The heart of an inferno reaching above and below sight.

Pyrodomon, here for them now.

No! Not now, Ahriman thought. *I need more time... I need more time!*

But there was no more time and the fire of the Rubric had come to claim them.

On the surface of the dead world, the fire arrived in Gilgamos' consciousness as a flash, blinding, as though a thermal bomb had just detonated in front of his mind's eye. His thoughts froze. Every process halted as white light and bright pain overwhelmed his sense of the warp.

He heard the scream of voices calling out as they burned. Their pain pierced him, shrill and clear. He could hear words in the roar. Names. Names he recognised. The names of brothers he had not seen alive or heard speak for centuries.

The pain rolled back.

Flashes of green light replaced the white.

The Rubricae had frozen in mid movement, the Dreadnoughts too. Above them the gunships and fighters that had begun to descend for extraction banked up, their flight paths ragged. The scarab swarms and centipede creatures crashed through them.

Gilgamos poured his will into a wall of force. He felt it buckle even as it formed. The swarms and creatures flowed forwards.

Aboard the *Hekaton*, Gaumata's thought form roared down the corridor. Sparks dragged from the air in its wake. It had the body of a lion. Four wings of orange-and-blue fire spread from its back. The head was near human. Silver tusks hung from its jaw. Its eyes were white stars. It was plunging down through the ship. Looking for the enemy. They had come from nowhere and were now everywhere. Images flashed through Gaumata's awareness: red tears falling in showers, gleaming like rubies. Harlequins, the murder dancers of the aeldari species. He had fought them once before and learnt that for all their speed, the truth of their lethal craft was confusion. They were weak and fragile and without their cloaks of lies, they held no power.

He sensed a cluster of them spinning down a passage and made the air burn with a shift of thought. It was too quick for them to dance aside. Paper skin and souls burned in seconds, and he was flying on. Commands passed from him to the Rubricae and brothers through the ship. They held every junction and could respond to every movement. Later there would be time to ask why the Harlequins had followed them here, but for now the reason for their attack did not matter, only that it would fail.

Gaumata was as a burning god, and in this realm, his will was truth. The warp was pouring through him, the tone of his thoughts and humours finding their echo without effort. An age of fire, Ctesias had called it, and he was right. The power of the flame was in the ascendancy, and this moment felt as though the whole universe were a pyre.

A blink of blackness. Sudden. As though the sun had gone out for the length of a heartbeat.

His thought form vanished.

He was tumbling back into his body. In his mind, the fire was an inferno, beyond his control, dazzling, shocking.

He slammed into his flesh and buckled to one knee. He was standing before the doors leading into the inner sanctum, where the personal domains of the Thousand Sons were, and the Serene Cages held their secrets. There were twenty-four Rubricae in the chamber with him: five Terminators and two sections of nine. Enough to break an army with him at their head. None of them moved as he forced a command out.

He stood, feeling blood shake from his lips inside his helm. The eyes of the Rubricae shone, and he could hear the dust-roar vibrating from them. To a mind that had taken fire into its heart, it was like an earthquake. He had the feeling that he was about to blast apart or ascend to a height of power he had never known.

Then the blast door blew in. Globules of molten metal flew out as the charges the Harlequins had attached to the other side detonated in a sequence that cleaved it from top to bottom.

A lone dancer walked from the ruin.

Gaumata rose, feeling his mind and flesh shake at the firestorm blazing in the warp.

Diamonds of colour and darkness scattered from the edge of the lone dancer's form. Its face was ivory, angular. Debris spun past it. Spheres of white-hot metal almost grazed it but did not touch it. On it came, unhurried, uncaring, as though it were walking a blade-edge line through chaos. Gaumata's sense glided out to it but he kept his distance. He could hear something in his head: a voice, empty and beautiful, a sing-song dirge sung by a soul in torment. It was revolting, terrifying. He pulled his thoughts up into the highest point of abstraction. The fire was there, filling his soul, embracing him as it always had. Fury leapt across his connection with his disciples and Rubricae. The alien's foot was rising to take another step. Gaumata's mind inhaled. He felt it catch memories, pieces of old pain and shame and loss: him holding his brother's hand as they took his father away, the lifeless arm hanging uncovered at the edge of the shroud; the teeth of a Wolf punching through his armour and the scream tearing from his lips. All of it went into the fire. He held it, felt it begin to eat the edge of his thoughts, and then released it.

The lone dancer began to run. A tongue of flame reached for it, but it was tumbling beneath and around it, body and movement sliding into the holes in space and slivers of seconds. Fast, so fast that Gaumata's mind and eyes saw it only as a staccato blur. His thoughts moved and the flames split, weaving through the air. The figure leapt, arms held close, spiralling. The fire reached for it, but it was not there. Gaumata felt the shock roll through him. The figure landed on the floor a pace from him and sprang back into the air. Gaumata whirled. The head of his morning star detached from its haft and whipped out on a rope of etheric flame. It arced into the space where the figure would be, and Gaumata poured his will into the weapon's core. The head blazed, heat cooking the air it passed through.

Pain exploded behind his eyes. The fire roaring through his mind flared brighter. The focus with which he held the flame in his thoughts slipped, and now it was blazing through him, ripping down the walls of control.

His swing quivered. The blaze in the morning star's head guttered.

And at that moment, as though it had been waiting for it, the Harlequin leapt. The head of the morning star passed under it. Ash and hologrammatic stars fluttered in its wake as the heat of the weapon burned the figure's cloak. The Harlequin reached down as it passed over Gaumata, its hand a shadow blur.

Gaumata felt the instant pass with perfect slowness, like the last images of a pict film juddering as they ran through a projector. The figure was right above him, looking down as he looked up. Its hand reached out as though to brush Gaumata's cheek. It touched him… and passed through his helm and skull. He felt it. Felt the fingers buzzing between substance and nothingness. He felt it reach into the meat of his brain as his thoughts formed, felt the ghost fingers close.

No death to an old enemy, he thought, no embrace of fire and fate. No redemption…

The Solitaire landed. Blood oozed from the handful of meat it had pulled from the sorcerer's skull. Behind it the body fell to the ground. The flames were guttering in the air. The ghost-driven suits of armour were twitching, their movements jamming. The Solitaire let the bloody mass fall from its hand. It walked on, towards the life that it had come to take.

'This is wrong,' shouted Ctesias into the firestorm. 'This is not salvation. It is annihilation.'

'What of the brothers that you and the cabal sacrificed to the

Rubric?' called Helio in reply. 'All of us made nothing, just pain and echoes drifting in an abyss. Annihilation indeed. I am the one that returned from that abyss. I am the voice and will of the Rubric and its Thousand Sons. *Our* moment to choose our fate is here.' The pressure of the wind was forcing Ctesias down; his thought form was coming apart, bits of his mind ripping away and tumbling into the burning wind.

'And do the rest make that choice with you,' asked Ctesias, 'or do you choose our fate alone?'

Helio shook his head slowly, the gesture sorrowful in its condemnation.

'I am sorry, Ctesias, but I remember you, and I do not remember you surviving the Rubric. You became like the rest. Like Ignis, like Ptollen...'

'No...' he tried to say, but Helio had turned and was walking away.

Ctesias gasped. A flash of light inside his sight. The idea of his flesh charring.

He was coming apart, burning, unravelling... into... memory...

He is an aspirant at the edge of a secret circle, watching as a sacrifice is made to something that shimmers in the air on the edge of being. The gasp of blood from a man's lips as he dies, and the voices surrounding the altar leap higher...

He is a warrior in red-and-ivory armour. The pages of a book sit open in front of him. They are crumbling but the words and symbols are just legible. There is smoke in the air as the archive burns. One of the humans comes at him, babbling about how the texts are dangerous. The man's rulers have recently accepted subjugation under the name of compliance. Ctesias' bolter blows him into shreds of meat...

He is a sorcerer in a tower on a planet of sorcerers. He looks out at the horizon, watches the light of the nine suns bend, and flocks

of Neverborn shimmer as they hunt for a weakness in the wards that
gleam in the air like nets. Ahriman is there, standing at the other
end of the chamber, waiting for an answer to his invitation to become
part of a conspiracy, a cabal. Ctesias lets out a breath of laughter and
turns to give his answer...

'All we are, in the end, are memories,' said a voice in the back of
his mind as though reading a lesson he had forgotten, 'Bundles
of things that happened carried from the past into the future in the
rags of our life.'

He cannot see Helio.

There is no past, there is no present. There will be nothing
but this. Nothing but fire.

'What is the point?' he will ask Ahriman. *'You say that we are*
going to save the Legion as though that is a complete reason and
explanation. But why does that matter? Why does our survival,
Ahriman?'

He tried to breathe, but the dust and ash poured in. Grey and
firelight, ashes and darkness...

'Ctesias.'

His name... Is that all he will be? A name that is not even
truly his, an echo repeating until it means nothing and is just
a cry of falling...

'Ctesias.'

A name... Is it his name? He cannot remember. There was
someone there, someone calling through the flames and swirl
of dust. He could... he could see them... Shadows... blurred
and ragged shapes. They were all around him.

'You are Ctesias,' said the voice, and now he could tell that it
was not one, but many. *'Stand, brother.'* The figures reached for
him, pulling him up. He was rising. Strength and power flowed
through his thoughts. He felt the idea of himself solidify. He
looked around, squinting at the burning dust. The figures were

pulling back. For a blink he thought he saw their faces, ghost smudges in the wind.

'Ignis?' he called. 'Ptollen?'

'*Brother…*' said the voice of the wind. Then the shadows were gone and Ctesias was rising, turning to look through the parting clouds of dust.

Helio paused in mid step, turned back. His eyelids blinked over the points of fire in his eyes.

'This is not as you remember it would be, is it?' said Ctesias. He felt himself smile. The wind rolled his voice into its roar. 'We are all so alike, all of the Thousand Sons. We believe that we know everything, see everything. Magnus thought he knew better than the Emperor. Ahriman thought that only he could save the Legion and defied Magnus. Now you believe that you, and only you, are our salvation… And like all the rest, you don't realise that your vision is flawed.'

Ctesias raised his hands, and the idea of his body changed. Arms grew from his sides. Claws and talons grew from his fingers. Blood and quicksilver dripped from their points. Wings unfolded from his back in pairs, one set opening after another until they haloed him with black feathers. His skin charred, splitting, the red beneath the glow of embers. His face was a shadow broken by eyes that were blank white holes and a skull's grin. This was his thought form, the shape of his long-mutilated and bartered soul. He hung in the dust wind for an instant, then flew at Helio.

Helio rose to meet him, a spiral of fire and burning dust. A moment beyond time extended in the gap between them. Then they were on each other. The burning wind ripped feathers from Ctesias' wings. Shreds of ethereal skin and blood scattered. His claws bit deep, ripping into the ghost substance of Helio's form. They locked together, their forms blurring, feathers and dust and claws and burning fangs. Ctesias could not last long, he knew, not against the inferno that fuelled Helio, but he did not need to. The talons of his mind dug into the core of Helio, reaching for the heart of his thoughts. He felt his mind close on a knot of half-remembered moments and scraps of tattered truth. Helio felt it too, and for an instant they both became still.

'You needed me to become whole,' called Ctesias. 'Without that spine of my memory you will be a mind of dust again.'

Sorrow dimmed Helio's light, and Ctesias felt the truth of the emotion wash through them.

'That is not the only reason I brought you here,' said Helio. 'I was trying to save you, too, Ctesias. Salvation is for all our brotherhood, even you. There is life in the flames, you see, brother. I remember what happens to you, otherwise, you see. You *are* the one that dies.'

Cold. The words falling through him like a silver coin tumbling down a well of night into black water.

'Then that is what must be,' said Ctesias, and he tore his memories from the heart of Helio.

The sea of Tizca... the impossible fortress... the library... all sat in his hands as he ripped free from Helio's grasp. They looked at each other – a devil of darkness and gold, and a storm of fire and dust holding the shape of a man. Ctesias paused, a sliver of time in a dream. The memories of what he had seen and understood in this dream journey sat in his claws, bleeding embers.

'Don't–' began Helio.

Ctesias crushed the memories. He felt a scream rip its way free. The image of Helio exploded into the dust wind. Golden burning fragments cut through Ctesias' thought form, pain and darkness and his cries tearing from him as the mindscape became nothing...

Ctesias' eyes opened, and the echo of the dream's scream gasped from his lips.

CHAPTER XVII

$\mathcal{A}$WOKEN

Red horizon. Golden sky. White and black feathers... Yellow tongues calling the names of his brothers... Ahriman saw the images fill his mind's eye.

Then it was gone, spiralling away, and he was shaking. His mind blinded by the after-image of the fire that had filled it...

'Ahriman!'

Coldness. A deluge poured over a blaze. The migraine smeared as it drained from his eyes. Maehekta was beside him. He could see her through the blaze as a cold blue outline. She was firing, bolter braced into the crook of her arm. Her presence, almost intolerable at other times, was now like cool water in a desert.

He rose. Maehekta stepped back. Power touched his thoughts. He felt the minds of Kiu and the others, still reeling from the inferno that had almost overwhelmed them. He pulled them into alignment with his own mind.

The xenos were closing, some ghosting through pillars and walls to cut Ahriman and his brothers off from the door to the surface. Ahriman caught the echo of the flame and pain lingering inside his skull and flung it out. White fire blazed from each of the Rubricae and sorcerers, pouring from eyes and hands. The fire curled through the air, weaving into a wall that rolled out. It struck the xenos. They kept coming, pushing their metal bodies through the flames even as they began to crumble. The beams of their gunfire reached through the fire. Ahriman reached his will through the minds of his brothers and broke reality into pieces. The beams of green light flickered, became liquid and mist. He held the fire and the wall of paradox for a second, enclosing them. The xenos halted. They stood beyond the ring of firelight and then walked backwards out of sight.

+What are they doing?+ asked Kiu.

The ground began to shake before Ahriman could answer. Structures in the cavern began to move. Splits opened in walls. Pyramids grew upwards. Canyons opened in the floor, plunging down into darkness. Ahriman twisted as the platform the Thousand Sons stood on lurched. Behind them, the door in the cavern wall was narrowing.

+Move,+ Ahriman willed, and then they were running towards the closing door to the world above.

Gilgamos felt the earth tremble. The centipede creatures reared back as though yanked by cords. The frozen Rubricae lurched. The light in their eyes dimmed for a moment. Gilgamos pushed his mind out. The guns of his brothers rose to his command, but the xenos were draining into the dust storm. The swarms of scarab creatures rose into the air, dissolving into the murk. The earth shook and shook again. There were figures in the dust, running figures, the blue of their armour smudged by the wind.

+Brothers?+ he called.

+Get the gunships down,+ came the thought-voice of Ahriman.

Gilgamos began to form an answer. A spear of dark stone burst from the ground behind Ahriman. It pushed up, thickening, shunting grey sand out of the way in a wave. Fissures opened. A handful of Rubricae tumbled into the abyss. Ahriman turned, staff flickering between white light and black absence. The Rubricae halted in their fall. Gilgamos reached out his own mind to pull them back to the ground. Another pillar burst from the sand, then another and another. The breaks in the ground were growing wider and wider, and new voids were opening. The gunships and fighters stooped from the sky above as the Thousand Sons closed ranks. Gilgamos looked at Ahriman as the first gunship dropped into a low hover. The scream of its engines vanished into the sound of grinding rock and wind.

Gilgamos pushed his mind up towards the ship that waited in orbit, calling to Gaumata.

Silence answered in echoes that filled his skull.

+Something has happened in orbit. I cannot sense Gaumata. My brother... I cannot... Something...+

Ahriman's sending sliced through the question.

+It shall be resolved.+

Gilgamos was about to reply when he finally saw the figure in sealed Terminator armour at Ahriman's side. He recognised the battleplate's lines, and then he saw the geometric designs running under the blue lacquer. The realisation sat for an instant, heavy, like a ball of cold metal forming in his skull. He had never liked all of his brothers of the Circle, but somehow he had imagined they would always survive. No matter what happened, they would endure. They had outlived the Flesh Change, survived the Rubric and exile. The doom of Pyrodomon would not touch them. A foolish belief, but one that in that instant, Gilgamos realised he had always held.

+Ignis...+ he sent.

+We must get clear now,+ willed Ahriman.

Gilgamos nodded, feeling a cold hollowness open in his mind as he turned and began to pull their forces in. Above them the engines of the drop-ships howled, as the world under their feet broke and split.

Ctesias gasped blood. His eyes opened. The hoops of the cages were melting as they rotated around him. He began to rise, head rolling with black bubbles and neon light.

The door to the chamber blew in. The spinning hoops of the cage tumbled, clanging. Failing wards blew out across the chamber. Ctesias rocked, then became very still.

The figure stepped through the space where the door had been. He knew what it was. Even with his mind spinning he could recognise what *this* was. He had taken many truths from the lips of the unwilling, and the truths of stolen and sacrificed souls were the coins of his hoarded knowledge. It was a Solitaire. *Arebennian* in the tongue of the aeldari. The one of their roaming dancers that gave its soul to the Dark Prince of Excess to play its role. Others wore the masks of death, but the Solitaires were its truth: death and slaughter and an eternity of torment. He had seen them in the conjured images of daemons and read of them in texts that he had learnt the aeldari's tongue to read.

'I am not going to try and defeat you,' he said in Aeldari, his tongue thick as it worked the alien sounds. 'I know I would not succeed if I tried.'

'I know,' said the Solitaire, in perfect High Gothic. The words sent fresh cold through Ctesias' shivering flesh.

In the aching depths of his mind Ctesias pulled a syllable of a broken name into his thoughts.

The Solitaire stepped closer, blinding speed made slow, made into a hiss or a sigh... It was beautiful, and as close to causing him to feel terror as he had felt in a long time. He kept his face still.

'You came for me before, didn't you?' he said to it. 'Your death-masked kin. I thought they were here for... someone else, but they were not. They and you are here for me.'

'Yes,' said the Solitaire.

'Why?'

'Because of what you would know.'

Ctesias dragged another link of the name into his mind.

'I have read that to speak to the Arebennian is to be cursed,' he said, and forced a smile to his mouth. 'And that to hear one of you reply is to forfeit all hope.'

'You are already cursed,' the Solitaire replied, 'and you have no hope left to steal.'

It took another slow step, and Ctesias knew that he had run out of time, that it had given him time to speak his part in the drama that they shared, and now, his part played, he would be pulled from the stage.

A bolt of cold lightning whipped from the door. The Solitaire whirled, tumbling aside as the energy arced after it. Lycomedes came forwards, his hand up, but the Solitaire was already a blur of broken light. Fast, so achingly fast, but the moment it had needed to dance aside had been enough.

Ctesias wrenched the last syllable of the daemon name into his mind and spoke. Blood sprayed from his lips, a red line ripped across reality. The daemon unfolded from the air like blood and entrails slipping from a slit skin. A crown of horns above a needle-filled mouth. Opalescent skin flowing over steel-cord muscles and soft flesh. Tatters of skin hung from silver hooks like a rippling cloak of silk, like a blood-spray halo vomited onto reality. The daemon gave a wordless cry of joy and agony and triumph, and bounded forwards. The Solitaire became a blur as it leapt. The daemon swelled, skin and mouth stretching and stretching. The two entwined, and there was a stretched instant, a blur of movement and violence, too quick to hold as anything but a blizzard of falling diamonds and the sound of razor edges drawing sparks from nothing. Then there was just blood dribbling from a folding sack of flesh and white light.

'Bind it now!' Ctesias shouted at Lycomedes, and began to call the daemon's name.

The Thousand Sons rose from the dead world and raced for their ships. The Harlequins had withdrawn as swiftly as they had come, along with the veils of illusion they had woven. Ahriman's mind reached out, connecting the brothers and command crew, his will pouring oil on the seas of confusion. Engines lit, and as the last gunships and strike fighters entered the hangars, the fleet was already pushing towards the edge of the system.

Behind them the tomb world of the Hyksos Dynasty remade itself. Megastructures pushed from beneath its skin of sand. Mountain ranges of pyramids appeared. Black chasms opened, each of them thousands of kilometres long. Huge crescents of black metal slid from the openings like the blades of folding knives. Lines of blue energy lit across their hulls. Clouds of lesser constructs glittered around them, spreading in a gold-and-silver mist.

In the primary hangar of the *Hekaton*, Ahriman staggered onto the deck and pulled his helm free. Around him the air screamed as gunships and strike fighters set down in washes of thruster flame. The image of the xenos ships taking to the void was still a grainy glow in the pict-feed from the gunships' sensors to his helm.

+Translate us to the warp,+ he commanded.

+The Navigator is gone,+ came the reply of one of his brothers who had remained with the ship. +We have no course prepared. We will be ripped–+

+We cannot be in realspace once those xenos ships start to move. Coordinate with all command crews. Translate into the warp then hold the ships steady in the ether fold. I will supply the psychic anchor. Do it now.+

He felt his brother confirm, the shimmer of understanding and obedience. He felt as though he was going to fall. Aches ran through his body. His mind was an unravelling mass of thoughts and impressions. He had nearly perished in the oubliette dimension, body bled of heat and life, mind starved of the warp. There was so much too that he could feel circling him, just on the edge of awareness and control. Ignis was gone, he could feel that revelation coming, that and all the other losses they had paid in coming this far. Too much: too much paid in pain and loss. Too much, but not yet enough.

A little further, he thought to himself, using the words like handholds to pull himself up the chasm in his mind. *A little further and I will set it all right.*

He felt the ship begin to move. Engine vibration shivered through his flesh, as his mind felt the tremor of the warp engines grinding through their waking. He straightened, let the thoughts and psychic residue of emotions fall from him.

A little further…

+We have taken the step, my brothers,+ he sent. +Though we are fewer, and the price is grave. We have taken the step towards not just salvation but eternity.+

CHAPTER XVIII

ℛEBORN

Silvanus woke. It was a slow sensation, not unlike surfacing after a soft, golden sleep. His eyes were shut, but his mind was bobbing up to the top of a bright bubble of forgotten dreams. He remembered being shot, though. When he was last awake, he had been shot... But now he didn't seem to care...

I have died, he thought, and felt the thought light euphoria in him. *The Emperor has taken me into His embrace... He gathered my soul as I died. I am free. I am free!*

His eyes opened. Rainbow light filled his eyes. The distorted image of a face bent across his sight, looming close. A finger tapped the space in front of him. Vibrations ripped through him.

Tap! Tap!

Panic lanced through him. He tried to gasp. There was fluid in his lungs. There were fangs in his mouth... No, in his *mouths.* He tried to twist and felt his flesh slam against the glass holding him.

+Be still.+ The command blasted the instinct to get free from Silvanus. He obeyed, panic fighting against the absolute authority of the thought-voice. He recognised it as Lycomedes, Ctesias' apprentice. +Understand, Navigator. Your physical form perished, but your consciousness was drained and distributed into your semi-clones.+

Silvanus felt the instinct to reply, to question and protest, but there was nowhere for those instincts to go except the clacking of his jaws against the glass.

+This circumstance was always a possibility, and one that the Circle predicted when they sanctioned the begetting of your semi-clones,+ continued Lycomedes, the sending cutting into Silvanus with the cold clarity of a surgical edge. +All is well. Once you have acclimatised, you will need to prepare to steer the ships. Ahriman himself will supply your course.+

Wait! Wait! screamed Silvanus, but if Lycomedes heard, he made no sign.

+I will now open your consciousness to your other semi-clone bodies.+

No!

He could not see. As though the flick of a blade had cut sight through the tank's glass. Then sight returned. Not just one view, but dozens, each from inside a different cylinder of fluid. In all the tanks in the navigation towers across the Exiles fleet, mouths opened and tried to howl.

The ships of the Hyksos gathered above the shell of their world. By the time the last of them slipped into the void, the orb that had been their tomb and prison was little more than a husk. Chasms criss-crossed its surface, opening to empty voids under the skin of its crust. The heavy core at its centre, long dead and old, sat open to the vacuum, a silent heart in a cage of flayed matter. Of the vaults, caverns and tunnels that had held the Hyksos, nothing remained. The canoptek engines of the dynasty had broken down and repurposed all the useful matter into the hulls of the ships. Each of those ships that had come from the world was a curved blade, of oil black and gold. The smallest of them sat in perfectly stacked formations. Beside them, the great tomb ships held to precise positions around the greatest of their number. It was a curve of darkness stretching thirty kilometres at its widest point, the flat of its blade supporting ranges of pyramids that rose to a single pinnacle, whose point glowed coldly blue.

The clouds of spider and scarab constructs moving over the ships began to drain into the hulls. Space around them distorted and shone as they started to fold and spindle physical reality. The sheet of stars creaked and shimmered, then the ships moved, sliding like sickle blades drawn through black velvet.

Ahriman watched as the craft of the Hyksos Dynasty slid from the orbit of their abandoned world. The black water filling the great mirror bowl at the centre of the *Hekaton*'s bridge rippled as it tried to hold the image of the ships while reality crumpled around them. He let the focus break and the mirror water cleared. He held his mind still for a moment. Part of his thoughts linked with his brothers commanding the other ships of their fleet. Another part connected with the Navigator-plural, Silvanus. Around him and the ships, the currents of the Great Ocean of the warp surged and broke, trying to rip them from their anchors. They were holding position close to the system that had held the Hyksos tomb world. The ships' warp engines and the minds of his brothers had been fighting the tides for long hours. Now the xenos had begun their journey they could slip free and follow.

Ahriman shifted the focus of his mind's eye and an image

formed in the mirror pool. Ghost patterns glittered in the dark. They were old runes, stolen from near-dead languages and belief systems. Just a few scratched marks, a little will and physical connection and they would lead him on through the night in the wake of Setekh and the Hyksos. He had not known of Setekh's nature, but in the underworld, he had realised that the only way to reach the dynasty's secrets of time was to let Setekh lead them there. He had marked the tombs, dusting their substance with devices that would leave a trace in the warp. The marks were tiny, meaningless to any who would look at them with mundane eyes, but in the warp, seen by the one who made them, they shone like the phosphorescence churned up by an ocean-going ship at night.

Looking at the golden threads in the dark water, Ahriman let himself smile inside his helm.

+Follow,+ he willed, and the ships of the Exiles slid into the tides of the Great Ocean.

Setekh stood at the centre of the court of the Hyksos. In the physical world, it was utterly still. The crypteks, overlords and vassals were statuesque beneath Setekh's dais. Beyond them, the walls of the court chamber rose to a ceiling that showed the stars passing in swirls and streaks. Outside those walls and the great pyramid above, the tomb ship and the rest of the dynastic fleet pushed through space, dragging paradox with them. Light flickered, swirled and folded in their wake. In a layer of reality next to the physical, the court was a blur. The tomb fleet was harvesting facts as it passed. They pulled every observable phenomenon from the void: the position of planets and stars, scraps of electromagnetic signals, flickers of radiation from long-past wars. Lower hierarchies of canoptek sifted it, compiled its meaning, and rolled it upwards to those above. Up and up the harvest of data went, until it reached the court nobility. There the crypteks gazed into the crystallised data and saw the past laid out for them in the light of wars yet to fade from the void. Occasionally, one would approach Setekh, supplicate himself, and present a fact. Setekh accepted each gift, consumed it, and added it to the map that hung in the centre of the court.

To a flesh eye, the map was a sphere of blue light. It was not just a map of space, but of the passing of time. Glyphs signifying stars, planets and spatial features glowed in its heart. To Setekh's sight, the map showed much more. The death and birth of stars flickered like ghosts. Tiny details glimmered. Different versions of past and future sat on top of each other.

It was far from complete. The dynasties that had betrayed him had taken his great work, the Key of Infinity. They would not have destroyed it; they did not have the courage or knowledge to do that. No, they had hidden it, locked it away, out of sight and reach. There would be signs to where it lay. Even after all this time, there would be a way to find it. He had already discounted many possibilities. To remove the rest, he would need to take direct steps. That would not be a problem though. The dynasties that had betrayed him still slept. The Silent King was gone, and who or what else could oppose him? And yet…

In the physical realm of the court, he turned his head and eyes. One of his overlords bowed and came closer. The overlord's name was Kheb'izzar, and in both life and death held the war name of 'the Scythe'. Setekh noticed a hitch in the movements of his inferior. The waking cycle and shift from the oubliette had perhaps seeded an error in Kheb'izzar's physical condition. Curious, but not a matter for the present.

– My phaeron – all is obedience to your will –

– The biological entity named as Ahriman –

– It is known, our phaeron –

– By our will it must die – it and all those that follow it – Find them – End them – I give this honour of annihilation to you –

Kheb'izzar bowed lower.

– From your will to the writing of eternity – Obedience –

Ctesias did not look around as Ahriman entered, but kept his gaze on the… *objects* in front of him.

'Your plan worked,' Ctesias said, deliberately speaking aloud.

'My improvisation, you mean?' said Ahriman.

Ctesias snorted. 'All improvisation requires preparation. Isn't that a maxim you used to teach?'

'It was,' said Ahriman.

They lapsed into silence. Ctesias did not look around at Ahriman or break the quiet. The bruises to his psyche still clung to his thoughts. He had found himself lost in moments of what might have been emotion if that had not been impossible. His thoughts felt leaden, filled with absences as much as content.

'You have recovered well from the effects of the aeldari venom,' said Ahriman at last. 'I am glad. Few do, I believe.'

'Aeldari venom… Yes. I suppose I should be grateful,' said Ctesias. 'Survival is not a natural state of being.' He nodded at the two other figures that stood at the centre of the room.

Ignis was utterly unmoving. His Terminator armour had changed. Its seams had sealed, and tongues of enamelled blue flame had spread across the orange, like a layer of metallic corral. Credence stood beside him, weapon mount slowly scanning the surrounding area as though waiting to meet a threat that would come at any second.

'We will restore him,' said Ahriman.

'Yes?' Ctesias shrugged. 'How well has that progressed so far? Ptollen, Ignis… all the rest. Outrun one doom and it just changes shape – first the Flesh Change, then the mutation once we fled into the Eye, now the Rubric... our salvation coming for us one at a time.'

'You doubt our cause?'

'Doubt it?' Ctesias gave a cold note of laughter. 'I never believed it in the first place, Ahriman. I just would rather fight against fate than submit to... whatever waits for a soul like me.'

Ahriman nodded. Silence slid back into place between them. 'The aeldari assassin that came for you–'

'A Solitaire,' Ctesias interrupted. 'That's what it was, one of their hollow souls.'

'Just so. It was weighing whether you knew something against your life. They are reading the strands of possibility and fate in their own way. They saw something that could change the future.'

'And here we are at the true point of this audience.' Ctesias smiled coldly and turned to look at Ahriman. Bright blue eyes looked back at him, sincere, unblinking. 'I have no idea what the aeldari thought I might know.'

'I know,' said Ahriman. He turned and moved towards the door. 'Find out.'

Gaumata opened his eyes as he felt his brother enter the temple. It was set at the heart of the *Pyromonarch*, down in the guts of the decks. Of all the places aboard the ship, this was the closest thing Gaumata had to a home. Others might set their sanctuaries on top of towers or under the light of stars. Gaumata had made his at the meeting point of the ship's plasma and heat ducts. Blue flames breathed and pulsed from vents set in the mouths of bronze creatures. Heat glowed and seeped from cracks in the basalt floor. The air shimmered and shifted with ghost images. Gaumata had taken his place at the temple's centre, floating on a disc of scotched silver. There alone he could bring his thoughts to perfect, burning focus.

+Hail, brother,+ he called as Gilgamos crossed the space from the temple doors. Gilgamos did not reply. His aura squirmed with indigo discomfort. The fire of the warp grated against his nature. He had always been a soul of water, even when he and Gaumata had been children. Always looking down into the depths of the seas, always trying to read what was in the depths while Gaumata turned his face and eyes to the sun. It was rare to have genuine siblings in the Legion, rarer still that they were twins, and rarer again that their abilities diverged so. There was a bond like no other between them, though. They made a whole: moon and sun, water and fire, action and reflection. And now Gaumata needed his brother's insight.

Gilgamos stopped nine paces from Gaumata. A flicker of will pulled a chunk of the heat-cracked floor under his feet into the air, so that he floated level with his brother.

+What is it?+ sent Gilgamos.

Gaumata shook his head once, then gestured. Burning marks unfolded in the air. Sigils on the temple's pillars and floor lit. In the warp a mesh of power enclosed them, separating and shielding them from any minds that might have been watching.

Gilgamos raised an eyebrow. +Layer upon layer of wards mark this ship. An enemy, even a powerful one, could never penetrate this far. Neither could one of the Neverborn. The only ones who could watch us here are our brothers...+

Gaumata floated closer to his brother. +What I need to tell you is for you alone.+

Gilgamos' clouded eyes held still, unblinking. +What has happened?+ he asked.

Gaumata paused. *I died*, he thought. He saw it again then. The lone Harlequin arcing above him. The fire of the Pyrodo-mon stealing his focus. The dancer's hand a blur as it reached through his helm and tore the meat of his mind from his skull. Over. Sensation ended. The scream as his soul began the endless drop into the tides of the warp. All his thoughts pulled apart. Oblivion opening its maw to eat...

And then...

Fire. Flame flooding the night, burning the night back. Sensation and thought and life kindling from nothing.

He had been amidst the fire. Agony beyond bearing. Searing to the point of annihilation. Light all around him. White, red, roaring. And he had been screaming without sound. He had seen a figure then, outlined in the flames. A shadow moving in the inferno, of the inferno. It had reached out to him. He had felt its hand grip him. Its touch was ice.

Not yet. The words had filled him, echoing like the soft fall of an avalanche. Then the hand had yanked him through the shroud of fire, up through the blaze of light and into a world where he was lying on the deck of the *Hekaton*, burn marks covering the floor around him like the shadow of an angel's wings. Alive. Gasping. Alive and whole.

+I have received something,+ Gaumata sent to his brother.

+What?+

Pyrodomon, he thought. *The fire that we thought was our doom is our salvation. I was dead. I had fallen beyond the moment of death as Pyrodomon came for us, but it did not destroy me; it saved me, brother.* The future, the present, the truth: all of it was not what he had thought it was. The fire had chosen him, had brought him back, and that had to be for a reason. For a purpose. That was what he had realised, and that was what he needed his brother to help him understand.

He looked at Gilgamos for a long moment, and then told of what the fire had given him.

+A revelation,+ sent Gaumata.

+Tell me,+ replied Gilgamos.

* * *

The temple was quiet as Ahriman crossed the threshold. Someone had left a bowl of oil burning on the floor in front of one the statues, but its flame was the only light. He sent patterns of power spinning into the warp as he walked towards it, their combinations hardening into a mesh that would turn aside any mind or eye that tried to see him. He was sorry for what he was doing, sorrier than any other would know, but sorrow did not mean he would stop. He could not stop. For the good of his brothers, for the good of his Legion and the salvation of all those he had wronged, he would not stop.

He reached the bowl of flames, paused, looked down into them. The glowing tongues danced across the mirror surface. He looked at his face, unchanged and unchanging, framed by fire.

'What do you see?' The voice came from the dark beside the statue.

'I see the universe straining a metaphor thin.'

Maehekta moved out of the shadows and looked down into the bowl of fire.

'Ah… yes,' she said, the echo of a smile on her lips. 'A reflection of yourself wreathed by fire, but not burned. The seeker of redemption and salvation in his torment.'

Ahriman looked at her. The dust of the tomb world still clung to her armour, and her weapons hung from her back. The truth trader was still looking down into the fire.

'I need more from you,' he said.

'Speak it.'

'Helio Isidorus must be protected.'

'And you think that I can do that better than you or your supremely powerful sorcerer brother?'

'You are not one of us, and that is why I want you to watch over him.'

Maehekta gave a slow nod of understanding. 'You do not fear those outside the Exiles, but those within.'

'There are things that have happened that I cannot explain – what happened to Ctesias, alterations to the clear chronology of events. Even now Gaumata meets with his twin behind a veil of secrecy.'

'You suspect treachery?'

'I suspect that until it is healed, our Legion will behave as it always has.'

'With suspicion, subtlety and guile?'

Ahriman met Maehekta's eyes, his face impassive, his mind still. He felt cold inside, down to his core. Always it was like this, always – ever since the Emperor had sent His Wolves to burn Prospero. It was as though the Thousand Sons could never be whole again but had to divide and turn on one another in ever smaller circles of deception and division. It was not even treachery, not really, any more than his own casting of the Rubric had been a betrayal of Magnus. They believed in their own minds that they had cause. Even those who hated him for what he had done were right, just as those that thought they should follow a different path did so because they thought they saw more clearly than him, or were stronger. None of them did see as clearly as he did, and none of them ever would. No one else bore the weight of the past as he did. No one else truly had the will to pay the price to set that past right. He was alone.

He shook himself, aware that Maehekta was still looking at him, eyes sharp in a face that bore a trace of sympathy.

'That is the other task I must ask you to perform.'

'Yes?'

'Watch and listen to what is happening amongst the Circle.'

'As only an outsider who trades in secrets and is impervious to sorcery can?'

'Indeed.'

'You should be worried about more than the Thousand Sons in your own ranks. The Pyrodomon affects all your gene-line, doesn't it? Those who remain with Magnus the Red, or who went to serve others?'

'Yes,' he nodded.

'They will blame you. Some may think you the cause. They will send forces against you.'

'It is possible. They will be dealt with.'

'Just like that,' she said. There was an edge of laughter in the words.

Silence filled the pause after.

'I thank you for your service,' said Ahriman, at last. 'You will be rewarded.'

He turned and took a step away from the fire.

'I have only the one price, Lord Ahriman,' said Maehekta. Ahriman turned and looked back at her. The light of the fire flickered over Maehekta's face, where twin dragons circled a broken skull. There was a desperation in her eyes that Ahriman did not need to examine his thoughts to see.

'When this is over, you shall have what we agreed. Your order will be remade. The Curators and all the secrets you carry for them will survive. I will make it so.'

'Then I shall do as you ask,' she said, and dipped her head. 'To help me, which of your brothers in the Circle *do* you trust?'

'None of them,' said Ahriman, turning away.

'Helio…' said Ahriman. No response. 'Helio Isidorus.'

Helio looked up, blinked once, slowly.

'Who are you?'

'I am Ahriman,' he began. 'I–'

But Helio's gaze had dropped. His eyelids fluttered over his eyes. His head twitched.

Ahriman felt the words form on his tongue. Something had happened. Helio had regressed even further than he had before. Was the manifestation of the Pyrodomon connected to it? It had to be. The Rubric was reaching through time and the blood of the Thousand Sons to claim what had escaped its flames before. Helio was the only one to have escaped those flames, but had the Pyrodomon taken some of what escaped back? How many more times would it be before Helio could not even remember his name, until he was just an echo trapped in a shell of flesh?

Time. He needed time, and that was the one thing that was running out.

'Helio Isidorus,' he said again, and again.

The eyes opened and looked up at him.

'Who are you?'

'I am Ahzek Ahriman.'

Helio shook his head.

'I am your brother,' Ahriman said.

'My brother?'

'You have many brothers. I am just one.'

'How many?'

Ahriman let out a breath.

'Fewer now than there were.'

'Fewer?'

Ahriman nodded. 'Fewer with every turning of the stars.'

'Why?'

'War. Betrayal. The cruelty of fate. They hunt us, brother. Hunt us down through time, and I can't yet break us free of them, and the sand of time runs swift...'

'I do not understand.'

'For that I am glad, at least.'

'What was his name?' Helio asked as Ahriman reached the door out of the chamber. He stopped and looked back over his shoulder at the only person he had ever been able to save. 'The last one of your... of our brothers that was lost, what was his name?'

He thought of the suit of armour then, standing still in a chamber forty decks down, its seams sealed, its eyes dark, the automaton Credence standing beside it. No command could make the automaton move from its place. And within the shell of armour just the soft roar of sand and dust, falling like the spent seconds of a life in an hourglass.

'Ignis,' Ahriman said, and shook his head, weary to his core. 'His name was Ignis.'

Helio Isidorus looked at him, and Ahriman almost thought he was about to say something else, but then he shook his head.

'I do not remember him being here. I am sorry.'

'Can you remember anything?'

Helio blinked.

'I don't know,' he said. 'I am... trying.'

Ahriman nodded, smiled.

'Good,' he said.

$\mathcal{I}$NTERLUDE IN $\mathcal{T}$WILIGHT

The principal players of *The Falling Moon* gathered in the ruins of an amphitheatre under the waning light of a star-ember. The ruins had been abandoned and then forgotten in the time when the Great Lament had seen the birth of their race's Thirsting Shadow in the warp. It had been a hiding place where the dissolute of their species had come to hide the worst of their excesses, a cup of secrets and screams clutched in the hands of the webway. Its makers had perished without ever returning. The spires and avenues had desiccated and crumbled, so that now the dust lay thick on the floors, and the towers stooped beneath the bowl of the false sky above. The star fragment that burned at the dome's apex cast the grey ruins in red light and rust-coloured shadows. The players had selected the place and the time carefully. The performance of an Interlude never had an audience, but it was still a beat in the arc of the emerging story, and so needed its setting as much as its entrances and exits.

Iyshak, Master of Players, arrived first. The black, blue and grey of the Speaker of Spaces had replaced the red and gold of the Murderer's Jest, and his steps bled a morose patience as he squatted atop a statue with three faces.

Yrlla, Shadowseer, the Voice of Many Ends, came next and began a slow pacing around the circle of the amphitheatre.

The players of the chorus followed, appearing from shadows to squat on the ruins, their masks the monotone of waiting.

Draillita, Mistress of Mimes, entered last and took her place, body and mask formed into a pose that could rival the ruins for stillness.

'The unwitting players have chosen, and so the path of the cycle turns,' said Yrlla.

'What follows all that has come so far?' asked Iyshak.

'Sorrow and the journey,' replied Yrlla.

~And at journey's end?~ asked Draillita.

'Hope. Betrayal. Suffering,' replied Yrlla.

Iyshak's head lolled low. Red and silver tears formed on his mask; its mouth had arched into a grimace of suffering. The faces of the chorus rose to mirror the movement. Tears glittered on the cheeks of their masks and fell in motes of fading holo-light. None of them had known what would come next, or what the cycle would demand before it closed. That was the way of the highest mythic cycles. The scenes and players grew and altered with the playing. Only the Shadowseer saw the whole arc and where it would close. Each player within their troupe took their place and followed their steps when they took the stage, but only the dance revealed their truth. The Solitaire had fallen, their soul gone to She Who Thirsts. They had come and played their last part. Had the Shadowseer seen that? Was it a moment that needed to occur for this saedath cycle to be completed?

'The lone player must dance again,' said Yrlla, as though in response to the unspoken question. 'Their mantle and mask must be taken.'

Iyshak stood.

'One more soul to walk into the mouth of She Who Thirsts...' he said and moved off into the ruins and distance, presence and voice fading. 'One more to dance to the Dark Prince's teeth...'

The players of the chorus followed, their movements muted, their outlines fraying to the grey and copper of twilight.

'As it must be,' said Yrlla, turning to follow the others.

Draillita waited until all the others of the masque had gone.

A Solitaire's mask lay on the floor of the amphitheatre as though it had always been there, waiting. A mist was rising through the ruins and curled through the eyeholes of the mask. Draillita looked at it. The hooks of two horns rose from the brow above a face of perfection and cruelty. She wanted to turn away from it but did not. She could hear a cold whispering hiss at the edge of her thoughts, a cruel smile given sound.

She took off her mask. In the quiet of twilight, there was no one to see her face beneath its shell. She threw it out of sight. She felt the layers of the roles she had played and those she might have played fall away. They were no longer hers. For the first time since she had become a Child of the Laughing God, she was herself. Not a role or a wearer of a smile. Just a soul. Just a choice to be made: play this last role at the price of her soul, or exit the stage never to return.

She reached for the Solitaire's mask. Inside her soul, she felt a hungering grin open in anticipation. She held her fingers still, then picked up the horned mask. It fitted over her face. The hiss of hunger in her soul became a shriek of glee.

She rose to her feet. Alone in the silence, she danced.

ABOUT THE AUTHOR

John French is the author of several Horus Heresy stories including the novels *The Solar War*, *Mortis*, *Praetorian of Dorn*, *Tallarn* and *Slaves to Darkness*, the novella *The Crimson Fist*, and the audio dramas *Dark Compliance*, *Templar* and *Warmaster*. For Warhammer 40,000 he has written *Resurrection*, *Incarnation* and *Divination* for The Horusian Wars and three tie-in audio dramas – the Scribe Award-winning *Agent of the Throne: Blood and Lies*, as well as *Agent of the Throne: Truth and Dreams* and *Agent of the Throne: Ashes and Oaths*. John has also written the Ahriman series and many short stories.

RENEGADES: HARROWMASTER
by Mike Brooks

Secrets and lies abound with the mysterious Alpha Legion, but as extinction becomes an ever-present reality for the Serpent's Teeth warband, Solomon Akurra seeks a new way of war...

An extract from
Renegades: Harrowmaster
by Mike Brooks

Jonn Brezik clutched his lasgun, muttered prayers under his breath, and hunkered further into the ditch in which he and seven others were crouching as the world shook around them. The weapon in his slightly trembling hands was an M35 M-Galaxy Short: solid, reliable and well maintained, with a fully charged clip, and a scrimshaw he had carved himself hanging off the barrel. He had another four ammo clips on his belt, along with the long, single-edged combat knife that had been his father's. He was not wearing the old man's flak vest – not a lot of point, given the state it had ended up in – and as enemy fire streaked overhead again, Jonn began to do the mental arithmetic of whether, right now, he would prefer to be in possession of a gun or functional body armour. The gun could kill the people shooting at him, that was for sure, but he would have to be accurate for that to work, and there didn't seem to be any shortage of the bastards. On the other hand, even the best armour would give out eventually, if he lacked any way of dissuading the other side from shooting at him–

'Brezik, you with us?'

Jonn jerked and blinked, then focused on the woman who had spoken. Suran Teeler, sixty years old at least, with a face that looked like a particularly hard rock had been hit repeatedly with another rock. She was staring at him with eyes like dark flint, and he forced himself to nod.

'Yeah. Yeah, I'm here.'

'You sure? Because you seem a bit distracted right now,' Teeler said. 'Which, given we're in the middle of a bastard *warzone*, is something of a feat.'

'I'll be fine, sarge,' Jonn replied. He closed his eyes for a moment, and sighed. 'It's just the dreams again. Feels like I haven't slept properly for a month.'

'You've been having them too?' Kanzad asked. He was a big man with a beard like a bush. 'The sky ripping open?'

Jonn looked over at him. He and Kanzad did not really get on – there was no enmity as such, no blood feud; they just rubbed each other the wrong way – but there was no mockery on the hairy face turned in his direction.

'Yeah,' he said slowly. 'The sky ripping open. Well, not just our sky. All the skies. What does that mean, if we're both having the same dream?'

'It means absolute jack-dung until we get out of here alive,' Teeler snapped. 'You want to compare dream notes after we're done, that's fine. Right now, I want your attention on the matter in hand! And Brezik?'

'Yes, sarge?' Jonn replied, clutching his lasgun a little tighter.

'Stop calling me "sarge".'

'Sorry, s– Sorry. Force of habit.'

A throaty drone grew in the air behind them, and Jonn looked up to see lights in the night sky, closing the distance at a tremendous speed. The drone grew into a whine, and then into a roar as the aircraft shot overhead: two Lightnings flanking an Avenger, all three heading further into the combat zone.

'That's the signal!' Teeler yelled, scrambling to her feet with a swiftness that belied her years. 'Go, go, go!'

Jonn leaped up and followed her, clambering out of the ditch and charging across the chewed-up ground beyond. He desperately tried to keep up some sort of speed without twisting an ankle in the great ruts and gouts torn into the earth by bombardments, and the repeated traversing of wheeled and tracked vehicles. He could see other groups just like his on either side, screaming their battle cries as they advanced on the enemy that were being savaged by aerial gunfire from their fighters. Jonn raised his voice to join in, adrenaline and fear squeezing his words until they came out as little more than a feral scream:

'FOR THE EMPEROR!'

Streams of fire began spewing skywards as the enemy finally got their anti-aircraft batteries online. Jonn heard the *thump-thump-thump* of Hydra quad autocannons, and one of the fighters – a Lightning, he thought, although it was hard to tell at this distance, and in the dark – came apart in a flower of flame, and scattered itself over the defenders below.

'Keep moving!' Teeler yelled as one or two in their group slowed slightly. 'We've got one shot at this!'

Jonn pressed on, despite the temptation to hang back and let others take the brunt of the enemy gunfire. Presenting the defenders with targets one at a time would only ensure they all died: this massed rush, so there were simply too many of them to kill in time, was the only way to close the distance and get into the enemy lines. Once there, the odds became far more even.

They passed through a line of metal posts, some no more than girders driven upright into the mud, and the fortifications ahead began to sparkle with ruby-red bolts of super-focused light. They had entered the kill-zone, the functional range of a lasgun, and the defenders now knew that their shots would not be wasted.

Kanzad jerked, then jerked again, then fell on his face. Jonn did not stop for him. He would not have stopped for anyone. Stopping meant dying. He charged onwards, his face contorted into a rictus of fear and hatred, daring the galaxy to come and take him.

The galaxy obliged.

The first las-bolt struck him in the right shoulder and burned straight through. It was a sharp pain, but a clean pain, and he staggered but kept moving. It was his trigger arm, and his lasgun was supported by a strap. So long as his left arm could aim the barrel and his right could pull the trigger, he was still in this fight.

The next shot hit him in the gut, puncturing the muscle wall of his stomach and doubling him over. He managed to retain his feet, just, but his momentum was gone. He began to curl up around the pain, and the stench of his own flash-cooked flesh. Eyes screwed up, face towards the ground, Jonn Brezik did not even see the last shot. It struck the top of his head, and killed him instantly.

'Die, heretic!' Stevaz Tai yelled, as his third las-bolt finally put the man down. He whooped, partly in excitement and partly in relief, but anxiety was still scrabbling at the back of his throat. Throne, there were just so *many* of them! Even as he shifted his aim and fired again, he thought he saw something off to the left, closing in fast on the Pendata Fourth's defensive line. He blinked and squinted in that direction, but some of the great floodlights had been taken out by that accursed aerial attack, and the shapes refused to resolve for him.

'Eyes front, trooper, and keep firing!' Sergeant Cade ordered, suiting actions to words with his laspistol. It was more for show than anything else, Stevaz assumed, since the heretics were probably still out of pistol range, but it would only be a matter of seconds until that was no longer the case. And those seconds could be important.

'Something to the left, sarge!' he shouted, although he snapped off another shot as he spoke. 'I didn't get a good look, but whatever it was, it was moving fast!'

'Was it in our sector?' Cade demanded.

'No, sarge!'

'Then it's Fifth Squad's responsibility, or Seventh's – not ours! We've got enemies enough in front of us,' Cade snapped, and Stevaz could not argue with that. He jerked backwards as an enemy las-bolt struck the dirt in front of him, and wiped his eyes to clear them of the mud that had spattered across his face.

'Full-auto!' Cade bellowed. 'Let 'em have it!'

Stevaz obediently flicked the selector on his lasgun and joined its voice to the whining chorus that sprang up along the trench. It would drain their power packs rapidly, but the sheer volume of fire should put paid to this latest assault before they needed to reload–

Something exploded off to his left, and it was all he could do not to whip around, lasrifle still blazing. It was immediately followed by screaming: high, desperate screams born not just of pain, but of utter terror.

'Sarge?!'

'Eyes front, trooper, or you'll be the one screaming!' Cade yelled, but there was a note of uncertainty in the sergeant's voice as he fired at the onrushing cultists. 'One problem at a time, or–'

Something large and dark flew into their midst from their left, and landed heavily on the trench floor. It clipped the back of Kanner's leg and she tripped backwards, and her cycle of full-auto shots tracked along Dannick's head and blew his skull to smithereens, then took Jusker in the shoulder. They both fell, and Cade roared in anger and frustration, and not a little fear, as his squad's output reduced drastically. Someone moved to help Jusker. Someone else fell backwards as a lucky shot from the onrushing enemy found the gap between helmet and trench top. Stevaz could not help himself: he turned and looked down at what had caused all this commotion.

It was a headless body, bearing the insignia of Fifth Squad.

Fear paralysed him. What had broken into their lines? What had decapitated this trooper, and hurled their body so easily into Fourth Squad's ranks? It couldn't have been the explosion he heard: what explosion would take someone's head off so neatly, but hurl their body this far?

Cade was shouting at him.

'Tai, get your arse back on the–'

The sergeant never got the chance to finish his sentence, because something came screaming over the top of the trench, and landed on him. The buzzing whine of a chainsword filled the air, along with a mist of blood, and then Sergeant Cade was bisected. His murderer turned towards Stevaz as the rest of the heretics' assault piled into the trench, rapidly overwhelming Fourth Squad.

Stevaz saw a snarl of fury on the face of a woman probably old enough to be his grandmother, and the light of bloodlust in her eyes. He raised his lasrifle, but her howling weapon batted it aside, and the rotating teeth tore it from his grip. He turned and ran, fumbling at his belt for the laspistol and combat knife that rested there, hoping he could at least outpace her until he had his secondary weapons drawn.

Too late, he realised he was running towards where Fifth Squad had been stationed.

He rounded a corner of the trench before he could stop himself, and collided with something enormous and very, very hard. He fell backwards into the mud, and looked up to see what he had run into.

Two glowing red eyes stared balefully down at him, and Stevaz nearly lost control of his bladder until he recognised them for what they were. The eye-lenses of a Space Marine helmet! The promised help had arrived! The lords of war were here on Pendata!

Then, despite the darkness, he took in the colour of the armour plate. It was not silver, but blue-green, and the pauldron did not display a black blade flanked by lightning strikes on a yellow background, but a three-headed serpent. His heart shrivelled inside his chest, because he suddenly realised what he must have seen, moving so fast towards Fifth Squad's lines.

'You're not Silver Templars,' he managed shakily.

The helmet tilted slightly, as though curious.

'No.'

A weapon with a muzzle as large as Stevaz's head was raised, and the bolt-shell it discharged detonated so forcefully that his entire upper body disintegrated.

Derqan Tel turned away from the dead Pendata trooper, and followed the rest of his team into the culvert that ran back from the front lines. No more defenders were coming from that direction: the Legion's human allies had breached the trenchlines now, and could be relied upon to make a mess of this first line of resistance.

'What is a Silver Templar?' he asked the legionnaire in front of him.

'No idea,' Sakran Morv replied. 'Why?' Morv was big even for an Astartes, and carried the squad's ancient autocannon.

'That mortal seemed to think I should be one,' Tel said. He

searched his memory, but drew a blank. 'I cannot think of a loyalist Chapter called the Silver Templars. You?'

'Perhaps he meant Black Templars,' Morv suggested. 'Although I think Va'kai would have recognised their insignia.'

Something wasn't sitting right in Tel's gut. Three loyalist strike cruisers had emerged from the warp since the Legion had made planetfall, and were now engaged in void combat overhead with the *Whisper*, the flagship of the Serpent's Teeth. Morv was correct: Krozier Va'kai, the *Whisper*'s captain, would know a Black Templars ship if he was shooting at it.

He activated his vox. 'Trayvar, have you heard of Silver Templars?'

'Is this really the time, Tel?' came the voice of Trayvar Thrice-Burned in reply. He was at the head of the advance, farther down the trench. He had also been the first into the defensive lines when Eighth Fang made their assault rush across the ground left dark by the destroyed floodlights; it was that sort of full-throated aggressiveness that had won him the renown he enjoyed, and also seen him doused in burning promethium no less than three times in one particularly brutal assault against a position held by the Salamanders Chapter.

'The mortal I just killed appeared to be expecting them,' Tel informed him. 'It could be a new Chapter. Or, as Morv pointed out,' he continued, 'a misremembering of the Black Templars.'

'Silver Templars, Black Templars,' the Thrice-Burned muttered. *'You'd think they would have some imagination, wouldn't you?'*

'The Imperium, endlessly repeating minor variations of the same tired routines?' Morv laughed. 'Surely not.'

'I'll vox it in,' Trayvar said. *'The Harrowmaster might know something.'*